ABOUT THE AUTHOR

Seraphina Madsen was born in San Rafael, California and grew up in Northern California and Maine. She attended Bates College and Kingston University in London. She became a French citizen in 2019 and now resides in the U.K. Her first novel, *Dodge and Burn,* was published by Dodo Ink in 2016 to critical acclaim and was longlisted for the Republic of Consciousness Prize.

Dodo Ink, an imprint of Dodo Publishing Co Ltd
66 Mayford Road,
Levenshulme,
Manchester,
M19 3DP

Cover design: Dan Stiles
Editing: Sam Mills
Copyediting: Andrew Gallix
Typography and typesetting: Ben Ottridge

ISBN: 9780993575884

Printed and bound by TJ Books Ltd, Padstow, England

This book was produced with the kind support
of Arts Council England

AURORA

SERAPHINA MADSEN

For Cleopatra and Cozmo

I.

The lynx are arguing and mating out there in the dark wood again, under the waxing moon and starlight. I can feel their shrill, guttural sounds, almost comical, a chaos of contours — blood-chilling, drunken shrieks of old women; of demons incarnate — coming from deep inside me, scratching in my throat. I want to scream, but nothing comes out. Horrifying. Such beautiful creatures with such hideous voices. The chandelier throws out a blue, red, and yellow fire that leaps around the room. Stacks of books with well-worn bindings, some newer than others, alive with silverfish, sitting on tables, on bookshelves, musky with mold spores, go to my head. The desk is covered in empty and partially-filled bottles of fizzy pop, the exact recipe of which is held in a secret vault in Waco, Texas. The bottle says it was invented by a doctor, presumably to make it sound healthy. Fortified with medicinal qualities, it's making my head drip like a urinal. Still, I can't get enough of it. There is no end to the thirst or the cigarettes I chain-smoke. There is a staunch mineral taste in my mouth.

And now to the point. This girl. A coincidence. An absence of contradiction. A link between contradictory terms. Perhaps this girl will always elude me. But I am compelled to write her down in an attempt to capture at least a part of her. The girl I want to understand was made with clay. As are all the daughters of Adam and Eve, she was molded into shape. I, myself, was created out of a volatile, shifting material — the fire of a scorching wind — as are all the jinn. Fabricated by the same maker, she and I are different and similar, or in any case, connected.

I've always held a fascination for the clay people. I admire their literature. None of my kind has ever written anything substantial in the language of the humans, which is odd because they have written so much about us. I, for one, feel the need to, so, here I am, word by word, forging chain lengths of sentences I sculpt with the scorching wind into form. I must remind myself that writing is not sculpture. But I aim to create a dynamic representation. I cannot tap away, step back and marvel at the hard marble transformed into the texture of skin, the fleshy thighs of Proserpina and the liquidity of her tears. Also, I am not Bernini. I want you to know she is like a thousand other girls, but she is also ancient, pre-biblical. A Pandora. She makes me shake and vibrate. I cannot contain myself. I want you to imagine you can smell her warm, earthy flesh and feel the little downy hairs on her arms because she really does have lovely limbs. She is as beautiful as the original Persephone. The moon is alive under her skin.

This is the how and the why of my encounter at the hands of the young woman. A meeting, which was also a liberation. A liberation with which I am at odds. Her very existence exacerbates my sketchy hold on the absolute and makes me want to scream. I am filled with venom. I am also in love with her. My nails are bitten to stubs; they are bleeding down my pencil and all over the page...

She was born in a trailer park across the river from Laughlin, Arizona — a glittering metropolis in the firmament of shining, sleepless cities where people gamble, consume drugs and alcohol, and cook illegal substances in sheds at all hours of the day and night, as her father did before he was shot and killed in a drug-related incident.

The child's mother gave birth to her outside, under the stars. Inside, the trailer was overheated, cramped, and sticky, with everyone smoking cigarettes and cooking drugs in tablespoons to make little crystal rocks.

Her mother had to get out of there. Passing through heavy veils of smoke spilt into the cool night air, wrapped in a bedsheet, naked underneath, unsure of how she had gotten that way, she walked down the steps and onto the dirt path. Something hard and muscly armed with a knife was on the inside of her belly, trying to push its way out. She needed to breathe. She felt like she was going to be sick.

Her body told her to squat in the dirt. She obeyed, screaming silently (no sound would come out). The water broke, gushing down her legs. Her uterus contracted with the stars overhead (stars which made no sense) as a black cat looked on from the top of one of the trailers. This went on for what seemed like a very long time. She felt herself tear. Finally, a warm, wet mush slid out. She couldn't help but think of a gigantic leech, slippery all down her legs. The baby squirmed in the dirt with a fleshy cord that grew from its belly, attached to something gelatinous.

In a moment of panic, the mother thought it might be her intestines, uterus, or bladder that had come out with the mewling form. She bent down. On her hands and knees, she inspected the blob attached to the cord. Everything was hazy and, at the same time, sharp, hyperreal. Straw and little rocks were stuck to the placenta. The baby was covered in a waxy substance and felt gritty to the touch.

In a state of shock, or something like sleepwalking, the mother took the wailing child from the ground and held it to her body, wrapping it in the folds of the bedsheet, the umbilical cord draped over her arm, the placenta hanging down. Looking upward, she was taken by the dome of sky and stars — a cathedral.

When she got to her mother's door she banged as hard as she could, leaving bloody handprints all over the glass and aluminium. Frantically, she pressed the doorbell — a small, illuminated rectangle smudged with dirt. Her mother emerged from a trapezoid of light, half asleep, behind the door in a polyester nightdress, her bouffant tied in a protective scarf, thinking perhaps this was a nightmare, her daughter wrapped in a sheet behind the bloodied glass carrying a blue, screaming infant. She didn't even know her daughter was pregnant.

The mother assured her daughter she had not lost her uterus, that all they needed to do was cut the umbilical cord, wash the baby, and everything would be alright. She would do everything. The grandmother took the wailing child in the sheet with the placenta hanging from it into her arms and told her daughter to get into the shower.

The grandmother filled a tub used for foot baths with warm soapy water in the kitchen. Carefully, she slid the hiccupping, shrieking infant into the water, where she managed to cut the umbilical cord. The thing oozed jelly that flew through the air as she tossed it with the placenta into the garbage disposal.

Finally clean and swaddled in a towel, snug against her grandmother's ample breast, the baby was red and rigid and would not stop screeching like a wild animal, fists clenched. The grandmother needed to put on something clean; her nightgown had gotten afterbirth on it.

In the shower, the child's mother did her best to clean off the blood and gore, rubbing floral-scented shower gel between her legs, over her face, her chest; watching the pink, bloodied water and dark red, gelatinous globs disappear down the drain. She wanted to stay in the warm, crystal water, the drops sparkling in the artificial light of the bathroom, perhaps forever.

Grandmother sat on the couch with the infant pressed to her chest, red, rigid, fists clenched, mewling. She tried to soothe the child with a finger that might be mistaken for a nipple, but this act offered no comfort. On the wall opposite, Jesus in a golden frame looked at them, bathed in golden light, a white lamb in his arms, head tilted in an attitude of grace and love. She kissed her grandchild's soft head. A little lamb. A child of God.

Through the baby's constant, feral wailing, Grandmother called again to her daughter, urging her to get out of the shower and come to the living room. After ten minutes by the shellacked Jesus face wall clock, she called out to her daughter again. Another five minutes. Grandmother got up, the baby still stiff, shrieking in her arms.

The bathroom was warm and thick, with white steam that poured over her upon entering. Sharply, Grandmother pulled back the shower curtain to find her daughter sitting on the tub floor — legs pressed to her chest through the white clouds, water pounding down, neck bent, face pressed to her knees. The daughter raised her head — eyes remote, like an alien. No light came from them; they were pure black. After seeing her daughter's eyes, it was obvious — there would be no shaking her out of that spine-chilling stupor to try and breastfeed the child.

Grandmother pulled out of the trailer park, kicking up dust, and navigated onto the main road under the yellow explosions of streetlights. The infant strapped to her chest with the seatbelt and pillow reinforcement, she drove to the nearest drugstore for baby formula.

Walking the aisles, Grandmother clutched the stiff, shrieking baby under the too-bright fluorescent lights, her whole body vibrating with the pain the child was in. Other shoppers and the check-out attendant looked at Grandmother like she was a murderer. If you've ever heard the screams of a newborn in withdrawal, they will haunt you for the rest of your life.

Back at the trailer, her daughter was gone, leaving behind wet footprints where she'd walked out and the bloody handprints on the glass door.

The baby was difficult to feed. After an hour by the Jesus clock, she turned blue. Uninsured, Grandmother hesitated, then dialed 911 and hoped for the best. Not long after, paramedics arrived. In the back of the speeding ambulance, the infant was racing toward death. Just before arrival she died for six minutes[1] and had to be resuscitated.

Following behind in her car the grandmother lost sight of the ambulance. In that moment, her chest felt like it was being pierced with a cold rod. Hands gripping the wheel, she focused on the road ahead, imagining her daughter in flashes, in the shower, walking out of the trailer soaking wet, maybe wrapped in a towel, maybe not.

In the Emergency waiting room, the infant's grandmother went to the front desk. She thought about giving a false name and address but couldn't bring herself to lie and broke down, explaining she didn't have any insurance, or any savings, that the baby was her daughter's. The person behind the desk said she could apply for emergency Medicaid which would cover both the emergency room and hospital care, but not the ambulance. She was given the forms. The grandmother found a chair and began filling in what she could.

Four hours passed. All around, in the air was the acrid scent of fear, coffee, unwashed bodies, chewing gum, chemical smells. She remained frozen, head bent, eyes closed, hands together in prayer begging the LORD to spare her granddaughter's life. Her eyes flipped open. She hadn't put a name on the form for the child. She had to

1. When I went back in time to observe, I followed her little departed soul floating toward the void like a pinpoint of light, until it was sucked back to earth and into the tiny body on a ventilator. From the very beginning, she knew about the abyss.

think of one. The child had to have a name. The person at the desk told her she could wait for the birth certificate to decide. But she couldn't. The thought the child might not survive, that she would go nameless through the gates of Heaven, was too much to bear. She had to decide now.

In her line of vision sat a stack of magazines on a side table. Grandmother got up and went to the pile. She picked up *Town & Country* and returned to her seat. The glossy pages had a dirty film from other people's touch; she got a tissue out of her bag to protect her fingers and turned the pages, her eyes greedily taking in the images. Sprawling estates, swimming pools, yachts, the immaculate shine of money, smiling people who mattered. Each story told a fairy tale of counts and countesses, Formula One drivers and their wives — important, fabulously wealthy individuals.

Skimming through the print, her eyes landed on a name: *Aurora*. It struck her as beautiful and unusual, a potential name for the child. In that moment the candy machine lit frantically on and off, followed by the ceiling lights, which hardly seemed possible because lights weren't supposed to flicker in hospitals, otherwise people would die. Grandmother was well aware the LORD moved in mysterious ways and couldn't understand how He would want to risk people dying by playing with the lights. All the same, she knew it was Him, giving her a sign. The candy machine. The lights. The child's name was to be Aurora.

Grandmother made a promise to Jesus then and there that she would not fail her grandchild as she had failed her daughter. She vowed to protect her beautiful baby angel. The little girl would not fall into drugs and go with Satan into the desert as her daughter had with the others, the ones with tattoos all over their bodies. Everyone knew they made bonfires and burned things, sang and danced to evoke the Antichrist, cut themselves with knives, sacrificed animals, wrote symbols and messages in blood on the rock faces in the desert. In sheds behind the trailers, they cooked drugs and sold them to children too young to buy alcohol. She had called the police and reported it and there had been raids, but still, it went on. How had all of this happened? How could she have failed so miserably? No, this child would be a shining light, a beacon of hope, her gift to the LORD and Jesus.

Grandmother came to a glorious spread — a great stone house with pink roses crawling up the sides, a terrace, a swimming pool with tiles made to look like an oriental carpet. In the background: trees, cypress, pine, a lawn and garden. The sky was a bright, china blue. In the centre of the frame, a woman with perfectly set hair held a baby in her arms, cheek to cheek, the glow of motherhood on her face. The husband had what Grandmother recognized as an aristocratic bone structure; one arm tight around his wife, the other held away, a cigar poking from his hand. These people, this world. This is what she wanted for her grandchild. She took the subscription card from the magazine and slipped it into her purse. If the LORD had communicated with her once through its glossy pages, perhaps He would again. He could do anything. Jesus's image had shown up in the most ordinary of places —

burnt into toast, etched into frying pans. And now the LORD spoke to her through a culture magazine, a very classy one, possibly the classiest. It made sense. Six hours later, a doctor came to tell her the child had stabilized. Total withdrawal from the opiates and amphetamines the mother had taken during pregnancy could take up to six months. Grandmother was told to go home and rest. The doctor looked tired and like he had no heart, the way he spoke. After she pleaded with him he let her look at the baby through a window, where she was being kept in a glass box with tubes and monitors everywhere. Grandmother would return the next day, and every day thereafter.

The infant Aurora lay inside the incubator for the first three weeks of life, trembling and wailing inconsolably, muscles clenched, sometimes gasping for breath as her tiny body purged itself of the poison. Social services got involved. She was given a birth certificate. Never again would she see, smell, or feel her mother's touch. Three days after giving birth, her mother fell unconscious after an accidental oxytocin overdose with a lit cigarette between her fingers. This started a fire that ended in the explosion of her trailer along with a methamphetamine manufacturing shed before the fire department arrived. Social Services granted custody of the child to her grandmother.

Upon taking the infant home, the doctors warned Grandmother of the dangers that came with the life of a crack baby. The child would most likely have learning disabilities and impaired motor skills. It was important to watch and observe, to catch out abnormalities, to take the child to a doctor at the first sign of anything unusual for diagnosis and treatment. Grandmother nodded, smiled, and thanked them. In her head, she knew they were no match for the LORD and that it was to Him she must appeal if her little grandchild was going to survive and thrive in this world.

In the months that followed, Grandmother warmed formula, cradling her infant grandchild in her arms and voluminous breasts, cooing, smelling the child's sweet skin, kissing her on the forehead. "May the LORD protect you, keep you safe." She prayed and closed her eyes, hoping that in the void she would reach God, that He would hear her and shine his light on the child.

This was the third child Grandmother would raise. The first drowned in Lake Mohave, a body of water everyone referred to as tranquil, on a camping trip. Eight years old. A boy. The second, Aurora's mother, as we are aware, went with Satan, and up in flames. LORD knew Grandmother had tried everything she could to stop this from happening. She had done her best to raise a God-fearing child, to keep her daughter clean and on the straight and narrow. What had she done wrong? The LORD forgave if you were repentant. She repented but didn't know what for exactly.

Grandmother prayed before every meal and down on her knees every night before bed, *Now I lay me down to sleep. I pray the Lord my soul to keep. If I should die before I wake, I pray to God my soul to take. If I should live for other days I pray the Lord to guide my ways.* They went to the megachurch every Sunday. She did not take the LORD's name in vain. She obeyed all His Commandments. This child would know and live and breathe and love the LORD and Jesus our Savior. She would live in the glory of Jesus and be protected.

Grandmother delighted in Aurora getting fat on infant formula. Watching her suckle the bottle, her little body growing more and more plump, delicious, irresistible to kiss, she buried her nose in the child's sweet smell. She was a beautiful baby, like the babies in T.V. commercials. Maybe even more beautiful.

Grandmother read *Town & Country*, religiously. The more she read the more she knew the world depicted in the pages was the kind of world she wanted for her grandchild. Aurora had to be amongst them, think like them, speak like them, behave like them from the very beginning. It was going to take money.

In her naiveté, Grandmother thought that if she took a couple of jobs from home, combined with her social security, she would be able to afford the education by saving up. If she had known the enormous sum she would have to accumulate, she most likely would have abandoned the project. But as it was, determined to watch Aurora grow into a woman of class, like the women on *Dynasty* and *Dallas,* with the power to wrap men around her little finger, she persevered. Aurora had to go to the best schools. The best kindergarten, the best elementary school, and all the way up to college. There, she would be surrounded by the monied elites, marry one of them, have his babies, secure her financial future. Any woman who married a multimillionaire and had his baby was entitled to half his fortune. Everyone knew that.

Grandmother worked stuffing envelopes with the din of the television in the background as she cast an eye on her little grandchild wiggling on the floor in her playpen, making pterodactyl noises, putting whatever she could get her hands on into her mouth, drooling on her toys, staring into space, crying when she was hungry or bored or frustrated or had spoiled a diaper. If life was a blur from lack of sleep, it was a happy one. Aurora was the angel of her grandmother's eye.

Worried Aurora would pick up a cheap trailer-park drawl and low-born mannerisms, Grandmother wouldn't allow her to play with the neighborhood children as she grew up. This left her in the company of a cat that appeared one morning in the kitchen sink.

Day and night, Grandmother plotted to rid the cat from her home. Black as pitch, sleek and shiny as an eel, its eyes lit a brilliant jade, the animal's distinct, clean lines reminded her of Egyptian cat statues she'd seen in witchcraft shops. The Egyptians who, in the Bible, were pagans and sinned against God. They worshipped cat bodies with human heads and human bodies with bird heads and cat heads. A black cat was not a good omen.

Grandmother crushed a Valium tablet and sprinkled it on a plate of canned tuna, then waited. The cat slinked out of whatever crevice it had been hiding in and approached the plate of tuna, eating it in chunks until it fell over, laying comatose on the kitchen floor, tongue lolling between its sharp incisors, limp as a dead rabbit.

This was how Aurora's grandmother found it the next time she got up to pour another cup of coffee and make toast. She put it in a shoe box without Aurora seeing (Aurora adored the animal — she adored all animals). Grandmother brought the box with the drugged cat to the car and stashed it under the passenger seat. She strapped Aurora in and gave her a packet of gummy worms to keep her occupied. They took a drive north to the Spirit Mountain area. Seeing a rest stop as good as any with a lot of scrub brush to hide the box in, Grandmother pulled over. After getting rid of the cat, she got back into the car, relieved, and turned on the radio to gospel music, singing along while Aurora slept, head slumped to the side in her car seat, the sight of her plump, flushed baby cheeks in the rearview mirror making her heart warm.

The next morning the cat was back in the kitchen sink. Licking its paws, it may as well have come through the drain as noxious vapors and materialized in cat form. The LORD and Jesus knew how many prayers Grandmother had sent up to cast the devil cat from her home.

In the end, there was no controlling the animal. It left mice hearts and tiny strings of intestines on the front steps as tributes. Like all felines, the cat was master of himself. He did not bow to anyone or anything. There was no shooing it out of the house with a broom. It always found its way back inside. Every night the animal shared Aurora's crib, his head nestled in the crook of her arm, the warm, purring body as close to hers as possible, paws wrapped around her little shoulder, a smile on its face; the room dimly illuminated by a plastic, phosphorescent Virgin Mary on the dresser, until the glow faded out, the room went dark and Aurora drifted off to sleep, her body vibrating with the cat's purrs so that it seemed like she too was a cat, purring herself to sleep. Aurora watched the cat with wide eyes as it jumped from the floor to the tabletops to the refrigerator where it sat, posing like a gargoyle. From the top of the television set it launched itself into her playpen. Aurora squealed, waved her arms and drooled with delight.

When Aurora could walk, she followed the cat outside into the front and back areas of the trailer, surrounded by a chain-link fence that marked their lot. Aurora knew she was never to crawl out under the fence with the cat. Once when she'd tried to, her grandmother came out of nowhere, grabbed her by the leg and pulled her through the dirt, smacking her bottom and yelling that she was never to do that again, that she was never allowed beyond the fence alone: anyone on the other side might take her away and she would never see her grandmother again. Aurora obeyed. She played with her plastic shovel and bucket, her second-hand Goodwill Barbie and her stuffed animal rabbit in the dirt, waiting for the cat to return with its kills. Aurora's fascination with the animal was absolute and bound with deep attachment and love, something the cat recognized and returned with the total dedication that lurks in the hearts of cats, despite their reputation for not caring whether humans live or die.

Aurora dug holes around the side of the trailer for the dead animals the cat brought back, collecting the prettiest stones to decorate the graves, eventually making a little cemetery. She didn't question why she was doing this; it was something instinctual, or something she'd seen on the television.

One day the cat delivered a house sparrow alive. She cupped the delicate creature in her hands, its tiny body resting there, feathers striped with brown and gold outlined in black, wings fluttering, eyes blinking. She felt its little heart beating in the palm of her hand. It was the most beautiful creature she'd ever seen up close besides the cat. The little bird gave a last flutter. The electric current of its life disappeared. She thought that if she buried it, one day it would rise again, like Christ. Even so, she felt a sinking, childhood sadness and cried as she made its grave.

The fact that Aurora was four years old and didn't speak but would instead meow, chirp, growl and sometimes hiss, was worrying. Her grandmother prayed every night for the cat to disappear. She didn't yet have enough money for pre-school, and wasn't going to change her mind about Aurora playing with the other children in the trailer park. She prayed to the LORD and Jesus for Aurora to grow out of her attachment to the cat and finally speak human words. Grandmother always kept the television on, hoping this would make a difference.

Finally, after paying off the ambulance ride to the hospital that had saved Aurora's life, Grandmother's bank account was healthy enough to enroll the child in the fanciest pre-school in Laughlin. On Aurora's first day, Grandmother was too proud to tell the teachers the child did not speak and would only make cat noises. She prayed Aurora would refrain from this feral way of communicating at school — that the LORD would strike her with His glory and put words in her mouth. For the first week, Aurora remained silent. The teachers assumed she was shy and tried everything they could to bring her out of her shell.

To Aurora the other children looked like uncoordinated, fleshy blobs, blubbering and screaming. They were nothing like the cat. She knew she had the same features as they did; the same smooth skin, hands, fingers, the same arms and legs, but she couldn't help but feel she wasn't really one of them. However, as time went on, Aurora stepped from the sidelines and shadows and began to participate, making paper-chain octopuses, dancing in circles with the other children, holding their hands, playing in the sand pit, herded around by her teachers from activity to activity. But what she really wanted was to be at home with the cat. The children were too loud and demanding.

Aurora knelt each night with her hands clasped beside her Grandmother, who knelt in the same attitude, imploring, "Lord Jesus, we need You. You died on the cross for our sins. I open the door of my life and receive You as my Savior and Lord. Thank You for forgiving our sins and giving us eternal life. Take control of the throne of our lives. Make us the kind of person You want us to be. Please bless my granddaughter and make her speak." She would finish with *Now I Lay Me Down to Sleep* before she said Amen.

After this, they would get into bed and Grandmother would read to Aurora from tomes of fairy tales she acquired at the Goodwill; stories in which Rapunzel, Sleeping Beauty, Snow White, Thumbelina and so on, are tortured by their families, and eventually saved by a prince with whom they live happily ever after. Aurora — wide-eyed, thumb in her mouth — listened to her grandmother, living in the stories through her soothing voice until she became drowsy and was carried off to sleep.

Aurora's favourite was *The Wild Swans*, where, in a kingdom, far, far away, there lived a widowed king with his twelve children: eleven princes and one princess. One day the king decides he needs a wife and a mother for his children. Unbeknownst to the king, he chooses a wicked queen who is a witch. Out of spite, the queen turns her stepsons into magnificent swans who are only allowed to become human again when the sun sets.

Next, the queen tries to bewitch the young princess, Elisa. But Elisa's goodness is too strong and she overcomes the witchcraft, so the queen covers her in mud and dirt and banishes her to the forest. Elisa's brothers, imprisoned in the form of swans swoop down and carry her to safety.

Here, Elisa is instructed by the queen of the fairies to gather stinging nettles in graveyards. Like this, she can knit shirts which will break the evil queen's spell, allowing her brothers to regain their human forms. Elisa must take a vow of silence. One word from her lips, and the word becomes a sword stuck into her brother's hearts. She endures painful blisters on her fingers from the nettle stings as she works.

During the course of her shirt-making, a handsome king from a faraway land happens upon her. Elisa cannot speak, but the king falls in love with her anyway. He takes her from the land of the faeries to his castle where he gives her a room to continue knitting her brothers' nettle shirts. He understands how important it is to her. The faerie queen has filled him in on Elisa's task and the selfless act has made him fall in love with her even more. Eventually, the king proposes to crown Elisa as his queen and wife. Elisa accepts, nodding her head. However, there's a problem. The Archbishop of the land believes Elisa is a witch because of all the nettle knitting and the fact she refuses to speak. He tries to convince the king she is a danger.

One night, Elisa runs out of nettles and is forced to collect more in a nearby church graveyard. From behind some bushes, the Archbishop is watching. Ghoulish spirits that devour the bodies of the dead carouse the churchyard. The Archbishop believes Elisa is in league with them. The statues of the saints shake their heads in protest, but the Archbishop misinterprets this sign as confirmation of Elisa's guilt. He reports the incident to the king as proof of witchcraft. The Archbishop then orders Elisa be put on trial for sorcery. Elisa can speak no word in her defense, and is sentenced to death by burning at the stake.

The brothers discover Elisa's plight and try to speak to the king but fail, thwarted by the rising sun that turns them into swans. Even as the tumbril bears Elisa away to execution, she continues knitting. This enrages the people, who are on the brink of snatching and ripping the shirts into pieces. Suddenly, the swans descend to rescue Elisa. The people interpret this as a sign from Heaven that she is innocent. Meanwhile, Elisa nearly finishes the last shirt, as the executioner continues to prepare for the burning. Elisa uses the last of her strength to throw each garment over the swans. Instantly, her brothers return to their human forms, all but the youngest who must forever live with a swan's wing instead of an arm, as she didn't have time to finish the last sleeve.

With her task completed, Elisa is free to speak — to tell the truth. But, alas, she cannot! She faints from exhaustion. Her brothers explain the situation in her stead. As they do so, the firewood around the stake miraculously takes root and bursts into flowers. The king plucks the topmost one and places it on Elisa's chest. She is revived by the white flower, and the king and Elisa are married.

Night after night Aurora's grandmother read her fairy tales. She prayed to the LORD for His grace, His intervention, to fill her granddaughter's mouth with words; make her communicate. On one such night, Grandmother pleading and crying to Jesus, Aurora gave in and said, in a perfect little voice, "It's okay, Grandma, don't cry". This made Grandmother cry harder. She pulled Aurora into her arms against her breasts, praising the LORD, thanking Jesus, squeezing the child so hard she nearly knocked the breath out of her.

Aurora proved bright. She had been reluctant to speak the language of her grandmother, of the other adults and children, because it seemed superfluous. The cat made more sense. But once she entered this world of words, there was no stopping her. In the car, she called out the street signs and speed limits, advising her grandmother to turn left or right or keep going straight. All of this was proof the LORD favoured the child, that His Grace was upon her, that He had a special mission for Aurora — to serve Him and His Son, Jesus Christ. Aurora was in the fold. She wasn't brain damaged like the doctors said she would be. It was a miracle.

At the breakfast table, the child sounded words off the coffee containers and cereal boxes, reading out the headlines of magazines as she drank her milk and ate her cereal. (Incidentally, it was here, eating a bowl of Frosted Flakes, that Aurora first came into contact with infinity on a can of Dutch hot chocolate which sat beside it, staring at the little braided Dutch girl in a blue dress, white pinafore, and white pointed cap on the label, who stood holding a can of the very same hot chocolate upon which another image of herself was presumably stamped, and so on. The second time she faced infinity, much later, was aged eleven, in front of funhouse mirrors at a carnival. Here, she was shaken by a relentless and ruthless infinity, recognizing reality as a form of illusion and illusion as a form of reality and felt compelled to embrace it. The tug and pull were overpowering. This was the abyss.)

On a trip to the Goodwill, they hit the jackpot and found more Jesus paraphernalia, statues, crosses for the walls, a lamp, and a rug that Grandmother placed strategically around the trailer so that His eyes were on them at all times. (His eyes and the eyes of owls. Because she also collected owl figurines.)

Each night Grandmother slipped her red, swollen fingers into a glass bowl filled with ice cubes and topped with water, as she watched evangelical channels, or else travel programs, or news for twenty minutes, after which, sleep would take her. The sewing and envelope stuffing along with a pension had been just enough to get by, save two thousand dollars, and send Aurora to the pre-school in Laughlin. The next step was kindergarten. She had seen a school mentioned in *Town & Country Magazine*, the Rudolf Steiner Waldorf. Children of the American elite and European aristocracy went there.

At the pre-school, Grandmother asked Aurora's teachers if they had heard of the school. She was met with raised eyebrows and screwed-up faces. "It might be 'right' for 'some' children," they said. And then something about it having 'alternative' ideas and 'rich hippies'. This reaction didn't deter Grandmother. If it was right for the European aristocracy, Hollywood people, the children of Formula One drivers, it was right for Aurora; her star was going to rise and burn bright. This was Grandmother's vision. It was clear the people at the pre-school school weren't going to help her, so she went to the public library. There, Grandmother stood before the librarian at the front desk, and stated her cause.

Never having heard anything like this before, the librarian, nevertheless, did not balk at the request and was in fact deeply moved and impressed by the grandmother's ambitious plan for her granddaughter. She agreed to help, found the address and telephone number of the only Waldorf school in the area, and wrote it down, adding, "If you decide it's right for your grandchild after visiting it, I can help you with application forms. Don't hesitate to come back".

The next day, at nine on the dot, Grandmother dialed the number. She was given an appointment with the head teacher for the following week.

The school sat on the outskirts of town, off the main highway, down a service road in the middle of nowhere. Red dust spooled into the air behind them; Grandmother held on to the steering wheel, her bouffant glistening with hairspray in the sun, navigating the dips and rocky parts of the road as they made their way toward the lone ranch in the distance, far-off mountains at the horizon, serrated like broken teeth. When they got there a painted sign with gold lettering stood to mark the entrance. This was the next step. They had to make a good impression. Grandmother made a kind of Scout's honour sign with her hand, kissed her pointer and middle fingers, pressed together, then placed them on the forehead of her dashboard Jesus. Grandmother closed her eyes and said a prayer. She looked at the child with pride, so beautifully formed, her hair shining with hairspray, her little bow lips, her little angel, "Here we are". She took the key out of the ignition, "With the LORD's help, this will be your next school. We're going to meet one of the teachers.

Remember Jesus and be on your best behaviour". Her eyes found Aurora's, who smiled back from the car seat, hands folded neatly in her lap, nodding in the cool blast of the air conditioning.

Once out of the car, a blast of hot, dry desert air hit them, burning their faces, bringing the smell of farm animal, herbs, and desert dust. The sound of children murmuring and wind chimes accompanied them up the flagstone walk to the door. Inside, it was cool and shadowy under the wooden eaves, with the scent of cured lumber and linseed oil soap drifting from the recesses. A young woman directed them to wait on one of the sofas.

In the interview, sitting with her purse on her lap, Grandmother listened dutifully, nodding her head when it seemed she was supposed to. She did not forget to smile. When the head teacher asked whether the school sounded like something she would want for her grandchild, she knew what she had to say and said it: "More than anything, I want the best education for my little girl. I know this school is the best. She's a sensitive, bright, child. I want her to rise in life. Her parents are gone, in Heaven — rest their souls — and I will do all that it takes to give my grandchild opportunities. I don't come from much. We live in the trailer park across the river. I want her to have the finest education she can. It's the only way she's going to rise in life. I know that now. It has been made very clear to me. It's the gift I want to give to her". She steeled herself, going through all the different ways to ask the head teacher about financing, then stopped and just came straight out with it. She could barely afford the nursery school and knew the Waldorf was going to be more expensive. Upon seeing the place, there was no doubt in her mind that this was the school for Aurora.

Grandmother's frank and humble manner immediately endeared her to the teacher, who said, "I can sense your deep commitment to Aurora's education and applaud you. The environment at Waldorf is one where we wish to encourage and nurture reverence for what is noble, true and beautiful". She smiled and looked at Aurora's small, open face; curious and calm and very cat-like.

"That's exactly what I want for her. I want her to grow to be noble and true and beautiful." Aurora's grandmother turned her head lovingly to the child and smiled.

The teacher nodded her head. "We do offer scholarships, if it's something that would interest you? I'll give you the application forms. We'll need them back in two months. We have an open house soon — ask our receptionist for the details. It is highly recommended you come and have a tour of the school".

Aurora's grandmother stepped out the school front doors into the sun, stunned. There was the possibility of a scholarship. The possibility Aurora could attend this school into high school if she was accepted. That would be the next decade accounted for — a golden path that led straight to the elite world of *Town & Country*. The teacher said she "applauded" her. This was like a standing ovation. She and Aurora had been tapped by Jesus. Yes, this was surely His hand. They were on the right path. The LORD and Jesus were shining down on them; showering them with gifts. They had to continue to please Them.

That afternoon Grandmother went to the librarian for help with the forms, not wanting to — because asking for help was a sign of weakness — but knowing if she didn't do it correctly, Aurora wouldn't get in.

The librarian was gracious and didn't make Aurora's grandmother feel like an idiot. Grandmother noted the elegant way the librarian's finger trailed across her forehead, pushing her hair into place, then fell to the counter where she took up a pen, wrote her number on a piece of paper and handed it over discreetly, like a secret. The two communicated over the telephone. In a matter of days, the librarian completed the applications. Grandmother baked a cake and drove to the library with Aurora in tow, signing and dating each line the librarian pointed to with her pen. Aurora gave the librarian a drawing she'd made for the occasion — at her grandmother's request, something with Jesus in it. A gigantic Jesus floated in mid-air in the page, upright, arms out, in the crucifixion position, with a halo — hearts flying from his outstretched hands. God sat in a cloud that rained flowers, crosses, and sunbeams on his Son. In the corner, holding hands, four small figures — herself, the cat, the librarian and her grandmother — stood side-by-side underneath a rainbow with a tiny cake that was difficult to make out. They did not stay to share the Angel cake; instead, Grandmother drove directly to the school where she delivered the application by hand.

The day of the open house, Aurora's grandmother brushed the little girl's hair until it shone and fashioned tight French braids that pulled her eyes up at the corners. This was the classiest kind of hairdo for a child. She dressed Aurora in a red corduroy, embroidered pinafore dress, a white-capped sleeve shirt, white socks, and black shoes with a buckle. She hoped the child would fit in and be presentable. They had to make a good impression if they were going to get the scholarship.

The Waldorf was a wonderland. The tour began at the playground. Delighted screams rang out. Children filled wooden buckets at a water pump and carried them to one of the pits, where they made sandcastles. Swings and climbing structures with rope bridges, towers, and slides crawled with frolicking children. At the far end was a koi pond with a waterfall. The students played in little log houses reminiscent of medieval Russian villages from storybooks, the eves carved with animals and flowers; the shutters decorated with hearts and acorns cut into them. A culturally-appropriated Inuit-esque totem pole stood in the center of one of the sand pits. From another pit, a great wooden dragon reared its head and back.

The tour group moved to the vegetable garden. Everything grown here was used in the school's kitchen. Next was the barn — a classic red prairie barn — where the goats, pigs, sheep and cows slept at night. During the day the animals were set out to pasture; even the pigs were free-range and lured back to the barn at night with food.

On the way to the stables, the tour guide pointed out older children in the distance practicing archery in the hard sheets of sun, with bows and arrows they had made themselves. Mares and stallions frolicked and ate grass in the fields. Next they visited the empty stables where polished tack hung from the walls; oiled saddles sat in their designated places. Strong whiffs of leather, oils and hay combined with the sweet smell of horses and went to Aurora's head.

Along the way, the tour guide explained that Waldorf children learned to milk cows, goats, and make goat's cheese. The sheep were sheared by professionals, after which the children washed the wool in eco-friendly soap and prepared it to knit their own hats, sweaters, toys — whatever. It was the kind of character-building climate a hippie, philosopher and survivalist would imagine for their child. Every morning the younger children went to collect eggs from the nests in the chicken coop.

Indoors, the fairy-tale folk theme continued in carved wood; each tiny chair, table, and desk crafted with care and skill. Chains of dried flowers hung from the wooden eaves. Tiled floors were covered with handwoven scatter rugs and sheepskins. At the front of the classroom hung a blackboard with lessons in chalk. The rooms were bright and colorful with painted cubbyholes and shelves stacked with art supplies, wooden toys, games, books, dressing-up costumes, jump ropes, etc. Here they did arts and crafts, drew pictures, made figures out of clay and beeswax. Aurora was enchanted. She wanted more than anything in the world to attend the Waldorf. After the tour, Grandmother drove straight home and spent the rest of the evening praying to Jesus.

Several weeks later, they learned that the interview with the head teacher was successful. Tears poured from Grandmother's eyes as she read the acceptance letter. Aurora asked why she was crying. She took the child into her arms and told her she was crying because she was happy; they had won the lottery: Aurora would be going to the Waldorf. Shivering with joy, she whispered in Aurora's little ear that God was watching and shining on her, and had sent them another blessing. Aurora was special; she had been chosen.

The first day of school, Aurora had never been so excited in her short life. Each morning the Waldorf children formed a circle — hand in tiny, warm hand — singing together to greet the day. There were special songs for everything; the children spent most of the day singing. Aurora loved it — the humming and vibrating of everyone's voices together; the words that were no longer just words but things that made you catch your breath, that set your head on fire with lyrics that spoke of "trusting the heart's inner light", a light which was like the sun and composed of the highest virtues: kindness, honesty and truth.

They sang on their excursions into the surrounding desert, looking for faeries with their teachers. There were songs for the birds and the lizards and the plants and the four directions. They sang for the goats and horses — soothing songs with calm, tranquilizing voices. There were songs for making arts and crafts, buzzing songs for when they used beeswax, songs for digging in the vegetable gardens. And they did it all together. Teamwork. Dreamwork. Working together harmoniously. Singing.

Of course, even with all this singing to keep them focused and harmonious, there were tantrums and upsets. Children got kicked and bitten and threw sand in each other's faces. They painted on one another and their clothes. A boy smuggled in a black permanent marker and gave a number of children tattoos all over their arms and faces before he was caught. There were power struggles, miscommunications; children who thought it would be funny to offer their urine up as lemonade from the windows of one of the Russian-style playhouses. One boy tried, on more than one occasion, to make Aurora eat little round goat turds. Another tried to pee on her in one of the sandpits. She was shocked, then awed by his ability, imagining how it would feel to possess something like that rubbery, wormy thing between your legs that could be turned into a squirt gun.

Grandmother noticed Aurora playing with "imaginary friends" around the time she began to read. She would find Aurora in a circle of her play teacups on the living-room floor, pretending to serve three people, plus the cat, whom Aurora now referred to as Tu-tu. Where she had gotten this name, Grandmother had no idea. The imaginary friends also had names: Nura, Putta, and Electra, whom she pronounced "Lectra". They were princesses.

When pressed further, as to where these invisible beings came from, Aurora simply explained they were three girls, all lit up, who could fly around the room. Thunderbolts came from Electra's fingertips. She could turn into pure energy and she ran through the wires. All of them could disappear into thin air. When asked what they talked about the child gave no clear answer. All Grandmother could make out was that these beings enjoyed tea parties and telling stories about the land they came from.

Now, Aurora's grandmother knew, as theologians do, that if God diverts His gaze from anything — for example, the hand and the pencil I am writing with — whatever it is will cease to exist. Not only that, but it will also be plunged into hellfire. How can something which doesn't exist be plunged into anything? But we will let this metaphysical question be for now, and just say that the business of the imaginary friends, the people Aurora spoke to in the thin air, and the cat, worried Grandmother deeply. She wondered whether the two were connected — if the demon cat had brought other demons into her home. She feared that for whatever reason, God was looking away.

Tossing and turning the matter in her mind, she couldn't be one hundred per cent certain. All she knew was that she had prayed herself blue in the face, imploring the LORD and Jesus to protect her grandchild. She and Aurora had never missed a Sunday at the megachurch. Perhaps this was a test of faith. Or a phase the child would grow out of.

As you may have guessed, the church was a great presence in Aurora's life. At church and through her grandmother, Aurora learned that her life was not her own, that there was a Creator to whom she owed it, the LORD. Jesus, who was His Son, had died for them on the cross and risen from the dead. He had done this because He loved her and all of humanity.

When Aurora asked about her parents, her grandmother told her they were far away, with the Angels. Aurora knew Angels from a young age. Her grandmother was always referring to them — she understood how they could be far away and remote, but also close by. She loved the Angels — they had wings and glowing haloes. Her grandmother had done her best to drill it into Aurora's head that her mother and father were up in a kingdom in the sky with the Angels, looking down on her. She would never be alone. They would always be up there, shining their loving light upon her.

There was also the Holy Spirit who was God's presence on earth. This presence could enter people and then they became holy, like the pastors. Satan was a fallen angel who was pure evil and would try every trick in the book to draw people into committing sins. He was God's immortal enemy, the cause of all that is wrong in the world, possessing people with demons and making them do horrible things. He could also shapeshift and pretend to be a snake, for example. Satan was the price one paid for forsaking God and Jesus. Eternal hell. Like the tattooed people in the trailer park Grandmother warned her about. Satan was in the fissures. Step on a crack, break your mother's back. Aurora was always looking out for Satan, who lurked in the shadows.

Aurora took the Sunday school group at the megachurch very seriously. One Sunday morning, in the middle of playtime, she stood up, put a toy gun to her head, and told the room she was ready to die for everyone's sins, like Jesus. She wasn't playing around, she meant what she said and was ready to die then and there for the sins of the world, so everyone could be free and live in Paradise. The rest of the children followed suit. There was a fight over the limited supply of plastic pistols, resulting in a brawl with children getting their hair pulled out, limbs scratched, a bitten face, bruises, one bloody lip with a broken tooth. The room was filled with roiling, screaming children. The teachers called for backup on the walkie-talkies.

The incident was contained by the time Aurora's grandmother arrived to collect her. Two of the Sunday school teachers explained what had transpired, and then began asking questions about Aurora's behavior at home, if she had noticed anything unusual. Grandmother told them nothing was out of the ordinary, except that Aurora had three imaginary friends, and she didn't know if that was normal or not. The teachers asked her exactly what went on between the child and the imaginary people and she explained that Aurora spoke to them, had tea parties, and danced. The word 'dance' changed the look on their faces; they became concerned. This made Grandmother confess that Aurora was also very fond of a black cat, who showed up out of nowhere and had settled in. The two teachers agreed they would have to take the matter to the pastors.

One of the Sunday school teachers led Aurora and her grandmother to a room like in a hotel with a bed, writing table, chest of drawers, a television and bathroom. There was a large mirror but no window. The teacher told the grandmother to press the first transparent button on the telephone if they needed anything, and that someone would be right back after the pastors were consulted. The teacher left and locked the door.

Aurora began to sob and tried to explain to her grandmother how she had wanted to die for everyone's sins like Jesus. She thought her teachers would be happy. Jesus was love. Aurora wanted to be love too. She wanted to sacrifice herself and be the love that saved the world.

Aurora's grandmother couldn't understand all the child was trying to say, and held her close, stroking her hair, telling her everything was going to be alright, saying prayers until Aurora calmed. She brought her to the bed and put the television on. There were two channels, one playing recordings of the pastor's sermons; the other a cartoon with Biblical stories made for a child's understanding. Her grandmother turned the channel to the cartoon while Aurora curled up on the bed and fell asleep, her red cheeks stained with tear tracks.

Several hours later three of the pastors came in and announced they were going to have to perform an exorcism immediately. They asked questions about how long she had been unconscious; if there were any markings that had recently appeared on the child's body. All her grandmother could think to say was that the child had cried, was very distraught, and was trying to say something which she couldn't understand but she said "Jesus", more than once. One of the pastors went to the bed and took the child, draping her in his arms, body dangling like a doll. The three left the room, one holding Aurora, and did not allow her grandmother to follow. They told her she could go home or wait there.

Aurora began to wake in the pastor's arms and didn't know where she was or if she was having a nightmare. She tried to scream, to shift, to get herself free. No scream came out. The pastor held her tighter as she squirmed. They took an elevator down several levels, got out, walked down a white, brightly-lit corridor and entered a door on the right. Inside was also bright and white. Aurora could not gauge the size of the room; she only saw the brightness, and behind it faint strokes of walls at odd angles. There was a shiny, cold silver table. They strapped her onto it. The pastors chanted, hissed and sprinkled water over her, ringing bells, scratching at her with crosses. One of them was the pastor who gave the sermons in front of all the people. He was someone Aurora recognized. He told her they were fighting Satan's army for her soul. He would rip the demon out and she would be free. They bellowed with spit flying from their mouths, reaching up toward the sky, pleading with the LORD and all the angels to do battle with Satan and his demons, to save the life of the innocent child. Tears streamed down Aurora's cheeks, she could not move; she was strapped to the steel table. Suddenly they began ripping her clothing, clawing at her with twisted faces, removing something hideous. Finally, she was able to scream.

This burst of terror animated them further. Aurora saw their eyes were crazy like the eyes of the people around the trailer park — the ones Aurora's grandmother told her had lost God. Aurora was unstrapped, carried to another part of the room and pushed naked into a claw-foot bathtub filled with ice cubes floating in a small amount of water. The pastors began their hallelujahs and other strange mutterings, then plunged her again and again down into the suffocating cold. Each time they pulled her out her head hummed with their voices, a murmuring Aurora did not understand. She was pushed under again and again until she couldn't feel anything anymore and left her body.

Here, she floated above the scene. She saw herself — her mortal flesh. Her body looked small and blue next to the pastors, one of whom held her in a red blanket while the others implored the sky, jumping and circling, their voices in rhythm, their movements like a dance. They took turns rubbing and shaking her. Aurora watched the scene in horror from her vantage point above.

An iridescent beetle whizzed across the room. It circled the pastors in their various machinations, one of them attempting to reanimate Aurora, then sat on the edge of the bath. Aurora followed the shiny green beetle, swooping downward, and suddenly found herself back in her body. She began to breathe and was met with a shower of prayers, all the pastors in tears over her.

Grandmother did not question why Aurora had been returned to her naked, wrapped in a red blanket, hair wet, whimpering and shaking. The child was too big to carry but she wanted to carry her, to hold her tight, all the way out of there. Instead, it was a pastor who took her in his arms. He told Grandmother not to hesitate to call them if there was any sign a demon had somehow remained. And to get rid of the cat. She told him she would and drove home.

In the car, Aurora began to cry. The sobs soon escalated to screeching at pitches so painful her grandmother had to pull over and hold her until the child fell asleep from exhaustion. When they arrived home, she found she was in fact able to lift the child's light frame, mostly legs, and carried Aurora from the car inside. Grandmother lay the child on the bed, dressed her in pyjamas and tucked her in. She stayed beside Aurora all night, stuffing envelopes, singing Bible songs, until she too drifted off. The child woke up at two a.m., crying, drenched in sweat, hysterical, inconsolable. From then on, Aurora had persistent nightmares of burrowing animals with claws, red shining eyes and sharp, bloodied teeth coming at her from within a network of tunnels...

Aurora keeps running from me. I am trying to catch her. My hands are sticky and covered in blood. Maybe it's the way I'm holding the pencil. I am at the part of the thrall where I am unravelling, in desperate need of the carbonated sugary drink, even though it's bloating my head and I vowed to stop drinking it.

I also need a typewriter, but then the noise might be too much, the tap, tap, tapping to no end. But the scribbling is also gnawing at my brain. I will gulp more of the artificial cherry beverage and have a cold bath with ice cubes and smoke a pipe with hashish and tobacco. Perhaps I'll be able to lie down, close my eyes and collect myself. But like all poets, I am always hungry. Aurora, my dark light, my black sun, this is why I must write everything down. If I leave this insanity that you have given me on the page, perhaps it will stay trapped there.

Writing about her is finally tiring me, but still, inside, there's a fuse vibrating.

In this room there is darkness save for the warm glow of a dim oil lamp. The moonlight casts hollowed silver beams over everything out there in the night. The wind slowly shakes things. In the hard light of the moon there is a peace which I cannot grasp. Everything out there is alien. The last time I slept, I remember there was a ram. Between its horns was an exchange of electromagnetic discharge — a nearly unbearable buzzing and a popping. Then gunshots woke me up.

My hands are freshly bandaged. It's easier to write. There must have been a point at which the acute pain stopped, which I do not recall exactly, because now it's just a dull ache. I ate a round of cucumber but after that, nothing else. I may even be sick. I've gone back on the artificial cherry pop. The effect it's having on me feels like an amphetamine and an opiate.

I have also resorted to a ballpoint pen — the pencil scraping against the page was beginning to cause mental strain; layer upon layer of pencil scratching growing in volume until I wanted to rip my head off. The pen is much quieter.

My handwriting has grown bad-tempered and secret. I am trying to make the writing like silver scaled fish, desperately leaping from the page, but also sober because the sober voice is the one I must always return to. My subject — the object of this writing — Aurora, risks sending me into a permanent delirium. Into a labyrinth from which I will never escape. But let us return to Aurora's story. Where was I?

Aurora began to be invited to playdates. Like this, she and her grandmother came to know the insides of the colossal, sprawling prefabricated houses and were dazzled by them. Her grandmother drank coffee and ate carrot layer cakes with cream cheese frosting in kitchens looking out onto swimming pools, while the girls played Barbie dolls in Barbie villages in playrooms the size of their entire trailer. The bathrooms were at least twice the size of their bedrooms. It made Aurora's grandmother sad she couldn't give her granddaughter the same, but she was glad the girl could at least see and experience it. She would have a point of reference.

In the company of the other mothers, no one paid much attention to Aurora's grandmother or her manner of dress. Nevertheless, she had her platinum-white hair washed and teased into a beehive twice a month at her local hair salon; made sure she was always very clean, smelled of soap, and mostly wore floral shirts and matching slacks. She told everyone the child's parents had died in a car accident. No one asked any further questions. All she had to do was eat cake, drink coffee and nod her head. They paid attention to Aurora, because she was a beautiful little girl who shined.

One day, one of the mothers commented on Aurora's outfits, and how pretty they were, then turned to her grandmother, to ask where she had gotten them. The school didn't allow the children to wear clothing with logos and encouraged all-natural fibers. This prompted Aurora's grandmother to make the child cotton pinafores and dresses, knit cardigans, create all her clothes by hand and sewing machine, in the style of a Russian peasant, in keeping with the fairy-tale theme the school promoted.

The mothers oohed and aahed and talked Grandmother into accepting bespoke orders at inflated sums, well beyond the norm for such things. Jesus had struck again, making everything possible. With the extra money, she sent Aurora to ballet lessons. The orders kept rolling in. Grandmother mulled over stopping the wedding dresses and envelopes altogether, what with the speed at which children grow out of things, but she didn't want to put all of her eggs in one basket. Hands ravaged, her fingers had developed thick callouses. Grandmother was on several expensive arthritis medications, but nothing could stop her. The LORD was working through those hands.

Nightmares with burrowing animals, claws, red reflective eyes, sharp, blood-dripping teeth scratching their way toward Aurora from within a network of tunnels continued. Now, there was also an octopus who wrapped its slimy, muscular arms around her body; the end of its tendril at her throat, squeezing the life out of her, leaving her choking and gasping for breath. Waking in the night to her own silent screams, her cat, Tu-tu, alert, sat at the foot of her bed like an ancient Egyptian statue, eyes shining in the dark.

Teachers at the Waldorf noticed Aurora had become withdrawn. She was tired and pale with dark rings around her eyes. One of them found her crying in the corner of the classroom. Aurora refused to say what was wrong. Two teachers spoke with Grandmother but she revealed nothing. She couldn't think of anything out of the ordinary that had happened, or any unusual behaviour. Busy as she was sewing, knitting, and licking envelopes, chauffeuring Aurora around to ballet, swimming, and gymnastics, she didn't have time to remark any great difference in her granddaughter. As she saw it, Aurora was still Aurora, polite and sweet. There were the nightmares. These were new, but she thought it was something the child would eventually grow out of, like the imaginary friends. Her granddaughter was turning out very nicely — everyone at the church said so.

The school decided to bring in a therapist. Aurora and her grandmother were to meet the woman once a week. Grandmother considered this intrusive and unnecessary — she didn't think Aurora needed to see a "head doctor". There was nothing wrong with the girl's mind. But if it was what she had to do to keep her grandchild in the school — if it was common practice, part of the workings of the institution — she would have to stay quiet. Plus it was free, covered under the health insurance that came with the scholarship.

And so, the therapy sessions began. What had happened, what was happening, Aurora could not speak about. It was as painful to stay quiet as it was to open her mouth and talk.

A transparent film kept her from what was real. The "real" was there, just beyond her grasp, veiled in cellophane. If she got too close to it, it would suffocate her. Was it there to protect her, to keep her from contamination, or to keep her from contaminating reality? It was something she'd been introduced to the night of the exorcism: the part of herself squeezed from her body by fear and terror, that separate self which was perhaps more herself than she had ever known — the one that was lighter than air, that would allow her to fly to the ends of the earth and beyond, further even, than the moon.

Aurora tried to appear normal for the therapist but behaved in a way that set off alarm bells. Her pupils became dilated. When asked about her parents, Aurora appeared to drift further away and explained they were in a better place, that they had become Angels, watching her from above. They were monitoring everything. Jesus was also watching. And God. When the therapist asked, "How do you feel about being watched by all these... invisible beings?" Aurora answered, "I hadn't thought about it," then paused and added, "maybe it's kind of creepy".

When the therapist broke the news to Aurora's grandmother that the child showed definite signs of having experienced trauma, Grandmother's face blushed red with shame. She knew it was the exorcism. But there had been no other option. The demons had to be thrown out. And it had worked: the imaginary friends were gone.

On top of all this, it was clear that one of the worst things in the entire world was to be trailer trash. Trailer trash had no money. They used toilet brushes to wash their backs. They peed on trees like dogs, and made bonfires with used tires, then breathed in the fumes and didn't know they were killing their brain cells. This is why trailer trash people were "retards". They were also "retards" because they were inbred, making babies with their brothers and sisters and cousins. Aurora prayed to Jesus and all the Angels to keep her secret. Somehow, little by little, the other children suspected it. They heard their parents say she was different, that she lived on the other side of the river and that this was why no one was ever invited to her home.

The most popular girls were the first to smell blood. They taunted Aurora, told her she stank, pulled her hair and kicked the backs of her legs, sending her crying into the corners of the little Russian playhouses. Then the boys joined in. And it was true. There was an almost imperceptible odor she carried that they did not — the faint pong of the Goodwill. Her grandmother did her best to keep the trailer and everything they wore clean, but it was there: the smell of poverty. It wafted in through the windows. It was in the cheap food they ate. The scent was subtly detectable in the fabric of the clothes Grandmother sold the Waldorf parents. They whispered amongst themselves that they put their orders through two washing cycles and added extra fabric softener in the dryer.

Aurora found herself shut out, which had the effect of a spell, enclosing her in a sphere by herself. The school's solution to the bullying was to lock her in a classroom at lunch and recess. Instead of sitting there by herself at a desk, she escaped through a window and made a b-line for the rabbit enclosure, took her favourite rabbit, a caramel and white baby bunny with short ears, stuck it in a little cross body bag she found in a cubbyhole someone had sewn in a leather working class, then climbed into the hayloft where the hollering and screaming of the other children was muffled and she could breathe in the smell of hay and rabbit fur, snuggle and play with the bunny, feed it carrots she stole from the vegetable garden, and pretend she was somewhere else.

Truth be told, she wanted vengeance on her classmates, on her teachers who had locked her in the classroom. Maybe she was trailer trash, but they weren't any better than she was. In fact, they were worse. They were the kind of people who would have crucified Jesus.

The next time Aurora and Grandmother went to the YMCA for swimming there was a new sign at the pool.

NOTICE PERSONS HAVING CURRENTLY ACTIVE DIARRHOEA OR WHO HAVE HAD ACTIVE DIARRHOEA WITHIN THE PREVIOUS 14 DAYS SHALL NOT BE ALLOWED TO ENTER THE POOL WATER.

Grandmother stood before the sign. "Well, this is probably because of the Mexicans."

Aurora said nothing, only looked up at her grandmother, reading her face, taking in her white, perfect French twist hairdo, her pink lipstick.

"Politicians. Making crazy laws because of Mexicans. The next thing you know, they'll be trying to keep us from buying guns." Grandmother carried her deceased husband's .45 semi-automatic Smith & Wesson in her purse and kept his shotgun in her bedroom closet. He'd taken her out into the desert to show her how to use them. When the time came, she planned on teaching Aurora but hoped instead that her granddaughter would get out of the trailer park and find a man who could protect her so that she wouldn't need to know how to use a gun. It wasn't exactly ladylike. "I don't know if you should swim in this pool anymore, baby girl."

"I know how to swim already. We don't need to come back here."

"Mexicans. Ruining this country." She shook her head, took Aurora's hand, and walked back to the changing rooms to get her out of her swimsuit. "I'll cancel the YMCA membership." She thought of the beautiful swimming pools at the McMansions Aurora's friends lived in. She prayed to Jesus that one day Aurora would have a pool of her own, even more magnificent, like the people in *Town & Country* magazine, with waterfalls and a hot tub on the side, where Aurora's children could play and swim in luxury.

Aurora and her grandmother continued to attend the megachurch every Sunday without fail. They were usually late. Aurora would say she had a fever, or else hide in the back corner of her closet with clothes piled on top of her. Grandmother would drag her out, which ended in her temperature being taken, found to be normal, and both of them getting into the car.

Terror sat on Aurora's chest, threatening to suffocate her all the way there, intensifying as they got closer. Once inside the great hall of the glittering, shining, stained glass dome, her gut continued to churn; her heart beat in her ears. Something alive and menacing vibrated violently inside her until she thought she might burst into flames. Please, please, please, please make it stop, she whispered to herself.

The congregation hailed the LORD and Jesus in a chaos of voices. Eyes closed, dusted with purple eyeshadow, head bent, Grandmother went into a trance. The air around them was heavy with perfume and sweat. The preacher shouted down from the stage. Aurora's blood ran cold. Her skin crawled. His vibrating, preacher voice went up and down through her body and the metal of the microphone: "I know I'm saved because I feel it right here! (thumping his chest) Right here! (pointing and poking at his heart) I would not trade this feeling I have for a stack of Ferraris as high as the Statue of Liberty! I would not trade the love of the LORD for a fleet of private jets, for helicopters, or mansions with fancy swimming pools! No! Not for cruise ships or any amount of money! Jesus walked across a sea of sins to save our souls! Jesus was so soul-hungry He died one death for us all, but He would have gladly died a million million times for each and every one of you! He would have endured ten billion nails in his body for every man, woman, and child on earth! This is how much Jesus loved humanity!"

The noise was deafening. In such a large space it seemed impossible to be claustrophobic, but everything pressed on Aurora — the voices, the devotees, the lights. Aurora looked down and thought, *Are these really my arms? Are these really my legs?* She looked up at the scene and a curious sensation overcame her; her field of vision narrowed — walls of darkness crept up behind her on all sides. She knew that when the tunnel closed she would be completely and utterly broken. She begged Jesus to make it stop.

Months wore on and turned into years of being forced to endure the pastor's sermons. Aurora couldn't stop thinking about what they had done to her. She knew it was evil. They were the imposters; they had been the ones possessed by demons. She was the sacrifice. She understood that now. Jesus had been on her side, and she had suffered as He had. Up there, on the stage, was a demon in the guise of a holy man. A false prophet, like the Bible warned about. Satan.

At the age of twelve, Aurora discovered Joseph Campbell's book, *The Hero with a Thousand Faces,* in the Waldorf library. As she no longer had any friends, she had plenty of time to read. She learned that the story of Jesus was not unique. Other figures in more ancient history had died and risen from the dead. They had also performed miracles. Certain details in the life of Jesus were eerily similar to pagan gods who had preceded Him. Then, there was the Buddha, also a historical figure, who had performed miracles and influenced men and women for thousands of years.

The Waldorf library was extensive. She borrowed books on the Celts, the ancient Greeks and Romans, Hinduism, Buddhism — everything the shelves marked History and Religion had to offer. Books were a Pandora's box, which she had opened and could not shut. She found Dee Brown's *Bury My Heart at Wounded Knee* and learned of the genocide on which her country was founded; the lies the U.S. government told, the cruelty and barbarism. Reading at night before bed — her face hot with rage, her heart sick in her chest, eyes swollen from crying — she would fall asleep under the glow of the Virgin Mary, exhausted; Tu-tu's warm body purring beside her. She sobbed into her pillow. She no longer believed in her grandmother's God. A God like that was evil. It was impossible to look away no matter how horrific the truths she learned turned out to be. The books Aurora read threw her into a pit of spiritual, historical, and existential chaos. She hadn't been told the whole truth. She had no idea what the truth was anymore.

One morning Aurora woke to find blood in her underpants. She knew this would happen. The blood stain made a heart shape in her underwear. She wondered if this was the shape of the hole it came out of. Aurora's grandmother had told her the day she bled from down there was the day she became a woman. Hair had also begun to grow under her arms and between her legs. It was disgusting, and shameful. She hadn't even developed breasts yet. Aurora prayed to the glow-in-the-dark Virgin Mary figurine on her bedside table to give her some, not to forget her. Now there would be this blood coming out of her for the rest of her days every month. She couldn't help but think of Jesus's blood. Jesus was also a victim of his father — that evil, cruel god.

At school, Aurora had become a ghost. The other girls didn't even want to waste their energy humiliating her. The teachers shunned her as well. She moved in her own orb, observing everyone else's drama. Orchestra practice was the only place she felt any sense of belonging to a greater whole. In the music she was a part of everything she had been denied. Although, everyone knew her oboe was second-hand and thought it was disgusting.

One morning over coffee and Danish sugar cookies from a tin, Grandmother flipped through *Town & Country*, her eyes landing on the name of a New England prep school. She'd questioned the kind of education Aurora was receiving. The hippy mentality at the Waldorf was beginning to irritate her. In the end, she realized, she didn't want Aurora to turn into one of those airheaded liberals. New England was conservative; it had Puritan values. The Arizona Waldorf people with their semi-feral, free-range children and New Age hippie-speak, wholemeal bread and toys made from hemp and banana leaves, did not have the elegance of the American aristocracy or international elite she ultimately wanted for Aurora. There were much finer houses in the world, finer clothes, finer cars, finer people than were to be found in Laughlin. Grandmother had seen and read enough of *Town & Country* to know these people in their McMansions were *nouveau riche* with appalling taste. She was hungry for more for her grandchild — tradition, yachts, villas in the south of France, private jets.

Grandmother didn't know who else to turn to, so she went back to the library. The librarian listened and again was impressed by her cunning and resolve. She told her that she did, indeed, have good taste. The prep school in question was one of the most prestigious in the country — the kind of place one finds American aristocracy and other privileged youth, children from highly educated, affluent backgrounds, old money, and powerful people in society. If Aurora was accepted and did well there, she would have a very good chance at a scholarship into the Ivy League. Harvard, for example. If she worked hard, managed to survive and thrive, she would have the education and connections to go anywhere.

After hearing this, Grandmother was moved to tears. It was exactly what she had wanted from the very beginning. A boarding school where Aurora would eat, sleep, converse, spend all her time with these well-mannered, elite people. She would become one of them — flesh of their flesh, mind of their mind. Decidedly, the prep school was the answer to her prayers. The perfect solution. The LORD had sent another message through the magazine. She patted herself on the back for catching it and for going to the library. The librarian was an angel, an agent of the LORD, sent down to make these dreams come true; to guide her grandchild, to fortify and prepare her for the world she was about to enter. Her grandmother agreed to bring Aurora to the library after school that very day to discuss everything. They had no time to waste.

Grandmother stood at the exit of the Waldorf, waiting for Aurora to emerge, turning over the possibilities in her mind, watching the children spill out from the school, looking for the child among the other children, many of whom were dressed in her Russian peasant creations.

On the way to the parking lot, Grandmother explained that they would be going straight to the library to speak to the librarian about a new direction for her life. Aurora, furious that she would have to miss ballet, picked up a rock, screamed like a feral animal, and threw it as hard as she could onto the ground where it bounced off another rock and hit a car's fender, making a dent. Face frozen in an expression of mortification, Grandmother hesitated, then told Aurora to get into the car. She did not look back, ducked into the driver's seat, turned the key and drove off.

Once in the passenger seat, Aurora made no sound, staring out the window at her ghostly reflection and the mountains, ballet bag in her lap, eyes like slits, annoyed she wasn't going to be able to practice the three pirouettes *en pointe* she had learned the previous week. The other children all had ballet studios at home. There wasn't enough floor space in the trailer for her to practice like they could. She only had one thin full-length mirror. These facts were keeping her from reaching her potential. Aurora silently seethed while her grandmother drove, eyes on the road.

"We're going to see the librarian now, no ifs ands or buts. She said she'll help you get into another school, one up north, in New England, where the best and brightest of the country go; where you can get a real education, the finest. But we've got to do it quick. This is the next step. I don't think the Waldorf is what we want for you, baby girl."

Staring out the window, despite her anger and frustration, Aurora mulled over the implications of what her grandmother had proposed. The prospect of another school, with new people who didn't know who she was, where she could begin again and get away from the girls who had made her life hell was very appealing. Plus, she would no longer have to dress like a Russian peasant. "You said it's in New England?"

"Yes. You would live there. You would be in the world I wanted for you from the very beginning, Aurora. You would get out of the trailer park sooner than I imagined. If you play your cards right, you won't ever come back."

"But I would miss you! And Tu-tu!" Aurora's face flushed hot, tears streaming down her face.

"Don't cry, sweet girl. The Lord is shining His light on you! You'll come home for all the vacations and see me and Tu-tu. If you work hard, you'll go to a good college, meet the right people, marry someone important, have children, go to charity balls like they do in *Town & Country*. Like they do on *Dynasty* and *Dallas*! You'll have a beautiful home, a swimming pool, vacations in Europe. The world will be open to you." The steel of determination set into Grandmother's face. "Because this is what I dreamed for you, Aurora. I want you to have the best of everything. This is why I've worked so hard."

Aurora had another burst of tears, laid her head on her grandmother's shoulder and said, yes, she would do it — she would listen to the librarian, do everything it took to get into the school. More than anything in the world, she wanted to make her grandmother proud.

In the librarian's office (she was now the head librarian), they got down to business. She had spoken with the admissions office at the Academy and learned the deadline for applications was in four months. Aurora was going to have to study to pass a standardized test and write two first-class essays if there was any chance of her being accepted. As luck or fate would have it, the librarian was from New England and knew their customs. She had a degree from a minor Ivy League college and knew what prep schools wanted. Straight away the librarian had gotten to work selecting books Aurora would have to read to prepare herself, now piled on her desk, facing Aurora with her grandmother, opposite. The librarian thought Aurora looked like a little cat — aloof, fierce, with a shine in her eyes.

After explaining everything they were to do, the librarian told Aurora she needed to know her level of commitment to the cause. Aurora looked squarely at the librarian. "I'll do it. Everything. I want to get into that school and succeed." Aurora saw the plan — the means to an end that had been laid out before her — and knew it was the way to elevate herself. If she succeeded, she could buy a house, maybe something in California, with a fountain and a swimming pool. She knew her grandmother was right. If she went to the best schools in the country and studied hard, she could become a lawyer, or a scientist. Maybe an astronaut. She could get to the stars, to the place where everything floated.

The librarian gave Aurora a workbook with practice tests for the standardized exams she would need to score highly on to gain entry into the Academy, told her to complete the first five of them, then to come back the day after next. Meanwhile, she would send for the application and scholarship forms.

In the car, Aurora begged her grandmother to drive to the ballet studio for the last hour (the first hour was in slippers with a lot of *barre* work and the second *en pointe*). Aurora dressed in the back seat on the way, jumped out of the car before the engine was turned off, and ran to the studio, where she hurriedly put on her *pointe* shoes. At the *barre*, stretching, Aurora watched as, one by one, each girl floated diagonally across the studio, practising her *grands jetés*.

Ordinarily, the instructor would have erupted and scolded anyone for being late, but today she said nothing when Aurora joined in with the next exercise, the *pas de chat*. When it came to pirouettes, Sindy, her rival, completed four in sequence. The room erupted into squeals and clapping. When it was Aurora's turn, she could only manage three. Her cheeks flushed red. She told herself if she was able to practice at home like everyone else, she would wipe the floor with all of them. A fury consumed her. She knew she had to find a way to control it or it would eat her alive.

As it so happens, this fury found its way into the fervor with which Aurora applied herself to the librarian's tutelage. They met every weekend. Aurora found a kindred spirit in the librarian. Another outsider. It's fair to say they found salvation in each other's company and the work at hand.

Aurora read passages from William Faulkner's *Absalom, Absalom!* out loud,

> ...*his very body was an empty hall echoing with sonorous defeated names; he was not a being, an entity, he was a commonwealth. He was a barracks filled with stubborn, back-looking ghosts...*

She was then asked to think about and write down what the passage represented in the greater context of the novel. Quick as a whip, time and time again, Aurora came up with winning answers: *Each narrator recounts the same story from their different perspectives. These reconstructions of past events by multiple narrators illustrate that history, personal or otherwise, is, in the end, irretrievable and imaginative. Identity becomes as intangible as a chimera, as fleeting as an echo.* Aurora's acuity — with its rage, drive, passion and urgency — secretly made the librarian weep.

They read essays written about the novel and interviews with Faulkner out loud:

INTERVIEWER: Mr. Faulkner, throughout your work there seems to be the theme that there's a curse upon the South. I was wondering if you could explain what this curse is and if there's any chance of the South to escape?

FAULKNER: The curse is slavery, which is an intolerable condition — no man shall be enslaved — and the South has got to work that curse out and it will, if it's let alone. It can't be compelled to do it. It must do it of its own will and desire, which I believe it will do if it's let alone.[2]

They discussed how the personal history of the protagonist in the novel was meant to mirror the rise and fall of plantation culture, this 'Southern curse of slavery', and how the protagonist's individual curse, his belief that he was superior to everyone around him, played into this. The story was a horror show of white supremacy that Aurora, in her limited life experience, could see was still going on. In the United States, if you have eyes, it is impossible to ignore. Aurora had heard her grandmother make racist comments. She was white trash but that was still better than Black. There were Black people in the congregation at church but Grandmother had made it clear, with hints and comments here and there that these 'people' were different from them, not as sophisticated. Aurora hadn't ever reflected on the situation before reading Faulkner and discussing it with the librarian.

When the librarian asked Aurora what she thought about racial inequality in the world today, Aurora told

2. Faulkner, William, et al. *Faulkner in the University: Class Conferences at the University of Virginia 1957-1958.* New York, Alfred A. Knopf, 1965.

her she was ashamed to be white. The words came out of her from somewhere in her gut, hit her heart on the way up and made her want to explode with tears and rage. She thought of the genocide; scenes from *Bury My Heart at Wounded Knee*. After this, they sat in silence. The librarian didn't ask Aurora to explain why. They both knew why and it was unspeakable. The librarian moved on to the next lesson.

When their discussions drifted by way of the religious, Aurora wanted to tell the librarian about the exorcism — what they had done to her. She wanted to scream it out loud, but an invisible hand tightened around her throat. The terror of telling made her mute. To speak would make it live again, give it power. It was the same every time she was about to tell the therapist — opening her mouth with no sound coming out. She thought the librarian would understand everything, that she would wash away the shame with her kind eyes and magic words. But Aurora found herself mute. Instead, she channeled her devotion into her work, into making the librarian proud...

Sitting here, I have the feeling that all is hollow and provisional. The lamp on my desk is lit; it makes shadows that quiver on the walls. My powers of expression feel weak. Everything is so hazy in my mind that the contours elude me. I'm working in a fog. If I'm going to capture her on this page, everything must be called into question. There were other women before her. Other female creatures, mythical and otherwise, I used to marvel at. But not like this. I am haunted by the realization that to objectify is to create. Fists clenched; I grind my teeth knowing it's simply one of the many tortures I must endure in writing this chronicle.

I cannot describe how it twists my insides to objectify this girl in order to make her exist for the imagination and the page — for you, the reader. The crucifixion in having to look at her this intensely, drink her in as I drink this fizzy soda pop that quenches my thirst, yet leaves me wanting more.

I move from one piece of evidence to another, from enigma to enigma, pursuing truth the way one hunts game. But I am the one in the trap. Far from marvelling at her, the object, I must treat her ironically. But how, when I am seduced and enchanted?

When I meditate on our capacity for self-deception, and this is true for the jinn as well as the sons and daughters of Adam and Eve, the more I see it as a measure of protection, as well as a hot poker I blind myself with in an act of self-harm. Rather than burn down the institutions and people who have wronged us, the rage is so acute we are forced to blind ourselves with the sizzling hot poker. We need the courage to face ourselves. I need courage. I thought the combination of soda pop and hashish gave me something, but if I'm honest with myself it has mainly resulted in a continuation of the unpleasant gushing sensation down my forehead and a burning in the tips of my fingers.

But back to the girl. Imagine a world in which we no longer deceived ourselves. But then I suppose we would be omniscient and living in the realm of the gods. No matter. We must try, we must keep on, like the lizards that jumped up and down for so many thousands of years they grew wings. I must come to the conclusion, draw out what it is I'm trying to convey to you so that you can see it and decide for yourself... I play with the snakes I write. Big fat snakes that hang in the trees waiting to suffocate me...

2.

And then it finally came. The letter from the elite New England prep school. Cradled in the next issue of *Town & Country* in the mailbox, Grandmother saw this as a sign from God. Aurora had just painted her nails and anyway couldn't bear to open it. If she failed at this, she had failed her grandmother, the librarian, the LORD and Jesus.

Grandmother put her glasses on and opened the envelope with a letter opener, Aurora balanced on the armrest of the couch, careful not to touch the fabric with her wet fingernails while she waved a pointed foot in a figure eight to dry the polish on her toes.

As Grandmother read the letter a little nerve ticked at the corner of her eye. Then tears, pride, relief, and elation spread across her face. She turned to Aurora and told her that she had succeeded. They called the librarian.

At the library, they presented the librarian with an angel food cake and flowers. Beside the librarian was a suitcase, which she pushed toward Aurora, "You've earned this: but you're also going to need it. My parting gift to you". For months the librarian had been buying items on eBay: Ralph

Lauren, Abercrombie and Fitch, Banana Republic, and J. Crew sweaters, blazers, tops, and skirts; a Burberry winter jacket, True Religion jeans, Ugg boots, loafers, ankle boots; a Chloé Paddington bag. These were basic items Aurora would need if she was going to have a chance in hell of blending in. Even Plato knew that class and conditioning have an inalterable effect on the individual. Psychology is another word for what the ancients called fate. Aurora was walking into a Bacchae horde. She was going to have to become one of them or they would capture her and rip her apart.

When Aurora got home, she took everything out — piece by piece — marveling at the craftsmanship of the bag, so grown up; such fine, soft leather. She broke down weeping, hands clasped, in front of the Virgin Mary with Tu-tu beside her.

Two days before Aurora was set to fly to New Hampshire, Tu-tu disappeared. She had never in her life been on foot beyond the chain-link fence that surrounded their trailer lot. She knew what she heard from her bedroom window — the murmur and conversations of neighbours erupting into screams, gunshots, the crash of rifle blasts, demented shrieking, dogs howling and barking, police sirens.

Aurora had only seen the park outside their lot from the car, protected from the people with tattooed bodies, wild eyes, rifles and shotguns, handguns at the smalls of their backs, dogs circling, appearing from behind a shed or truck or just milling around, carrying out their lives on the other side of the glass. Her grandmother made it clear to her granddaughter that if any of them were to get a hold of her, they would rip her apart limb from limb. There would be nothing her grandmother could do. This was why Aurora couldn't go beyond their boundary lines. "Pretend the fence is electrified," her grandmother used to tell her when she was a small child. Once Aurora had reached a certain age, she had figured it out for herself; Grandmother didn't need to tell her these things, it was self-evident. She saw and heard and felt the electric violence all around them on the other side of the fence.

But there she was, running, softly calling for Tu-tu, past the trailers on their lots, crouching to look under cars, trawling the ditches, her heart in her throat. Grandmother was out shopping. There had been no one to stop her. People in their yards looked at her as she passed through the lines of trailers and outbuildings, some of them called to her, asking if she was looking for her pussy — laughing, making crude remarks — but she did not heed them and moved on.

When she found herself at the edge of the park, she followed the razor-wire fence north, calling for Tu-tu out into the desert beyond where her voice evaporated into thin air. A place in the fence had been cut large enough for a sizable dog to pass through. Aurora got on her hands and knees and crawled to the other side.

Land and sky spread out wild and free. Desert air filled her lungs. Scrub brush was everywhere, shining in the sun. The heat brought out the desert scents. On the ground, debris littered her path: spent shotgun cartridges, batteries, rusty soup cans, chunks of yellow foam, six-pack plastic rings, transparent candy-colored lighters, a car seat. Sage flickered silvery green with cholla cacti here and there sprouting from the red, rocky ground, their spiked limbs reaching out, an army of them, grains of sand hissing in the wind around them. Aurora thought the cacti bore a resemblance to coral formations at the bottom of the ocean she'd seen on television.

She began again to call for Tu-tu, scanning the area, feeling naked and exposed, miniature in that vastness. When she fell silent, she could hear the brush leaves and branches tapping in the breeze as if they were talking to one another, as if they were aware of her and alert. There was the call of a bird of prey and cactus wrens. Lizards like the ones Tu-tu caught darted in the dust and under rocks.

Above, the white, violent sun made aureoles around everything. Aurora sat on the hard ground where she cried long, bitter tears for the cat, forgetting where she was; sobbing until she didn't feel like anything more than a burning hot piece of sun. She kept silent when voices came, carried on the wind. Getting up slowly she stood and watched.

Four figures — men — approached in the distance along the razor-wire fence. One carried a shotgun; another a rifle. They had a big black-and-white billy goat on a rope with horns like the devil, pulling out in front of them. As they approached, she saw that two looked older; the others younger — maybe in their late teens. One of the younger ones cleared his throat, spitting off to the side. They were coming directly at her. There wasn't anywhere to hide.

Bracing herself, Aurora told herself to move, to appear cool and collected, with her heart beating wildly as though it had gotten away from her and at any moment would spread its wings and fly away. Their voices came closer, and she heard them talk about firing rock salt out of the shotgun, and then frozen Vienna sausages. They wondered if a sausage would kill the goat. They would aim for the heart.

She began to walk back toward the hole in the fence, praying to Jesus to let her pass without incident, without being grabbed and pulled behind a rock and raped before they killed the goat.

When the men took notice of her, she felt her blood beat, urging her forward. She kept her head held high, continuing at an even pace. The younger ones began to hoot and whistle and broke into dance, shouting obscenities, with the goat dancing too, braying and kicking his hind legs. Aurora kept walking with her eye on the hole in the fence.

The group of men and the goat veered in her direction to get a better look at her. Once they were only feet away (she had nearly made it to the hole), one of the older ones, who stank (sweat, beer, goat, motor oil, chemicals) grabbed her by the arm. When she turned away, he grabbed her by the face with his dirt-stained hand and said, looking into her eyes, he thought he knew her, she was so and so's daughter. The way he said it, he respected her old man.

Before Aurora could answer he let her go and pushed her, telling her to get on her way, while one of the others said she was looking for her pussy. They chuckled and guffawed, and another said he would help her find it, then: "It ain't rape if she enjoys it!" They laughed some more and watched her walk away. She heard one of them say he didn't think they should have let her go, but the sausages were melting, and they had to fire them while they were good and frozen.

Walking home, Aurora wished she'd brought along the gun her grandmother kept in the box under her bed. Or found out where they lived and burned their houses down. The man had known her father. Her father was with the Angels now. There was no use in thinking of him. She would never know him. He was one of those men with guns and tattoos her grandmother warned her about. He probably wasn't an Angel.

Upon her arrival, the trailer was empty. Tu-tu hadn't returned. The Jesus clock ticked. A sweet, yeasty smell filled the trailer from the doughnuts her grandmother had made that morning — fried in the deep pan, with the grease in a jar next to the sink. Her grandmother was still out grocery shopping. Aurora felt her head begin to dissolve like she was going to faint, slid to the floor and cried.

Her face flat on the cool linoleum, she remembered something the librarian had told her — something she read, from Tennessee Williams — and whispered it to herself: "The world is violent and mercurial — it will have its way with you. We are saved only by love — love for each other and the love that we pour into the art we feel compelled to share: being a parent; being a writer;

being a painter; being a friend. We live in a perpetually burning building, and what we must save from it, all the time, is love". The words consumed her and she broke down again, for what felt like hours, crying until her eyes were red and raw. She thought of her mother and father looking down on her, floating in space.

When Grandmother came in with the groceries, she dropped them at the entry, shocked to find Aurora on the kitchen floor, her cheeks red and seamed with tears; her face bloated from crying. Grandmother tried to cradle her little girl who was no longer a child, sweetly telling Aurora everything would be alright. She helped Aurora off the floor, onto the couch and went to the freezer for ice, wrapped it in a cloth and put it to her swollen face. Aurora said nothing about the men with the goat she met on the road, or her phantom parents, floating above her, their sad eyes pained in replica of hers, in replicas of Jesus.

Evening came. Tu-tu did not return. Aurora moved her food around the plate and forced herself to eat enough to satisfy her grandmother, then went to bed, where she lay until it grew dark, alert to every sound, listening for Tu-Tu. She lay with her hands clasped in prayer under her chin, eyes on the Virgin Mary statue, beseeching the Virgin to bring Tu-tu back safe and sound.

The night became a vigil. It went on and on. Again and again, Aurora charged the Virgin's phosphorescence with her flashlight to make it glow and prayed. Eventually, her suffering and concentration became so fierce the idol began to move — its plastic, glow-in-the-dark surface turned into a fleshy substance, the Virgin's arms rustling in the folds of her robe, rising toward heaven; her sweet, delicate face tilting upward, alive, soft and glowing. The abnormality of the situation should have been overwhelming, yet Aurora found she was calm, bolted to reality with a high degree of clarity and focus. She had, in fact, never felt so alive, or seen as clearly. All sins were washed clean. It felt like being in the sun and being home, protected from all evil — everything was understood. The next thing she knew she was spat out of this reverie, back into the dark, into her room with the unmoving Virgin, the sound of coyotes and a shotgun blast.

The next day, Grandmother drove Aurora to the airport. Crossing the bridge over the Colorado River, Aurora felt a chill in her gut. They passed the larger-than-life river boat hotel casino, and sailed into the city, its windows glinting and reflecting the fractured morning light. She made it a point not to look in the direction of the megachurch. She didn't ever want to see that place again and said a prayer to Jesus and the Virgin that she would never have to. In that moment the vision of the Virgin in the night came to her. The Virgin had moved. The Virgin Mother had inhabited the idol. Aurora knew now her life would never be the same. The thing that was destined to happen was happening.

Grandmother sat tall in the driver's seat, her swollen knuckles resting on the wheel, her lacquered nails shining, along with her white hairsprayed hairdo. This was the next stage. Aurora was leaving the nest. Everything she'd done had brought Aurora to this point.

Aurora vowed to make her grandmother proud and promised to call and write as often as she could.

"I know you will, sweet girl," Grandmother said, looking over with tears in her eyes. "Don't make me cry now Aurora, I'm driving. I hope you know how proud I am of you." She turned her head back to the road. "Keep Jesus in your heart, and you will not falter."

At the departure gates they said their last goodbyes. Grandmother hugged Aurora tight. Aurora thought she might suffocate in that bosom turning her cheek and taking in, the scent of lipstick, face cream, sugar and fat from the doughnuts mixed with the faint acridness of old people's skin. Grandmother told Aurora to trust in Jesus, to keep Him in her heart.

Aurora gathered her things and walked ahead, turning back once to give a quick wave. She was off, into the future, alone, leaving Arizona and her old life behind, now part of the swarm of the airport, untethered and exposed.

It was Aurora's first time on an airplane. She chose a window seat when the check-in agent had asked her preference. Once airborne, Aurora pressed her cheek to the cool, acrylic pane and looked out, imagining herself in the clouds. This is what the Angels saw. This was part of their world.

Six hours later, Aurora got a taxi from the airport to the Academy. Stepping out of the car, she noticed the air was different. It stuck to the skin, soft and heavy on her exposed limbs. Trees made flickering canopies above. Shadows danced on the ground. Pathways darted everywhere through shrubbery and manicured freshly mown lawns. Colonial and gothic revival red-brick buildings crawling with ivy made Aurora feel that she had stepped into a fairy book. The air was swollen with the scent of green, living things.

It was still warm, summery. Aurora walked trailing her suitcase, Chloé bag over her shoulder, the buzz of flirtation, illicit, late-night drinks on rooftops, and uncomplicated flings in the air. Dressed in her white, short-sleeved Burberry shirt with check piping around the edges of the chest pocket and a short, pleated, navy J.Crew skirt, her black, Italian leather Banana Republic loafers felt molded to her feet. She didn't even need to wear socks. Aurora stopped to look at the map she'd been sent in her orientation package, studying it, looking for her dorm. This marked her out as fresh meat, a lamb lost in the woods.

Everywhere around her polished people advanced — some with boyfriends or girlfriends; others with parents — all of them healthy, illustrious, smiling, with bright shining hair and faces, exalted, brimming over with optimism. Aurora's mind sent her a flash of scenes from *The Stepford Wives*. She continued on, following the map, passing groups of girls in Chanel miniskirts and denim cut-offs wafting Calvin Klein perfume. Everyone and everything sparkled and glowed in the early September light.

Aurora found herself in front of a tall, red-brick building, an all-female dormitory where she was meant to spend the entirety of the four years. Stone steps led to great wooden and glass doors flanked with white columns. This was her new home. She was greeted by a student dorm proctor to whom she showed her orientation documents and was led to her room on the top floor.

Standing in the empty space, the noxious odor of fresh paint making her dizzy, Aurora noted her roommate had not yet arrived. She went to the dormer windows and opened them. Outside she could see the roofs of other buildings, the church steeple, the crowns of trees. Voices from the quad carried upward into the room. Standing there, suitcase at her feet, the building was nothing like the trailer with its flimsy, fake wood-paneled walls. This was a fortress. Aurora didn't know which bed to take. She sat down on the wooden floor and looked up at the apex ceiling, the eves, the slanted walls, then went through the Chloé bag — lip balm, a ripped boarding card, a pink, sparkly pen her grandmother had given her; watermelon bubblegum she'd bought at the airport, letters and the map from the prep school; two hundred dollars cash from her grandmother zipped in the inside pocket.

When the door opened she was still sitting there, staring into space, high on paint fumes. In came her roommate, Sylvia, hugging a bowl with a Siamese fighting fish inside, preceded by her glamorous mother, Mrs Belmont, followed by their driver, carrying a potted palm. Mrs Belmont was light on her feet and spoke with a clipped tone, "Hell-o! You must be Sylvia's roommate!" She introduced herself, then joked the room wasn't much bigger than a walk-in closet but was good for building character, living like a monk. She had, in fact, arranged for her daughter to stay in one of the Academy's larger rooms after giving the school a six-million-dollar donation.

AURORA

Aurora got up from the floor and introduced herself. The driver left the room and came back with one of the student proctors, carrying a steamer trunk between them. Behind were two more proctors with four suitcases. Leaving the trunk and suitcases where Mrs Belmont indicated, they all disappeared, leaving the three alone. Mrs Belmont asked Aurora where her parents were, and where she came from.

Blood beat in Aurora's ears. "My parents passed, my father before I was born, my mother not long after. I was raised by my grandmother in Arizona. I got a scholarship to come here." Aurora was struck red with shame, feeling she'd said too much, or not enough, or not the right thing.

Mrs Belmont's hand rose to her chest and then her throat, her face flashing white, "Oh my dear child, I'm so sorry, I — well your grandmother must be a wonderful person, to have brought you up so well!" Unbeknownst to Sylvia, beside the large dorm room, Mrs Belmont had also requested she be placed with a student on an academic scholarship, rather than one of her friends who were, truth be told, allowed to run too wild. Rooming with an underprivileged girl would give Sylvia a dose of reality.[3]

---

3. Sylvia's mother did not know the details, but that summer Sylvia had run riot on Martha's Vineyard and in NYC with five of her friends. She took up smoking cigarettes and cannabis, drinking alcohol and tried cocaine at one of the house parties. She kissed two guys and three girls and held a boy's penis, not knowing what to do with it. He had put his hand over hers and jerked off until he came, which was genuinely astonishing to her because she'd never even seen porn before. The boy was handsome with a cherubic face and floppy hair, of her ilk, and told everyone he knew she'd given him a hand job. All summer she denied it. Word got round to Sylvia's mother that her daughter was in with a group of girls who were out of control and was brought home for the last week of summer.

"Yes, she is. I'm very lucky to have been raised by her."
Aurora had immediately captured Mrs Belmont's heart.
The delicate, gentle, blushing girl she saw before her, with
the bright, open face — positively angelic — perfectly
proportioned with bowed lips and large, glittering eyes.
What was not to love? The hardship and tragedy made
Mrs Belmont want to take Aurora in her arms like an
orphaned seal pup and adopt her. She knew her daughter
felt likewise as they exchanged glances, moving closer to
Aurora, touching a strand of her hair, and putting her
arm around her. Mrs Belmont gave Aurora a squeeze
and told her she was welcome to come home with Sylvia
any weekend. They didn't live that far away and would
send a helicopter. If she wanted, she could also come for
the next school break, unless she had to fly back to her
grandmother. They would be delighted if she came to the
house to stay. "Your grandmother? Is she here?"

Aurora replied in the negative, looking down, Mrs
Belmont admiring her long dark lashes.

"You've got to come to orientation with us, you can't
go on your own." The room was beginning to close in
on Mrs Belmont. She ushered the two girls out of the
room, down the corridors and flights of stairs, out into the
sunshine on the quad where the business of the parents
and moving in was peaking. The three went together to
register, have the girls' photos taken for their identification
cards, and then on to the assembly hall where the Dean
would speak.

Mrs Belmont sat between the two girls. Aurora secretly
observed tiny details about Mrs Belmont — the shade of

her lipstick, the curve of her leg — drinking her in. The atmosphere in the hall had nothing of the showman carnival outpourings Aurora was used to at the megachurch when people with authority and power occupied the stage. People in the seats listened intently, here and there speaking in hushed tones among each other. Academic excellence, team spirit, heritage, curfews, and advisors, were among the topics the Dean rallied home with gravity, urgency, vim and vigour. Mrs Belmont turned to smile at Aurora more than once. Afterward, the three took a tour around the campus, visiting the library, the church, the sports centre, the stables, ballet studios, cafeteria, the pond, etc. All of this was surrounded by one thousand acres of forest. To go outside the school boundary, one needed to secure a day pass. To leave for the weekend one needed written permission from a parent. Mrs Belmont did not seem suited to this much walking in kitten heels and suggested they go to dinner in town. It was the first time Aurora had ever been in a restaurant besides McDonalds. The driver was waiting in the school parking lot, dressed in a suit and tie — immaculate — holding the door of the shining black Mercedes limousine open, sleek and discreet. Aurora caught a glimpse of the dashboard. It belonged in a cockpit. On the slippery leather seats, Aurora breathed in the scent of wealth: expensive cowhide, electronic components, plastic smells, a hint of the driver's cologne. When they took off, they glided along as though inches above the tarmac. Sylvia looked out the window, turning to smile once at Aurora who mostly stared ahead at the back of the seat and Mrs Belmont. They dined at a Chinese restaurant. Aurora had seen people eating in restaurants plenty of times on T.V. so it wasn't completely foreign to her. Mrs Belmont ordered all the appetizers for them to taste, a soup, and a main dish with rice, then asked Sylvia and Aurora what they wanted and ordered for them. They drank jasmine tea. Thankfully, Aurora had learned to use chopsticks at the Waldorf school and did not have to resort to a fork. In fact, she was quite good at it — a natural. With the check came the fortune cookies. Sylvia got *To truly find yourself you should play hide and seek alone.* Aurora cracked hers and read it aloud as Sylvia had: *Love is like sweet nectarine, good to the last drop.* Mrs Belmont read hers, then pushed it out of the way and made a move to leave. Aurora wanted to reach across the table and see what it said, take it as a memento, but felt intuitively that the act would have been frowned upon. Leave the fortune where it lies, she told herself. You will never know.

Mrs Belmont walked her daughter and Aurora back to the dorm from the parking lot, up the flights of stairs to their attic room and had a last look around, making offhand comments here and there about where Sylvia might put the lamp, the radio, the alarm clock, the bowl with her Siamese fighting fish. She said they needed a sofa underneath the dormer windows and would order one and have it delivered. And like that, Mrs Belmont disappeared in a puff of silk, cashmere and woodsy perfume, leaving Aurora and Sylvia to their own devices.

Hanging clothes in her closet, Sylvia told Aurora she could borrow anything she wanted. They were a similar height and build. They wore the same shoe size. Both girls had dark coppery blonde hair, hazel eyes. Later, they would find they looked enough alike that their identities would often be confused when they walked around campus alone.

What Aurora would later find out was that Sylvia's reputation preceded her. She was a member of the American aristocracy, her father from the way back South — plantations, cotton, human trafficking, slavery — whose family had been forced to diversify their wealth when their main source of income became illegal. The winning investment turned out to be a certain fizzy drink, a celebrated soda pop which had become an empire. Mrs Belmont was a New England aristocrat. They met at a debutante gala in New York. Sylvia's brother had graduated from the school the year before and was now a freshman at Stanford. His father wasn't happy about this and would have preferred the Ivy League but Sylvia's brother wanted warmer climes and was rebellious, like Sylvia.

Aurora had never met anyone as chic and self-possessed as Sylvia. She came back from class to find her on the bed with her face in the first volume of Simone de Beauvoir's *The Second Sex*, in French; a French-English dictionary beside her, the air in the room smelling of cigarettes. Her hair was generally dishevelled like Brigitte Bardot or Kate Moss, giving the impression she had just gotten out of bed. Everything about her suggested a devil-may-care sophistication without vanity. She brushed her hair with a wooden boar bristle brush to get the snarls out, the only type of brush that didn't break your hair and made it shine, only using it before she washed her hair, never after. They smelled practically the same, both of them using Sylvia's strawberry shampoo, vanilla conditioner and peach bodywash, their intimacy consummated by using the same razors to shave their legs and underarms until Sylvia simply divided the packages she bought and gave half to Aurora because she suspected her roommate couldn't afford them. They sent their laundry off together. Sylvia was generous with her twenty or so tubes of chapstick and lip gloss and encouraged Aurora to use them.

More often than not they went to breakfast, lunch and dinner in the cafeteria together — a place that would have been much more dangerous for Aurora if she hadn't been shielded by Sylvia's glamour and status. Aurora followed Sylvia's lead. She had never seen so much food, so much choice, but did not take advantage of it, wanting to put a bagel with sausages and eggs on her plate but instead taking only an apple, a coffee and a spoonful of peanut butter to Sylvia's measly outpouring of cereal, a satsuma and diet coke. They sat with Sylvia's friends, blue bloods, children of Wall Street scions, famous writers and actors. It was tacitly understood that Aurora was Sylvia's project and not to be messed with. However, Sylvia did not consider Aurora a project. She was incapable of seeing anyone in those terms: she had a higher emotional IQ than any of them and a deep need to trawl the heights and depths of the human condition, which made her sensitive to psychological and social issues. After several months, Aurora had successfully put each girl in her place with subtle, cutting retorts and astute, sometimes hilarious observations delivered in an understated, deadpan tone; squinting her eyes, she eventually won them over with calculated, muddled looks of bewilderment, dizzy, punch-drunkenness, silence, grace, and aptitude for listening and offering thought-provoking advice. Inside though, she was a mess and felt out of her depth but knew all she could do was soldier on, to take each insult as it came. Above all else, she wanted Sylvia to be proud of her.

Most of these girls had boyfriends who attended other prep schools, or even college. Some of the boys went to the Academy. All of them were on the hockey team, or else lacrosse, or wrestling teams, and most had bad habits, most notably, wadding chewing tobacco in their bottom lip that they spat unceremoniously onto the ground or into sawed-off Coke cans when indoors. This surprised Aurora. Not even the trailer park people did this. They smoked cigarettes. These girls were constantly in the process of trying to find a suitable match for Sylvia and Aurora, who remained uninterested.

After Sylvia's experience with a boy that summer whose penis reminded her of a sea cucumber she'd stroked at a man-made tide pool in an aquarium, she was turned off by the whole idea of sex with primitive prep school boys, preferring to smoke cigarettes, and read Simone de Beauvoir. When Sylvia thought about the male sex she fantasized about meeting her own Jean-Paul Belmondo or Alain Delon when she summered in France. She saw herself as either Anna Karina or Jean Seberg depending on her mood.

For her part, Aurora was terrified of losing her virginity before marriage. The shame it would bring on her grandmother if she ever found out — a shame she feared she would not be able to live with or hide, tainted the way she saw these boys whom she feared and desired. She thought that if she lost her virginity her grandmother knew her so well she would sense it in the tone of her voice. Aurora telephoned her grandmother every weekend from one of the payphones in the dorm, refusing Sylvia's offer to call from her cell phone until Sylvia bought her one under the pretext that she needed it in case of emergency. She told Grandmother she missed her, that she was studying hard and made sure to add she was praying to Jesus. She told her about Sylvia and how she'd been invited to her house for the weekend and that soon they were going to fly there in a helicopter. Of course, this news was music to her grandmother's ears; proof that the LORD and Jesus were looking out for her, that Aurora was on the right path. She was being accepted into the bosom of the Establishment.

Aurora always asked if Tu-tu had returned and each time felt her heart drop.

Aurora studied hard, spending a great deal of time in the library — a concrete pitted, Brutalist monolith with massive sheets and portholes of glass against the cold that descended at night. The library was a hive of academic industry: a cavernous place for trysts, making out between the stacks, hand jobs, sex. Vents blasted hot air and dust, wafting the tang of books mixed with cashmere, expensive perfume and bodily odors through the stacks. There were glassed-in booths for watching films and listening to music. Aurora wandered through the labyrinth using the information she gathered from the card catalogues like a map to buried treasure, after which she would find a hiding place, away from probing eyes, where she could devour them and take notes.

Aurora would arrive back at the dorm after dark from the library. By October the heat had been turned on automatically and was impossible to adjust — rooms were either boiling hot or if you had a dud radiator, frigid at night. Their room was a furnace, the radiator ticking, unstoppable, the faint smell of burning iron mixing with earthy, autumn scents blowing in through the open windows. Aurora would enter the room and look at Sylvia in wonder — her dishevelled, dark blonde hair catching the light; the figure she made on the bed in a camisole and high-waisted black lacy underwear like a French movie star — and remind herself that where she was, was real. Sylvia was real. The room was real. Stretched out on the bed, Sylvia read in the sphere of conical lamp light, the turquoise and red Siamese fighting fish unfurling its fins, flitting around in its glass globe behind her — casting its shadow, swimming on the ceiling.

At ten p.m. a dorm proctor would knock on doors to make sure everyone was in their room for the night. The two would continue to read in bed, making notes in the margins of the pages and in their notebooks. Sylvia was currently in thrall to Simone de Beauvoir and would scribble down English translations of sentences she was particularly impressed by — ones that electrified her and caught her off guard. She read them out loud to Aurora: "The body is not a thing, it is a situation: it is our grasp on the world and our sketch of our project...What would Prince Charming have for occupation if he had not to awaken the Sleeping Beauty?"

"*Touché!*" (This was a word Aurora had picked up from Sylvia.)

"Or, what do you think of this: 'Art, literature, and philosophy are attempts to found the world anew on a human freedom.'"

"Yes."

"Elaborate."

"I'm not going to argue with Simone de Beauvoir."

"*Quel dommage!*" Sylvia would turn back to her book and note taking.

The two often talked, giggled, smoked cigarettes, until three in the morning, sleeping four hours before breakfast and ballet, classes, lunch, horseback riding in the afternoon, more classes, then dinner. Sylvia planned on trying out for the lacrosse team in February. Aurora didn't intend to add any more activities to her plate. She needed to maintain her grade point average.

They gave one another manicures and pedicures over conversations on religion, myth, feminism, the nature of reality — both girls agreeing that all religions appeared to be echoes and refractions of one another, from the same source or sources, and that women had been relegated to inferior positions with the Original Sin in the Garden of Eden, etc. There were patterns. Christianity had been twisted and was rooted in much older pagan ground. Sylvia casually mentioned the Dionysian, Eleusinian and Orphic mysteries. Later, Aurora searched for sources in the library, using up valuable study time. Her curiosity could not be contained.

As for the Eleusinian mysteries, Aurora learned that what little remained of their existence could be found in lines of poetry, eroded inscriptions, cult symbols, vase shards, vandalized sanctuaries, puzzling frescos, begetting more questions than answers. Ultimately, the Mystery was an experience. A culmination of symbolic acts. A purging of sin through beatific visions, to be reborn and unified with the godhead, quite likely under the influence of a hallucinogenic drink made with ergot. It was a series of events — organized madness designed to provoke ecstatic experiences, spiritual catharsis, death and rebirth.

Aurora found notes from a seminar, "Visions", by Carl Jung given in 1930:

Therefore, those mystery cults were all concerned with the hope of immortality. It was the going back to god, to eat the divine body and drink the divine blood...whatever the sacred drink or food may have been...

(Aurora, moving her finger under the words...)

A spiritual bath... being submerged under water means going down into the unconscious, and there in the depths one is no longer single and separated, one is all-embracing, one is the creative god himself... This extraordinary experience is really the purpose in going into the unconscious, and that was a conscious act in the old mystery teachings.

In another book, Aurora went on to learn that according to the Orphic view, the soul is divine, of celestial origin — a God among a society of Gods — before inhabiting a body on earth, sinking, as Empedocles says "into a strange garment of flesh", where the soul enters upon what Orphics variously called the "circle" or "wheel of generation" and the "circle of Necessity" — a long and weary circuit of birth and death which must be traversed before it can return to the place from whence it came. An angel fallen into earthly flesh. In Orphic language, the soul must be made pure. The original sins washed clean. The normal duration of this circuit, according to Empedocles, is thrice ten thousand seasons, by which, in all probability, meant ten thousand years. Aurora saw correlations with Buddhism.

Sitting on the floor in the stacks, peering into one of the books resting on her knees, Aurora felt eyes on her, a heat, and turned her head in their direction. There was a boy, of the artsy poetry ilk, standing alone in one of the beams of light that fell from the ceiling, pretending to read a book. They met one another's eyes. Aurora let the book slide down her legs into her lap and picked up another, opening it randomly. Her eyes fell on part of a lecture given by Jung:

And so, in the antique mysteries the initiate was always transformed into Helios, a cosmic being. She had to climb through fantasy circles up to the sun... This is not poetry. Mind you, this is history and psychology. You should not think of these things merely as poetical metaphors. In the history of mystery cults or comparative religions these are sacred metaphors in which man's psychology has expressed itself since time immemorial... And I warn you not to assume they are mere words... Anybody who has had the corresponding experiences knows that these words are not mere metaphors, they are very poor attempts of man to characterize powerful psychological facts of an overwhelming nature, and they may transform human beings completely.

Aurora looked up from the book. The boy was still there. Air vents fired up from the floors and making the building seem alive. Aurora sat in the pull, the beam of the boy's focus and observation, and then got up, leaving the books on the floor, turning the corner around the stacks. She thought of the lines Sylvia had read her from Simone de Beauvoir: "The body is not a thing, it is a situation: it is our grasp on the world and our sketch of our project... What would Prince Charming have for occupation if he had not to awaken the Sleeping Beauty?"

SERAPHINA MADSEN

After Simone de Beauvoir, Sylvia turned her attention to
the Surrealists, while Aurora remained fixated on Jung.
Long into the night the girls held discussions, turning
their gaze toward animistic ideas, alphabetic letters and
symbols. They would end up in bed whispering, finding
correlations. By now they had brought their bed frames
into the basement for storage and put their mattresses
together on the floor, making a double bed. (Word
got around that they were lesbians and they moved to
the top of the list in the *Black Book*, an actual book
consisting of a rating system and guide to the most
fuckable girls on campus, passed around from boy to
boy — a kind of holy book so venerated it never got
desecrated or lost.)

Things were coming together. Aurora and Sylvia decided
that the very act of reading was an intensely concentrated
form of animism because words and symbols become
archetypes and attract elemental powers — the basis for
religion and witchery. What is written down on the page
and drawn on the wall speaks to us in much the same way
as flora and fauna, streams, shadows, thunder, wind, fire,
etc. speak to hunters and trackers, to the animists who still
exist to this day, to people who carry on ancient traditions,
to poets. It was the spectre of thought, making contact.
These realizations thrilled them.

Aurora and Sylvia's classes — History, Biology, English
Literature, etc. — were dull and laughable compared to
what they were learning on their own. The teachers found
them smug, but couldn't fault their work. Both of them

were maintaining 3.9-grade point averages. Always on top of their coursework, finding shortcuts, speed reading, knowing what to dismiss and what to hone in on, the two were free to hunt through the school library's religion and history stacks; chasing down more and more sources for their extracurricular project through the bibliographies, requesting them through inter-library loans. They sat in bed at night, reading each other passages, such as this one from Stuart Harris-Logan, ethnographer and folklorist:

> This experience of the self, freed from psychological limitations is what many mystics in various cultures have deemed to be the 'true self'. . . We can define trance, then, as a technique which not only brings the practitioner into contact with the spirits, but also with the most free and sacred parts of their essential self.

And from André Breton's *Manifestoes of Surrealism*:

> Let us not lose sight of the fact that the idea of Surrealism aims quite simply at the total recovery of our psychic force by a means which is nothing other than the dizzying descent into ourselves, the systematic illumination of hidden places and the progressive darkening of other places, the perpetual excursion into the midst of forbidden territory, and that there is no real danger of its activities coming to an end so long as man still manages to distinguish an animal from a flame or a stone.

The Surrealists swooped in on Aurora. They called to her like the sirens to Odysseus, but she had not stopped up her ears and was carried away. Odysseus did not know what he was missing. To access the most free and essential, sacred parts of their true selves! The words fell on the girls' tongues like nectar.

"You know, the surrealist approach to knowledge is essentially an occult approach. It's aimed at a universal, coherent synthesis of different forms of thought that enable the subversion and transformation of reality." It was this realization from Sylvia that led them to the *Hermetica*, *Nag Hammadi*, *Vedas*, Coptic and Demotic texts, Egyptian-Greek wisdom texts, Bön texts from the ancient, native Tibetan folk-religion predating Buddhism, books on paganism and nature worship, the Druids, ancient Greeks and Romans, the Vikings and Celts, polytheists, animists, Swedenborg. Sylvia ordered books from the internet — rare, expensive books from university presses or else reprints of old books that had lost their copyrights sold on eBay.

They learned that each element — fire, water, air, earth and ether — has a type of consciousness. Elemental consciousness is more rudimentary than the one found in humans. When a four-element creature, such as a human, is drawn into the sphere of a single element, such as fire, they are flooded with the vitality of that particular force and can easily be poisoned by an overdose while being starved of the other three elements they need to maintain their existence. However, if one can communicate with the elementals, in a trance or meditative state, they will offer their knowledge, aid and allegiance. Like the capricious sprites and nymphs of the ancient Greek and Roman worlds, the nature spirits of the Celtic, Germanic, and Slavic tribes, the Shintō religion and countless cultures across the globe and time. They might be saving your life one minute and destroying you the next.

"Do you realize what this means? Everything is true! The sylphs and naiads, the spirits of the trees and streams! They live! They exist!" A deranged euphoria played in Sylvia's wild, flashing gold green eyes. Breathless, she began pacing the room, crying "The oracles, the Druids! It's all true! All of it!"

The natural world called to them. Drawn to the forest at the edge of the school's northeastern perimeter, not far from their dormitory, the two meditated by candlelight in their room, then went on their morning run through the woods, following paths beaten to dirt over ice and exposed tree roots, bounding across the river that ran through its narrower points. They loped through the pine woods under the stars in the pre-dawn, gambolled through dead leaves, mud, ice and snow, ran in sub-zero temperatures, their breath white in the silvery, gelatinous glow of the moonlight reflecting from the birch trees, from the banks and drifts of snow.

Chasing after one another in their frolicking, they sometimes tripped on roots or rocks, or slipped on ice, tumbling to the ground, rolling over like puppies, sitting up, winded, gasping until they burst out laughing, their sharp white teeth and pretty pink tongues not exactly human. By meditating, focusing their attention on the practices and beliefs in their animist and occult books, they were transforming themselves, receptive to forces in nature; attracting them so to speak. They were shifting themselves and their world closer to that of the elementals simply by being open to their existence, and like this, the elementals could get a hold of them.

In spite of the euphoria they experienced, Aurora and Sylvia did not suspect they were, in fact, being possessed by the elements on their forest runs, charging them with a potent, rudimental vitality; making their eyes flash with a new élan — as green and penetrating as a cat's — and their hair shine rose gold in the dawn. They flew between the trees, through the snow, over boulders, drunk on the unstable energies that had infected them. These nature spirits would often not let go even when Sylvia and Aurora left the forest. Thus, the girls were not merely girls anymore. They had acquired aspects that were non-human. Walking around campus, they were enchanted; their heavy, slant-eyed gazes taking in everything and nothing, reveling in the moment, as light as air, riding the magnetic energy of the earth, their bodies repelling magnets that allowed them to float. Anyone who got too close to them felt dizzy. They were becoming something they felt they had little control over but didn't care, like being in the throes of inebriation for example, except this particular poison heightened one's attractiveness, making the eyes shine, the skin and hair glimmer, casting an aura of incomprehensible, maddening splendor about the person. No creature was immune. Birds and rabbits followed them on their runs. People on campus found themselves trailing behind them, at one point realizing they had no idea what they were doing, where they were going. Aurora and Sylvia went about their lives, oblivious in their enchanted bubble.

The two lit candles[4] and engaged in surrealist practices — automatic writing and drawing — which they taped to the walls. They studied the paintings of Leonora Carrington, reminiscent of illustrations from fairy stories, and the absurdist worlds of Lewis Carroll, where traditional alchemical, Kabbalistic, magical symbols and references frequently appeared. There was also Hilma af Klint, who predated the Surrealists, yet went into trances to produce the first abstract compositions known in Western art history, years before Wassily Kandinsky, Piet Mondrian and Kazimir Malevich. Her works were understood to be gateways to other dimensions, calling for interpretation on a narrative, metaphorical, esoteric level. They evoked primordial geometry, sought out new forms in artistic, spiritual, political, and scientific systems with humanistic motifs, namely transcendence and love. All of which fed into the Surrealists' idea of myth explaining aspects of the psyche, the omnipotence of thought, the uncensored creative impulses of the unconscious, the "revolution of the mind" that André Breton, Max Ernst, André Masson, Salvador Dalí, Yves Tanguy, René Magritte, Man Ray, and others embraced and were engulfed by.

It was exciting, the most exciting thing either girl had ever encountered; the most total liberation they had ever seen expressed — the role of the artist as magician, the purpose

4. This was of course a fire hazard, forbidden on campus.

of art as a means towards self-knowledge, transformation, illumination. With her evangelical upbringing, Aurora knew her grandmother would not approve of any of this. There were things she would never be open to or understand. The more Aurora thought about it, the more she knew her grandmother was a fanatic. She had let the pastors do what they did to her. No matter how much her grandmother loved her, she had let them do it. And no matter how much her grandmother said she liked Black people, she was racist. And her grandmother hated Mexicans. This was something she didn't try to hide. Pieces of the puzzle were falling into place and Aurora didn't like the picture that was forming.

The time finally came to go to Sylvia's house in upstate New York. While Sylvia's friends had spent their weekends partying in Martha's Vineyard with their boyfriends or on short trips to the Bahamas, she had remained on campus with Aurora, chasing Surrealist material and copies of ancient manuscripts, devouring books such as Alexandra David-Néel's *Magic and Mystery in Tibet.* In a time when women of society did not go anywhere unchaperoned, David-Neel trekked across the plains and mountains of Tibet for fourteen years, studying Buddhism, Bön, and Tibetan Tantra; met with the Dalai Lama, meditated in caves and frozen, wind-swept, winter mountains with yogi hermits, lamas and magicians where she learned mental visualization exercises to create disembodied thought forms, had visions. She practiced yoga through which she learned to control the body-heat mechanism in a way similar to bees, allowing her to live naked in sub-zero temperatures. The secret teachings enabled a subtle fire which warms the generative fluid and drives the energy all through the body along tiny channels of psychic energy to keep one warm.

Sylvia and Aurora took schoolwork and a few of their Surrealist and occult books to the helicopter that waited for them in a field — one the school allowed the few students with helicopters to use as a landing pad. The helicopter was a thing of beauty: black, insect-like with a vertical gold stripe around its center. Aurora followed Sylvia through the uplift of wind, climbing behind her, Sylvia pulling the sliding door shut behind before they got into the passenger seats, where they secured their bags and buckled themselves in. Sylvia took out her headset, and put it over her ears. Aurora did the same. Everything went slightly fuzzy, vibrating with the engine behind them and the rotor wash pounding the cockpit. The pilot flicked switches and went through security measures. They taxied and then pulled up, the nose pitching forward and down. Rising slowly, with a bump they suddenly leapt into the air and away they went, above the school, the forest, the town, everything in miniature below. Sylvia asked Aurora if she was okay over the mouthpiece. Aurora gave the thumbs up, unable to speak. Seeing the world this way, from inside the metal and glass machine, was debilitating; Aurora felt like she was on the verge of spooling out of herself. If she'd had wings and was flying on her own it would have been magnificent.

Sylvia did not tap Aurora on the shoulder and point when the house came into view. They descended on what appeared to be a page out of *Town & Country Magazine*; a long tree-lined road led to an ivory edifice built from quarried stone pillowed on site. The mansion may as well have been a castle stranded in a fairy wood. Added to this was a swimming pool, two guest cottages, tennis courts, stables, a riding arena, a pond. Stone walls delineated separate sections of gardens, that led to outbuildings. They landed on one of the manicured lawns. Sylvia thanked the pilot as they climbed out of the helicopter, the blades winding down as they made their way to the house.

The grandeur of the twenty thousand square foot Georgian-style mansion took Aurora's breath away. They entered through the back by way of the kitchen. A conservatory roof illuminated the white marble floors. An island in oak and black marble made to look like an Edwardian display cabinet sat in the middle. To the left was a glassed-in pantry and scullery with hand-blown glass windows. They trapsed through the kitchen and into a corridor which met the wood-pannelled entry hall where green, black, white and pink marble had been set to make a three-dimensional pattern on the floor. A crystal chandelier the size of an SUV shaped like an inverted Christmas tree caught the light above them. Sylvia turned to Aurora, "Welcome to my humble abode," then continued on, taking the winding, central staircase.

The tour of the house included ten bedrooms, fifteen bathrooms, two half bathrooms, a billiard room, smoking room, three studies, a home theatre, a dining room, kitchen, atrium, two sitting rooms, a wine cellar, an indoor pool, sauna, steam room, and two libraries.

Mrs Belmont greeted Aurora with open arms, gently placing her hands on her shoulders and kissing her on each side of the cheek. She told Aurora to make herself at home, then disappeared. Later, Aurora would note that Mrs Belmont was generally absent. She caught sight of her talking on the telephone, drinking wine or scotch, fluttering around the magnificent palace with a battalion of servants at her beck and call.

After settling into their bedrooms, Sylvia pulled a bell for a maid and when she arrived ordered snacks. They ate in Sylvia's bed like it was a picnic. After this, Sylvia blindfolded Aurora and took her by the hand, leading her to her father's smoking lounge where she pulled the blind off. They stood before a Rothko. Sylvia's breath had the sweet tang of pomegranate juice. She whispered in Aurora's ear, "Stay still and watch". They remained silent, hand in hand. After a time, the Rothko began to breathe. Then came a hum and a glow. The painting, existing on the wall and inside each girl, became a communion. Sylvia was the first to speak, "Van Gogh is like this too". Sylvia spoke with the electric thrill of the experience in her eyes: "We're going to stand before all the Rothkos and Van Goghs and they'll be a part of us, forever. We'll listen to the murmur".

Aurora wondered whether, with their thoughts aimed at the painting, they were charging it as it was charging them — leaving a piece of themselves in the painting's aura, as the painting left a piece of itself within theirs? Sylvia responded aloud, "Yes, yes, yes".

They returned to Sylvia's house nearly every weekend after this. Generally, a normal day would begin waking up to one another, entangled or otherwise, luxurious breakfasts of which they would eat very little, then a round of studying, followed by horseback riding; after which came lunch, a nap, a swim, a bath, then the steam room and sauna. At night, they would read and occasionally watch a film in the home-movie theater. Sometimes, during a film or at night in bed, Sylvia's eyes would become glazed and far off, like telescopes, and she would speak with a cotton-packed, floating sensation taking over her body: "Maybe it was consciousness itself, a living, vibrating thing, that created the universe...". Aurora thought Sylvia was the loveliest creature she had ever encountered.

One night, in the middle of watching *Planet of the Apes*, Sylvia broke from Aurora's side and calmly, purposefully, walked out of the room. She came back with a pen knife. Pulling the largest blade out to get her friend's full attention, her eyes locked on Aurora's sweet face. She held the knife and recited: "For the Woman whom I prefer, Here is Festival — Where my Hands are cut, Her fingers will be found inside".[5] She then cut her own palm and after reached for Aurora's hand, which Aurora gave willingly, to be cut in the same manner. They pressed their hands together, clasping with wet palms, mixing their blood to seal their pact. They ended up getting blood everywhere.

5. Sylvia had read the chapter on Emily Dickinson in Camille Paglia's *Sexual Personae* when she was writing an essay on the poet.

Aurora was worried but Sylvia didn't care, knowing the servants would take care of it. Somehow, whatever mess or stain she made throughout her life, a servant's hand would miraculously make it disappear.

On one of these weekends, Sylvia braided Aurora's hair on the bed, her gaze shifting now and then to the full-length antique mirror that sat in the corner of the room. According to the books they'd been reading, mirrors could be used to access other dimensions. Yes, it was dangerous. But why not?

Aurora remained still, luxuriating in the sensation of Sylvia's fingers going through her hair: "I know what you're thinking".

Not skipping a beat, Sylvia responded: "As Breton says — we cross through with a shudder into what the occultists call *dangerous* country".

"Are you not afraid?"

"I think we're ready. The mirror is perfect."

"Yes, it looks old."

"It's seen some things."

"I'm not sure."

"Whether we should do it?"

"Yes."

"I have *Psychic Self-Defense* in my bag."

"Maybe it won't even work."

"Let's find out!"

"Okay."

After finishing Aurora's milkmaid braid, Sylvia slid off the bed and dug out *Psychic Self-Defense* from her school bag. She returned to the bed, flipping through the pages until she found the pages dealing with the desired operation:

1. Look at the mirror and see it as a two-dimensional plane.
2. Now shift your way of looking at the mirror and notice whatever is behind you in the room.
3. Now look into the pupils of your eyes.
4. Think, or say if you are alone... [here one chooses whatever it is they want to evoke, ask, or see, and the appropriate words and symbols to coax a reply.]

The girls committed the instructions to memory. This was their protection, just as astronauts have spacesuits to survive the compression of the cosmic void of space that would otherwise asphyxiate them and set them on fire. So it is when venturing into the plane of the Unseen, one needs a membrane — a sphere of sensation made impenetrable to any outside and disturbing influence. With such an aura, one can go anywhere, do anything, meet any entity without fear or anxiety that one's person could be assailed successfully. In theory.

The two girls stood before the mirror and followed the prescribed instructions. Again and again, they repeated the steps until the only reality they had known — the reality in which they had spent the majority of their lives — dissolved. They were no longer in the mirror, or in reality, but occupied a place in between, which felt infinite. Physically they were still in the house, in the bedroom, standing in their nightgowns, barefoot before the glass, eyes set in concentrated slits as though trying to bend spoons with their minds, rigid and stationary. Inside the room, which was not Sylvia's room but another dimension, a Pan or devil appeared — unsummoned and unwanted.

At the sight of this creature the two girls became paralyzed. The thing placed itself between the girls and the lit stairway to the outer world and safety, its eyes glowed red; it bared sharp, bright teeth, snarling in such a way they could feel the vibrations in their ribs, their teeth, in the hairs of their inner ears, through every organ and bone in their body. The creature's stench made both girls want to vomit, which made the breathing techniques they needed to anchor themselves practically intolerable, but still, they managed.

With persistence and grit, the two were finally able to override their panic. They made several attempts to maneuver around the creature. But the horrific, supremely disgusting, slavering and growling entity blocked their every move, threatening to suck the souls out of their eye sockets and send them to the abode of the damned. The evil thing did not advance but functioned as a moving barrier to every possible exit. It crossed Aurora's mind that in the outer world they stood catatonic before the mirror. What would happen if they were found? Would they be taken to the hospital? Would they be trapped in that hell forever?

Finally, the entity attached itself to Sylvia. It lacked the strength to possess both of them at once. Aurora found herself on the floor, cheek pressed to the Persian carpet, drool at the corner of her mouth. Eyes locked on the base of the mirror, dust motes falling. She turned her head. Sylvia was beside her — feverish, sweating, eyes rolled back in her skull, lolling her head back and forth, breathing heavily, a rasp in her throat. Aurora sat up, grabbed her friend's hand, and called out for help.

The first person to hear her cry was Mrs Belmont, who came rushing up the main stairwell, appearing in Sylvia's room as though she had been beamed there by a Star Trek transporter, her movements light as air. She fell to her knees and knelt beside Sylvia, putting her hand to her daughter's forehead, saying Sylvia's name over and over again. She turned to Aurora, sorrow in her drugged-up eyes, asking what had happened.

Aurora feared she would sound insane if she said they were trying to enter another dimension through the mirror, and lied, telling Mrs Belmont Sylvia had felt unwell and then fell to the floor. Together they lifted Sylvia up into bed.

The doctor was called from the telephone in the hall. Aurora stayed beside Sylvia, holding her clammy hand, watching her struggle to breathe with panic in her throat, running ice cold through her stomach. She noticed a purple sheen had settled into Sylvia's eyelids which were swollen shut. Thin trails of tears made tracks down her hot, flushed cheeks. Sylvia groaned.

The doctor arrived within the hour. He took out a cold stethoscope and put it to Sylvia's chest. Both Mrs Belmont and Aurora held Sylvia down in the bed to keep her from rocking back and forth. The doctor then took her temperature, which confirmed a fever. He tried to look into her ears but she wouldn't stay still. He also had no luck looking down her throat with her head thrashing from side to side. Her lymph nodes weren't swollen, perplexing him. His diagnosis was nevertheless the flu. He prescribed antibiotics, told Mrs Belmont to keep Sylvia in bed, full of liquids, and to contact him if she worsened. The next day, they were supposed to be at the Academy. Aurora pleaded with Mrs Belmont to let her stay by Sylvia's side. Against Mrs Belmont's better judgement, she agreed, for she could not resist Aurora's charms. Aurora knew what she had to do. She had to follow the steps laid out by Dion Fortune in *Psychic Self-Defense* to rid Sylvia of the entity.

That first night the tapping on the walls and ceiling began. A foul odour of sewage-clogged drains rose up and hovered, filling the room, making it difficult to breathe. A cool, opaque humidity slithered in, spreading out and settling as a clammy film on the girls' skin.

The second evening, around midnight, an orb floated in the mist above their bed. The two lay side by side watching it — Sylvia only vaguely, her vision impaired. Eyes closed, Aurora attempted to meditate, breathing in the prescribed manner to achieve a hypnogogic state.

With no success in entering the world of the Unseen that night, Aurora spent the day wiping Sylvia's forehead with a cool, damp washcloth, giving her sips of water and Coca-Cola, reading to her from Simone de Beauvoir. Aurora got used to the latrine stench and came to appreciate the beauty of the gauzy sheaths of putrid green haze that filled the room like water in an aquarium. Again and again, holding Sylvia's hand, she would attempt to pitch herself into a trance state and go beyond the Veil to find the entity that had attached itself to Sylvia and destroy it in psychic combat.[6]

After three days and three nights of ghosts and confused, nagging, fantastical dreams — nights that witnessed the resurrection of a long lost, barbaric, infantile, and animal world where no border lies between reality and unreality or action and dream — the fever had not broken. The night the full moon rose, its light like a metal sheet, cutting through the break in the curtains, Aurora held Sylvia's hand and did the exercises. Out of the chartreuse haze whipped a grey cord, more like a writhing tentacle, that led her to Sylvia's astral body — glowing, suspended in the vapors. The tentacle with suckers had attached itself to Sylvia and was draining her life force. Aurora imagined a hatchet and pulled it out of the air, then went to work hacking at the fleshy cord again and again, using the full force of her will, pieces of gore spraying across her face, chest, arms, until finally the demonic entity was cut free. Curling up, the tentacle swiftly withdrew with a high-pitched noise and static.

---

6. For those who doubt or even laugh and find this ludicrous, who's to say that what goes on in the imagination, the psyche, is any less important than what goes on in everyday reality? Occult teachings are predicated on the idea that humans have two types of consciousness, one which is necessary for everyday thinking; the second, a state of consciousness needed to function as sorcerer and seer. *Logic will get you from A to B. Imagination will take you everywhere.* The mind and creative thought are the mothers of invention. Invention finds its way into the creation of reality. It's a two-way street. Doubt at your own peril.

For Aurora and Sylvia to try and pierce the Unseen world on their own had clearly been ill-advised and reckless. But they were only children and believed what they'd read in Dion Fortune and *The Complete Golden Dawn System of Magic*, that one could become initiated simply by doing the meditations and following the instructions. While this is true, it's certainly not responsible. They were lucky to have survived the ordeal.

The next morning, snow was falling. Sub-zero wind cut in through the cracked open window, giving the girls shivers of ecstasy. The scent of snow and pine would haunt them forever. Drained of energy from the psychic battle, red-cheeked and red-lipped with dark circles under their eyes, their bodies aching, covered in bruises, they lay like rag dolls. For three days they existed on Reece's peanut butter cups, Sprite, and Coca-Cola — the only things Sylvia wanted to eat — and were finally recovered enough to return to the Academy.

In their first steps outside, they were struck by the endlessness of the sky and the intensity of its winter blueness — slowly, almost imperceptibly expanding. The air, the trees, the rocks, birds, everything in the natural world was exquisite with a pinprick of menace. Things were reminiscent of what they had been but certainly not the same. They'd returned to something that resembled what they had known before but the old one was dead and gone forever; they would never revisit it. This one vibrated with electricity. Aurora touched Sylvia's cheek.

Skin had never felt so soft. Sylvia wanted to bite Aurora's lip and make it bleed and taste the blood.

Piercing through the Veil and winning a battle attracted the attention of more elementals on their morning runs, who came at Sylvia and Aurora from every angle. The shine of an otherworldly vitality came back to them every time they engaged with the nature spirits; their eyes blazed green, their hair gleamed, their lips red as cherries. Boys began to notice them. In fact, everywhere they went heads turned, as though magnetized.

The first evening they returned to the Academy, side by side in bed, staring up at the ceiling, Sylvia and Aurora's conversations turned to Christianity, with Sylvia ruthlessly, passionately cataloguing the Catholic and Protestant churches' hypocrisy; how they were, in effect, evil empires, devoted first and foremost to the creation of wealth and power, bringing bloodshed, torture, and genocide everywhere they went. They spread ideas like diseases, and these diseases ultimately subjugated the general population by giving them just enough hope and ecstasy to keep them in their place, all the while creating the illusion they were moving forward. Christianity. It was a form of poison. Like the drugs rapists slip into their victims' drinks to violate them.

Aurora told Sylvia what the pastors at the church had done to her. Sylvia grit her teeth. Her face flushed, swamped with rage, she wrapped her body around Aurora, hugging her, cursing the pastors and the church, describing all the ways she would kill them. She raised her arms and cried out — "By the power of God and the Holy Spirit, eradicate those devils in the guise of men from the face of the earth! Send them to the asshole of the universe!" Both girls began to laugh. "Jesus loves you! And Jesus loves it when you give me money!" The two were in hysterics: "So come on down to our Happy Holy Mega House and get mega blessed! Where our pastors, who may even be criminals, will work miracles on all your non-specific illnesses! For only ten percent of your pre-tax income per annum!". And so on, until they fell asleep, limb to limb, heads together on the mattresses they pushed together on the floor, not waking until the late afternoon.

Sylvia began to skip classes, more interested in her extra-curricular studies than what the Academy had to offer. Aurora would find her in the late afternoon, legs over the armrest of her leather club chair, reading Swedenborg's *The White Horse*. Sitting by the window smoking a cigarette, exhaling, Aurora reflects out loud, "What would you say if I told you that sometimes I feel to the point of delirium that I am pure thought?"

... If only I could kiss Aurora's cheek right now, this instant. Touch her soft, apple-scented skin with my lips.

It occurs to me that Aurora is my *zâhir* and this strikes chords of horror in my heart. The possibility is so terrifying I cannot adequately explain it here. In its most common form, *zâhir* signifies entities or things with the terrible power of being unforgettable (Aurora). The image of the thing or being eventually drives one insane (again, Aurora).

And if we're going to get into the power of words, the creation of everything — as so many of the ancient texts proclaim — was made possible by the Word. The Creator spoke, bringing the universe into being with the power and vibration of the Word. Never forget, vibration is one thing, metaphor, another. As everyone knows, for centuries mystics have been searching for this Word, the word that is capable of manifesting the thing it describes. It is the "word with its own light".

Being a jinn, of course I was forced to study the Qu'ran (even though not all jinn are Muslim; some are Christian). From Prophet Muhammad comes, "The first thing Allāh created was my Soul, and the first thing Allāh created was the Pen, and the first thing Allāh created was the Intellect." All three arrived simultaneously in the universe, and are referred to as 'Light'. So here we have the "'Word'" and its connection to the "'Light'". Please bear with me as I try to elucidate.

The way I see it, there is light in language, as there is light in the language of genetic code. Indeed, there are luminous bodies — biophotons — embedded in every strand of DNA. The two are inseparable, as space is inseparable from time. And they are necessary for communication and creation. Much like the communication that happens in fiber optics. There is a transfer of information through the light.

At this moment it seems incredibly important, vital, to realize that in order the fact that to see anything clearly, one must be in the presence of that which is luminous. And I must see clearly. This is the thing. Only God and the blind can create miracles in the dark; as for the rest of us, light gives form to creation.

And as it is, everything must communicate, even rocks. As DNA communicates through the light of biophotons and technological devices through the light of fiber optics, one can see how communication and light — these transformative substances — are necessary for creation and life. And so, I finally refer here to light because it is a vessel of communication; it is the beginning and the continuation. And in this girl, whom I cannot exorcize from my thoughts, there is light... No. I will crumple up these last pages and toss them into the fire; I'll watch the paper burn blue, turn black at the edges, devoured. I hate reading all that meta bullshit in literature. I will begin again. There have been so many failures. I am a cage in search of a bird. I think I now know what Kafka meant... She is not a Venus: she is a Diana, the cold queen of the night, the female reflection in the mirror's silver...

At night, in bed — Sylvia reading Regardie's *The Complete Golden Dawn,* they wondered whether going through the mirror, piercing the world of the Unseen on their own had been ill-advised and reckless, something they shouldn't attempt again. When Dion Fortune did this kind of thing for the first time she had been under the guidance of a master. Alexandra David-Neel had been instructed by lamas. They wondered whether they in fact needed a Master.

In the campus library, Aurora came across a book from the 17th century entitled *The Art of Worldly Wisdom* by Balthasar Gracián. She stopped when she got to a certain passage, then read and reread it again:

> Know how to be all things to all men. A discreet Proteus — a scholar among scholars, a saint among saints. That is the art of winning over everyone, for like attracts like. Take note of temperaments and adapt yourself to each person you meet — follow the lead of the serious and jovial in turn, changing your mood discreetly.

The words fell into her. She burned with shame. They were missing pieces of a puzzle. With a conscious clarity, she realized that the entire time she had been doing exactly this, going through a process of calculated metamorphosis — blotting out her trailer trash origins. At the Waldorf, at the Academy. She had studied Sylvia and her friends. The way they spoke, the way they dressed — gathering up verbal and non-verbal cues, code words, committing everything to memory, pressing it all into her psyche until it became second nature. She now spoke like Sylvia, in the manner of the educated New England elite. She dressed like Sylvia. She ate like Sylvia. She showered like Sylvia. She smelled like Sylvia. The book was telling her that there was nothing wrong in wanting to take a conscious part in one's own creation. In fact, no one had been born perfect, and it was one's duty to chisel oneself into something that shined:

In your affairs, create suspense. It's neither useful nor pleasurable to show all your cards. Not immediately revealing everything fuels anticipation, especially when a person's elevated position means expectations are greater. It bespeaks mystery in everything and, with this very secrecy, arouses awe. Even when explaining yourself, you should avoid complete frankness, just as you shouldn't open yourself up to everyone in all your dealings. Cautious silence is the refuge of good sense.

A decision openly declared is never respected; instead, it opens the way to criticism, and if things turn out badly, you'll be unhappy twice over. Imitate divinity's way of doing things to keep people attentive and alert.

The height of perfection. No one is born complete; perfect yourself and your activities day by day until you become a truly consummate being, your talents and your qualities all perfected. This will be evident in the excellence of your taste, the refinement of your intellect, the maturity of your judgement, the purity of your will. Some never manage to be complete; something is always missing. Others take a long time. The consummate man, wise in word and sensible in deed, is admitted into, and even sought out for, the singular company of the discreet.

Impeccability. Grace. Perfection. Discretion. No one is born complete. She would be her own making and she would not be ashamed. She would pay attention. She would scrub the trailer park out. No trace of it would remain. In the

school library film archives, Aurora began studying classic
femmes fatales: Rita Hayworth, Lauren Bacall, Brigitte
Bardot, Sophia Loren, Ava Gardner, Marilyn Monroe,
Romy Schneider, Grace Kelly, Isabelle Adjani, Monica
Bellucci. Jean Seberg in Godard's *Breathless*, Anna Karina,
Corinne Marchand in *Cléo from 5 to 7* (even though the
man Cléo fell for at the end was an idiot). She watched
B-movie noirs: *Blonde Ice* was one of them — "Ice in her
heart, icicles in her veins". A mood of cynicism, flashbacks,
voiceover narration; the dreamlike quality of hopelessly
tangled plot with German expressionist composition and
angles. Aurora let it seep into her. Corruption, fatalism,
moral ambiguity, violence and brutality mixed with erotic
elements; hardboiled narrative and dialogue — an urban
setting, a private detective, a femme fatale, an antihero,
crime, rain-slicked city streets, neon signs, venetian blinds,
and cigarettes, low-key lighting. There was a scene where
the blonde — the femme fatale with a heart of ice — and
the private detective — dressed in a tuxedo — are in a
smoky parlor together and she asks, "Is there something
criminal in my being ambitious?" The detective stands and
looks down at her as though he's speaking to a child, "Why
no, criminal? Of course not. Unless your ambitions take a
perverse form and you'll stop at nothing, right or wrong
to get what you want". She looks up at him — confident,
her skin glowing like the moon, eyes wide as saucers,
eyebrows raised: "They say the female of the species is
deadlier than the male". Aurora sat rapt, in calculation,
the lights from the television screen flickering across
her face.

The power these women wielded was palpable, anchoring itself deep into her imagination, her limbs, nerves, blood, gut, breath and beating heart. Whenever she walked into a room — the classroom, the cafeteria, the ballet studio — she summoned them up, all of them, in different combinations, variations, potencies, in a way that was intuitive and vague but at the same time commanding, hard; something she could feel taking over her entire being. She looked at herself in mirrors. She observed people around her, their movements, particularities, ticks she found attractive and captivating, harvesting information, processing, ingesting it, using it like photosynthesis. *Cautious silence is the refuge of good sense. Imitate divinity's way of doing things to keep people attentive and alert.*

A passage from a biography on Marilyn Monroe held a key. Marilyn was in New York City with a friend, walking down the street like anyone else, unnoticed. Suddenly she turned and said, "Do you want to see Marilyn Monroe?", then continued walking. People began to point and shout, car horns rang out, traffic stopped, people called from their windows, "Marilyn!" There was something one could turn on and off — a magnetic field. Of course, whatever it was, it wasn't foolproof. It had not saved Marilyn on whose deathbed side table sat bottles of sedatives, soporifics, tranquilizers, opiates, amphetamines, and sleeping pills — a vial of Nembutal, found empty, next to her corpse. By thinking so much, Aurora became echo and abyss, extracting all that she could, imbibing inviolable secrets to nourish and create herself (which seems almost vampiric to me now). Sphinx-like in her silences, she took on an Orphic quality. Symbols want to keep their secrets.

Aurora and Sylvia's realizations, or revelations, along with the elementals who continued to infect them on their forest runs, shot the two girls to the moon. Out there, in the depths of space, they saw and realized the vast ocean of darkness pricked with stars, where everything they'd known before was encapsulated on a little glowing island floating and spinning in the void. They had become something 'other'. In ballet class they stupefied the teacher and other dancers, moving in tandem without looking at each other, their movements controlled and efficient, charging the room, their mercurial forms reflected in the walls of mirrors to infinity. They left their audience unsettled, a liquid rattle in their eyes, not knowing how to believe or react to what they had just seen.

Smoking a cigarette, taking a break from writing a paper on Emily Dickinson, Aurora could see the church steeple from the dorm window. She would never forget how Sylvia had come to her with a knife, reciting: "For the Woman whom I prefer, Here is Festival — Where my Hands are cut, Her fingers will be found inside" and they had become blood sisters. That was just before they entered the Unseen world through the mirror.

And now she also saw, thanks to Joseph Campbell, the paganism in Christianity. The blood, the sacrifice; the invisible, incomprehensible forces at work in the universe twisting fate. Aurora marveled at how easily Dickinson cut God's hand off and banished Him:

Those—dying then,
Knew where they went—
They went to God's Right Hand—
That Hand is amputated now
And God cannot be found—

The abdication of Belief
Makes the Behavior small—
Better an ignis fatuus
Than no illume at all—

The professor said Dickinson may have been referring to John Milton's *Paradise Lost*, lines 631–642, when Satan is compared to a will-o'-the-wisp, or *ignis fatuus*, leading Eve to the Tree of Knowledge of Good and Evil. She'd also pointed out that Dickinson's bride figures are always rape victims, duped by their lovers — the trickster, Death. And then there was this:

A single Screw of Flesh
Is all that pins the Soul
That stands for Deity, to mine,
Opon my side the Vail —

Once witnessed of the Gauze —
Its name is put away

As far from mine, as if no
plight
Had printed yesterday,

In tender — solemn Alphabet,
My eyes just turned to see —
When it was smuggled by
my sight
Into Eternity —

More Hands — to hold — These
are but Two —
One more new-mailed Nerve
Just granted, for the Peril's
sake —
Some striding — Giant — Love —

So greater than the Gods
can show,
They slink before the Clay,
That not for all their Heaven
can boast
Will let it's Keepsake — go

More riddles. Love, she seemed to be saying, was
something the gods are incapable of showing the people
of clay (humans); the gods "slink" around the humans,
pinning their souls like butterflies in trophy showcases to
the walls. Dickinson didn't seem to have much reverence
for Jesus either:

The Auctioneer of Parting
His "Going, going, gone"
Shouts even from the Crucifix,
And brings his Hammer down —
He only sells the Wilderness,
The prices of Despair
Range from a single human Heart
To Two — not any more —

Jesus as an auctioneer, taking hearts away from people and selling them off. There was so much sadomasochism and gore in Emily Dickinson. But frankly, no more or less than any religion had ever offered. The Bible was a slaughterhouse.

My Life had stood — a Loaded Gun —
In Corners — till a Day
The Owner passed — identified —
And carried Me away —

And now We roam in Sovereign Woods —
And now We hunt the Doe —
And every time I speak for Him
The Mountains straight reply —

That night, in her journal, Aurora wrote:

November 3rd
You are crucified by your own limitations. You have choices. You can be the loaded gun. Your mother, your

father, you'll never know what part of them is inside you. Don't waste this chance. You have the power to be anything. Find it, use it. Sylvia believes in you. Sylvia is sublime. Stay in this world. Do not fall. Do not falter.

3.

That summer, Aurora accompanied Sylvia to her house on Martha's Vineyard. Grandmother's arthritis had gotten much worse — she'd stopped sewing wedding dresses and making outfits for the Waldorf children, so had very little disposable income and couldn't afford Aurora's plane ticket home, but didn't tell Aurora this. She told the child she'd miss her and would see her soon, but that going with her friend was a great opportunity and no doubt the work of Jesus. It was clearly His Will, his Plan.

In town they couldn't go anywhere without Sylvia being stopped by people she knew and barely knew to chat, which she did with the nonchalant air of a European film star, until her impatience consumed her (Aurora could see her smoldering), and she cut the person or persons off with a charismatic little smile and a *Ciao!* Sylvia had no interest in the silly parties that took place on the island. She'd done all that the previous summer.

They stood by their decision to stay away from occult practices. The only questionable thing they got involved with was remote viewing, something they decided wasn't exactly occult if the U.S. military used it. They followed instructions from an unclassified CIA manual they found on the internet, entitled, "A Suggested Remote Viewing Training Procedure".

The manual was written and compiled by consultants from a research institute called SRI International, founded by trustees of Stanford University. Aurora and Sylvia would sit quietly, one of them recording a coordinate, or target, on a piece of paper — for example, a location, Paris — while the other sat at their desk with paper, pencil, and clay and closed their eyes, concentrating on "the signal line", a sensory, visual, and/or emotional impression related to the target, which generally appeared in the mind in scraps like jigsaw pieces. They would draw and/or write these impressions down, whatever came to them, then shape a representation of what they had experienced in clay. With this, they reconstructed and made sense of the information they'd received. Sylvia came closer to hitting the targets than Aurora.

During these experiments Aurora often found herself at a high altitude above the ground, looking down as if from an airplane, the curvature of the earth visible. She would then descend with views of rocky mountains, forests, plains, flying over small towns with illuminated telephone polls in the crepuscular light. Once she saw a train moving along its tracks. She wrote the words "altitude view", "patchwork grass in green and gold", "farmland", "snaking rivers", "snaking roads", "fuzzy forests", "flattened mountains", "towns at night", "highway", "crackling sounds", "yellow, orange, lights", "pickup truck", "gasoline skunk smell", "wood, tree, earth smells", "cigar stink".

And again and again, night after night, Aurora dreamt of Tu-tu. He was walking across the country to find her. When she woke it was a stab in her chest to realize the cat wasn't there, that it had been a dream; that she would most likely never see him again until the next time she dreamt him, or perhaps, in the afterlife.

The two ate frozen yoghurt, crushed on boys from afar, read, swam, rode horses. On one occasion they went sailing with Sylvia's uncle who was a high-functioning alcoholic, his beady sea glass eyes sunken into an untrustworthy, doughy face, stoic in his middle age, constantly offering them whisky and cigarettes. Declining the whisky, they drank Diet Coke instead.

Flashes of Sylvia's mother appeared here and there throughout the house, coming and going, her skin radiant, perfectly glowing — she was sometimes flustered with minute signs of dejection, her face like a beautiful Midwestern sky with fast blowing clouds over the plains, flickering in the shadows and light, one moment concerned, the next brightening into a smile, followed by thinly veiled ticks of despondence — even when she was there she was partially elsewhere.

"Fuck it. We'll go to Paris and the Côte d'Azur. I'm bored already." Aurora thought Sylvia was joking. But no. Stunned that Aurora didn't have a passport, she called the passport office and found out what they needed to obtain one. Aurora called her grandmother and had her send her birth certificate and fax a statement of consent. With these, they were able to get a passport in three days. Sylvia bought airplane tickets with her unlimited credit card. She found her mother in the bedroom, in the walk-in closet to be more precise, highball on the rocks in her hand, told her what their plans were, and to let the people at the apartment in Paris and the house in Cannes know they were coming. Mrs Belmont didn't make any moves to subvert their plans, one arm crossed beneath her bosom supporting the other; the ice in her highball glass popping, tinkling against the crystal.

The next day the driver took them to a private airfield where they boarded one of Sylvia's father's company jets with their luggage, books for school, and half of their occult library. They sat in wide leather seats like armchairs, smoked cigarettes and drank Diet Coke while Sylvia marked out the locations of cafés the Surrealists had frequented on her map of Paris.

They would go to the Deux Magots where F. Scott Fitzgerald, Gertrude Stein, and Hemingway's Lost Generation drank absinthe shoulder to shoulder with Picasso, André Breton, Miró, Sartre, Simone de Beauvoir, Camus and a host of other Surrealists, Existentialists, and members of the avant-garde. The café had also been the haunt of Symbolist poets — Stéphane Mallarmé, Paul Verlaine and Arthur Rimbaud.

The Hôtel Mistral in Rue Cels was on the map. Here, Sartre and Simone de Beauvoir had rented rooms when they were teachers. It was also where de Beauvoir began her first novel *L'Invitée*. La Closerie des Lilas marked the place Sartre and de Beauvoir held a 'Socialism and Freedom' meeting in 1941 after Sartre returned from a prisoner of war camp. Then, at No. 11 Rue Victor-Schoelcher, overlooking the Montparnasse Cemetery, was where de Beauvoir lived with Claude Lanzmann. "She fell in love with him when she was forty-four and he was twenty-six. They lived there together until she died," Sylvia explained, her dark eyelashes in an attitude of reverence.

The jet flew over green and gold patches of farmland, clusters of houses, swathes of woodland, silvery rivers, and then over something that looked like a metropolis but was not Paris, skating along high above the Seine, finally crossing over it and landing in Paris–Le Bourget Airport, six miles outside the city. A driver met them at the airport in a Mercedes. Entering Paris, the city swooped in on Aurora from all sides. She felt like she was in some kind of snow globe, the air conditioning on full blast, the world outside the stuff of fairy tales — towers, gigantic ornate cupolas and spires, rows of buildings in white stone with blue grey mansard roofs, some of them metal, glinting in the sun; narrow cobbled streets, ancient, golden brick edifices with wisteria climbing up the walls to the terraces. Sylvia's apartment was on the top floor of an historic private mansion — Avenue de la Motte-Picquet, 7th arrondissement — with a private elevator, caretaker services and security, soaring four-meter-high ceilings, original period details, renovated with the finest materials and designer touches. From the enormous wraparound balcony, the Eiffel Tower was in plain view. It was one of several properties Sylvia's family owned in the capital. They sat in cushioned wicker armchairs in the heat, smoked cigarettes and drank Diet Coke.

"Let's go to Les Deux Magots." Sylvia carefully flicked cigarette ash into the nearby ashtray.

"Yeah, I'm ready whenever you are."

"I think first though, a shower is in order." Sylvia stubbed her cigarette out and got up.

Aurora stayed behind, finishing her cigarette, head spinning from the rush of nicotine. A falling object caught the corner of her eye — she turned and saw a tiny, grey piece of fluff making peeping noises on a chair cushion about eight feet away. She got up to inspect it. A tiny bird, the size of a cotton ball, flailed its wings, then began screeching, its mouth stretched open. There was terror in its pinprick eyes. Black streaks stretched back along its head, making it look like a bandit. Aurora picked the miniature creature up gently, holding it in her palm, lightly stroking its pale yellow, fluffy cheeks and underbelly with her index finger. "Don't worry, I'm not going to hurt you. I'm going to find your mommy."

Looking up and down for a nest, listening for other chicks, she found nothing. That settled it. She was, from that moment, a bird mother.

Sylvia was taken instantly by the chick and called the driver to bring them to the nearest pet shop, where they could get food for it. She rummaged around in the master bedroom walk-in closet and found a little Tiffany box with tissue paper they could use to carry it for the time being. The tiny chick was so delicate they feared they would accidentaly crush it in their hands. "It looks thirsty," Aurora mused; she went to the kitchen, found a small bowl and filled it with water, but the bird wouldn't drink.

"We need a pipette," Sylvia observed.

At the pet shop, the woman told them they should return it to the nest, but still sold them dried as well as fresh bugs and worms in containers of dirt plus seeds to feed it, along with nesting material. In the car, they held a small, live worm in front of it, its beak no bigger than the sharpened end of a pencil lead. The tiny thing screeched, opening its mouth as wide as it could. Aurora was afraid that if they just dropped it in the bird would choke so she held it there until eventually it took the worm into its mouth and swallowed it.

"Well, let's go to Les Deux Magots. We have everything it needs." Sylvia leaned forward between the front seats and gave the driver their destination in French.

The fabled café, with its elegant stone façade and ironwork balconies, sat on a corner with green awnings and people crowded around small circular tables, seated on chic bamboo and woven plastic bistro chairs. The driver stopped in front to let them out. Sylvia asked the waiter if they could have a table outside and they were led to a table in the terrace garden surrounded by shrubbery. Aurora felt grown up for the first time in her life. She was in Paris, sitting in the café where the Surrealists had written their manifesto.

Sylvia wasted no time ordering champagne. Aurora left the chick in Sylvia's care while she went to the bathroom. The interior of the café looked untouched since the days of Art Deco, with chandeliers, columns, red leather banquettes and brass reflecting in wall-length mirrors. The carved faces on the gigantic Chinese figurines — stuck to the top of two columns beside one another — were grotesque, like demons. The bathroom had a latrine smell and was nothing to write home about.

Aurora arrived back at the table to champagne and the bird calling out from the Tiffany box for more food. Sylvia had her sunglasses on and was smoking a cigarette. She raised her glass, "To us". Aurora clinked glasses with Sylvia, took a sip and sat down, occupying herself with feeding the bird another worm and giving it beads of water from an eye dropper. Aurora refused a cigarette from Sylvia. She didn't want the chick to be exposed to smoke, however she didn't say this, and in fact they sat, not speaking, just existing comfortably in their chairs, in the hum of Paris, and the conversations around them, looking at their menus — bistro staples, duck à l'orange, chicken supreme, beefsteak, omelettes, quiches, croque-monsieurs, salads, and sandwiches made with Poilâne bread. There were also wild Burgundy snails and Petrossian caviar with toast and cream. Dessert included Pierre Hermé's pastries, macarons, and an assortment of *glaces*.

They both ordered salads. Sylvia chose a bottle of the most expensive wine, which was Hermitage. Aurora noticed that the bill came to over five hundred euros. As they ate it became immediately clear that Les Deux Magots was now an American tourist hotspot. Across the road, the Brasserie Lipp looked more chic. Sylvia decided they would go there for a coffee: "My illusions have now been shattered," she looked around disapprovingly, "Of course. What was I thinking?" She stubbed out her cigarette.

Aurora understood this to mean that there was, of course, no way of going back in time to try and grasp a particle of the first Surrealists' world. The present epoch had swallowed all of that up. If they wanted to be in the presence of the next groundbreaking movement they were going to have to find it by other means — means which they were unlikely to acquire in the short space of time they planned on staying in Paris. Artists in the modern age are underground. They don't sit in cafes writing manifestos.

But more than anything, more than the question of where the next philosophical, artistic movement might be taking place, Aurora was preoccupied with the chick, worrying it wouldn't make it. She remembered the tiny bird Tu-tu brought to her, barely alive, that had died in her hand. "What do you think we should call her, or him?"

Sylvia gave this some thought: "Dinky". Sylvia paid the bill and they moved with Dinky to the Brasserie Lipp.

After their coffee, they went back to the apartment in a taxi. Sylvia went to take a nap while Aurora sat on the terrace and fed Dinky every forty minutes or so. In between, she read Leonora Carrington's *The Hearing Trumpet* while kestrels flew overhead[7].

7. Little did she know, it was a kestrel nesting in the Eiffel Tower that had dropped the Eurasian blue tit hatchling from its talons onto the terrace. The emanations that fizzed from Aurora — still possessed by the elementals — had disrupted the kestrel's navigation.

Sylvia didn't wake up until seven the next morning. Aurora took the guest bedroom and tended to the chick all night, terrified it would die. She'd brought her glow-in-the-dark Virgin Mary, who she now saw not as a symbol of Christendom but as the more ancient Artemis — "Lady of the wild animals", virgin goddess of savage nature, the moon, defender of innocence and purity, huntress, attended by water nymphs. Aurora prayed to the glowing goddess to protect the little bird.

The next morning Sylvia padded into Aurora's room, feet sticking to the parquet, dressed in a navy blue, oversized silk pajama top — fresh face glowing, hair disheveled, eyes smudged with kohl — and climbed into bed, her skin sugary, vanilla-scented, mixed with the slight acridity of champagne, the earthy odor of her hair losing the fragrance of shampoo, and said: "Today we should go to the Pompidou. I want to see Breton's Wall". She touched Aurora's hair and kissed her cheek, both of them sinking into each other's beauty, wanting to amalgamate, but keep their essential selves so that they could feel the merger more intensely.

Rustling in the box on the bedside table, Dinky called out to be fed. She, or he, had grown in the night. Aurora rolled over and fed the chick from the box of earth and worms. Afterward, she cupped the little bird in her hands and held it to her cheek. Dinky crawled into her hair and began making a nest.

"Do you think Dinky's male or female?" Sylvia stretched her arms upward.

"I have no idea."

"Let's just say she's a girl," Sylvia got out of bed, "I'm going to see about breakfast. I'll ask Madeleine — or is it Sophie? — to put it out for us on the terrace". When they arrived, they'd briefly met the maid, dressed in a traditional black-and-white uniform.

They had a leisurely breakfast — coffee with milk, croissants, strawberries, fresh squeezed orange juice with vitamins. Aurora untangled Dinky from her hair and put her in the Tiffany box.

"These croissants are the food of the gods." This was the only statement made throughout breakfast.

The driver let them off in front of the museum, which resembled a giant futuristic boiler or scientific device with its massive pipes, but was also somehow nautical with the prominent air vents that looked like they belonged on a cruise ship. They walked in past security with Dinky nestled in Aurora's hair. Once they were out of sight, Aurora transferred the chick into the box. Sylvia bought tickets.

They found themselves before a portrait of Guillaume Apollinaire by Giorgio de Chirico. "Apollinaire looks like your uncle. In sunglasses."

"It's actually Orpheus. Apollinaire is the shadow lantern figure in the back with the half circle. The semicircle is the premonitory aspect — depicting where he'd get hit in the head with shrapnel."

They moved on to Joan Miró's *La Sieste* with its amorphous forms reminiscent of objects in the process of disintegrating, silhouetted against an indefinite deep space.

They moved on to Max Ernst's *Ubu Imperator*. Sylvia read a line from the description of the work: "Behind the buffoonery of power alluded to by Ubu as a spinning top, the whole traditional aesthetic of rational construction and geometric perspective is also ridiculed".

"I wonder why he wanted to evoke the Tower of Pisa."

Next came Man Ray's Le *Violon d'Ingres*. "This is so famous."

Aurora looked in on Dinky in her box, then stroked her head to make sure she was still alive.

"I love the image of woman as a cello. Total stroke of genius," Sylvia turned to Aurora, "He got Lee Miller into photography. And then he flipped out that she was just as good or even better than he was."

"They discovered how to solarize photos to give them that ghostly, glowing look. But some historians credit Miller completely. She was so gorgeous. I'm obsessed with her. What a badass".

Moving on to the next work, Sylvia sighed, "When Lee Miller set sail for Paris in 1929 she had a whole string of lovers so they flipped a coin to decide who got to see her off. One of the guys who lost the coin flip swooped down beside the boat in a biplane to shower her in roses. She was also a war photographer."

"I know."

"There's a famous photo of her in Hitler's bathtub".

"I've seen it."

They came to Salvador Dalí's *Lion, Cheval, Dormeuse invisibles*. "This is an example of his paranoiac criticism."

Aurora got as close to the painting as she could, "The brushstrokes are so precise. It looks like it was made by a leprechaun".

"His style is so iconic it almost seems like a parody of itself now."

"Yeah, but when you see it up close, the real thing; how it's made, the little, impossible details, it doesn't."

"True."

Next was Victor Brauner's *Loup-table*. "God, I love this."

"It's incredible." Aurora had always found foxes enchanting.

"Let's go to Breton's Wall."

They stood before it — two hundred and fifty-five works of art and found objects — tourist knick-knacks, masks, pottery, decorated frames, dolls, whistles, ex-votos, sugar skulls, a carved whalebone, a box of mummified cicadas, an Egyptian amulet, a Tatanua mask, a fossilized sea urchin, a Mayan doll, pebbles from the bed of a river, an Iroquois mask, a Victorian glass display case of butterflies, Picabia's painting *Le Double Monde* to the right of Miró's *Tête* with paintings by Jean Degottex — *Pollen noir* — sitting on the upper part of the wall along with René Duvillier's *Fleur d'écume*. In the geometric center of this forest sat a photograph of Breton's last companion.

"That's his last wife, Elisa," Sylvia whispered into Aurora's ear and pointed. "She was an artist and writer and the inspiration behind Breton's *Arcane 17*. Her daughter tragically drowned at a young age and in the final prose quartet of *Arcane 17*, Breton compares her death to the death and resurrection of the Egyptian god Osiris".

Elisa. The name of the princess in Aurora's favourite fairytale.

"It says the painting by Rousseau, *Nature morte aux cerises*, interweaves the stories linked to it in a round of images, visions and speculations as presented in myth, popular stories and legends," Sylvia was still whispering.

Dinky cried out for more food, peeping frantically from inside the box. Aurora sat down on the nearest bench to feed her. Sylvia remained standing in front of the wall, then came to sit beside Aurora. "In Breton's *L'Art magique* he said that art has a 'magical' dimension when its meaning eclipses, exceeds and opposes its 'formal' dimension — its realization as a 'beautiful' object. The 'magical' work is neither particularly 'beautiful' nor 'true'. 'Magical' art, more than anything else, is a bridge."

"Maybe it's also a ladder. Or a portal." Dinky greedily ate the worms Aurora fed her, her little wings spread at her sides. She looked like a miniature penguin.

"Yes, it's definitely a portal. And probably also a ladder." Sylvia gave Dinky a little stroke on the head, "I think there's a Rothko here. Let's go find it."

The two girls rode the transparent tube elevator, slowly conveyed above Paris until they could see the Eiffel Tower and the Sacré-Cœur through the glass streaked with dust.

They came to *Sans titre (Noir, Rouge sur Noir sur Rouge)*, painted in 1964, and stood before it. Crimson reds darkened into browns to form a floating square

AURORA

hole of blacks. It appeared to vibrate. What is more the
vibrations seemed to be emitting sound — the sound of a
pregnant void, of blood, mud; a sand-packed sky spitting
tiny particles invisible to the naked eye, while at the
same time sucking everything in — indifferent blackness
devouring the light, bringing it to ecstasy.

"Jesus Christ! That is so intense," Sylvia murmured.

Aurora could not speak. Tears ran down her face. Dinky
was also silent.

Sylvia pulled Aurora by the arm, away from the magnetic
field, soft, dense, fervid, until they got far enough away
from the painting's orbit and the air thinned out.

"I think we've seen enough. I need to go outside."

Aurora looked at Sylvia, not speaking. The expression
on her face said everything. They took a packed elevator
down to get out as quickly as possible, Aurora fearing
the stress of their surroundings was too much for Dinky,
wanting to scream but holding it in like a rabbit caught
between two headlights.

Outside the museum, Sylvia lit a cigarette, "I need a
glass of wine. Let's go to a café. I love it how we can just
go anywhere and drink here."

"I think we should have left Dinky at the apartment and
asked Madeleine — or is it Sophie? — to feed her every
forty minutes. Maybe we should go back." Her heart beating
wildly, Aurora pulled the top off the Tiffany box. Dinky
looked up at them and opened her little beak, then threw
around some nesting material. "Thank god, she seems okay."

"She looks fine. I think we should go to lunch near here,
and then back to the apartment."

They found a café and ordered salads with the most expensive wine on the menu. Sylvia was drunk after two glasses of wine and smoking again. "I think I've had enough of Paris. We could stay another day and go to the Louvre, then to Cannes, or we could just go to Cannes tomorrow. What do you think?"

"I don't know — whatever you want to do."

"I mean, we're here, so we could go to the Louvre. You've never been there."

"Yeah, that would be cool. I don't know if Dinky can handle it though. I think the museum was too much for her today."

"The maid could feed her."

"I don't know."

"Let's just go for like an hour."

"Okay."

"Then you can say you've been there at least. It's really cool. There are amazing ancient Egyptian and Roman statues and artefacts."

"Sure."

"We can go in the morning when it opens, then come back here, get our stuff and fly to Cannes in the evening."

"Sounds good."

They took a taxi back to the apartment.

"You look tired, Aurora. You didn't sleep all night. If you want a nap, I'll feed Dinky."

"Thanks." Aurora walked to her room, thinking Sylvia was a different person in Paris; more American, but still chic. The cotton sheets were fresh and soft as silk and smelled pleasantly of a foreign laundry detergent. She sunk her head into the down pillow. In her dream she was with her grandmother, but they were in a ranch house from the Sixties and Tu-tu was running from room to room chasing a rat. Her consciousness moved from this to other scenes, in and out, and she found herself in a medium-sized town — lost — trying to get back home when a red balloon came floating by. She grabbed onto its string and was lifted into the sky, higher and higher. Terrified, she knew she would die if she let go. The balloon took her over mountains and forests and then turned into an umbrella. Falling through the stratospheres she landed on top of a Mack truck moving down a highway and immediately passed through its roof like a ghost when the umbrella evaporated. The truck driver didn't seem to notice she was there. She wondered where they were headed – scenic views of mountains and forests flashed past out the window — and how she was going to get back to Tu-tu. After this, she was catapulted into darkness, into the tunnels with the glowing red-eyed, sharp-toothed rodents of her childhood nightmares.

Half-awake, the diurnal rhythms attempted to pull Aurora up into the waking world with their marionette strings. Aurora fought, digging in the mud, claustrophobic, struggling to breathe with dirt in her throat, clawing her way out, the last convulsions of sleep pressing its body down on her, doing all it could to keep her encased in its realm.

Finally free, with a heavy head, Aurora came to and realized where she was. She got out of bed and walked through the empty rooms; through the salon in the gold and pink light and out onto the terrace where the viscous, soft, steady, air clung to her, and the expanse of sky glowed azure and magenta with violet clouds high above the rooftops stained with tangerine — the liquid gold light of the sun was sinking into hazy lilac crimson bands at the horizon, with the Eiffel Tower standing in the centre of it all — like a gigantic syringe. Sylvia was smoking a cigarette. Dinky rustled in her nest and cried out. Sylvia set the cigarette in a nearby ashtray and took a beetle out of the paper bag on the table to feed her. "Anyway."

Aurora stood there pink and gold in the light. "Anyway what?"

"I just said, anyway."

"Oh."

"How did you sleep?"

"Not well."

"Why? What happened?"

"I don't want to talk about it."

"Why?"

"I want to forget it."

"It's good for people to talk about their dreams, or nightmares."

"I'm not people."

"Everyone is people."

"I'm not."

"True. In this light you're more like an angel. Enigmatic. Ravishing. Terrifying. Sublime." Sylvia stubbed her cigarette out and lit another one. "Do you want to go out to eat? Or stay in?"

"Let's stay in."

They ordered Chinese food and ate on the terrace by candlelight. Afterward, they went to their separate rooms to read, Aurora taking Dinky to feed her throughout the night.

In the morning they were served croissants and café au lait out of bowls on the terrace as usual with Dinky beside them in her box which had been freshly cleaned. The amount of excrement she produced was astonishing for such a small creature.

"Jesus Christ! Dinky looks like she grew twice her size in the night."

Aurora took the bird out of the box and held her in her hand. "Yeah, her feathers are getting brighter." Dinky twitched her head left and right in a way that was mechanical, looking back and forth at the two humans.

"Maybe she'll fly soon."

The driver stopped in front of the Metro entrance at the Louvre and told the girls to enter the museum that way to avoid the lines at the pyramid which already wound around the glass structure. He also said the museum was free for people under eighteen and to show their identification when they got tickets. Underground, the halls were polished, sand-colored stone with glass ceilings that let trapezoidal prisms of sunlight in. In places, gigantic blocks of rock made up the bottom part of the walls — remnants of the original royal palace fortifications.

They got past security with Dinky in the Tiffany bag, went to get their tickets, then took the Richelieu entrance, walking across the polished marble floors, the beams of light from the ceiling illuminating the classical statues. Up a marbled staircase with columns on either side, they came to *The Code of Hammurabi* carved in black stone, then went through a recreation of the temple where the Code was found, flanked with winged bearded deities, their heads human, their bodies bulls. After this, they wandered through halls with ancient Egyptian objects. The sheer volume of artifacts was exhausting.

Down a set of stairs was the famous Sphinx. They took more stairs upward and came to rooms with Ancient Greek artifacts and moved on the Greco-Roman area with enormous columns and the highest ceilings Aurora had ever seen in her life, higher than the ceilings at the megachurch, and more glorious, painted with intricate scenes from antiquity, shining with gold.

In the *Art funéraire du Proche-Orient* section, Salle 181 — *Les cultes*, they wandered among idols and stopped in front of Podium 9 *Le Mythraeum de Sidon*. Both of them were drawn to an entirely naked male figure in and amongst the other figurines. He was beautifully formed, as perfect as a Greek god with a lion's head and angel wings on his back. Wrapped around his body was a snake with its head coiled on his chest, hissing. The lion's head had its mouth wide-open, canines exposed, tongue sticking out. In his hands, held stiffly by his side, the figure carried two keys. Behind his legs was a tree stump.

"Surrealism before Surrealism," Sylvia mused. "I think I'm in love with him." Reading the plaque explaining the figure, "He's Syrian. Lion-headed figure of the Mithraic Mysteries, from the late 4th-century, discovered by the journalist Edmond Durighello in 1887. The function of a round hole in the back of his head is doubtful. Identification of the head as that of Aion is an approximation. There is general agreement that the figure has something to do with Time, and that it has many of the iconographic characteristics of Aion. However, the figure's name and function are not actually known". Sylvia turned to Aurora, "I want him."

"I wonder if he's wearing a lion's head or if his head is actually a lion's." One could have imagined he was an angel wearing a mask — a hollowed-out lion head he had killed. Bewitched by its menace and beauty, the icon made the young women's blood run hot. They wanted to break the glass and possess it, as they stood mesmerized, their phantom reflections in the glass staring back at themselves.

"We'll never know. It's like Schrödinger 's cat — both I guess."

The figure continued to command their attention and hold them in his thrall for some time: they couldn't take their eyes off him. "Not much is known about the Mithraic Mysteries," remarked Sylvia.

Eventually, they turned away from him and continued up more stairs until they came to the headless Winged Victory statue, then turned right into another set of rooms where panels of early Christian scenes hung from the walls. A winged Jesus hovered above the ground shooting a spider web from his wrist onto a monk. They stood in front of a scene with ashen-faced Christian zombies. One of the priests had a meat cleaver stuck into his head.

When they got to Artemis, they did not turn to enter the room with the *Mona Lisa*. Under elaborate dome ceilings with painted scenes and golden eagles in relief they came to Napoleon's *Coronation* and *Liberty Leading the People*. Walking past more and more of the gigantic paintings, they stopped in front of *Pandemonium* marked with the year 1841, which depicted Satan trying to convince other angels to join him.

After this they entered the neoclassical section with white statues everywhere and came upon *Cupid and Psyche*, the masterpiece by Italian sculptor Antonio Canova, depicting the moment Cupid wakes Psyche from a death-like sleep that had been induced by a toxic gas inside a flask, by touching her with one of his arrows. She had been sent to the Underworld by Venus to retrieve the flask and told not to open it. Which, of course she did.

From inside the Tiffany bag, Dinky's cries reached a fever pitch, prompting a few people nearby in the crowd to look around. Aurora held little parts of beetles to her open beak, pushing them in again and again until she was satiated. She stroked the bird's head. It jumped onto her finger, clutching on with its little talons. Aurora could not help but lift the chick from the box, against her better judgment, and hold her up in front of her face. It was at this moment Dinky decided to fly. Aurora felt the flutter of little wings, and instinctively threw the little bird up into the air, where it flew off and landed on Cupid's shoulder.

"Good God," Sylvia giggled.

Members of the crowd noticed Dinky who sat there moving her head from side to side, taking the scene in. Some began taking photos. Aurora remained calm and held out her hand, calling to the little bird who then flew from Cupid's shoulder to perch again on her finger. Aurora cupped Dinky in her hands. "Let's go."

At the apartment the girls packed their bags for Cannes. Dinky now had a feeling for the air and flew around everywhere, chirping, perching on a chair or a lamp, or one of their shoulders, nibbling their earlobes, sometimes dropping excrement, which didn't worry Sylvia because she knew the help would clean it up.

"We're going to need a birdcage to carry her from the car to the plane. I think I saw a decorative one in the salon." Sylvia climbed on top of a chair to retrieve the brass cage and set it in the hall with the rest of their luggage. Aurora filled the bottom with nesting material and sprinkled beetles everywhere. She also filled an eggcup with water and set it in, hoping it wouldn't tip over. With Dinky in the cage, they got into the car and drove to the private airport. Sylvia's jet was ready to rock. She'd called her mother the day before to arrange the flight.

Leaving the tarmac, Aurora wondered if she would ever see Paris again. The flight was uneventful. The eggcup fell over and spilled. Aurora filled it again with Evian. Sylvia read, smoked cigarettes, and drank Orangina. Aurora looked out the window. Approaching Nice, they flew over the snowcapped Alps, the turquoise curve of the Mediterranean coast spanning out to the horizon in the distance. Down below hardly seemed real. Aurora was about to land into yet another world even more magnificent than the last. Experiencing more and more of reality, life for Aurora was becoming more and more make-believe.

Sylvia's compound had two swimming pools: one with a waterfall; another the shape of a nautilus shell. Two guest cottages sat at different points, built into the sides of the hills, overlooking the Mediterranean. The main villa was also set into the rock slope and had been restored by Sylvia's parents to its original Art Deco grandeur. Inside, the high ceilings and casement windows flooded the house with light; the living spaces flowing outwards to shady terraces, fusing the interior with the exterior, where one was met with views of the mountains curving around the glowing blue sea, even more spectacular from the towers.

They did not leave the grounds for the entire month, spending their time reading in the shade, eating the most exquisite bread, cheese and fruit Aurora had ever tasted; drinking apricot juice, preparing for the next year at the Academy, studying books from their Surrealist/occult library, swimming in the pool with the waterfall, watching Dinky grow, her feathers brighten. The little bird darted through the air, following the two around, perching on their open books and the tops of deckchairs, dropping excrement all over the place; eating crumbs from the table, hunting spiders and insects in the trees, watching over the girls at night as they read to one another in bed, their downy arms and silky, freshly waxed legs entangled, the cacophony of cicadas, night birds, and frogs, coming in through the open windows from the dark outside.

Aurora read from Jung:

The woman whose fate it is to be a disturbing element is not solely destructive, the worker of change is herself changed and the glare of the fire she ignites both illuminates and enlightens all the victims, what seems a senseless upheaval becomes a process of purification

So that all that is vain
Might dwindle and wane (Faust, Part II)

If a woman of this type remains unconscious of the meaning of her function, if she does not know that she is

Part of that power which would
Ever work evil but engender good (Faust, Part I)

she will herself perish by the sword she brings. But consciousness can transform her into a deliverer and a redeemer

In the mornings or at dusk when the heat was bearable, they took walks in the hills with Dinky flitting along, through the forests of pine, cedar, lark and ash, oak and fig trees, past olive groves which had been cultivated for two thousand years, now abandoned. They crossed the crumbling walls and half foundations of old stone cottages, picking up rocks, observing wasps.

Leaving the south of France was like leaving a fairy tale. The views from the private jet of the hills and the Alps, the red-tiled roofs of the villages — the Mediterranean, becoming smaller and smaller as they ascended into the clouds. Upon Aurora and Sylvia's return to the Academy, they found their room filled with the nauseating stench of rotting aquatic life. The Siamese fighting fish was dead, decaying in two inches of putrid water left at the bottom of its bowl. In their hurry to leave, they had forgotten about it. Aurora's head swam; tears gushed from her eyes. She wanted to perform a proper burial. Sylvia pinched her nose, said there was nothing left to bury and took the bowl outside to the nearest dumpster. The next day she ordered another bowl and another fish from the nearest pet shop.

Their dormitory room was smaller than they remembered. It might even have been smaller than Sylvia's mother's walk-in closet. They burned essential oils, and kept the windows open to air the place. Dinky flew in and out, discovering her new habitat, flying back to the safety of their room, to Aurora who she saw as her savior and protector, never leaving her side for any length of time. The bird followed the two girls to the cafeteria, to class, to ballet, skimming through the air, dropping excreta along the way. The story spread like wildfire: how Aurora had rescued the bird in Paris, that they'd brought it back in Sylvia's private jet.

The faculty wasn't pleased with the distraction but found they had no way of keeping the bird out of the classroom. When Aurora's grandmother and Sylvia's parents were notified, Sylvia had a long talk with her mother on the telephone. Mrs Belmont called the Dean and transferred two hundred thousand dollars to the school so they could keep it. Still, not everyone was happy. Students and faculty members got hit with the droppings that flew out of her in the hallways and complained. In the school dining room — walking across the quad — everyone stared and whispered. Everywhere, they were prodded with eyes. They had both become more beautiful over the summer. Aurora's bust had grown. And now they were accompanied by a little bird like something out of a Disney princess film.

As if by fate, in their second year, Aurora and Sylvia fell in with a clique of girls from California. The Californians had been admiring the two from afar. Previously, Aurora and Sylvia had been so entangled in one another and their world they had barely noticed the Californians, who were, in fact, the most popular girls at the school — one year older than Aurora and Sylvia — throwing parties in the house they rented off campus, showing up to class late, sauntering in wearing miniskirts and oversized sweatshirts, braless, with bedhead hair and smudged eyeliner.

The ice was finally broken when, at the end of a ballet session in the changing room, Madison, one of the Californians — round-faced, healthy, with an athletic physique, one hundred and seventeen pounds, an enviable 35-27-35, the total, impossible California dream, complete with doe-eyes and blonde hair — managed to catch Sylvia's eye. The two smiled at one another, Madison's lips shiny with pink lip gloss, Sylvia's eyes striking Madison's with an electric discharge[8]. The Californians were having a party that weekend (it was rare a weekend went by they did not have a party in some form or another). Madison took a sparkly blue pen and Hello Kitty notebook from her bag, then drew a map from the campus to their house with the date and time of the party written on it, folding the paper and handing it to Sylvia, who was immediately taken by Madison's bubbly handwriting and the cute way she drew the directions to make it look like a pirate's treasure map.

The night of the party Aurora and Sylvia listened to Mazzy Star, singing along to *Fade Into You*, dancing and smoking cigarettes, drinking Diet Coke, trying on outfits.

"Aurora, have you ever even ever had any hard alcohol?" Sylvia stood in front of the mirror, trying to make a chignon.

"No."

"Maybe just stick to wine. I mean, if you do, just take a couple of sips and wait to see what happens. I don't want you getting date raped."

Aurora's grandmother had said as much about alcohol. She had called it the nectar of Satan and made Aurora promise not to let it touch her lips until she turned twenty-

---

8. The elementals had grabbed hold of her again on one of the morning runs in the forest with Aurora, but would soon let go of her.

one and even then — it wasn't ladylike. Really, only whores drank alcohol. Like wearing makeup — which also made you a whore — it wasn't recommended. However, as everyone knows, Jesus had turned water into wine.

The Californians' house was a short walk off campus, down tree-lined residential streets with grand houses set back from the road, each surrounded by landscaped gardens. Dinky sailed and swooped through the air, hovering now and then, resting on Aurora's shoulder or Sylvia's head. They followed Madison's map to an imposing Gothic Revival-esque mansion with dormer windows and a tower, built on stone foundations that made it look like it had emerged from the bedrock. The edifice was covered in weathered, grey shingles, its porches, balconies and general asymmetrical construction designed to encourage a tactile interaction with the out-of-doors, the shingles acting to camouflage the hulking form in its surroundings. Dominant canopies of red pine, mixed with balsam fir, hemlock, red spruce, white pine, and a few paper birches inhabited the peripheries. An imposing oak stood alone on the front lawn, knee deep in snow.

Walking onto the property, up the shoveled walkway, Aurora and Sylvia sensed an invisible line. They were crossing a meridian from which they could never turn back. They were entering into the world of the house. On the porch Sylvia pressed the bell — Dinky safely nestled in Aurora's mittened hands — their breath fuming white into the air, vaporizing. The door flung open to reveal Harlow — already half drunk, barefoot, toenails painted neon pink, in denim hotpants and a sparkly, tight, knit top with one arm bare and "Babe" embroidered in cursive across the chest. "Hey! So glad you could make it! And you brought your little bird! So cute!" She welcomed them into the rose-paneled reception hall, their hair flying in the frigid gust that met with shimmering columns of heat from the wood fires and gas radiators inside. Behind Harlow, a grand rosewood staircase wound upward to the higher levels. Blondie's *Heart of Glass* played in one of the rooms, above the buzz and murmur of conversation.

"It's so great to see you two! What can I get you to drink? We've got some really awesome wine." Harlow led them to a sitting room, then disappeared and returned to put a glass of white wine in each of their hands, excusing herself when the doorbell rang again.

There, Aurora and Sylvia stood — in the middle of the living room — their first social event at the Academy, surrounded by their peers, none of whom were of drinking or smoking age, but were nonetheless drinking and smoking. Frail blue trails of smoke wafted from the ends of American Spirit cigarettes and spliffs, rising and dispersing to join the dirty violet plane that hung above everything, submerging and bluing the chandelier in soft, pearly clouds.

People were sprawled on chairs and sofas, others standing in twos and threes, deep in sparkling conversation, smiling with white shining teeth, kissing, flirting, posing, dancing. The two stood together, taking in the scene, drinking their wine. Dinky flew off through one of the archways to find a place with clear air. When they had drained their glasses, Sylvia took one of the opened bottles from a tub of ice, brought it over and poured them some more: "Be always drunken! It's the only way. So as not to feel the horrible burden of time that breaks your back and bends you to the earth, you must be continually drunk! But on what? Wine, poetry or virtue, as you wish. But be drunk. And if sometimes, on the steps of a palace or the green grass of a ditch, in the mournful solitude of your room, you wake again, drunkenness already diminishing or gone, ask the wind, the wave, the star, the bird, the clock, everything that is flying, everything that is groaning, everything that is rolling, everything that is singing, everything that is speaking... ask what time it is and wind, wave, star, bird, clock will answer you: 'It is time to be drunk! So as not to be the martyred slaves of time, be drunk, be continually drunk! On wine, on poetry or on virtue as you wish!'" Sylvia concluded her rendition of Baudelaire, then walked away and came back with a bottle of absinthe and poured some into their already full wine glasses. "Sip! Sip! My sweet angel!"

With the alcohol inside her, Aurora felt herself begin to lift and spread out like helium, carried away. The ancient Greeks and Romans were right. The rising of religious ecstasy — ritual madness. She felt possessed.

At the end of the glass, neither Aurora nor Sylvia knew where one ended and the other began. It was in that moment, surrounded by strangers, that they began to realize the extent to which they had become connected. It sent a shiver of terror up their spines. They looked at one another with the glowing eyes of wild animals and went off in separate directions. Sylvia strode out and disappeared into other rooms where more people congregated.

Aurora put her glass down and went back out through the hall, feeling eyes on her as she made her exit, then drunkenly followed hallways, hand trailing along the wallpaper. She caught up with Dinky, flying up from off a table lamp, following her as she ducked in and out of rooms, excusing herself as she slid past other partygoers, where finally she slipped out a back door, into the garden, Dinky behind her.

Standing in the half-light of a lantern beam, she looked hard at her fingers around the clear stem of the new, full wine glass someone had handed her along the way and wondered how her hand could be her hand when she could barely recognize it. She took a sip of wine and then another and another with Dinky flitting around her head, barely tasting the wine in the cold, tipping it back to empty it, eventually pressing it down onto a garden table piled with snow. Breathing in, the air was a cool knife running itself back and forth, flaying her lungs. Dinky skittered off through the air into the trees at the periphery of the garden to look for seeds she smelled in the neighbour's bird feeder.

Aurora's body felt only vaguely familiar; she stood weightless, numb, jelly-like, taking in the waving tree line, the hard-packed snow under a thin frozen sheet that glittered in the moonlight. The stars penetrated her with

AURORA

their rays, causing some sort of interference in her brain. The dark pines swayed, throwing off grains of snow to the wind. She became aware that the trees knew she was there. It was, in fact, the wind which had developed a strong attraction to her. Ushering Aurora away[9], further from the house, the air full of silver sparkles (always a sign the veil is thin), the elementals had their way with her, in the reckless, oral darkness, vibrating with thin impulse; spinning her round and round, lifting her off the ground, a tide breaking against her, contorting her body into pitches of rapture, into a gem-like flame.[10] The stars were speaking to her now, ravishing and chilling in that vastness — in her teeth the sensation of biting on tinfoil with metal fillings. Round and round she spun, penetrating worlds, sequels to each other — calculated where once they were only a suspicion.

With dawn and the first lights, the air spirits spat Aurora out before exposing her to lethal levels of their potency. They didn't want to ruin her — she was particularly amusing to play with. Laid out in the snow, Dinky burrowed under her hair, clinging to her neck for warmth. Everything was stained pink in the morning light; Aurora's exposed skin turning a pale blue. Jolted by a part of her primal brain to move or die, she made it to her feet, Dinky following her to the door where she struggled to turn the knob, then

---

9. The elementals of Air, as all occultists know, are puckish rogues.
10. Mountaineers know this particular terror with which the great hills can obsess them, a curious oppression of the spirits by the overwhelming grandeur of nature. This same force, when not at poisonous levels of concentration, inspires a passion for the love of the hills or sea as poets have celebrated so gloriously in their poems.

resorted to banging her hands against the glass. Eventually, someone came, speechless at the sight of her: her violet skin, frosted hair, eyebrows and eyelashes, Dinky hovering and pecking at the glass. The girl led Aurora to the sitting room, where there was a fire; Dinky flitting through the air behind them. She told Aurora to lay down on the sofa and covered her in blankets, where Aurora fell asleep, her body numb, burning, feeling herself fall into void. Dinky perched on the side table — chirping, airing her wings — then flew off to look for food in the kitchen.

When Aurora finally awoke, she was in a bed, and a room, all foreign to her, with no recollection of how she had gotten there. She was awake but felt as though she was still in a dream. Dinky was chirping from the edge of a lampshade, then made clicking, purring noises. It appeared to be afternoon; dusk was falling. Curtains were drawn across the sash windows. High up a circular leaded glass window filled the room with gentle light. The sheets were smooth and pressed and smelled of fresh laundry. The comforter and pillows were filled with eiderdown, like the ones at Sylvia's house. Dinky flitted around the room and landed on the edge of a glass of water on the bedside table, dipping her beak in, drinking with verge and vigour. From here she flew to the windowsill, where she preened herself. Every surface gleamed with polish, the chest of drawers, the writing desk, the bedside tables. Aurora tried to remember where she was, what had happened. The glass of water refracted wobbling light on the nightstand.

Her bladder was full. She was thirsty. Through an open door she saw an en-suite bathroom. Twisting and turning Aurora maneuvered herself out from inside the smooth cotton cocoon, pushing against her will to remain in the soft warmth. She felt drugged, her body sore, as she made her way as quickly as possible to relieve herself.

At the sink she turned on the cold tap and drank. She looked at her reflection: her eyes smudged with eyeliner and gold glitter that sparkled on her cheeks, here and there all over her face. She closed her eyes. Thought-forms blazed with stained-glass saints and animals. Opening them again she took in the bathroom — shiny mint-green tiles bordered in black around the sink, the bathtub, the toilet — all of it wouldn't have looked out of place in a turn-of-the-century doll house. She raised her arms. A wave of sickness. Dizzy, Dinky flitting around her, she held onto the sink, then managed to turn the tap on and splash her face with water. She sunk to the tiles with her back against the bathtub, feeling its coolness in the heat of the room while a breeze from the drafty window washed over her; a welcome, reviving chill. She was unwashed and smelled. Her hair was greasy. She took her tights off, slipped out of her dress and stood up in her bra and underwear, then began washing her underarms with a washcloth and the fragrant floral soap in the soap dish. Not knowing what to do with the tights, she left them on the bathroom floor, along with the dress.

Standing in her underwear, in the dry heat of the room, the central heating cranked up to eighty degrees, she decided she didn't need clothing. Curiosity getting the better of her, rather than wait in the room for someone to come and tell her where she was, she stepped out into the hallway — Dinky perched on her finger. She listened for people, movement, but heard nothing except the house — clocks ticking and the wind outside. Downstairs the kitchen was empty. On one of the counters sat a bowl of red grapes. Dinky flew from her finger and alighted on the side of the bowl, pecking at them. Aurora took three for herself and ate them one by one, staring out the window, and thought she had never tasted grapes this tart and sweet and juicy. Tracing her steps back into the hall, she continued to look for life in the house, for her coat and shoes, for any clues as to where she was. The front door opened. "My god! Aurora! You scared the bejesus out of me. I thought you were a ghost! How are you? You've been asleep for two days!"

It was Madison, one of the girls who lived in the house, the one who had invited Sylvia to the party — the doe-eyed blonde with the perfect body. She was also in Aurora's ballet class. And here it all came back to her. She was standing in the Californian's house, half naked. Here, in the hall, before Madison, she felt like a pretender — an intruder in their world. Aurora found she couldn't speak. Her lips parted, but nothing came out. Dinky came flying through the hall and landed on a side table, ruffling her wings.

"Oh! Your bird! We left some seeds in your room for it to eat. It didn't want to come out of the room. Sylvia couldn't even get it to come out." Madison was trying to behave normally. "Are you okay?"

Aurora nodded her head.

The glimmer in Aurora's eyes unsettled Madison. When she spoke her voice sounded strange, a tone she hadn't ever heard herself make before.

"I'll bet you're hungry. Come with me, we'll find you something to eat."

Aurora and Dinky followed Madison into the kitchen. Dinky alighted on top of the refrigerator while Aurora stood there, watching Madison move things around, rifling through the cupboards. "Some hot chocolate?"

Aurora nodded. Again, Madison was taken aback by the alien shine[11] in Aurora's eyes. She felt as though an ice-cold finger was poking its way around in her gut. "A grilled cheese sandwich? I'm good at making those."

Aurora nodded again. She didn't know what else to do.

Opening more cupboards, Madison found an electric griddle and a pot and set them on the counter along with the bread and cheese, butter, milk, cocoa powder and a spatula. Dinky flew to the sink faucet, chirping.

The two sat at the kitchen table in silence: Madison trying not to watch Aurora drink the hot chocolate; Aurora drinking it like someone stoned on barbiturates — slowly, each motion heavy. The more Madison looked at her, the more deranged she felt, slowly spooling out of herself.[12] Madison wanted to know everything about her. She wanted to lose herself in Aurora, to be consumed by whatever it was that was consuming her; whatever it was that Aurora had, that was making her drunk, her

---

11. Residue from her night with the elementals.
12. The discharge of intense emissions coming from Aurora's night with the elementals was affecting her.

brain and body transfigured so that she wasn't herself anymore. She wanted to climb out of her skin and into Aurora's.

Dora, another one of the Californian clique, drifted in with an air of calm, her dark, heavy eyelashes framing the most beautiful eyes Aurora had ever seen — her face the face of an angel. "The sleeping beauty has awoken. We were going to call a doctor if you didn't wake up soon. You've been sleeping for nearly three days. How are you feeling?" She noted that Madison was looking strange, maybe even a bit creeped out, and that Aurora was drinking her hot chocolate as though in a dream.

Aurora looked up, wanting to communicate.

Madison turned to Dora. "She hasn't spoken a word."

"I guess she'll say something when she's got something to say." Dora turned to Aurora. "You can stay here as long as you like. It's obvious you're going through something. That's cool, we're here for you."

Aurora set the hot chocolate down, smiled at them with infinitely sad eyes, got up and disappeared through the doorway, Dinky skimming through the air behind her, down the corridor, up the flights of stairs; Aurora's fingertips gliding across the wallpaper, wandering until she finally found the room she had come from. She climbed into bed and hid under the blankets, the hum of the elementals vibrating through her nervous system.

Another twenty-four hours passed before Aurora got out of bed and ran a bath. Sitting in the water she burned with shame. What was she doing, in this house, with these people? Why had Sylvia abandoned her? She wanted to be back in her bed, in the dorm where she belonged. She had to get out of there.

There was a knock at the door. "Aurora?" Sylvia came through into the bathroom, Dinky flying in after her and landing on the faucet. Sylvia had cut her long hair into a shoulder-length bob with bangs and dyed it ice blonde. Her voice was husky, as though she'd been up late smoking cigarettes. "How are you?" Sylvia perched on the tiled ledge of the bathtub. She dipped a finger into the water. They had seen one another naked hundreds of times; they had showered and bathed together, but now Aurora wanted to cover herself up, grow a tail like a mermaid and disappear into the sea.

Using her voice for the first time in nearly four days Aurora responded — "I don't know" — then submerged herself in the green bathwater, staying under for as long as she could. When she came up, Sylvia spoke again. "Dora, Madison and Harlow have invited us to live here with them. I moved in yesterday. What do you think?" Dinky flew past them and into the bedroom.

The house was certainly more luxurious than the dormitory, where they had to share a bathroom with everyone else on the floor. "That's wonderful," Aurora smiled, unsettling Sylvia in a way she couldn't put her finger on.

"So, you'll move in too?"

Aurora couldn't figure out whether Sylvia wanted her there or not. "Yes, of course, if you don't mind — if you want me here."

"Why wouldn't I want you here?" Sylvia smiled as though nothing had happened, as though they were still blood sisters, partners in crime, even though it didn't feel that way.

"I don't know, I was just —. Could I borrow something of yours, I don't have any clean clothes here."

"Of course." And with that Sylvia slipped off the side of the bathtub, leaving Aurora alone in the water. Sylvia had cut her loose, like she had cut the tentacle from Sylvia during their scrying disaster. She felt a deep sadness but also lighter, unhinged — capable of things she could hardly grasp.

That night, in her diary she wrote:

October 3

When photons are being observed they act like particles, and when they aren't, they behave like waves. Could it be that humans feel they need to be seen in order to exist in a certain way, like photons? Is this what God is for: to observe, to judge, to keep us as particles, to stop us from becoming waves? I don't want my every movement to be observed. I don't want Him or the angels, or Jesus, or my parents in Heaven to see everything I'm doing. I don't want all these eyes on me. I want to live. I want to be free. A figure observing, you can turn the world upside down.

Be still my beating heart. I am in thrall to her mind. Do you not see, even at this point, how I could be anything but enraptured? The hand that holds this pencil will not stop scribbling. I suspect a case of hypergraphia. Aurora doesn't give up looking for ways to live in the infinite while still being alive in the temporal human body. She doesn't want her heart to stop beating, her lungs like wings to ever stop filling with air, carrying her up, up, up; she never wants the blood that feeds it all to quit flowing. She is ALIVE. She is on her way to a stage of illumination. And miraculously — at such a tender age — she knows, subconsciously, that for the mind to tap into its full power, the concrete must serve the mysterious.[13]

I'm growing more and more fond of this cabin every day. No one bothers me here. I like the tang in the air of cured wood from the walls and ceiling, the smell of the cast-iron stove, the pine and ash and moss and all the forest fragrances drifting in through the cracked open windows. The rushing wind through the stands of trees, all the varieties of tiny, delicate birds hopping from branch to branch, calling out; the chattering of squirrels and chipmunks, the owls at night. And the stars. I'm so sick of the artificial lights that kill the stars I may never go back to a city again. I feel like I could spend eternity here, except that it is painful to write. Under ordinary circumstances it would be so easy to stop, but I am held here at this desk with a terrible suction. I know the tiniest details about

---

13. When the intellectual force pours out into the absolute, it meets resistance. At variance with the main current, it swirls into eddies. The intellect is the Ariadne's string — you cannot let go of it, you cannot let it be destroyed, or you will fall into oblivion, madness, death. If you succeed in holding on to the intellect while venturing into the absolute you will have all the untapped power you desire, you will not fatigue, you will be capable of feats that appear supernatural to the ordinary person, but which are as natural as fire or air.

her. Because the future is affecting the past. I can think of nothing else. She is here, before me, locked away. In case you haven't guessed it already, I'm from the gutter of obscuredom. And I learnt a lot there. And I'm still here, learning. And laughing. But I digress...

To move off campus, Aurora and Sylvia had to provide written permission from their legal guardians. The Californians' parents had an agreement with one of the school monitors to check in on the girls — a special arrangement the Dean had been wrangled into by their parents. The monitor had been promptly dispatched by Harlow, Dora, and Madison who paid her not to visit and to give reports of their good conduct to the school.

Grandmother was overjoyed to hear her granddaughter's voice over the phone. Aurora explained she had an opportunity to move off campus into a house with some girls from California. She needed her written permission to do so. Her grandmother asked questions about the others and said she'd gotten the postcard from Paris and was so happy she was making the right kind of friends. Aurora apologized for not calling every week and for not writing to the librarian like she'd promised. Grandmother said she understood, that Aurora must be very busy with her studies and social life and not to worry.

When Grandmother put the phone down she thanked Jesus and cried, tears sliding down her cheeks, between her breasts to her navel. With her hands locked in prayer she stared up at one of the images of Christ on the wall —

His big sad eyes and dirty blonde hair – and begged Him to continue to watch over and guide her granddaughter.

Aurora felt guilty for not writing and calling her grandmother every week like she'd promised. She could respect and love her grandmother for raising her, for loving her, for making sacrifices to give her a better life, but she was also ashamed of her and wasn't sure if she could bear seeing her again. She didn't know what to say to her.

The buzz of life in the house intensified with its two, or rather, three new inhabitants, including Dinky. Appearing out of thin air, the bird's bobbing, swooping flight pattern through the hallways gave the house a sense of fairy-tale magic. She would alight on a table edge, head raised, chest puffed out, tilting her head this way and that, then fly up to a chandelier where she would hop from crystal to crystal, hang upside down and drop, flying forward, backward, making loop-the-loops, showcasing her aerial acrobatics. Never mind that as she took wing and glided around droppings flew out of her onto the furniture, the lampshades, the walls, their persons.

Aurora came to see that Dora and Madison were thick as thieves, having known one another from kindergarten at the Waldorf in Malibu. Harlow had joined the same Waldorf school at ten and missed out on the seminal years that had bonded them. Like Aurora, Harlow spent more time in her room than the others, but unlike Aurora she wasn't studying so much as writing song lyrics, poetry, making offerings to angels at her altar; listening, singing along, and dancing to Mazzy Star, Portishead, Massive Attack, Eminem, or talking to her mother on the phone so often the others became annoyed, and another phone line had to be put in. Every morning, she practised Transcendental Meditation.

From the beginning Sylvia waltzed around like she had always belonged there because wherever Sylvia was she was cherished and venerated. Her new ice blonde haircut and the way she carried herself gave off California skater girl and CBGB New York City vibes. She seamlessly paired this new look with remnants of her New Wave French film star/New England prep school girl persona and began to wear sparkly eyeliner and lip gloss every day like the Californians.

It wasn't long before Sylvia forgot about the time she nearly died attempting to scry in the mirror with Aurora and broke her promise to stay away from the arcane. Aurora watched without comment as Sylvia picked up *The Hero with A Thousand Faces* or *The Power of Myth*, offering up a gateway philosophy that would eventually lead to more complex, esoteric proceedings. Sylvia would walk dramatically around the room, reading from the books, her voice a boomerang, cutting the air, flying back to her, whizzing past the Californian's heads. "People say that what we're all seeking is a meaning for life. I don't think that's what we're really seeking. I think what we're seeking is an experience of being alive, so that our life experiences on the purely physical plane will have resonance within our own innermost being and reality, so that we actually feel the rapture of being alive." Or "All the gods, all the heavens, all the hells, are within you... The goal of life is to make your heartbeat match the beat of the universe, to match your nature with Nature... Where you stumble and fall, there you will find gold... The cave you fear to enter holds the treasure you seek".

The Californians began to pay attention. Every night before bed, they sat in one of the living rooms by the fire and drank wine Harlow's parents sent in cases every month under the condition she did not take drugs or consume alcohol outside the house or hold parties (these were well-intentioned promises, but not ones Harlow had been able to keep in that atmosphere of chaos, revelry, and depravity). Night after night, Sylvia led them down the rabbit hole, reading from Breton's *Manifestoes of Surrealism*, Agrippa, E.E. Evans-Prichard's *Witchcraft, Oracles, and Magic Among the Azande;* an essential anthology of Antonin Artaud's writings on the occult, magic, the theater, mind and body, the cosmos, rebellion, and revolution in its deepest sense; Michel Carrouges's *La mystique du surhomme*, Kingsley's *Ancient Philosophy, Mystery, and Magic: Empedocles and Pythagorean Tradition; The Mirror of Magic* by Kurt Seligmann, with quotes from poets like Octavio Paz on Breton:

...the word revelation shines in many of Breton's texts. Speaking is the noblest activity of all: revealing what is hidden, bringing the buried word back to life, calling forth our double, that Other which is us but which we never allow to resist — our suppressed half. Then quite clearly, revelation is resurrection, exposure, initiation. It is a word that calls for rites and ceremonies.

Little by little, and then at break-neck speed, Sylvia introduced the Californians to pieces of her occult library. Quotes and ideas from Empedocles[14], Paracelsus[15], Regardie, Helena P. Blavatsky's *Isis Unveiled*, Emma Hardinge Britten's *Ghost Land, or, Researches into the Mysteries of Occultism*, Cornelius Agrippa, Jonathan Pollock's *Opium and the occult: Antonin Artaud and Samuel Taylor Coleridge*, Paschal Beverly Randolph's *Dealings with the Dead*, André Breton's *The Magnetic Fields*, along with his "Letter to Seers" in which he praised "these young women, the only guardians of the Great Secret"; Pierre Mabille's *Mirror of the Marvelous*, C.G. Jung's *The Archetypes and the Collective Unconscious*, *Tertium Organum* by the Russian philosopher-occultist Piotr Ouspensky, etc. were a breadcrumb trails with which she was luring the others into the woods, into the depths of the psyche, to adventure — to the revelation of the true functioning of thought. Sylvia had become delirious in the process of constructing maps in her head, in her notebooks, drunk on the possibilities, the connections.

14. Greek scientist and philosopher of the 5th century B.C.E., is credited, among other things, with the opinion that the embryo is shaped by the imagination of the mother at the moment of conception, proven by the fact that women who have fallen in love with statues often give birth to children that resemble them.

15. 16th c. alchemist who believed nature could be read as a book, full of hidden messages from God that could only be perceived and understood if one learned how to recognize and read the "signatures of things". The universe is a theater of mirrors, a mosaic of hieroglyphs to be decoded. Everything in nature is a sign. The tiniest object hides a secret.

A new Surrealism. A unique interpretation. The girls would take charge. They would learn the history and spin the wheel on to new frontiers. *With sorcery, as everyone knows, there is no stopping it.* Sylvia was not going to give up. Because it's impossible to bring a hammer to a standstill in mid-air once it's been flung.

Little had Sylvia realized, Madison, Dora, and Harlow, coming from an elite Californian lifestyle, were already well acquainted with New Age ideas — ideas which overlapped with the mystical knowledge, philosophy and anthropological studies Sylvia and Aurora had immersed themselves in before they decided it was too dangerous. The Californians knew Jungian terms like "synchronicity", and what the "collective unconscious" was. They were familiar with certain Buddhist and Native American ideas, such as the belief that everything in nature is sacred; that animals have souls, that there's a balance humankind must maintain with their environment. They believed that dreams could predict future events and send important messages. They also believed one hundred percent in the existence of U.F.Os and ghosts because they had seen them with their own eyes. What's more, as children, all three had begun Transcendental Meditation as part of the curriculum in school; their minds were fertile for the kind of work Sylvia would soon propose.

Out of the Californians, Harlow had more occult knowledge than anyone. Her mother was a New Age fanatic, psychic to a long list of Hollywood stars. She had engaged a group of monks to cleanse and bless the house before the girls moved in. She wasn't going to let her child and her friends live in a cesspool of negative energy. You never knew what these old houses held. Their compound in Malibu was cleared regularly by a medicine woman of the Chumash tribe. It was preferable to have someone qualified in the ancestral land of the place do the clearing, but Harlow's mother couldn't find anyone with those credentials at such short notice. Most tribes that once were native to New Hampshire had ended up on reservations in Canada and she hadn't been able to get through to anyone before the girls were due to move in. Instead, she found a group of willing Buddhist monks.

Thus Harlow had grown up in an atmosphere which stressed the spiritual, the Unseen, the other planes. She watched as her mother magnetized objects and erected altars with crystals, semi-precious stones, flowers, incense, idols, invoking angels with whom she spoke telepathically. It was a given that people could influence events with their minds, communicate in thought forms, and that spirits — disembodied, energetic entities — moved around in the world. There were fairies in the woods. She and her mother spoke to butterflies and lizards, birds, flowers, trees, ants, bumblebees and other creatures who also carried messages. It was a nuanced and complex system. For example, beetle symbolism takes on different meanings. It can symbolize rebirth, renewal, the sun, and life, but can also have a negative significance like the devil's symbol, death, and other ill omens. Worlds existed out there beyond the naked eye if you used all your senses to perceive them. Magic was everywhere.

As for Dora and Madison, they were sufficiently indoctrinated into these kinds of beliefs by osmosis. As everyone knows, California is the birthplace of hippies and the New Age. It was impossible to escape these ideas in any mid-upper-class to upper-class household, and even more impossible if one had gone to the Waldorf like Dora and Madison had. Hippies had come from all over the country to California since the Sixties, their culture and ideologies eventually embedding themselves into the fabric of the everyday. Dora and Madison were well aware of the existence of "energy suckers", very much like the concept of "psychic vampires" in the terminology of the occultists. There were people who sucked the life force out of you. You didn't want to become an energy sucker — they were the worst kind of people. Dora and Madison wholeheartedly believed in auras and out-of-body experiences and watched paranormal television shows as though they were documentaries. The cosmic law that everything moves in circles, whatever thought-forms we send out, unless absorbed by the object at which they're directed, will boomerang back on the sender, was known to them. Karma. It could be a bitch. Reincarnation was possible; this went along with the ghosts, plus Buddhists believed in reincarnation and at least half of the families who went to the Waldorf were Buddhists, or semi-Buddhists. Buddhists were Zen. California cool. Chilled-out.

In the evenings, at impromptu gatherings by the fire, the Californians began to present passages related to the ideas in the books Sylvia had introduced them to. Dora read from a letter Arthur Rimbaud sent to Paul Demeny:

I say one must be a seer, make oneself a seer.

The Poet makes himself a seer by a long, rational and immense disordering of all the senses. All forms of love, suffering, madness: he searches himself; he consumes all the poisons in himself, to keep only their quintessence. Unspeakable torture, where he needs all his faith, every superhuman strength, during which he becomes the great patient, the great criminal, the great accursed — and the supreme Knower, among men! — Because he arrives at the unknown! Because he has cultivated his soul, already rich, more than others! He arrives at the unknown, and when, maddened, he ends up by losing the knowledge of his visions: he has still seen them! Let him die charging among those unutterable, unnameable things: other fearful workers will come: they'll start from the horizons where the first have fallen!...

I'll go on:

So the poet is truly the thief of fire, then.

This set them all on fire. It was a rallying cry to forge a path into the lands of the mystics, the oracles at Delphi, the Druids, the First Nations of North America, the ways of ancient civilizations of South America, the First Nations of Australia and New Zealand, followers of Bön. There would be blood. But it was worth it. They drank red wine and exalted in their newfound knowledge. Aurora joined in the spirit of bacchanalia. However, deep inside her, the little warning light that had been activated after the scrying incident with Sylvia continued to blink on and off.

Sylvia reached a feverish pitch when she discovered a book entitled *The Cosmic Serpent, DNA and the Origins of Knowledge*, written in what can only be described as gonzo style. In the account, the author — Dr Jeremy Narby — an anthropologist, describes his field study in the Peruvian Amazon with the aim of learning how indigenous people use the plants in their environment. This new material also shocked Aurora to her very core. It was a revelation. The idea that DNA could communicate across life forms via the use of entheogens was a disintegration of the fourth wall that allowed her to see deeper into the fabric of reality. Here was an example, in the present day, of humans taking psychoactive substances in a ritual setting, communicating with plant life and bringing back proof in the form of art and knowledge.

Against the general code of anthropology, although it had been done before a couple of times in history with disastrous results, Dr Jeremy Narby had taken part in rituals where he drank a psychoactive ayahuasca brew his contacts — medicine people from the Asháninka tribe — had told him was the means to converse with the spirits of the jungle plants.

Where had they obtained these complex combinations of plants? The Ashǎninka told Narby spirits had given them the formulas with which to make medicines coveted by pharmaceutical companies! Eighty percent of Western medication comes from plant combinations these same Amazonian tribal people had been creating for centuries. Sylvia wanted all of them to fly to the Peruvian Amazon like Jeremy Narby had and be introduced to the mysteries of nature.

Furthermore, when Dr Narby showed drawings the Ashǎninka medicine people made under the influence of ayahuasca to a molecular biologist, they confirmed the accurate depiction of molecular structures immediately. Did the drug give them the ability to see on the molecular level? It certainly gave them the ability to concoct medicinal recipes which worked so well they were being used in modern-day medicine by major pharmaceutical companies.

All of this brought Sylvia to the understanding the Surrealists had reached: that ancient civilizations — the Greeks, Egyptians and Romans, the Native Americans, the Celts, the Vikings, the Germanic tribes, peoples who worshipped the earth — might very well have communicated with the spirit worlds in a similar fashion. Modern people were the barbarians! They were the dullards who didn't understand the true reality of things! Humanity's birthright — knowledge that allowed them to communicate with nature — had been stolen from them by Christianity and science. Harlow had heard this all before from her mother; Madison and Dora had been

primed by their Waldorf education to see that Sylvia
was making a lot of sense. Aurora could not disagree. It
was exciting.

Sylvia then moved on to *Food of the Gods: The Search for
the original Tree of Knowledge,* by Terrence McKenna,
also gonzo in style; an ethnobiological, historical subset
of gonzo, if there was such a thing. At any rate, one
of the key ideas in Terrence McKenna's book was that
psilocybin mushrooms were responsible for the advent of
religion in prehistoric human society, as well as the great
leap in brain development which precipitated the creation
of artistic expression. Eating the mushrooms led to God
and to self-reflection. Whether this was the beginning of
religion and birth of art is what Sylvia wanted to see for
herself. The Californians were hooked. There was talk of
flying to the Peruvian rainforest. They wanted to witness
and experience the birth of art and religion; to speak with
plants. Of course, this was all possible since each one
of them, apart from Aurora, possessed an "unlimited"
credit card.

When they first began throwing around these fanciful
ideas, Aurora didn't take them seriously. Then again,
Sylvia's family did have a private jet. And the girls were
truly crazy enough to try and pull off something like that.
Yes, it was dangerous. But she only had one life. True,
the occult wasn't something you played around with. But
she was dedicated. She wanted to know, to discover, to
steel and surrender herself. Yes, the scrying incident had
gone wrong. But they had pulled through. Sylvia had

clearly forgotten or ripped up the pact they'd made not to tempt fate again and tossed it to the wind. Maybe Sylvia was right.

Aurora listened in silence as Sylvia lectured on about ayahuasca ceremonies, the Eleusinian and Orphic Mysteries, The Golden Dawn, psilocybin mushrooms, holding her and the Californians in thrall.

The Californians began to do more of their own research.

"This is insane. According to Epiphanius, there was this sect called the Borborites who had a ritual where instead of bread and wine they drank semen and menstrual blood. All the female members were called "Virgins", but they still had sex — only the man couldn't ejaculate inside them. If one of them accidentally got pregnant they kept the woman's "virginity" intact by aborting the fetus, then prepared it with honey, spices and aromatics, and ate it," Dora looked up from the book she was paraphrasing to eyes filled with horror, the girls around her frozen, wine glasses in their hands.

"We are sure as hell not doing that," Madison was the first to speak, "I mean, maybe I'd drink semen from some hot guy mixed with my own menstrual blood if it was going to lead to enlightenment, but I definitely wouldn't eat an embryo."

"I think I'm going to be sick," blood drained out of Harlow's face, she put her glass down and left the room.

"Obviously, they didn't do this kind of thing lightly and there were nutjobs in antiquity, just like there are nutjobs today and that's part of our work, to sort the truth out from all the insane bullshit," Sylvia held the wine glass stem in her fingers, silver nail polish catching the light, "We must dissect, dismember, dismantle, denude, all with the aim of uncovering, discovering, revealing, laying bare, unmasking the naked, unvarnished, unveiled, and unalloyed truth to get to the heart of the matter."

Aurora figured all of this was exactly what her grandmother had warned her about when she spoke of false prophets and Satanism defiling Christianity. But Sylvia was right. There were nutjobs, and then there was the truth.

The next night was dedicated to 'sex magic', which Sylvia came to the conclusion was a concept wholly corrupted by Western "New Age Tantric practices" conceived by the likes of Theodor Reuss and Aleister Crowley. Their *Ordo Templi Orientis* cult and its off-shoots were defilements and misinterpretations of Tantric philosophy, the Kabbalah, Ancient Egyptian texts, medieval occult bullshit, and generic Oriental exotica rather than anything based on what one could consider true esoteric knowledge, which had led to the "life-affirming" techniques of self-improvement that fit quite nicely with American capitalism and consumer culture. Basically a "McDonaldisation of occultism," transmitting a form of "McGnosis".[16]

Harlow swung her legs from the armrest, got up from the sofa she'd been lounging on, went to the fireplace and threw her crystal glass of absinthe into the fire where it exploded into blue flames, "Everything my mother told me about Tantric sex was bullshit."

16. Sylvia got this from Peter König's paper "The OTO Phenomenon".

"I mean, maybe not everything," Dora tried to console her.

"You give new meaning to the word Molotov cocktail, by the way," Aurora observed.

"I'll drink to that," Madison raised her glass.

Still staring into the fire, the heat on her face, Harlow answered, deadpan, "I think it has to be vodka to fulfill the Molotov element."

Dinky clung to a crystal on the chandelier where she'd taken refuge from the breaking glass and explosion of fire, dropping excrement that landed on the side table next to Sylvia.

Aurora weighed in, "I mean, yeah, Russ and Crowley were making their own interpretations from ancient texts, the same thing the alchemists and humanists were doing in the fifteenth century. They were appropriating Neo-Pythagoreanism, Neo-Platonism, Alexandrian hermeticism, the Jewish Kabbalah, Paracelsus, trying to establish relationships, see the universal correspondences, the main one being the idea that the cosmos is alive, which is also a core pagan belief," ideas ticked in Aurora's head, "In essence, Tantra relates to a vast array of beliefs and philosophies in the esoteric traditions of Hinduism and Buddhism with religious and practical instructions to becoming Awakened or aware of the true nature of reality, which is what we're after."

Harlow cut in, "We know all this. Tantra is power and energy with teachings and techniques that tap into the spiritual force that flows throughout the cosmos, throughout our bodies — a means to spiritual liberation, even wealth, fame, and supernatural abilities. But, what's real and what's not?"

"Yeah, totally. That's what we want to do, harness this power to have supernatural abilities." Madison tilted her head slightly to the side in agreement and contemplation.

Sylvia stepped in, "And this knowledge can be twisted and used for the wrong reasons. Like I said, "McGnosis". And sexual abuse. And brainwashing. So, number one, we don't want to mess around with gurus.

"Then, rather than being used for social liberation, tantric texts like the *Kaulajnananirnaya* or the *Brihat Tantrasara* have historically acted as a mode of suppression to affirm the authority of the male brahmans who claimed they were the only ones skillful enough to handle the dangerous energies in the cosmos. Which is all completely at odds with our surrealist principles –"

"Obviously." Madison looked at the ceiling, then took another sip of wine.

Sylvia continued, "What we seek are forms of socio-political transgression — to undermine the class system and subvert the status quo. I mean, there's definitely misogyny in the *Bhagavad Gita* which made me want to scream and set the book on fire, and from what I've seen and read, Hindu texts present diverse and conflicting views on the position of women, ranging from feminine leadership as the highest goddess, to limiting gender roles and considering women unclean when they have their periods. I don't know. We have to keep looking. I mean, there's also legitimate knowledge in there. Like I keep saying, we have to sift through it."

"Right. So back to sex magic. *Shakti*, harnessing the power coursing through the universe. Supernatural shit." This came from Madison.

"Well, I've been taking notes, and there was some seriously crazy sex magic shit going on in the The Fraternitas Saturni, this group in Berlin during the late nineteen twenties," Dora pulled out a notebook from the pile of books at her feet and began flipping through the pages.

"Do tell." Madison leaned forward, edging closer to Dora.

"Well, obviously 'fraternitas' refers to men."

"I don't care. I like men," Madison reached out, drunkenly, and made a circular motion, pointing to everyone in the room, "Who doesn't like men?"

"Yeah, I'm a feminist, but I don't hate men. We don't hate men, do we?" Harlow was on the floor in front of the fire practicing splits.

"I like hot men. Who aren't assholes. Jake Knox is hot," Dora turned her head in Madison's direction, making a reference to one of the boys on campus.

"I don't hate men, but I think I'm bisexual. Probably everyone is bisexual to some degree," Sylvia offered.

Harlow stared into the fire. "Maybe I'm bi-curious."

Aurora remained silent. She didn't know what she was. She'd spent her earliest years loving Jesus. She'd also loved the Virgin Mary. But, upon reflection, the love she had for Jesus was not the same love she'd had for Mary. Maybe she did think Jesus was hot. She loved Mary like she loved the Angels.

"Aurora, who do you prefer, men or women? Or both?" Madison's eyes ground to a halt in Aurora's.

"Hot men who aren't assholes," then, "Women are also hot. Kate Moss is hot." There had been times she wanted to kiss Sylvia on the mouth, to bite her lip, get a droplet of Sylvia's blood on her tongue. And then, when Sylvia had cut both their hands and recited Emily Dickinson, and they pressed their palms together, she felt a rising and rush previously unknown to her. And when they slept, arms and legs, bodies entangled, feeling one another breathe, she had wanted to kiss Sylvia all over. To lick her, to taste her skin. Taking showers together, their bodies in the flashing water droplets and drifts of steam, slick and wet and shining, Aurora thought Sylvia was as beautiful as a water nymph.

"Yeah, and Tyra Banks," Madison added.

"Jesus Christ those are models," Sylvia balked. "What about Lisa Bonet in *Angel Heart*?"

"Can we please not? You know everyone calls me Lisa Bonet café-o-lait." Recently, a group of boys on campus had started a trend, harassing Dora with this epithet.

"But she's super-hot, and so are you. I think you look like her," Madison was the only one who could get away with saying this.

"Jesus Christ. Not you too."

Madison slipped off the sofa, wine glass in hand, and went to Dora, trying to put her arms around her, dropping the glass on the floor, red wine seeping into the carpet[17],

---

17. None of them cared about any messes they made. It would all be cleaned, every stain would magically disappear, because of the three women who came to clean the house every week.

and ended up kneeling in front of Dora, her head on Dora's knees. Dora looked down and stroked Madison's hair, "You're so drunk."

"I know. But I want to hear about sex magic."

"I cannot fucking believe you. You want to hear about the Fraternitas Saturni?"

Madison lifted her head and nodded.

"Ok," Dora picked up her notebook. "Here we go. The phallus was viewed as the earthly manifestation of divine power, with semen as its vehicle. The vagina symbolized chaos as the creative ground of being. These people did not accept homosexuality. In short, they were homophobes.

"So, the female would be the medium who facilitates workings in the astral sphere. She has to be totally subjugated to the magus sexually –"

"Boooo," Madison remained on the floor at Dora's feet.

"Does that mean you don't want me to continue?"

"No, go on."

"The magus gets his dominance over her by rubbing his semen on the woman's solar plexus —"

"So basically, don't ever let a guy rub his semen on your solar plexus unless you want him to dominate you," Harlow chimed in from her place in front of the fire, still going through her splits.

"Right, and when she was on her period she also had to drink the magus' semen regularly. Sperm is one of the most potent ingredients in magical creations, but its 'fluidic forces' must be consciously directed by the mental and imaginative power of the magus; otherwise, it is completely useless.

"So, one of the things they did with this sex magic was to create astral beings. The magus' sperm had to be combined with the female's bodily fluids and they would take this from her vagina after their 'ritual sex'. They called these solar and lunar fluidic forces, and together, this spiritual combination had the power to create astral beings.

"So, the magus and his medium would be protected by a magical circle during the ritual to keep out astral vampires. Sometimes they all used cannabis or opium to enhance the power of their visualizations and for fumigation purposes to keep the negative energies away. They then tied the astral being to a symbol or kabbalistic name written on parchment with the mixture of the solar and lunar fluids. With the astral being they have created and captured, they could then use it for all kinds of practical magic work, calling it forth with the symbol they had tied it to. As a side note, this procedure was completely different from the invocations or evocations of already existing angels, demons, or other spiritual beings.

"There are more rituals for different purposes, but they all have the circle and the mixing of the fluids," Dora put the notebook down.

"Yeah, I mean this is part of all the questionable stuff," Sylvia spoke and at the same time was writing in her notebook.

"Is there more?" Madison looked up at Dora from the floor.

"Yeah. Do you want me to go on?"

Madison's face lit up. "Yes! Yes! Yes!"

"Yeah, why not?" Harlow was now practicing arabesques.

"Fire away." This came from Sylvia.

"Yeah." Aurora was trying to decide whether having this information inside her head would corrupt her, or whether all knowledge was power, and she should try and find out as much about everything as there was to know.

"Okay. So, sex magic was also used for the activation and development of the chakras. For this they used certain runic and yogic positions. There were degrees, like a hierarchy. In the eighteenth degree there was a rite of initiation where the magus and medium had ritual intercourse in front of the members who also had to be holders of the eighteenth-degree. In the course of this ritual, a living black cock is decapitated —"

"Oh my God! No!"

"They mean a rooster! A black rooster!"

"You can't really go to bed with that image in your head now."

Harlow stood still, breathing deeply, in and out.

"Go on." Ester wouldn't have minded if Dora had been talking about a live man's penis, however horrible and gruesome that would have been.

"A living black cock is decapitated, and its blood spilled over the couple while they are engaged in intercourse. The magus must ejaculate outside the vagina through vigorous rubbing of the penis by the female partner, while the other sisters and brothers of the eighteenth degree yell ecstatically. In the end, a clean white cloth is placed over the couple." Dora concluded, "It is not certain that this rite has ever been put into actual practice, and if so, how often".

Everyone sat quietly with the image in their minds. Not because they wanted to.

Madison got up from the floor and went looking for more red wine, or the absinthe bottle or whatever she could find.

"Have any of you read about Kremmerz?"

Dora and Aurora shook their heads.

Sylvia continued, "His real name, or his first name, was Ciro Formisano, alive between 1861 and 1930. Kremmerz was the name he got after he attained a certain degree. He was known in Italy and France as one of the great figures on the Italian magical scene, next to Julius Evola and Arturo Reghini. I read Kremmerz in French because nothing he wrote has been translated into English.

"One of his major points is that there's an important distinction between love directed by the mind, which is impure, and love directed by the heart — dedicated to the angels — which is pure. He wrote about teachings, never going into any great detail unfortunately, that induce the 'lighting of a psychic fire'.

"This 'lighting of the fire' is based on the complementary magnetism of the female — which he called passive — and male — which he called active — polarities. The fire happens when a man and a woman are very attracted to one another, very aroused, but cannot release it through any kind of sexual relationship. The man and the woman use this erotic energy and the fluids that come from it to enter transcendent states. The energy also has to be more than purely physical, otherwise the power, or magical current or *shakti* or whatever it is, gets paralyzed and can't flow properly. I'm not sure what happens if it isn't done right — maybe the people psychically explode or die or go insane or something. Anyway, the purpose is the attainment of a transcendent androgynous state, which is reminiscent of practices by the occult group *Fedeli d'Amore* in the Middle Ages."

Madison had found champagne in the kitchen and was using her teeth to pull the foil from the muselet.

"No, no, Madison, you're going to break a tooth." Harlow took the bottle from her.

"It's fine, I can get them crowned." Madison was not yet slurring her words but was clearly inebriated. "Like Tom Cruise. His teeth are amazing."

"Are we really going to have champagne now? It's one a.m.." Harlow held the bottle, waiting for everyone's approval.

"Why not?" Dora was looking through her notes.

"Do you guys want me to go on, or is this boring you?"

"Aurora?" Harlow tipped the live end of the bottle toward her.

"It's never a bad time for champagne." Aurora did not actually believe this; she was only saying what she thought everyone wanted to hear.

Harlow tore off the foil, which looked like it had been attacked by a rabbit, eased the cork forward, untwisted the wire cage and let the cork pop. "Go on Sylvia, we're in it now." Standing with the froth overflowing onto the carpet, Harlow mused, "Where are the champagne glasses?" then, "Fuck it". She swilled from the bottle and passed it to Sylvia.

"Okay. Further down the rabbit hole it is." Sylvia chugged from the bottle and handed it to Aurora. "So where was I? As a boy, Kremmerz, then Ciro, was in the midst of members of a pagan and strongly anti-Christian group called Scuola di Napoli (School of Naples). This group supposedly devoted itself to alchemical and magical workings, but unfortunately we have no documentary proof that it actually existed.

"The School of Naples was believed to hail back to the Prince Raimondo di Sangro di Sansevero, Duke of Torremaggiore, in the eighteenth century. Di Sangro was the first Grand Master of Freemasonry in Naples and a known alchemist rumored to have tried to create a homunculus. The Prince was excommunicated by the Pope and eventually died by accidentally poisoning himself in the course of one of his alchemical experiments.

"Enter a fake, self-appointed count, Count Cagliostro, also from Naples, who was in the Prince's circle. The Count traveled to Germany where he may well have come into contact with groups of alchemists such as The Order of the Golden and Rosy Cross. It is after this that the Count came into possession of secret 'Egyptian' degrees, which, legend has it, he passed on to three important members of an *Ordine Egizio*, out of which came Kremmerz's *Ordine Osirideo Egizio*.

"The first to receive the secret Egyptian rites was the Baron Nicola Giuseppe Spedalieri, a pupil of Eliphas Lévi.

The second was the lawyer Giustiniano Lebano, also a contact of Lévi's, who owned a considerable library of occult works. Occultists from all over of Europe came to visit him: Sir Edward Bulwer Lytton, Helena P. Blavatsky, Dr. Franz Hartmann, and — you guessed it! — Kremmerz.

"Sadly, all Lebano's papers, manuscripts, and books were lost when his wife committed suicide by setting herself, along with the library, on fire, to atone for her husband's magical wrongdoings.

"The third person to receive the secret Egyptian rites was Pasquale de Servis, who lived in the house in Naples where the young Kremmerz, grew up —"

Confused, Madison interrupted her. "I thought this was supposed to be about sex magic?"

"She's setting it up, it's like a bedtime fairytale."

"Exactly. Provenance, Madison, provenance. It's super important." Sylvia lit a cigarette.

"How do you know all this?" Harlow was now prone in front of the fire, which she had been poking and feeding.

"I've been studying it for like, almost two years."

"How do you find time to do that plus everything else?"

"Well, let's just say I don't have a great GPA. I mean, it's okay. I do the bare minimum for class."

"Yeah, I mean, you'll get into the Ivy League anyway."

"I don't know, I might go to Stanford, or Berkeley."

"Okay, okay, okay, what about the sex magic stuff?" Madison could barely keep her eyes open.

"Do you want me to go on?"

"Let's go to bed. We can continue the sex magic stuff later."

"A world without men would be horrible. But fuck the patriarchy! We need to harness our own *shakti* on our own terms." Madison said this from her position at Dora's feet, her eyelids heavy, words slow. "We need them for sex magic."

Dora tilted her head, insouciant, sublime.

"I'm really not so sure a matriarchy is the answer. Women can be ruthless bitches too." Sylvia smoked her cigarette, elbow bent on the sofa armrest, chin resting in her palm.

"Oh my god, you are so right!" Madison said this with inebriated enthusiasm.

"I'm going to bed." Harlow got up from her place at the fire, her line of sight set on the archway that led to the hall and through which she disappeared.

The next night Sylvia began, a freshly lit cigarette smouldering between her fingers. "Okay, so I think I need to go into more historical detail before I get into any juicy sex magic specifics — sorry Madison, I know you just want to get to it but we need background, then theories, then rituals. And after that, we can see if we want to do anything with the information. Because, at this point my reading is just a drop in the ocean and even if I spent my entire lifetime studying this, I would only manage to scratch the surface...

"I don't see any clear lines back to antiquity in regard to actual rituals. The people who have the clearest lines are probably indigenous people in Australia, New Zealand, throughout the Pacific, North and South America; seers or sages of Yungdrung Bon, Shinto; certain people from Africa who haven't been tainted by Christianity. And I'm not even sure any of them have anything like sex magic —"

"What are you saying? I'm so confused." Madison rotated a ring on her finger back and forth.

"What I'm trying to say, is that all the stuff I talked about yesterday — the stuff Dora was talking about — it's all heavily laden with Christianity, even the so-called 'Egyptian' rites and secret knowledge that mage guy Kremmenz supposedly had that he got from the Prince and the Count. So much of what we call 'magic' — the search for the Philosopher's Stone, for supernatural powers — are rampant with Christianity and Christian iconography. It's mixed in with Kabbalah stuff and rites, statutes, that the Israelites supposedly learned from the ancient Egyptians."

"Okay, what about *The Kybalion*?" Harlow's mother had mentioned it many times and said it had the hermetic philosophy of ancient Egypt and Greece with rituals and practical sorcery.

"That was written in 1908 under a pseudonym by this American occultist who started the New Thought movement."

"Jesus Christ! How do you know all this?"

"I don't know — I just read and absorb things. Yeah, *The Kybalion* is supposed to have ancient knowledge, which comes from hermetic sources but in reality, we only have fragments of hermetic teachings. There are the Coptic *Nag Hammadi* texts found in Egypt, but they aren't complete. So, we have bits and pieces — we have astrology, for example — and they got mixed with Christianity and the Kabbalah and Celtic and other pagan knowledge, and these are basically the occult treatises we have today."

"Okay, so where does that leave us?" Harlow turned her freckled face toward Sylvia.

"Paschal Beverly Randolph, a Black man, born free in New York City in 1825, with no father, mother, or family, somehow managed to survive in the notorious 'Five Points', the most impoverished, violent slum at the time, and on top of this succeeded in obtaining enough education, so that by his early twenties he was able to take up the profession of barber in Upstate New York.

"He discovered the Spiritualist movement, of which, as you recall, Dion Fortune was a part, decided to try mediumship and quickly found his calling as a trance speaker, first mediating for famous figures from American history such as Thomas Paine and Thomas Jefferson, then moved on to calling up more illustrious dead people such as Zarathustra. Through these trance sessions, he figured out how to travel in the spirit world. He then moved beyond Spiritualism. The power of sex magic coupled with psychoactive drugs was the genie Randolph would let out of the bottle and loose upon the world.

"In 1855 and 1857 he travelled to Europe and the Near East where he encountered Mesmerism and mirror magic by the likes of the Orphic Circle and Berlin Club. The members used drugs, crystals, and magic mirrors to separate the 'flying souls' of their young subjects and send them on occult missions around the earth, or on clairvoyant journeys in the vast celestial hierarchy. Only the female seers, not the mages, were allowed on these missions. Randolph did not actually experience any of the rituals in the Orphic Circle or Berlin Club first-hand. It was on his trip to Europe that he first heard of them —"

"So, he unleashed sex magic with drugs on the world, but these people had done it before him, and he wasn't even a part of their group?" This came from Dora.

"The Orphic Circle and Berlin Club sound more interesting to me than this Randolph guy." Madison dipped a finger into her mimosa, stirred it, then put her finger in her mouth.

"Yeah, they really do." Harlow turned her head in Madison's direction.

"Well, go read *Ghost Land: Or Researches Into the Mysteries of Occultism* by Emma Hardinge Britten, who was one of the young women they used as a seeress," Sylvia offered, "and report back."

"What is that supposed to mean?" Madison batted her eyelashes.

"I was trying to impart what I thought was important to facilitate this discussion and what I've read on Randolph is more interesting, is all I'm saying." Chain-smoking, Sylvia reached for her pack of cigarettes, put one in her mouth and hastily lit it with a match.

"Okay." Madison crossed her legs.

"Do you want me to go on? The Berlin Club is the Fraternitas Saturni which Dora already talked about — the ones who made a circle and decapitated a black rooster and wrote sigils in sperm and women's cum on parchment to trap the entities they made."

"Ah, okay, right," Madison nodded.

"So, the Randolph guy —" this came from Aurora.

"I don't even know where I was." Sylvia took a drag of her cigarette. "Okay, basically." She stopped, then started again. "Maybe it's all bullshit. In any case, he didn't write the specifics of the sex magic instructions down but one of his followers — Maria de Naglowska — supposedly used his insights to create her own system. She wrote quite a lot on the subject. Maybe we should all try reading her for our next meeting, say in like two weeks or something, to give us time." Sylvia took another drag and exhaled. "She had this theory that by knowing Satan one could know God. She argues that Satan is the negation and therefore part of God and that it was out of this dialectic that Jesus was born. But that had nothing to do with Randolph — that was her theory."

"I think we're wasting our time with Satan. And this mangled Christianity," Aurora mused.

"Hard to swallow for an evangelical." Madison turned and smiled at Aurora.

"Well, admittedly de Naglowska was a bit batshit. She thought that a genuinely pure woman is one who has dedicated herself to a higher Force, meaning Satan; one who doesn't want anything for herself, and can turn violent, base men into sages by satisfying their carnal desires. She wrote this crazy novel with some kind of Ayn Rand hidden philosophical message, where the heroine gets raped but then — plot twist — it turns out that she was the one who actually raped him as it was the only way to enlighten him." Sylvia flicked ash from her cigarette into a nearby ashtray.

"I don't know, I mean having sex in a circle of witches yelling ecstatically as rooster blood and sperm is sprayed all over me, and then writing a symbol on parchment with the blood and sex fluids to create an entity that will give me supernatural powers sounds kind of hot." Madison was now doing shots of tequila which were acting like rocket fuel on her brain and tongue. "We need to find more practical stuff like that."

"I was trying to give us philosophy, concepts, ideas we could work with. But no. You didn't want to hear about Randolph."

"We want ancient stuff. Pagan stuff. Oracles. The derangement of the senses, psychedelic drugs, orgies in the woods." Madison raised her shot glass to all of them.

"Yeah, the only problem is that we don't know exactly what those pagans did — they didn't write it down," Dora interjected.

"Okay. So, quantum physics teaches us that photons change from a particle to a wave when they're being observed. Observation has something to do with all of this. Maybe it's our will, our intention. Our eyes and our minds on things have the ability to change how they behave." Aurora's eyes grew brighter and seemed to glow[18].

Sylvia caught the intellectual spark Aurora had thrown out and came to attention. "Yes. There's a theory that observation creates reality. You're on to something

18. Due to the elementals, still in possession of her

Aurora. When Randolph went into his trances and was able to travel astrally, or whatever, travel in the other realms, he said..." She picked up a book beside her on the end table, cigarette still lit, and flipped through it, ash falling on the sofa. ". . . Here, *The eye did not see, but I was all sight. There was no organ of locomotion... but my spirit seemed to be all motion, and it knew instinctively, that by the power of the thought-wish it could reach any point within the boundaries of earth where it longed and willed to be ...*'" Sylvia looked up from the page. "He talks about being able to access and use this thing he called the Aeth which was a boundless, undefinable, unimaginable ocean of liquid fire that fills and animates creation and is the basis for all magical power." Sylvia's eyes became remote, in contemplation. "God as Light, accessible through the secrets of sexual magic ..."

"Maybe this is *shakti*?" Harlow offered.

"Maybe." Dora too, was lost in thought.

"... the 'practice of separation' of the solar Self and the alchemical creation, through sexual magic, of a second subtle 'glorious body' to survive the physical death of the mortal frame ..." Sylvia continued with her interior dialog, out loud.

"Okay, so when we go into a trance, we can find this liquid fire ocean of creation, and if we do it while having sex, then —" Madison got up, headed for the kitchen to get more champagne. "I think we've had a breakthrough. We need to find a way to get to the liquid fire ocean."

"That's why I was trying to tell you about Randolph."

"Yeah, I get it now." Madison disappeared into the hallway.

"So, Randolph writes about this process he calls 'blending' —"

"Wait for Madison to get back." Dora lifted her chin and turned her eyes toward the archway. They sat, saying nothing: Harlow examining her hair for split ends, Aurora, hand outstretched, trying to get Dinky to come down from the chandelier; Sylvia looking through her book for the passage she wanted to read.

Madison returned with a bottle of champagne gripped in each hand, gave one to Harlow to open, tore the foil off hers with her teeth, then untwisted the agraffe until the cork was loose, dislodging it with a gentle *poof!*, smoke pouring out like a fired pistol. Harlow's bottle popped like a rock star's. Madison bent down and took as much of the stream as she could into her mouth. It ran down her chin, her neck, between her breasts and onto the carpet. They filled everyone's glass.

Sylvia continued on the subject of Randolph in the background, "Blending. Randolph had his first experience with a state he called 'blending', or *Atrilism*, or 'mixed-identities' during his Spiritualist period, when he went into a trance and blended, or mixed, identities with a dead lover. As he progressed and went beyond the world of human souls he came into contact with other, more elevated and exalted entities in the cosmic hierarchy and found that this blending process was universal. He was able to merge with them in the same way, so that he could experience the power, knowledge, and wisdom of these entities. I'll read what he says about it:

By slow degrees I felt that my own personality was not lost to me, but completely swallowed up, so to speak, in that of a far more potent mentality. A subtlety of thought, perception and understanding became mine at times, altogether greater than I had ever known before; and occasionally, during these strange blendings of my being with another, I felt that other's feelings, thought that other's thoughts...

The book also says Randolph realized the key to the process, and indeed the key to all the secrets of the universe, lay in sex — sex not borne of lust but pure love. Like I said before, he never wrote any specific instructions down, but it's assumed he taught his students, one of whom was Maria de Naglowska, the weird sex magic Satanic woman."

"Jesus Christ!" Madison sighed.

By slow degrees I felt that my own personality was not lost to me, but completely swallowed up. Aurora ran the words through her head. This is how she felt when she watched the film stars in the library.[19] Her thoughts bubbled. She remembered something she'd written down in her notebook in reference to trance and yoga. "Wait a minute, I might have something." She flipped through pages, skimming over passages marked "Trance" until she came to the one she was looking for. "This might be something we could use. It's from Eliade's *Shamanism: Archaic Techniques of Ecstasy*. I actually got the quote

19. Ironically, the truth was that, as she was trying to possess, she was being possessed, or infected, by the elementals, the nature spirits, charging her with their vitality, pushing her to the edge of her capacity for existence, stirring her atavistic depths.

from *Singing with Blackbirds: The Survival of Primal Celtic Shamanism in Later Folk-Traditions* by Stuart Harris-Logan. Okay,

> In Yogic meditation manipulation of the breath is key to achieving a trance state... this power enables the yogic to detach himself from the world and even in some measure destroy it. Because yogic liberation is equivalent to completely breaking all ties with the cosmos; for a *jivan-mukta*, the universe no longer exists... it seems to us significant that Indian spirituality, seeking a means of metaphysical liberation, employed a technique of archaic magic reputedly able to abolish physical laws and play a part in the very constitution of the universe."

Aurora looked up from the page.

"What is a *jivan-mukta*?" Dora met Aurora's eyes.

"It's a kind of saint." Sylvia stretched her arms over her head. "A *jivan-mukta* is one with the Godhead, fully liberated from conditioning by space-time, causation, karma; in a state of unbounded illumination, consciousness, bliss. They're alive but it's like their consciousness has ascended to a kind of heaven or nirvana." Her arms came down. She reached for her pack of cigarettes.

"Aurora, you look like you're glowing." Madison had taken one of Harlow's clove cigarettes and was smoking it. "I mean really glowing — like blue or green or something. Like, glow-in-the-dark."

"Yeah, she is."

"Maybe it's your aura."

Aurora looked at her arms. Dinky flit around her. "I don't see anything." She tried to look natural, as though nothing had happened. She felt foreign things writhing inside her.

In the next meeting, Sylvia began with Terence McKenna and his psychoactive mushroom theories, reading aloud from *Food of the Gods*:

I believe that the use of hallucinogenic mushrooms on the grasslands of Africa gave us the model for all religions to follow. And when, after long centuries of slow forgetting, migration, and climatic change, the knowledge of the mystery was finally lost, we in our anguish traded partnership for dominance, traded harmony with nature for rape of nature, traded poetry for the sophistry of science. In short, we traded our birth right as partners in the drama of the living mind of the planet for the broken pot shards of history, warfare, neurosis, and — if we do not quickly awaken to our predicament — planetary catastrophe.

The book was filled with warnings such as these — against the dangers of technology, the Industrial Revolution, ecocide. They had all seen the oil spills on the news — the chemical spills, the rivers that caught fire, the water that took flame when lit with a lighter as it streamed from the faucets in people's kitchens. They agreed Nature was being raped. They knew there were islands of plastic garbage in the Pacific and that radioactive waste found its way into the oceans and rivers. Pollution was tearing holes in the ozone. Terence McKenna was right. If there was a way to speak with and listen to plants and the elements this would be a major accomplishment. The worship of Nature, paganism, and benevolent sorcery were a way to heal the planet.

"Of course, we could die, taking all this psychoactive shit." Harlow shook her auburn hair out over her shoulders, then swooped forward and up with a flushed face. She was practicing her barre work using the back of the sofa to steady herself.

"Yes. It's true." Dora gave a knowing nod. "We could jump out the window, fall down the stairs and break our necks."

Madison stared ahead, her lips stained red from wine. "We could lose our minds.".

Sylvia paced the room, "But, imagine! If taking entheogens allows us to experience the thing that made humanity aware of the nature spirits, of the gods, and was the catalyst of art, don't we have a duty as artists, especially surrealist artists of the occult, to try them? It isn't supposed to be easy! Danger is unavoidable for growth."

Aurora, ever anchored to reason, secretly wondered whether Sylvia's positivity was in fact toxic, devoid of an acute sense of the potential danger that lay ahead if they continued on this path of blind sorcery and drugs. Nevertheless, she could not deny that it was exciting.

Beside *Food of the Gods*, Sylvia read from Robert Gordon Wasson's *The Wondrous Mushroom* — passages concerning the Aztec deity, *Xochipilli*, the Prince of Flowers, god of the ecstatic mushroom trance, of light, of youth, dance, music, games, poetry, art, summer, the rising sun, of butterflies and warmth.

"There are things we need to know, that we may have to risk dying for." Madison's eyes were clear as fresh ice. She looked as though she had sold her soul to the devil.

They all agreed with Madison, sharing her reverent enthusiasm. Sylvia thought art and love were worth dying for. They all agreed to that too.

"When art and love are gone, there isn't any point in living," Dora mused. "But then, maybe that would be impossible, as long as people exist, art and love will too."

"Maybe," Harlow offered. "The end of art and love would be the end of humanity."

Aurora agreed with all of this.

"We've got to get serious now. We have to decide how we're going to create our surrealist group. We have to think about art projects." She took a sip of wine, musing, "Eventually, exhibitions of our work could be put on in L.A., New York, London, Paris, Amsterdam, Buenos Aires.

"Through our work the attendees will have the opportunity to cross to the place Beyond the Veil — the Unseen worlds. Some might remain there forever. It would be known that to go to one of our exhibitions risked one's sanity. But, obviously, the gains would be immense if one survived. What do you think?" Sylvia looked at each girl and saw their faces lighting up.

"Yes! Cast spells to influence events! Drink wine, take mushrooms, derange our senses and make art! Have ritual sex!" Madison was one hundred percent on board. "We will raise storms! We will levitate under the full moon!" It was the most exciting proposition she had entertained in her short life. "Where are we going to get the mushrooms? We could fly to Amsterdam!"

In the library, they learned the *psilocybe semilanceata*, or Liberty Cap mushroom, grew in the United States as well as Europe. A grassland fungi, it appeared in autumn and was most commonly found on pasture and parkland that hadn't been enriched with artificial fertilizer. They discussed waiting until the autumn to go hunting for them, or using other channels — a dealer on campus perhaps, or someone in their network of friends in California. All Madison wanted to do was to go to Amsterdam. They could bring some back on Sylvia's father's jet. Harlow thought they should try an infamous druggie on campus — the son of a Supreme Court judge. He lived in a dorm known for its rampant drug use, which despite this, held one of the highest collective GPAs on campus. Most people stayed away from this dorm, unless they were looking for a wild time. Before they met Sylvia and Aurora, Madison, Dora, and Harlow had gone to parties there. The previous semester a group of its residents tried to make ether in the basement and nearly blew the building up. Only one person had been expelled. Madison and Harlow volunteered to speak with the son of the Supreme Court judge. Aurora was curious. She wanted to go along.

The notorious dorm was named after a Puritan minister, founder of one of the original Thirteen Colonies. It sat on its own, behind the quad, five storeys tall, a circular drive with a stone staircase that led to imposing front doors. With its austere lines and red bricks, it resembled a Victorian prison. Pirate flags hung from several windows. Madison, Harlow, and Aurora mounted the stairs in the dusk. Girls were forbidden in the male dormitories after dark, but they didn't plan on staying long. Inside the building, stale hops, the odour of acrid, noxious, and unclean adolescent boys rose from the recesses, cured into the wood panelling from nearly two hundred years of habitation.

The judge's son's room was easy to find; the first boy they asked knew the room number. Walking down the high-ceilinged corridor, their shoes sticking to the floor in places from beer residue, making sounds like adhesive tape being pulled off a surface, they came to the door marked fifteen. Madison knocked. They thought they could hear music inside. Nothing. She knocked again. With bated breath they waited, staring into each other's faces until Harlow burst out laughing and Madison shooshed her, laughing too, and knocked again. Aurora only smiled.

The door opened. Cannabis smoke emptied into the hall, soft and humid on their faces, engulfing them, spreading out down the hallway. They found themselves face to face with the judge's son: tall, slightly stooped, wearing long shorts and a check flannel shirt. Music was playing in the background. "Hello," he said, his head bent, squinting and shielding his eyes from the light in the corridor.

Harlow was the first to respond. "You don't know us, but we were wondering if we could have a word with you, about something." They looked at him with hopeful eyes and smiles on their faces.

He did know them. They had never formally met but he knew them from campus and the Black Book. "I see, well, you're way too young to be cops, so come in," he made a sweeping gesture. They walked inside the darkened room lit with candles, a lava lamp and two red lights shining from the eyes of a gigantic rubber pig head nailed above the doorway. The judge's son put the roll of fabric softener back over the gap in the bottom of the door to keep the cannabis smell from drifting into the hall. Two young men sat on a couch in front of a steamer trunk that served as a coffee table. Reclined on the bed lay a young woman in a cashmere sweater, miniskirt and tights. A song with an unpleasant mixture of psychedelic, proggy sounds, jazz and folk, with cloying, goofy, lyrics laughing in the face of everything that matters played from a hi-fi set up in the corner.

The judge's son told Madison, Harlow, and Aurora to make themselves at home, to sit on the bed. The young woman shifted, sitting up and sliding into position with her legs to the side. Everyone said hello to one another. The judge's son's retinue was more or less sedated. "So what brings you here?" he asked, sitting down on a chair.

"We thought you might be able to help us," Harlow began, "We're looking for Liberty cap and/or amanita mushrooms. We wanted to make some tea with them and use it as part of a pagan ritual and film it for our art class."

His face lit up. "Right on. I'm down with this project." He nodded his head. "Sounds awesome."

Madison spoke. "So you'll help us then?"

"Yeah, I can help you. How much do you need?"

"Enough to make tea for five people."

He scratched his chin. "So, twenty-five grams I'd say. I can get Mexican a lot easier than Liberty caps."

"We specifically need the Liberty caps or *amanita muscaria* because that's what the Druids would have had access to."

"I see, yes — your project."

"We're going to perform at least five rituals. So we'd need a hundred and twenty-five grams?"

"Yeah, sounds right."

"We can leave it with you? You think you can get it?"

"Of course I can." He gave them a reassuring smile. Harlow smiled back.

"We're not playing around. I just want to make sure, that you aren't either. We don't have a lot of time to waste." This came from Madison.

"I know people. I can get LSD, ecstasy, Mexican mushrooms very easily in D.C. I'm going down there in a few weeks and I'll see what I can do. No one's ever mentioned Liberty caps to me before, but I know what they are. I had them in Amsterdam last summer."

The girl on the bed took a bong from the floor and packed a bud into the bowl. She turned to offer it to Madison. Madison graciously accepted, then passed it to

Harlow, who put the tube to her mouth while Madison lit the bowl. Harlow bowed her head and sucked, the water gurgling, until the embers burnt out. It had been a generous bud. The girl packed the bowl again. Harlow lit the bong for Madison. Aurora couldn't finish hers and passed it to Harlow. This was the first time Aurora had smoked weed.

They sat silently in their own little worlds, saying nothing in the cannabis fog — the hideous music wrapping itself around them, warping the scene into a nightmare — auras around the candles in the distorted light, glittering in its refractions.

Out of nowhere, one of the boys spoke. "It's a weapon to have a woman who looks like Britney Spears and is a professional seducer designed to turn a man into a boy again, so they can delete his memory and put him back in primary school. It is also a crime where I come from. And we do punish it." He looked in the girls' direction. "You *are* innocent in my eyes..."

"Whitaker —". The son of the Supreme Court judge turned toward his friend, his eyes slits, communicating with his tone that Whitaker sounded insane and needed to stop talking.

Harlow and Madison found themselves rising from the bed, thanking the judge's son, saying goodbye to everyone; Aurora following them like the orb of light she felt she had become: the three leaving through the door with the life-size plastic pig head mounted above it, eyes glowing red, into the brightly lit hall — the light so hard it was like hitting a wall they somehow passed through like ghosts, and kept on going.

The next thing they knew they were outside, walking in the night, under the stars, across campus to their house — mouths and throats dry, thirsty — with thoughts that spiralled, then tapered off into dead, empty space. They couldn't hold a conversation and laughed hysterically, miming all the way home, falling in the snow, where they made snow angels in slow motion — freezing cold lumps of snow sliding down their necks, down their backs, making them squirm and cry out. Somehow, they made it home and were greeted by Sylvia, Dora and Dinky in the entrance hall. The three walked several paces, fell to the floor, writhing on their backs and stomachs and thought they might die of laughter.

The next evening the girls drank wine sprawled out on the sofas, Dora's head in Madison's lap, gazing into the fire — crackling and hissing, letting off a blowtorch sound, eating the logs — while Harlow smudged the room with lavender. Aurora was curled up in a chair, Dinky flitting around her head until she descended on a lampshade and dropped a turd onto the polished surface of the side table. Sylvia read from Dion Fortune:

There are two gates, and two only, by which the attacker can gain entrance to the city of Mansoul, and these are the Self-preservation Instinct and the Sex Instinct. How does the attacker proceed? If he wants to perform a psychic murder, he must fill his own soul with the rage of destruction until it overflows. If he wants to perform a psychic rape, he must fill his soul with lust and cruelty. The cold rage of cruelty is essential to effectual operations of this nature. Now what happens when he does this? He has sounded a ringing keynote in the Abyss. It will be answered.

Psychic Self-Defense was a logical jumping-off point as what they needed to know, first of all, was how to protect themselves against malefic entities from the Invisible Worlds. Going beyond the Veil was not make-believe or child's play. The books made this fact clear. They were in danger of ending up in an insane asylum, and even dying. Fortune's instructions had succeeded in cutting the entity from Sylvia during the infamous scrying session. They needed to prepare, to strengthen themselves and their foundations; to practice breathing techniques, meditate, become capable of a perfect concentration of mind, so that when in trance their subconscious would be constant and fully realized. Dion Fortune made it clear that a chain was no stronger than its weakest link — if one of the team couldn't handle the forces, everybody would suffer: a ritual lodge was no place for the well-meaning ineffectual.

Of course, the casual racist and pro-eugenics remarks Fortune made were repulsive. Ultimately, she wasn't anyone to aspire or look up to. She had valuable occult knowledge, but as a human being she was deplorable. However, they decided not to throw the baby out with the bathwater. Their wine drinking also went against what Dion Fortune and other occultists advised. Alcohol and drugs in any amount were not to be consumed when handling Invisible Forces, according to the Spiritualists.

The girls had wholeheartedly decided they would disregard this and go the way of prehistoric humans, the ancient Greeks, Romans, Celts, pagans, Rimbaud et al. and consume ethnogens, drink wine and spirits. The purpose of art was not to represent reality but to access greater truths through the "systematic derangement of the senses," which in itself was another form of reality.

As the evenings progressed, they moved on to other works. Sylvia passed around a book she'd won on eBay called *Hints to Young Students of Occultism*, published in 1917 in Los Angeles. This complemented the Dion Fortune, offering a host of essential teachings, such as:

> The student's will should always be in control. Under no circumstances should it be surrendered to anything or anybody. It is his purpose to know himself and his environment; to obtain first-hand knowledge of the mysteries of life; to purify his vehicles of consciousness and develop his spiritual powers that he may be the greatest possible assistance in spreading the light and helping others forward... The student should work steadily at the development of his heart qualities, for his future safety lies there.

It was glaringly obvious that all the books were addressed to men. This made the girls furious and strengthened their resolve to become forces of nature using occult knowledge to, amongst other things, reorder the world, set women alongside men in the social power dynamic.

The next night Sylvia introduced them to a book entitled *Harmonic Overtones: Magical Vibration in Voice and Music*[20]:

> Our consciousness determines the vibration of our brainwaves. Our brain radiates various brainwaves depending on the state we are in. When we're excited or working hard the beta waves (12 Hz and higher up) are dominant; when more relaxed we are producing alpha waves (8-12 Hz), when very relaxed or in meditation the brainwaves are predominantly theta (4-8 Hz), and when in very deep meditation, or sleeping, we produce mostly delta (4 Hz and lower). Various combinations of these states are possible throughout our days and nights. Music can certainly influence our brain states, and so can overtones. Many listeners at overtone concerts report a complete change of consciousness, lasting from half an hour to several days...

Sylvia read from her notes. "The transformative effects of overtone harmonics were known to the ancient Celts, Tuvans, Mongolians, Chinese, Greeks, Romans, Hindus, to name a few. There's a Neolithic temple at Göbekli Tepe in Turkey, the oldest known archaeological site, dated seven thousand years before the Egyptian pyramids, where archaeoacoustic analysis led to the discovery that the hunter-gatherers who built it also knew about overtone harmonics.

20. Dick De Ruiter. Harmonic Overtones : Magical Vibrations in Voice and Music. Havelte, Binkey Kok, 2003.

"Located on a hilltop, there are human-made baths that lead to concentric stone-built structures — sort of like Stonehenge — with massive, T-shaped standing limestone pillars, and in the center of this shrine, there's a limestone pillar that 'sings' when you delicately tap it. The pillar was made to look like a human with hands and a belt carved in relief and then there are unexplained symbols around the throat. There are loads of symbols carved into the limestone — bulls, snakes, symbols that resemble ancient Egyptian symbols.

"There is no doubt, according to the archaeologists, that the site of Göbekli Tepe was not a settlement, but a site belonging to the religious sphere — a sacred space — and not a settlement, since the excavation has revealed no residential buildings. Göbekli Tepe seems to have been a regional center, where communities met to engage in complex rites. The resonance base sound of the singing pillar and its harmonics are all in the range of 65-145Hz, which affects brain activity.

"The majority of ancient sites — from Sogmatar in south-east Turkey to Xaghra Stone Circle in Gozo, Malta; from the Alatri Acropolis in Italy to Felix Romulian Palace in Serbia and Epidauros in Greece — are all placed over sources of natural low frequencies or magnetic fields, which affect the human body and brain activity. Same with a large group of sacred sites in England, Bosnia, Serbia, Slovenia, Macedonia, and Portugal. Then there is the Hal Saflieni Hypogeum in Malta, dating back five thousand years to the Bronze Age," Sylvia put her index finger to the page, "There are three levels, making a labyrinth of elliptical chambers connected by corridors. One of the chambers is carved out of solid limestone and has been named 'the Oracle Chamber' because it has an echo behavior whereby sounds made at certain pitches can be heard throughout the entire structure, amplified to the point that you can feel the sound vibrating in your bone and tissue as much as hearing it with your ears. And yes, like the other sites I just talked about, this happens when the sounds are at the right hertz to affect brain activity and induce a trance state —"

"This is incredible. This is what I was talking about! We need to go back as far as possible. Forget all the Christ stuff." Madison gesticulated with a champagne glass in her hand above Dora's head. "We should go there, take mushrooms and do a sex magic ritual."

"It's a UNESCO Heritage site, so I don't think that's going to happen." Sylvia reached for her cigarette pack. "We should form a band and use overtone harmonics to put people into a trance."

"Yes! Dora, you on your synthesizer and all your electronic gear, Madison on the violin, Sylvia, with your cello, I'll play the flute. Aurora, you have your oboe, I can also sing — this would be awesome!" Harlow's voice, grainy from the champagne and cigarette smoke, was exuberant.

"We can all sing." Madison raised her empty champagne glass, got up from the sofa, and turned around until she set eyes on one of the champagne bottles on ice in the wine chiller.

"When do we start?"

Sylvia closed her notebook. "Tomorrow night. Be there or be square."

They decided to use a den on the ground floor as their music studio. Dora set up her Minimoog synthesizer and Korg Volca. Sylvia sat on a chair with her cello; the rest of them stood.

"So, maybe one of us start with something, and the rest joins in. Maybe the cello," Dora offered.

Bow in her hand, fingers on the cello's neck, fingertips on the strings, Sylvia was filled with an ice-hot terror. In her classical training she had been bound to complex scores laden with incredibly specific instructions. She sat, everyone around her quiet, giving her the space to find and collect herself — to freefall into the overwhelming vastness and unbearable reduction of her own psyche.

Everyone stood around her holding their instruments, breathing. Sylvia came to terms with the fact she didn't have to hold the bow or move her fingers as she had been trained. She knew the instrument and could have her way with it. She was free to explore. She chose the key — a B major jazz scale — then took the bow, gently rubbing it against the strings in an in and up-and-down sawing motion which she imagined moving in a similar way to a butterfly, then tapped the B string, D, C, A, sawing on like a butterfly's movements until her bow hand went free and made sweeping gestures, her fingers pressing down, gamboling over the strings.

Aurora joined in with her oboe, filling the space with a starry-eyed reverie. Madison let Aurora go on, then came in with her violin, striking dark, solemn chords that lifted and cut and plunged down again, to which Harlow added wafting, ethereal notes on her flute. Dora waited until the right moment and brought in a minimal melody with four keys on the Minimoog, slightly adjusting the bass and intensity, moving the repeat rate up and down to create a sonic sensation of lift-off, then generated a beat sequence on her Korg Volca and let that drop. They went on like this for several hours. The session died out naturally due to the intensity and exhaustion of their exertion, even though they didn't want it to end, or part of them didn't. The same vortex that bound them in its ecstasy was also one that could or would completely unravel them. Madison cursed that they hadn't recorded it.

"Well, we didn't know it was going to sound that good. We'll record from now on." Harlow was on the floor, legs crossed, her flute wet with spit, pressed across her lap.

"I doubt we can do that again." Madison was not a believer.

"We can." Aurora said this without knowing she was going to say it. It came out of her from somewhere deep inside that knew things the surface did not — the place the elementals often hid in their possession of her[21]. And, in fact, the nature spirits had taken part, amplifying and reveling in the sonic concoction, here and there opening shimmering punctures in the veil, not quite large enough for a human soul to pass through.

---

21. Unlike Sylvia, who the nature spirits had abandoned, Aurora was unable to let go of the cord of reason, the Ariadne's string which kept the elementals from destroying her completely, so that she was able to bear the weight of them.

Skipping classes[22], they stayed up all night playing music; drinking wine. Making music in the den became a drug. Singing bowls were procured to bring in more overtone harmonics. They experimented with a capella. In this enthrallment, with the addition of the elementals working through Aurora, they entered a trance state that threatened to knock them into the world Beyond the Veil, where Aurora and Sylvia had wrestled with the entity in the mirror. However, mostly they just hovered there, at the entrance, in a limbic space, which gave them an eerie, dreamy sound. When Aurora sang, the elementals took over completely, charging her voice with raw emotion that gave her delicate contralto a harrowing edge. She never remembered singing anything and only heard herself on the tape playback. It was disturbing.

Waking from sixteen-hour sessions with puffy eyes and splotches on their faces, they started over with martinis and olives for breakfast. Being on a scholarship, Aurora could not afford to miss one lecture or drop a grade in any of her subjects and absented herself from the morning music making sessions, unless it was on a weekend, and went to class with sunglasses on, Dinky following her through the halls, perching on top of doors, riding on her shoulder, flying between the other students, circling back, accompanying her to her desk in the classrooms. She studied in the library in the late afternoons — until it closed on the nights she didn't meet with the other girls.

They waited on tenterhooks for the mushrooms to arrive, hoping the son of the Supreme court judge wasn't going to let them down. Harlow, Sylvia, Dora, and

22. All but Aurora.

Madison were dead set on playing under the influence. Jimi Hendrix, Jim Morrison, John Coltrane, Janis Joplin, The Rolling Stones — to name but a few of the musicians they idolized — had well-known breakthroughs with psychedelics. Even the Beatles had taken LSD. They wanted in. Aurora was hesitant, holding on to her string of reason. She had a nagging feeling it was too soon. Every now and then during their fireside occult sessions she would get the creeping feeling of the entity she and Sylvia had encountered through the mirror, its claws at her neck, fingering her hair.

After five weeks, the judge's son came through and delivered one hundred and twenty-five grams of dried Liberty caps. He said he was still trying to get the fly agaric and would let them know. "Apparently the amanita can't be commercially cultivated, due to its mycorrhizal relationship with the roots of pine trees. The Liberty caps come from Oregon. It took a while because I had to use different contacts from my usual. Sorry for the wait." The son of the Supreme Court judge stood in the entrance hall and handed the bag filled with dried mushrooms to Harlow, who opened it and sniffed the contents, noting the nutty, sour smell, then passed the bag to the others to examine while the son of the judge explained, "Note the stems marked with purple and blue spirals, which I assume indicates a high presence of hallucinogenic potency. A friend of mine who took them last weekend got lost in the Botanic garden in D.C. and thought he was in Egypt."

"They don't smell rotten."

"No." He smiled, a reassuring, dimpled smile. "And you do know the Liberty caps and the fly agaric are completely different? One has psilocybin, the other, the amanita, has some other crazy shit."

"Yeah, we've read about the amanita. How much do we owe you?"

"Two hundred and fifty bucks." The judge's son looked at Harlow with his cool, blue, bloodshot eyes. "Yeah, that amanita shit is strong as the devil."

She left him in the hall to get the money and came back. "Thank you. Let us know if you get the amanita. We really appreciate it."

"Will do!" He turned and as he was turning said, "And let me know how that project gets on."

"Yeah, you bet." Sylvia shut the door, and they all convened in one of the sitting rooms, just off the entrance hall. Harlow emptied the contents onto the coffee table. The caps were tiny, golden and wrinkled like wizened nuts; soft to the touch with little nipples at the top on thin, delicate stems. Sylvia bent down to sniff them. The mushrooms had a sweet, acrid scent, reminiscent of walnuts.

"They're beautiful." Aurora touched one lightly.

"I read on the internet you can put them in honey."

"Yes, and the honey has to sit for at least a month to draw the psilocybin out."

"You have to get it into tiny pieces, preferably with a coffee grinder." Sylvia's eyes were cool as ice. "That will give us time to decide what we're going to do." In the kitchen, they put the mushrooms in the grinder; divided the dust between two jars of honey, stirring the opaque, sappy substance until it had devoured every shred of mushroom, then stashed the jars away — high on a shelf in the pantry — to infuse. Thankfully, with the mushrooms stored away, suspended in honey, blackening as they released their psychotropic chemicals into the sweet amber syrup, the girls had put aside the folly of flying to the Amazon to look for the Asháninka tribe and take ayahuasca. The trip to Amsterdam for magic mushrooms was also completely forgotten.

Madison thrived on the power their music making gave them. However, she wanted more. She wanted witchery. She had tasted blood and wanted to swim in it. Time and time again, her mind turned to the act of sorcery. She wanted it now. She thought they should try something innocuous, like calling a storm, and brought to their attention *De lamiis liber: item de commentitiis jejuniis* (or *The Book on Witches*) written in 1577 by the Dutch physician and demonologist Johann Weyer (aka Wierus). Witches were said to bring rain "by casting flint stones behind their backs towards the west, or flinging a little sand into the air, or striking a river with a broom and so sprinkling the wet of it towards heaven, stirring water with the finger in a hole in the ground, or boiling hogs' bristles in a pot".

The girls had read accounts by other folklorists with similar instructions, involving brooms made of heather to flick water; stir cauldrons. Harlow was immediately on board, suggesting they form a circle in the forest, sing to the elements of thunder and lightning, dance, play their instruments, fling sand into the air, throw flint stones behind their backs in a westerly direction.

Still haunted by the sensation of the entity from the mirror slinking around her, breathing on her neck, tangling its claws in her hair — for the first time Aurora voiced caution. "Messing with one entity from the Unseen Realm like Sylvia and I did is dangerous — here you're speaking of two or more. We don't know the will of these gods or spirits. I mean, even though our practice is dedicated to the Light, you can never avoid the Dark. So, there's always a chance of being sucked to the dark side. I'm not sure we're ready." As soon as the words had left her mouth, Aurora regretted them. No one wanted to hear words of caution. The chill was palpable. She was a buzz kill.

Madison slumped slightly and tilted her head. Everyone sat in their positions until Madison came alive again and uttered, "Whatever doesn't kill you makes you stronger". Widening her eyes, she declared: "There are things we need to know, that we may have to risk dying for".

Everyone agreed, even Aurora. There were things worth dying for.

Sylvia, holding an unlit cigarette, flipped her Zippo lighter open and observed, "What's that Hemingway quote? 'The world breaks everyone and afterward many are strong at the broken places. But those that will not break it kills.'"

Several weeks later, they held a convocation in the nearby woods at the river's edge, with the intention of calling a storm. Madison was, in the end, victorious. Aurora's notes of caution were reflected upon by each of them, silently, creeping into their inner dialogues but never brought to the light of day. To do so would be to hex the group and their endeavor. They pushed all doubt back into the dark recesses, where they had faith it would be smothered. A new mood swept over the group. *With sorcery, as everyone knows, there is no stopping it.* Impossible to rein in the axe after it's been thrown: all one can do is hold on and feel the impact. The five were becoming intimate with the far side of themselves. They had glowed in the dark and they wanted more. What had come slowly and carefully, at first, was now bursting, accelerating, creating friction and sparks. Aurora felt the full force of their determination and knew no actions or words she could offer would deter them.

Madison ordered heather from the Scottish Highlands to make brooms. The day before the ceremony to call the storm, the five sat in a circle in the attic and wove the heather — singing a cappella as they worked, with Harlow beatboxing. Light fell in on them at angles through the dormer windows, arms and fingers busy — the air, their bodies, vibrating; humming with their songs. Aurora hadn't changed her mind about the danger and foolhardiness of invoking the elementals but sat and sang and wove her broom with the others, fighting back any misgivings she had. She had to sacrifice herself for the good of the whole.

The five went out four hours before dawn on a clear night. The stars glittered; the moon cast a mercury glow over the forest. Dressed in floor length mink and arctic fox fur coats Sylvia had stolen from her mother's closet, they followed a well-trodden path through the trees — their lamps making soft, moving orbs of light, the clouds of their breath illuminated faintly above them; their Airwalk moon boots marching over the packed ground, crunching through the snow.

Dora wore a faux fur wolf head hat, Harlow, a faux bear head hat, Madison a helmet with horns over a wool beanie, Sylvia a raccoon hat, Aurora a trapper cap with Dinky nestled into the nape of her neck, their hair loose, walking single file, wearing backpacks with their brooms and supplies. In each mittened hand, they carried a lantern. Faces painted with menstrual blood — the vital fluid that bound them to Nature like tides to the moon — they reasoned the blood of their fertility was like the song that calls to the shark in the deep ocean. The forces of Nature were predatory as well as life-giving and nurturing. This sentiment was echoed in *The Golden Bough*, where the high priest of Cybele cuts his arms, offering his blood, after which his assistants whirl about him, wrapped in a frenzy of ecstasy, slashing their bodies with potsherds and knives "in order to bespatter the altar and the sacred tree with their flowing blood".

Veering off the icy, well-trodden path in the woods and into the deep powdery snow, they found the tracks they'd left the day before, marching under glittering ice-encrusted branches and icicles. Kicking their way through the snowfall they came to the place where they'd carved out a circle with a fire pit at its center, filled with logs and kindling on top, ready to be set alight. Not far off, the river crept through the wood, shimmering, catching the moonlight, throwing it out into the night. The pit walls they'd dug had hardened; everything glistened in the monochrome light. Bare tree branches sheathed in ice seesawed in the wind. The girls placed their lanterns on top of the raised snow shelf, making a wheel of light, then went to work on the bonfire.

Sylvia was the last to arrive at the altar pit, her Bolex and D.A.T recorder slung over her shoulder. She wanted footage of people performing occult rituals to add to her video collage for her final art project. The thought occurred to her that filming would turn what they were doing from ritual to spectacle and nothing would happen. Sylvia left her backpack with the others, took her video and audio recording equipment, and retraced their steps through the snow, into the thick wood, so that she could film an approach to the scene.

With only eighteen minutes on a roll of film, if she couldn't reload the camera in the sub-zero conditions, eighteen minutes would be all she had of this night. She might be able to reload next to the fire. Despite her mittens, she managed to turn the camera on, panning the forest skyline with stars. She took wide shots and close-ups of an icicle with other icicles in the background, seeming to glow. She moved forward, doing her best to give the impression of a disembodied eye floating through the dark forest, between the pines, in the blue light of the full moon. The forest was the main character. It was the most important thing. Everything that played out within it was like the forest dreaming, thinking, bringing thought to fruition.

Coasting along, Sylvia captured the thread-like rays of bonfire light scattered through the tangle of branches. The girls were singing. She checked again to make sure her audio recorder was on. It was. It had been recording from the beginning. Following the filaments of light through the dark silhouettes of the trees, a cocoon of light emerged with the naked, dancing young women inside it. They were miniature in that drop of light — in the belly of the forest — growing larger as Sylvia approached through the snow.

Drawn to the bonfire like a moth to a flame. This is what she wanted the eye of the camera to evoke. A moth. In the cold, the camera seemed to move by itself, breaking the line of action as she turned around the scene, closer and closer, swooping around the naked dancing bodies — Dinky rushing and diving through the air above them, the hot and cold currents under her wings. Flame and shadow — a feverish, wet sheen illuminating their skin; a slow, fertile nightmare and dream, elucidated little by little. Sylvia let the camera drop into the snow, and took off her clothes.

Dancing in a circle, agile and slippery as eels in the ocean, the five girls passed through into the mouth of the Beyond. Visions of twinning serpents, a vibrating hoop, a gyrating wheel — the ouroboros — spun through their heads. Breaking free of one another, they continued to dance in their own orbits within the circle, round and round, leaping into arabesques, spinning in a frenzy of nimble movements, amid a meteoric bombardment of atoms falling grain by grain, the bloodied faces of the girls, tearing through the soldered air.

With dawn, the forest was bathed in a pink glow. Their fire now reduced to embers, the girls began to turn blue, their bodies scattered in the snow, thrown out of the enthrallment. Illuminated branches frozen in ice made clicking sounds in the wind. Grains of snow hissed, swept across the frozen crust.

They had not called a storm. Nothing had happened. What they did not know, however, was that they had attracted the attention of maenads who were hiding and watching. Huddled behind trees and boulders, dressed in fawn skins, ivy wreaths around their heads, some with bull helmets in honor of their god, others wearing snakes, their long sticks wrapped in ivy tipped with pinecones in the grip of their hands. Peeking out from their hiding places they watched the five dance in the wheel of lantern light around the bonfire. Intrigued by the rite, the maenads did not rush to rip them apart, but instead became bewitched, stock still; the snakes winding around their arms and up and down their bodies, waving their heads, tasting the air with their tongues. When they had seen enough, they disappeared back into the heavy mist, returning to the world from whence they had come, where they would continue on their way, racing through the forest, pursuing Dionysus, killing every animal in sight.

"We've got to get up." Raising her head, Sylvia made an attempt to mobilize the blue bodies bathed in pink light, thrown about on the snow, the bitter, cutting wind slashing their bodies.

Dora responded, barely moving her lips. "We're going to freeze to death." Her eyebrows and eyelashes were crusted with ice.

Aurora lay in the snow, Madison beside her, her outstretched arm crossing Aurora's ankle. Not feeling her body, gazing at the pink and blue sky, the soft clouds, Aurora thought she might like to go to sleep forever there. Madison wanted to speak but found she could not move her lips, shifting her eyes to gaze in shock at her naked body, a violet blue. Before all this, before this moment, the girls had thought themselves immortal. Now they saw death, tasted it, felt it creeping in, numb, with the colors of a bruise.

Not far from Harlow the emergency foil blankets gleamed in the sun. She pulled herself across the burning snow toward one of them and managed to wrap it around herself. Later, she would not know how she got to her feet — which, by now, were nothing more than numb stumps — gather the rest of the blankets, bundle up each girl, and start the fire again. She took the girls one by one and rolled them to the fire, making a pile as best she could, then lay on top of them until their naked bodies began to thaw. Dinky appeared from an abandoned nest in the hollow of a nearby oak, hopping over their bodies covered in foil, flitting around them in the heat.

The fire and each other's body heat warmed them enough to untangle themselves, get up and grab their furs. They shoved their numb feet through thermal underwear bottoms, into moon boots, picked their backpacks up from the ground, left the lanterns and trudged back through the deep snow. Battered, their heads like meat staked with ice picks, they marched on.

They had overestimated themselves. The next day, the five cut their hands and made a blood pact forbidding the invocation of elementals or entities, until they had a guide and protector. They all agreed they would perform rituals to call for this guide — but that was all.

Harlow decided it was a good time to perform a purification ritual. Her mother had been nagging her about it. Even though the house had undergone a purification by the Buddhist monks before they moved in, regular cleansings needed to be carried out. Harlow had been taught how to cleanse spaces by her mother, who had learned it from someone who had learned it from a member of the La Jolla Band of Luiseño Indians who used sage. However, because Harlow and her mother were not indigenous people and sage was becoming rare, out of respect, it was improper to use the herb. Instead, they would use lavender.

Gathered in the attic — dressed in flowing silk white robes they ordered on the internet, daisy chains in their hair — Harlow explained how they had to let the lavender do its thing without standing in its way. Work with it, get to know it. Become an empty vessel to receive its power. There were countless ways to do this, but she was going to do it the way her mother taught her. Harlow got everyone to repeat the words, gestures and song until she felt they were ready to perform the ritual for real. I will not divulge details of the ceremony here.

Afterward, in the haze of lavender smoke, they all joined hands. Instead of closing the ceremony — still in a trance state — Harlow was taken in another direction, remotely aware she was moving into territory unknown to her and began, "We gather here today as a sisterhood," moving the group in a deosil — clockwise — circular motion, "To advance in the sacred arts, to use whatever power we gain for good". The five girls sped up, dancing round and round, chanting the line that had come to Harlow on the spot, faster and faster, until they became a blurry vortex.

Twirling, spinning, whirling — they became sleepy. Their eyes darted back and forth behind their eyelids. The five passed into a state that mimics REM sleep, but with the signal reversed — an operation which leads to hallucinations or visions, forms of waking or lucid dreams. As the circle gyrated, they were flung into the dimension of visionaries and mystics.

The five girls found themselves alone, in a wilderness, their bodies strewn haphazardly, as though they had been dropped from the sky. The air was cool and humid, fragrant with woodland scents. Birds chattered in the trees and brush amongst the rustling of forest creatures. Sunlight streamed through the trees, awakening them into this waking dream.

Aurora came to with her body draped on a tree limb and slipped, breaking through cracking branches, cutting and bruising herself all the way down, until she dropped to the moss-covered ground with a thump. Dazed, head aching, she sat up. She found she was under a very large, old oak, its leaves shimmering in the golden light. The forest floor was cool and damp. Beyond the perimeter of the oak lay a forest. She got to her feet, brushed herself off, neglecting the leaves that had attached themselves to her hair, and scanned the area for paths.

"Hello!" Dora called out.

"Yes! It's Harlow!"

"It's Madison! I'm over here!"

"Over here!" Aurora called out with hands cupped around her mouth, then stood still and waited. The girls continued to call out, but never found one another. Instead, they each met someone else.

Dora awoke in a sunlit meadow with poppies swaying above her, mesmerized by the floating orb-like shapes in pale shimmering pink, translucent peach, lilac electric blue and vibrant, glowing red. Colors had never been so alive. The flowers shook in the breeze overhead with the sun's rays spraying down like diamonds from an impossibly blue sky.

She sat up, her hands pressed to the weedy ground, the damp tang of earth mixing with the honeyed scents of grasses and flowers. Ants crawled up her legs, into her underwear, biting her so that she jumped up, frantically brushing them off, stomping her feet and ran through the tall grasses and general verdure teeming with all kinds of insects clinging to the grass and flower stalks, jumping, flying, pollinating. Tiny crickets sprang from the undergrowth, flying in hordes in all directions.

The meadow was surrounded by forest. At the Waldorf she had learned orienteering. Theoretically, she knew what to do in this kind of situation. She had often thought about the day something like this might happen and had looked upon it with terror. This was the first time she'd been by herself, out there alone — for real. Once she got out of the meadow, she thought she'd look for something to use as a marker to flag trees, bushes, and rocks. Wading through the field, the sticky, stringy plant caught up in her shoes. Butterflies darted over the meadow.

"Hello!" Dora called out, cupping her hands to her mouth. Harlow, then Madison, and finally Aurora returned her call. She did not hear Sylvia. They were there somewhere, but she couldn't make out what direction their voices had come from. Kicking her way through the tall stalks of grass — the metallic sounds of insects in her ears — she called again. This time, only Harlow answered. The voice seemed as though it came from the sky, as if there was a dome above her with Harlow calling from the other side. She continued walking, leaving a trampled path.

From out of nowhere, like a heatwave mirage, there in the wildflowers stood a maiden with a bow and quiver, a fawn at her side. Next to her was a man with the head of a lion and the wings of an angel folded behind his back. A snake wrapped itself around the man's naked torso, its tongue slithering in and out to taste the air. The two beings with the fawn were more real than anything she had ever laid eyes on, and were radiating something — a force, a light. She wanted to ask them who they were but didn't dare. Then everything went blank.

Aurora found herself by a brook in the wood. She sat up in the pine needles, then rose and walked to the water's edge, crouching down. There were rocks below the surface with rainbow scaled fish shuttling downstream through crystalline water. Diamond reflections of light sprayed across her face. On the other side were more trees. She was in the middle of a dense forest. At the back of her neck, she felt a presence and turned. The doe appeared first, then Diana with her bow. Aurora knew the goddess straight away, there was a voice inside her who told her it was so. With Diana was a man, a god, Aion. The god they'd seen the statue of in the Louvre, come to life, with his lion's head and the wings of a bird folded, gleaming like a shield, held up behind him. A snake wrapped itself around his body, like a pet. He held a ring with two keys. In her mind's eye flashed an orb and the symbol for eternity. Aurora knelt before them. Diana instructed her to rise with a clear, firm voice, then raised her arm, turning her wrist in a circular motion,

I spin, I spin, around, around
And close my eyes

AURORA

And let the bile arise
From the sacred region of the Souls' Profound
Then gaze upon the world; how strange how new!
The earth and heaven are one
The horizon line is gone
The sky how green!
The land how fair and blue
Perplexing items fade from my large view
And thought which vexed me with its false and true
Is swallowed up in Intuition; this
    This is the sole true mode
    Of reaching God[23].

After this, everything went black. Aurora awoke back in the attic room on her side with one arm outstretched, the other bent over her head. She lay like this, not moving, hair spilt across her face, shining in the last rays of sun, eyes illuminated, glowing, searching for something to hold on to. Everything she saw from that angle in the attic room was recognizable, but remote, as if it were all a remembered dream, and where she had just come from was the true reality.

Meanwhile, on the other side — in the realm of the Unseen — Madison landed in a bush in the fragrant, black dirt, scratches all over, leaves in her hair, and fought her way out of the tangle. When she emerged from the brambles, she found herself in a grove of birch and walked through the fractured sunlight, dust motes floating dreamily from the canopies to the forest floor. She heard Dora call out,

23. Dowden, Edward, "The Secret of the Universe" (1843–1913)

then heard Harlow answer. Another cry came from further away. She couldn't make out who it was. They were here — somewhere. She had to keep walking. "Hellll-ooooo!" she bellowed, then stopped to listen. A fawn appeared between the stand of birch, then a man with a lion's head, and a woman. Upon sight of them, Madison was struck with terror, wonder. They took her breath away. Where was she? What was this place? Although it looked like earth, it did not feel like earth, and in fact it felt more real than any place she had ever known. Shortly after, everything went black. Madison came to in the attic room, her cheek to the floorboards.

The five girls came to in a broken circle where they had fallen to the floor — one here, another there; wrists over ankles, arms over legs — with the sensation they had been far, far away on a long journey and returned. One by one, they sat up and stared drowsily at their surroundings. Dora was the first to speak. "What just happened?"

"That was far out." Madison stared ahead, dazed.

"I think we've been initiated." Sylvia's eyes blazed.

Harlow and Sylvia had also encountered the doe, the goddess and the god. Diana had spoken to them, but they couldn't remember what she had said.

With Harlow leading them, the five had stumbled into a technique used by the ancients to pierce through into the Unseen plane of vision, where they encountered Diana and the lion-headed god Aurora and Sylvia had seen a statue of in the Louvre. This was monumental, although something they would not repeat straight away.

They returned to earth, as it were, with burning questions: what did it all mean; how to proceed from there? They had broken their pact — venturing into the Unseen world — yet they had done it unwittingly. Perhaps this meant they were ready? Had the world called to them, or had they simply fallen through by chance?

Sylvia typed the lion-headed god's name into the Internet, which came up with:

Aion (Greek: Αἰών) is a Hellenistic deity associated with time, the orb or circle encompassing the universe, and the zodiac.

The "time" which Aion represents is perpetual, unbounded, ritual, and cyclical: The future is a returning version of the past, later called *aevum* (see Vedic Sanskrit *Rtú*). This kind of time contrasts with empirical, linear, progressive, and historical time that Chronos represented, which divides into past, present, and future.

In the latter part of the Classical era, he became associated with mystery religions concerned with the afterlife, such as the mysteries of Cybele, the Dionysian mysteries, Orphic religion, and the Mithraic mysteries. In Latin, the concept of the deity may appear as Aeternitas, Anna Perenna, or Saeculum. He is typically in the company of an earth or mother goddess such as Tellus or Cybele, as on the Parabiago plate.[24]

24. Aion (deity), From Wikipedia, the free encyclopedia

The girls went to the library for further information and found a photograph of the statuette in the Louvre. Dora made a photocopy of the image and sent it to an online company that made three-dimensional sculptures from photos of people's pets. They hadn't ever done anything like Aion before, but he did have a lion head, so they agreed and provided them with a decent representation in bronze, to sit beside Harlow's Saint-Gaudens Diana statue on the newly made altar they'd set up in the attic. As the months passed, they continued to process their experience, making sketches and writing about the experience, composing songs for their band, which they decided to call Trashfire Carnival, in reference to Terrence McKenna's belief that modern society was headed for ruin and ecocide if it continued on its present path.

Running on her own through the forest in the predawn (Sylvia no longer accompanied her) Aurora was followed by a pack of boys. Catcalling and leering, they reminded her of the men with the goat in the trailer park, just before she left for the Academy. When she turned her head to look at them, they also called to mind the pastors with their wild, frenzied eyes – their hunger and contempt. Aurora ran. Her heart beat in her throat. Blood boomed in her ears. Without thinking, she invoked Diana and Aion to come to her aid.

In that liminal cavity, shifting from darkness to first-light, the membrane between worlds was thin enough that the elementals who possessed Aurora were able to lure the god and goddess through the mist and set them on the boys, with the purpose of amusing themselves, watching the spectacle unfold.

The sound and vibration of the boys' voices in the air and feet on the ground behind Aurora disappeared. All went quiet. She turned, and in place of their running, taunting forms echoing off the trees and ice she saw rabbits, bounding in a group, one by one scampering off into the undergrowth.

The goddess turned the boys to rabbits for forty-eight hours. They tore through the brush with terror in their chests, just enough to keep them going — below the threshold that would make their hearts explode, as rabbit hearts are known to do in the face of terrifying circumstances. Forty-eight hours was a rabbit lifetime from their perspectives, thanks to Aion. The boys had no recollection of their transformation when they found themselves in the forest, dirty, covered in excrement. Their exposed skin was cracked, red and wind-whipped, peeling off; their shoes gone, their clothing torn; one of them frostbitten, resulting in the amputation of a finger. The boys remembered nothing, were never the same, and never bothered Aurora again.

Of course, Aurora had reason to be afraid. Everyone on campus knew there were boys among them who hid the hearts of demons. There were rumours of savagery, rape, gang rape. When some of them got drunk, they could turn into beasts. The identities of the boys who had committed these monstrosities could never be pinned down for certain. Different names got thrown around. X and his friend might have bragged they'd had a threesome with Y and gone into detail about what she had done to them and what they had done to her. People would whisper and mark her as a slut. When asked, Y would say it was all lies out of fear and shame. No act of violence was never officially confirmed by the Academy. The administration had their own police. They did their own investigations. It was always hush-hush. Boys were never expelled. Lawyers came secretly. Girl Y, who was accused of being a slut and taking on two or three guys at once, might leave the institution, never to be seen or heard from again. There might be rumours she was sent to an elite school in Scotland or Switzerland where she was rubbing shoulders with European aristocrats and royalty and had picked up an accent.

The secrecy of women's powers, hidden deep within them — the magic of propagation, the conception of a life, this act of sovereignty — mystifies and terrifies men, even though they are part of the equation. Like womankind itself, it is an intricate, disturbing, impenetrable mystery that no one can escape. There isn't anyone alive who hasn't been inside a womb, cradled in this underworld where a little glob of fertilized flesh incubates and grows into a fully formed being. Men cannot hatch a new life from inside themselves or nourish it with the milk of their bodies, unless of course, they were at one point a biological woman. When faced with someone who can, biological men are beguiled — scared stiff. This incredible power will never cease to amaze them. From terror, violence often arises, foolishly thinking it is just, and can be contained.

When Aurora arrived home from her run, shaken, the dangers she faced pulsating in her veins, dangers which even seemed a part of her, of her physicality, she ran into Dora and Dinky on the stairs.

Dora knew something had happened. She felt Aurora vibrating with it, "Are you okay?"

Aurora told her about the boys who had been chasing her in the wood, and then disappeared into thin air.

"Maybe you're in shock. Are you sure you didn't black out or anything?"

"I don't think so. I panicked, kept running, then I couldn't hear them anymore. I turned around and saw rabbits. I feel like I'm losing my mind."

"Did you recognize any of them?"

"No, I don't think so."

Dora hesitated, resting her hand on the banister, "My freshman year, I drank too much at a party. I passed out, woke up and a guy was pulling my skirt down. Somehow, I hit him with a lamp and ran."

"That's horrific. Who did that to you?"

"I can't even remember his face. I think I blocked it out. He called me a nigger. East Coast preppy hick. Probably inbred. Fuck him." She paused, then said, "I thought I saw him once, but couldn't be sure".

The grandfather clock in the hall chimed the hour.

"Fuck those assholes."

Dora continued down the stairs. "Stay safe."

"You too."

Aurora kept on up the stairs, Dinky flitting in the air around her, sensing something was wrong.

The girls began work on art projects in line with their occult surrealist visions. Sylvia made film clips inspired by Tarkovsky. She also wanted to evoke the moods and atmospheres of Leonora Carrington and Remedios Varo's paintings. Aiming to embrace the abstract in long takes, she worked on building viewer immersion with sound design to mirror the inner workings of the characters, to construct personas through action that would create a mounting pressure in the scene before cutting it. Sylvia sought to do the impossible — to fuse what cannot be fused entirely: a spiritual and corporeal synthesis. She wanted to capture the unity of nothing less than the cosmos, like in Varos's *Papilla Estelar*, in which a woman spoon-feeds ground stardust to a caged crescent moon.

Dora aimed to be the next Niki de Saint Phalle. She loved the aritst's *tires* series with the violent splashes of paint that dripped over clusters of mundane found objects and de Saint Phalle's shooting paintings but thought her sculptures were tacky and grotesque. Dora was in the process of making a mold for a larger-than-life-sized statue of a goddess with moose antlers — her body adorned with ritual scars — brandishing a crossbow, in the midst of battle. She was working on finding a source of osmium – one the toughest metals known to humankind. Once it had been poured and hardened she would shoot the sculpture with an M-16, Kalashnikov, and/or a sawed-off shotgun.

Madison and Harlow turned primarily to wheat pasting, a direct-action guerrilla art form used to communicate with the masses. They'd seen a documentary on the subject and decided to get involved. Wheat pasting enabled them to deploy nuanced, complex messages at numerous locations with minimal effort and risk, as opposed to straightforward graffiti, which they'd dabbled in here and there, but which required a lot of stealth. They'd come close to getting caught by campus security and off campus police on several occasions. Taking cues from the Situationists, they made absurd, fantastical maps, collages with famous people's faces, spray-painting things like FINISH YOUR HOMEWORK. REVISE FOR EXAMS. DO AS YOU'RE TOLD. DIE. or, THE EYE CAN BLOW A FUSE AT ANY TIME. or, AION FOREVER! on the Academy's brick and concrete walls. Anywhere they could, they pasted images of Diana and Aion with mazes behind them. They had stickers made, which they stuck everywhere — on bathroom walls, the backs of chairs, the drinks machines in the cafeteria, lampposts. The administration was actively seeking the perpetrators. No one turned them in, even though their celebrity was in the process of becoming an all-consuming monster.

The Californians, along with Sylvia and Aurora, had a certain amount of notoriety before they began their group. The Californians, being obviously from California in their manner, accent and dress, with their penchant for throwing wild parties, got themselves noticed quickly. From the beginning, Sylvia's reputation had preceded her. Aurora's name had been made through her association with Sylvia. Now that they had joined forces, were suspected of witchcraft, of defacing campus property with cryptic, absurd images and slogans, they were on their way to superstardom, hated and admired, dissected and venerated, at the top of the list in the little Black Book and in everyone's mind as among the most coveted girls on campus, their fans imagining them while they masturbated. (This is one of the unfortunate prices of fame one does not often consider.)

Aurora's contribution to the fine arts vein of their surrealist occult movement took shape in the school's art studio, where she worked on a five-by-twelve feet rectangular board set on the ground. She used oil and acrylic paint mixed with dust from the floor. Entitled *The Life You Save Could Be Mine*, the painting was inspired by the death of James Dean and the string of violence associated with the car that killed him.

In an interview just before his death, Dean appeared nervous and at one point blundered his lines, changing the popular saying, "The life you save could be your own" with "The life you save could be mine", as part of a public service announcement on road safety. Not long after, in September 1955, Dean was killed in a horrific car accident while driving his Porsche Spyder, which he'd named Little Bastard. Many believed the car was cursed.

When Little Bastard was towed away from the scene of Dean's death and taken to a garage, the engine slipped out and fell onto a mechanic, shattering both of his legs. Eventually, the engine was bought by a doctor, who put it into his racing car and was nearly killed when the car flipped over during a race. Another driver in the same race, who had Little Bastard's driveshaft fitted to his car, crashed and died. When the Porsche was being repaired, the garage it sat in was destroyed by fire, along with all the vehicles inside — except for Little Bastard.

Later, the car was displayed in Sacramento but fell off its mount and broke a teenager's hip. A driver who was hauling Little Bastard on a flatbed truck was killed instantly when the Porsche fell on him after he was thrown from his truck in a road accident. The mishaps surrounding the car continued until 1960, when the Porsche wreckage, en route to Los Angeles on another truck, mysteriously vanished. (To this day, Little Bastard's whereabouts are unknown.)

Aurora stood in front of the painting contemplating the horrifying and bloodthirsty chain of events as she worked, face to face with incidents that seemed to defy reason. Her mind ticked with questions wrapped up in ideas of the individual, coincidence, malicious forces in the universe. The painting put its claws in her, threatening to rip out her beating heart with its explosions and torpedoes of paint splattered against multi-layered backgrounds — gauze and sunsets, blue-green twilight skies — where pieces of broken sunglasses, aspirin, a tuft of blonde hair like a tumbleweed, sat in coagulating blobs of crimson oil paint; here a page ripped out from a road map, pieces of an address book, a comet-like blaze shooting across the centre. This was what she had so far. It needed more objects epoxied to it and she wanted to paint ladders and crosses to symbolize the passing from life to death and death to life. In her more indulgent, asinine moments, she fantasized about performing a ritual to make the painting into a vehicle and a weapon, drawing Little Bastard's spirit into the canvas like a genie to a lamp, then burning it to rid the world of the evil entity. If something like this was even possible. It went against everything she had been trying to communicate to the four others and sounded like something Sylvia and Madison would want to try. Aurora remembered something Sylvia said that had stuck with her, something she read out of her notebook from H.P. Lovecraft: *The process of delving into the black abyss is to me the keenest form of fascination.* Even Aurora was not immune to the pull. *With sorcery, as everyone knows, there is no stopping it.*

Aurora spent more and more time by herself in the library. She found a documentary entitled *The Corporation.* She learned that modern day money was made by federal banks out of thin air. Private, elite groups had power over these global federal reserves. Even the American Federal Reserve wasn't owned by the government, despite what the name implied. Because money was now untethered from the gold standard, debt had become valuable, a commodity. It created more money. When someone took out a loan, this wasn't backed by anything, more money was simply willed out of nothing, numbers added to a balance sheet in a computer. The entire system was built on faith and manipulation. In short, it was fragile – a gigantic pyramid scheme. It was insane. There was nothing rational about it. The entire world was fuelled by money that groups of wealthy, powerful men were creating out of nothing and then charging interest on. It was obscene. The other girls didn't care about finance. They didn't know they were sitting on a ticking time bomb. Even Aurora could see this wasn't sustainable. Aurora wasn't going to be the one to tell them. She felt like robbing a bank.

Aurora had tried to assimilate, to take note of everything the others said, the details of their gilded realms, to drop names like they did, to wear lip gloss, the voice in her head repeating, *Know how to be all things to all people. A discreet Proteus — a scholar among scholars, a saint among saints. That is the art of winning over everyone, for like attracts like... In your affairs, create suspense. Admiration at their novelty means respect for your success. It's neither useful nor pleasurable to show all your cards. Not immediately revealing everything fuels anticipation, especially when a person's elevated position means expectations are greater...*

Despite all this, the creeping feeling she would never truly be accepted tightened around her heart and gut like a snare. She thought she could hear their whispers in the ventilation shafts, echoing from the vent cage in her bedroom: *Aurora...Her bird shits all over the place, it's disgusting...Aurora...She never contributes...She keeps missing our band rehearsals...She uses all our stuff, eats all our food, we always pay for her...Aurora...She's vampiric!...I can hear her talking in her sleep, saying crazy shit...I think she's been stealing my razors...She's so fucking annoying...* The words came in drips like water torture, interrupting her reading, her sleep, gushing through the room, bouncing off the tiles in the bathroom when she was taking a bath. What was she saying in her sleep? Did they know she was trailer trash? She burned with shame. She told herself their money was artificial. One day it was going to come crashing down like a house of cards. Their upbringings were fake. They were circling the drain. They didn't know what really mattered. Their money wasn't the squeaky-clean bath they thought it was. It had corrupted them. Made them weak. She wasn't the dirty one. She was a survivor. She stood in front of the bathroom mirror trying a new look with gold eyeshadow, fingering the dust just past her eyebrow, down the corner of her eye, then took a brush and outlined everything in black. *Fuck them...fuck them...fuck them...*she screamed inside. The eyeshadow made her look insane and hideous.

One evening, Harlow, waving a burning lavender bundle in the air during one of their fireside occult sessions, mused, "When are we ever going to have mushroom tea and make music?"

"I don't know, like right now?" Madison took a sip of wine.

The honey came out. Tea was made. Careful not to boil the water which would spoil the psilocybin, they added black tea to the teapot. After waiting for it to brew, the tea was poured into delicate cups decorated with peonies, pastel colors and butterflies, part of a Wedgwood afternoon tea set that had come with the house and sat in a cupboard behind glass. They went into the den where their instruments and microphones were set up.

After about forty minutes, the walls began to breathe. Harlow noted that her violin was also breathing. Madison could not take her eyes from a framed poster of Leonora Carrington's *And Then We Saw the Daughter of the Minotaur* they had hung in the room to inspire them, the figures now alive, the colors changing rapidly, clouds in the image moving as if pushed by wind across the plains. The daughter of the Minotaur grew and opened her mouth, but no sound came out. Madison felt she was being attacked by paranoia and time itself.

Harlow's violin slid between her legs, hitting the floor with a twang and a bump. She was overtaken by waves of nausea and sleep, dropping to her knees and then all fours, crawling out of the room, up the stairs and to her bed — a monumental achievement, through a melting, writhing universe — where she pressed her face into the pillow and clawed at her hair, convinced she was hearing ghosts slipping into her room from the floors below.

Dora's trip took a distinct sine-wave form with periods of extreme euphoria and an opiate-like body feeling. She didn't want to play music, much less listen to it. The idea of being in music's thrall terrified her. After a euphoric peak came a fit of terror, which was then followed by a sense of "This is it..." Her body felt like it was dying. She was in the throes of death. She forgot she'd drunk the mushroom tea, then realized that she hadn't forgotten, it just somehow ceased being relevant. She knew she was on her way to being eternally insane. She had superhuman powers. More and more twisted thoughts rallied around her, including the idea that what she was experiencing was Logos, somewhere between Terrence McKenna's and Aristotle's conception; that the entire logic and balance of the universe, the thing which binds matter together, the process of organization into hierarchies, this Logos, which has complete knowledge of the individual, was communicating the entire history of genetic information, the entire history of the universe and beyond, and that, being under the influence of psychedelics, she was able to experience this on an intimate level. In the future, she thought, humankind will master these realms, apply engineering and science to these inner worlds, which are currently the most mysterious thing we are capable of exploring, probably more so than space which we can only explore to the extent that we are still dependent on combustible fuel. But ultimately, she kept coming back to the realization that, IN THE END, NOTHING MATTERS AND NOW I HAVE BECOME A GOD AND WILL DIE SOON! In spite of this insanity, Dora had a grain of reason left inside her, shining brightly, telling her to stay as still and as silent as possible, that that would be the best way out. At one point, she focused on the words of bell hooks to keep her from completely unravelling: "Action, like a sacrament, is the visible form of an invisible spirit, an outward manifestation of an inward power."

Sylvia saw what she could only describe as a slot machine, infinitely long and tall, that adjusted in perspective according to the position her head took. Where the symbols should have been were pictures of herself in different emotional and physical states. The picture in the center of her range of vision was the emotion she felt fully, but the slot machine was circling at such an alarming rate she felt what she estimated to be ten emotions every second. Her facial muscles worked to accommodate each emotion, and she felt herself losing control of her face. This was followed by extreme pain, then euphoria for a millisecond each. She realized, to her horror, that she was experiencing everything at once. Finally, the slot machine rested on a single face: Madness. It was a picture of herself in green, clawing at her eyes. She then realized what was going to happen: When the machine adds the sum total of all she has been, she will be defined, and she will die.

Sylvia: This is awful.

Aurora: I know.

Sylvia: I need to forget all of this. (She starts to cry.)

Aurora: We poisoned ourselves, we just need to sleep, and when we wake up, it'll be like nothing ever happened.

Sylvia: I am going to die. Call 911, right now.

The marvellous befalls only those who sacrifice to its cult.[25] They had underestimated the mushrooms. When Madison came to, she was in an ambulance. She was told she had been Tasered by a policeman after crossing a traffic intersection. She had left the house in a state of

25. Jacqueline Chénieux-Gendron

undress under the auspices of the daughter of the Minotaur who sent a moth-like creature to guide her through the labyrinth, naked and unafraid, in search of the truth. On Madison's head she placed a crown, which was actually a tiny galaxy — a complete cosmos in miniature — in which gossamer clouds of a blue-white material floated upward, anchored by a small glowing orb in the centre. Madison had walked into town where she had tried to get into several people's cars as they pulled out of a gas station. She had then had gone into the station and opened cans of beer, pouring them over her head, ripping packets of chips and beef jerky from their places near the cash register. After this she ran out into an intersection where the police couldn't contain her.

At the hospital, Madison was diagnosed with a brain haemorrhage, a fractured nasal bone, a bruised rib, and lacerations all over her feet and body. For two days she was in the ICU and spent another four there altogether. The doctors were close to having to drill into her head to relieve the pressure, but thankfully did not have to do this, so that she survived without any enduring injuries. This was, of course, a scandal at the school. No one, however, could prove the episode was drug related. Madison was seen by a psychologist, who determined she'd had a psychotic break and needed to be monitored. Madison's mother arrived after two days. She was vacationing in a private island spa retreat, undergoing an intensive program.

Madison wasn't happy to see her mother. She'd been desperate to get away from her parents. It had been her idea to go to a prep school in New England. She wondered how it was even possible she'd come from her mother and father and nearly convinced herself she'd been adopted. What her mother looked like underneath all the spray tan and makeup was mostly a mystery. She'd once caught a glimpse of her sickly face without it. The visage was just as horrifying as when it was painted. The unmade-up face made Madison think of the harpies from ancient Greece she'd learned about in school whose description fitted her mother to a T: repulsive little half human, birdlike creatures with anaemic, pale faces from starving themselves, who carry with them foul odours and contaminate everything they come into contact with. How she had been born from the womb of this harpy was incomprehensible. Rarely in her mother or father's company, she had been raised by nannies and became attached to the first few, but when she realized they would all leave eventually, her heart hardened and made it impossible to form any kind of deep, lasting bond. Plus, when she found out they'd been paid to take care of her, that killed everything. Madison's mother did not stay long and did not insist she come home.

The Californians and Sylvia had planned to spend the winter break in Aspen and the Bahamas, but this fell through in the midst of Madison's hospitalization. They decided to bunk up at Sylvia's house in New York instead, so Madison could recuperate.

One fine day the Christie's catalogue arrived in the mail. Sylvia loved the Christie's catalogue and was flipping through it over breakfast when she dropped her toast.

Sylvia Plath's deck of Grimaud Tarot de Marseilles was listed — a gift from Ted Hughes. Sylvia had to have it. Madison suggested they do a sex magic ritual. Everyone was inwardly horrified except for Sylvia who was up for anything. "We could construct the rites ourselves and I could film it." She took a vitamin from her glass bowl of vitamins and swallowed it with orange juice. "We can all wear masks and it will be surrealist."

Aurora, her throat tight, unable to swallow after Sylvia's suggestion, looked at Madison who was also swallowing her vitamins. After Madison's psilocybin experience and her monumental accident, Aurora didn't think Madison had changed much. But maybe that wasn't true. If anything, Madison had become harder. Maybe she was in the process of making herself into a diamond. She felt she was finally beginning to understand, to see all of them, shining diamonds, to love them for what they were and what they were trying to accomplish. Madison caught Aurora looking at her. She screwed her face up into the equivalent of a FUCK YOU, raising her fork with a melon square stuck to the end of it into the air: "It's Britney, bitch!" They all broke out into laughter.

"Aurora, why is your skin so luminescent? What are you using on it?" In Sylvia's tone was the sting of accusation. Dinky flew to Aurora's side and sat on top of her nest of bed hair.

"Nothing. Nothing unusual. Just that facial bar soap by the sink."

"Clinique?"

"Yeah, I guess so."

"In the green plastic case?"

"Yeah. Although I didn't use it today."

"You look like you're wearing makeup, or sparkles or something."

"I can assure you I'm not."

"Going back to the more important point, Sylvia, if you film the sex magic sacrament, you won't be part of the ritual." Harlow held a strawberry by its stem and had been about to take a bite before the sex ceremony suggestion came up but was now simply holding the strawberry, uneaten. "I for one, am not so sure about this." She looked at the others, unnerved.

"What are you suggesting, exactly?" Dora tilted her head in Sylvia's direction, elbow on the table, resting her jaw in her upturned palm.

"I mean, I don't know exactly. It's for us to determine." She turned her flashing eyes, hazel lined with black kohl, on the group.

Later, all of them gathered in Sylvia's bedroom, sitting, lounging on her bed. Sylvia sat, legs bent like a resting deer, a well-thumbed paperback copy of *Ariel* beside her. "What you have to understand, is that in Plath's collection," she said, pointing to her copy, "there's a direct correlation between the Major Arcana and the first twenty-two poems. The only academic, or person, who has entertained this idea is Mary Kurtzman in an article she wrote for *The Centennial Review*. I only happened to find it because I was researching a paper for English on Plath. Like, one of the only things I've written for school this semester, but anyway.

"Kurtzman claimed that Plath used the Thoth Tarot, but that deck didn't exist in Plath's lifetime! Now we know what she used. The oldest deck — the Tarot de Marseille! So, these are probably the cards she used for *Ariel*!" Everyone on the bed felt Sylvia erupt and go up like a flare. "I mean! This is beyond monumental." Her eyes became serious, intense, electric.

The others fully appreciated the titanic importance of the cards and sat in silence. Harlow passed around clove cigarettes.

"It's well known that Shakespeare, Chaucer, Dante, Blake, W. B. Yeats, Samuel Taylor Coleridge, T. S. Eliot, and so on, wove mystic symbolism and narrative into their work, tapping into the reader's subconscious to create a subliminal yet intense experience. Sylvia knew this. And she did the same. And that pack of tarot cards was part of it. We must get it!"

"So, what do you suggest, as far as a ritual?" Aurora sat upright at the edge of the bed, twisting her torso to the centre so everyone was in view, her legs hanging down, toenails painted fuchsia.

"Maybe we could do it in the wine cellar."

"That would be so totally bacchanalian."

"I can order a ton of wisteria and candles and we can put them up everywhere. We'll wear flowers in our hair and read from *Ariel*, walking round and round in a circle." Sylvia took a drag from her clove cigarette. "And maybe we can be naked and make offerings of grapes."

"I'm fine with being naked but I don't think we should specifically do a sex ritual, like with sex." Harlow tapped her cigarette in an ashtray.

Dora agreed. "Yeah, I mean, we don't know enough about it, and it doesn't seem especially relevant."

Sylvia turned her head. "Madison?"

"I mean, yeah, but what about the thing where you get the sexual fluids and mix them with rooster blood and write on parchment? That seems like it would be effective?"

"Okay, so how do you propose we do this? Do we find some guy or are we all going to have a lesbian orgy?"

"I mean, I'm willing to be the sorceress or witch or virgin sacrifice or whatever and we can find a guy in town and lure him here."

"You're still recovering from your injuries. I'm not so sure that's a good idea."

"It's been like four weeks. The doctor said my nose would heal in three. Otherwise, I didn't break anything else."

"So why didn't we go to Aspen and the Bahamas then?"

"We can still go."

"I just really don't feel like partying after the mushroom thing, and that's all we'd do in Aspen and the Bahamas."

"But you feel like doing a sex ritual?"

"Yeah."

"Okay."

"So, where did you say we're going to get this guy?"

"I don't know, do you know anyone around here Sylvia?"

"I mean, everyone's probably in Aspen or the Bahamas."

"Okay, so should we fly to Aspen and do it there then? We can just go to a party and pick one up. It shouldn't be too difficult."

"We could, yes. My parents have a house there and no one's in it right now to my knowledge. My brother's in Saint Lucia."

"Maybe it shouldn't be anyone from school or anyone we know. They're just going to tell everyone."

"True."

"We need to find someone who doesn't know who we are."

"We also need to be sure he doesn't have a disease."

"True."

"Also, he's supposed to be a magus. I'm not sure how easy it's going to be to find one of those."

"Well, I'm not really a seeress or a witch yet or whatever."

"So maybe we shouldn't be doing this."

"Maybe we should just keep it low-key and read Sylvia Plath poems."

"I don't know. What would Sylvia do?"

"I'm on the fence about this. There are a lot of variables."

"I meant Sylvia Plath."

"Oh. Well, when she met Ted Hughes for the first time at a party he stole her earrings and she bit his cheek, drawing blood, in retaliation. So, Sylvia would probably have voted for the sex magic."

"I thought we also said we weren't going to do any sorcery. We made a blood pact."

"True. But then Diana and Aion came to us, so that seemed like it was divine license to go ahead."

"I mean, I'd like to make love with Aion. Maybe we could conjure him up again."

"Maybe we could do the ritual in the Beyond!"

"We all got separated when we were there though. And who knows if we can fall through again?"

The five sat in contemplation.

"Maybe we could get a rent boy or a male escort or prostitute or whatever you call them?"

"And make him wear a lion head."

"I don't know where we're going to get a lion head."

"eBay?"

"We also need wings for him and a snake."

"Maybe we could get the prostitute online too."

"Are you sure about this, Madison?"

"Yes, I'm sure. We also need to get a rooster."

"No, we're not cutting a rooster's throat."

"I'm not sure about the snake — I mean, can you rent a snake?"

"We're getting the rooster and cutting its throat. You eat chicken, don't you?"

Aurora sat silently, her poker face serene in the vaults of sun that illuminated them all, relieved she wasn't going to have to take part in an orgy with the others. Madison was going to sacrifice herself to the cause, and apparently delighted in it. She thought about her grandmother and that if she knew about any of this she would be horrified.

The five huddled around Sylvia with her MacBook on her lap, looking for male prostitutes through an escort service called Gentlemen 4 Hire. Madison was to be the ritual sacrifice, so ultimately, she would have the last word. They scrolled through photos and clicked on twenty or so profiles before they found the best candidate, the one whose face and body most resembled the kind of god Madison wanted to have sex with. They then looked for a lion's head and found an ancient Roman gladiator replica helmet — handmade — crafted with brass powder, polyester resin, fiberglass, and patina that was bronze and silver and magnificent. It looked enough like the head of the Aion statuette in the Louvre, but instead of completely obscuring the face, the massive top incisors fell alongside the wearer's eyes with the bottom incisors following the jawline so that the face was visible inside lion's open mouth.

"This is perfect. We can get next day delivery."

"Okay, so how are we going to do this?"

"We need to set up the wine cellar."

"Should we call the service and see if the guy is available tomorrow night?"

"What is the moon like tomorrow?"

Sylvia looked for moon phases on her laptop. "Oh my God, there's a full moon in Leo on the sixth."

"That's in three days."

"It says that the heart — aorta, blood circulation, blood pressure, and heart rate — are influenced under this sign and full moon, and it isn't a good time to have surgery."

"Well, we're not going to perform any surgery."

"Let's see if the guy is available for the sixth."

"Madison, you call him."

"What do I say?"

"Don't tell him you're underage."

"You have to see if he's okay with wearing a gladiator helmet, wings, a snake, and having four other women watch."

"The snake is kind of weird. How do you wear a snake?"

"What about being sprayed with rooster blood during the act?"

"Maybe we can negotiate that when he comes."

"He's probably going to insist on wearing a condom."

"We *need* to mix our sex fluids and write with it on the parchment. How are we going to do that?"

"Maybe we can get it out of his condom, and you mix it with your fluids and the rooster blood."

"Oh my God, this is sounding complicated."

Dora took the laptop from Sylvia to look for snakes.

"What are we even going to write on the parchment?"

"I think we should write one of Sylvia's poems."

"Jesus Christ, how are we going to do that? We'd have to do a short one."

"Or maybe just a few lines?"

"We'll use a calligraphy pen. Sylvia, do you have one, or can you order one now?"

"Let's just see if the guy is available and agrees to our requirements."

"The snake is going to be difficult."

"No, actually we can buy a snake, and then we can just keep it as a pet. It says here that gopher snakes make great pets — that they're muscular, long serpents and can be intimidating because of their size. However, there's little to fear because they are non-venomous. In fact, they are important to keeping the rodent population in check and maintaining their local ecosystems, according to Stanford University. We can have one delivered here from this pet shop."

"Where are we going to get a rooster?"

"Maybe our chef would know. He'd know what knife to use. I'll bet he could get one for us."

"I thought you were supposed to cut their heads off with an axe?"

"Is he going to tell your mother?"

"I'll ask him to keep it between us."

"Okay. Just call the guy and see if he can do it."

"The escort?"

"Yes. Call him now." Sylvia took the cordless phone on her bedside table from its cradle and handed it to Madison.

"Okay. Read me the number." Sylvia read the numbers out, Madison dialled. "Hello? Yes. I was calling about Gabriel. Is he available on the evening of the sixth?... Yes, all evening, until the morning, the break of dawn, just to be sure...Great...No, that's fine...Would he be willing to wear a gladiator helmet?...And angel wings?...No, I would provide them for him. What about a snake? I have a harmless, non-venomous snake here and I'd like the snake to crawl on his body...Yes, of course I'll pay more for all of this. Also, I have four friends, women, who will be present. Is that a problem?...Like I said, that's no problem if there's an extra charge...Let's see, just a second." Madison put her hand over the bottom of the receiver. "What time should he arrive?"

"When it's dark."

"Maybe before midnight, like eleven."

Madison removed her hand and spoke into the phone, "Could he come at eleven p.m.?...Yes, that's great...Yes... Yes, okay, just a second." She clasped her hand over the mouthpiece again. "Can someone get my credit card? It's in my purse in my bedroom. The dark purple one, Miu Miu." She spoke into the phone, "Just a moment."

Dora left to get the card and came back.

"Thank you very much. Yes, I look forward to meeting him." Madison pressed the button to hang up and handed the phone to Sylvia. "Oh my God, I just hired an escort!"

"If you don't want to do this when he gets here, it's fine, you know that."

"Yes, yes, I know. I'm totally cool with it." Madison flipped her head around, blonde ponytail flying across Dora's face, "I'm buzzing!"

Sylvia ordered the gladiator helmet, parchment, and a calligraphy pen. They discussed flowers, then found what looked like a perfect set of wings and ordered the gopher snake.

The night of the full moon was negative seventeen degrees; the air outside so cold it felt sticky. Everything was covered in snow and glowed. The girls could see the rabbit in the moon: hyperreal, a yolky, luminescent yellow, the craters that made up the rabbit stained with lilac. Harlow had set crystals into the snow on the terrace to absorb the moonlight. The girls wore Sylvia's mother's furs, naked underneath, with wisteria blossoms in their hair. When all the crystals were collected, they went inside to wait for Gabriel.

Aurora had never seen or been a part of an actual sex act. She hadn't ever watched any porn. Sylvia had been introduced to porn only recently, with the Californians, who had seen porn together, age twelve, at Madison's house. Her father had a collection of reels from the seventies under lock and key in his study[26]. The thrill of it all made Aurora felt like she was in a dream, floating in and out of the edges of reality, her heart beating hard in her chest, her head filled with helium. It seemed that at any moment she would lose control and float off the ground.

They smoked clove cigarettes in one of the sitting rooms and drank champagne while they waited. Sylvia's mother had already gone to bed, safely medicated with sleeping pills. She wouldn't wake up until the afternoon. Dinky stayed clear of the smoke, flying in and out of the room, perching on various surfaces, finally settling on top of a pearl nautilus shell, part of an Art Nouveau lamp with a bronze, stylized kelp stalk around which a weeping mermaid in a surge of grief clings and wraps her tail.

---

26. The girls had watched the pornographic film, *Alice in Wonderland*, where Alice is a librarian who dreams herself into Wonderland, goes on adventures and is seduced by the King of Hearts. She goes to bed with him but is caught in the act by the Queen. Alice is then convicted of being a virgin and sentenced to oral sex with the Queen. This was one of the milder films, but highly erotic. The other titles were less imaginative with more graphic sex, however, nothing as soul destroying as what would come in the eighties, nineties, two-thousands.

AURORA

The doorbell rang. "Madison, you go and get it and bring him in here."

Madison stubbed her cigarette out and went to get the door. The girls heard echoes of conversation in the hall. Madison and Gabriel entered the room. "These are my friends: Dora, Harlow, Sylvia, and Aurora." Each of them gave a little wave of the hand — silver painted fingernails flashing — to indicate which name belonged to whom. "Come and sit down — have some champagne. We'll explain what we'd like you to do and then you can tell us if you're up for it."

"Good evening, ladies." Gabriel grinned like a man-boy, reminiscent of Tom Cruise, his grin giving way to a sly smirk. He sat down in an armchair. Madison brought him a glass of champagne.

"So, we want to perform a sex ritual to obtain Sylvia Plath's deck of tarot cards. You and I would have sex in the middle of the room — in this case, the wine cellar, on a table. These beautiful girls, or women, will be dancing in a circle around us, chanting Sylvia Plath's poems." Madison hesitated, not knowing how to explain the part with the rooster. "You'll be wearing a gladiator helmet. I asked the agency and they said that was fine."

"Yeah, a gladiator helmet sounds cool. I'm going to need another payment if there's sex involved."

"No problem. How much?"

"Two thousand."

"That's fine." Madison turned to Sylvia. "Maybe you should get the cash now, except, there *is* another thing." Madison threw back the remaining champagne in her glass. "This is like a kind of voodoo ritual. We wanted to cut off a rooster's head and have the blood sprinkled on us while we're having sex."

Gabriel, beautiful as a god — his chiselled poker face unmoving — sat contemplating the situation, then said, "Okay, but that will be five thousand for a total of seven thousand. Up front, in cash".

Madison cried out, "Amazing!" The other girls smiled, wrapped in their furs, naked underneath, flowers in their hair, champagne glasses in hand, in shock that all of this was going to happen.

Sylvia rose from the sofa. "Let me go get the cash and I'll be right back." Sylvia knew the combination to her mother's safe. Her mother was sleeping, barely breathing, her smooth face reflecting the moonlight that lit the room. She had forgotten to draw the curtains. Sylvia entered her walk-in closet and punched the code in, the numbers lighting up. She counted five thousand dollars in hundreds and went back downstairs. Everyone was drinking champagne, smoking clove cigarettes, laughing at some witty story Gabriel had been telling. Sylvia went looking through drawers for an envelope, found one, shoved the cash in and handed it to Gabriel. "Please count it to make sure it's right."

He raised his head to her and smiled — "Thank you" — counted it out while the girls continued smoking, sipping their champagne. "Perfect."

"Right, so I'll explain a bit further. In this ritual you're supposed to be Aion, one of the primordial Greek gods — the god of perpetual time and eternity."

"The 'time' he represents isn't linear, it's a perpetual, unbounded, ritual, cyclic conception of time."

"Okay." Gabriel stubbed out his cigarette. "I think I know what you mean, I've got a huge uroboros tattooed on my back."

"No —"

"Yes."

The girls froze, then looked at Gabriel and one another. They all knew what this was: Jungian synchronicity. No one said anything. If they spoke it out loud it would ruin the spell.

"So, you're okay with snakes?"

"The agency said something about a non-venomous snake. What were you thinking?" Gabriel focused his attention on Madison, his dark eyes sulky, brooding.

"We've got a gopher snake. It's perfectly harmless. It goes with the wings and the gladiator helmet. To make you into Aion. I don't know, we hadn't really thought about it. In the depictions we have of Aion the snake is twisted around his body."

"I see."

"I mean, what do you think?"

"Could I get a whisky?"

"Yeah, sure." Madison looked to Sylvia who had already gotten up and was making her way to the drink cabinet.

"Well, I mean, if it's harmless, like you say, I'll see if I can get it to wrap itself around me. A god's gotta do what a god's gotta do, right?"

"Thank you for being so amenable." Sylvia handed Gabriel the whisky.

They had made the wine cellar into a cave of wisteria, hanging and twisting branches with flowers from the bottles and their cradles, from the chandelier that dropped out of the domed, gold-painted plaster ceiling, so that all the walls were covered, and a waterfall of wisteria and crystals hung in the centre over a mahogany table, also covered in wisteria blooms. The rooster was loose in the cellar, crowing, padding around in circles, marking his territory. It was not a black rooster; it was more rainbow-colored with an orange red neck and a magnificent, green iridescent tail the colour of beetle wings. The cockerel had his own unique attitude, and yes, baggage. He had no idea what was about to happen to him. He did not understand that the tree stump and the axe in the corner were for him.

Glass lanterns with candles were lit and sat on the floor, the light bobbing here and there in the gold on the ceiling. The six walked through the solid mahogany double doors, Dinky flitting in amongst them, into the sweet, heady rush of wisteria, and stepped barefoot across the dark tiled floors, the girls without their furs, only flowers in their hair, Gabriel naked, the helmet and wings on, the bright yellow snake wound around his arm.

The girls were chanting "The Rabbit Catcher", circling the table, Harlow playing the singing bowl, casting eerie tones through their bodies, driving the cockerel wild, making its head swing and stagger as though drunk, while Gabriel and Madison followed them in the procession three times around, finally mounting the table, while the girls continued their revolutions.

No one knew what was going to happen. They decided to surrender to the forces at play and improvise. They only knew they would chant the poem, walk in a circle, play the singing bowl, chop the rooster's head off, spray the copulating couple with its blood mid coitus, then gather the fluids in the singing bowl and use the calligraphy pen to write the astrological symbol for Scorpio on the parchment, as Plath was born on October the twenty-seventh.

Naked, dancing and chanting "The Rabbit Catcher", the singing bowl and wisteria fumes going to her head, Aurora concentrated on the lines of the poem, on her body, with Gabriel's wings and buttocks, his golden lion helmet glinting, Madison's legs around him, flashing in the corners of her eyes — Madison and Gabriel pressed together, see-sawing their bodies, Madison flipped around and mounted from behind, Gabriel's wings beating the air, the snake slipping from his neck, Madison's murmurs strung through the octaves of the singing bowl. At one point, when Gabriel was taking Madison from behind, Sylvia grabbed the rooster by its neck in a swooping motion, shuttling it to the tree stump, where she held its body and knocked its head down onto the block, stunning it for the moment it took to grab the axe and deftly cut its head off. Blood spurted everywhere. Sylvia held the rooster up toward the table where Gabriel and Madison were engaged, the snake writing in Madison's grip, and moved closer, directing the surges of blood back and forth with the rooster kicking and flapping its wings, spraying blood all over them, over herself, over Aurora and the girls dancing and chanting with blood raining down. And then from nowhere, one of the girls bent down and came up again blowing gold dust over Gabriel and Madison and all in the circle, which Sylvia had joined, letting the rooster fall and run headless until it collapsed. The fucking intensified; there were moans. Gabriel called out, then pulled his phallus out of Madison, spraying her buttocks and back with his semen (he did not wear a condom). Aurora and the girls continued to dance in a circle, chanting, the singing bowl filling the air, Madison on all fours, flowers still stuck in her bloodied hair, the snake in her hand, her blood-sprayed face looking back at Gabriel on his knees, his face, his chest, his wings, mottled in blood, glittering with gold, sparkling. He pulled Madison up from behind and held her to him, her hands on his thighs, her back on his chest, kissed her on her neck, on the cheek as she turned her head, then shifted her around to face him, sperm, blood, dripping down, flower petals stuck to her back. They kissed on the mouth, her legs around his waist.

After this, Gabriel jumped onto floor, wings and penis bobbing. Madison remained on the table, holding the snake to her breast. The dancing had stopped. Everyone stood back, pressed up against the wall of wisteria, chanting with the singing bowl, deranging their brains and the air. Dinky flitted around the room haphazardly, over Madison on the table of flowers, who, still clutching the snake, gestured to Sylvia with an outstretched arm. Sylvia knew she wanted the parchment and ducked down to get it from its place on the floor underneath the table and handed it to her.

Still in possession of the snake, Madison wiped her hand along her back to collect the mixture of sperm and blood, then put her hand between her legs to mix it with the fluids there. She used her index finger to draw the Scorpio symbol onto the paper, then held it up for all to see. After, she lay down, placed it on her abdomen and held the snake to her chest.

The next morning at breakfast they did not speak of the night before. They did not dare, for fear their words would break something.[27] The five ate and took their vitamins in reverent silence. Dinky flitted around the room chirping, pecking at seeds they'd laid out for her. Madison, and all of them — especially Sylvia with her exquisitely executed rooster sacrifice — felt they had achieved something monumental, that they had taken part in the workings of things, taken the ship's wheel, so to speak, and turned it together, altering the course of the universe. Aurora had no doubt she was one of them. She belonged. Whatever happened, they were inseparable. What they had done would last forever, as long as the universe existed. Aurora called to Dinky, who alighted on her finger and was fed a grape.

The day of the auction, the girls were back at school. They all sat on Harlow's bed, staring at Sylvia, drinking Diet Coke and smoking clove cigarettes. Sylvia posed as her mother, successfully answering the security questions. The

27. Sylvia had gone back into her mother's safe and paid the help to take care of the wine cellar, to not say a word to her parents about what they found there. They would never look at her the same way again. The scene was disturbing and unholy.

auction ended at just over two hundred thousand dollars. Sylvia hung up the phone, stared ahead in a suspended state of animation, eyes wide as saucers, gripping the down comforter, fingers digging into it, and screamed. The girls knew this meant victory and danced around the smoky room like crazed sugar plum faeries. Her parents were going to kill her, but they wouldn't contest the payment because they had too much pride and beside all this, her mother had named her after the poet. She had room to finesse.

The girls celebrated with bottles of champagne, smoking more cigarettes, dancing to old Francophone songs, "Ça Plane Pour Moi", making themselves into airplanes, "Laisse tomber les filles", "Hippie hippie hourrah", "Café crème", "Problèmes d'amour", etc, dancing until they passed out from drunkenness.

The next morning everyone except Aurora slept in. Alone in the kitchen she poured herself cereal. *Food of the Gods* was lying on the kitchen countertop. As she ate, she flipped through the book's pages, landing on a passage which chilled her blood:

Not to know one's true identity is to be a mad, disensouled thing — a golem. And, indeed, this image, sickeningly Orwellian, applies to the mass of human beings now living in the high-tech industrial democracies. Their authenticity lies in their ability to obey and follow mass style changes that are conveyed through the media. Immersed in junk food, trash media, and crypto-fascist politics, they are condemned to toxic lives of low awareness. Sedated by the prescripted daily television fix, they are a living dead, lost to all but the act of consuming.

Did she actually *know* her true identity? Had she become disensouled? No. She had a soul. She could feel it. It was there. But she had been moulding herself into a shapeshifting creature, a fluid personality with endless possibilities, like Whitman in his *Leaves of Grass. Do I contradict myself? / Very well then I contradict myself / (I am large, I contain multitudes.)* She could not pin herself down. Was this wrong? Did she have to know who she was? Did anyone? Did it matter? Did the universe need a centre?

She could see how society was marching toward Aldous Huxley's *Brave New World*, enslaved, lobotomized by the technology they loved; technology into which they poured their hearts and souls. Aurora understood that the 'crypto-fascist politics' would be the result if the world continued its current path, although she couldn't imagine fascism coming to the U.S.A.

Upon reflection she decided the soul could be infinite and perhaps this was even part of the solution. She wasn't one of these consumerist zombies. However, she might be worse, because she consumed and knew the consequences, and yet kept consuming. Scenes of people like the walking dead, or asleep as Gurdjieff called them, eyes glazed in the thrall of consuming, had dug themselves in, these fat, white grubs, their brains infected by parasites the media had inserted there and left to incubate and spread.

The Surrealists, the Situationists, they had been trying to make people see, to wake them up with bizarre assemblages of ordinary objects, dream-like scenes and symbolic images, unexpected, illogical juxtapositions — slaps in the face. Surrealism wanted to wrap you in its cocoon so you could incubate and grow wings. .

What she, Sylvia, Dora, Madison, and Harlow, and all the Surrealists had embarked upon, was the antidote. They were fighting against this golem mindset, in the pursuit of art and knowledge. It was like Leonora Carrington's novel *The Hearing Trumpet*. They were searching for a knowledge so powerful that it did not merely transform the individual, but the entire world. A new utopian age in which humanity diminishes in importance. A new community in which goats, cats, and werewolves, in the case of Carrington's novel, are their equals.

Aurora decided that, in fact, part of being an artist was divining and inventing oneself, willing oneself into existence out of the darkness.

Plath's tarot cards arrived at Sylvia's house addressed to her mother. Two days after the auction, Sylvia had told her mother about the transgression on the phone. Her mother didn't say anything except that she should come home that weekend

Sylvia arranged for one of the limousines to come and collect everyone for the six-hour journey to her house. On the way, they were only allowed soft drinks from the minibar. She didn't want anyone showing up drunk, or even with the faintest whiff of alcohol on them. Cigarettes were also verboten but Harlow had brought a pack of Djarum Black Kretek clove cigarettes. After a short discussion it was agreed they could smoke them. The clove cigarettes went well with the Diet Coke. Of course, each of them had to take turns riding with their heads out the sunroof, wind ratting their hair, tears flying out of the corners of their eyes, until the driver eventually pulled over when they wouldn't stop and told them they were going to get themselves killed and to cut it out. Aurora held on to Dinky the entire time so she wouldn't be sucked out. The five arrived with tangled hair, smelling of cloves, and managed to miss Mrs Belmont who was in her room resting, as she had taken too much Valium. Staff took their bags to their bedrooms.

Sylvia woke her mother, who told her she'd put the cards in her closet safe. Sylvia retrieved the package and brought it to the bed, sitting there with her mother in a moment of reverence, not daring touch the box that housed the cards. Her mother sat up, supported by eiderdown pillows, a goddess perpetually descending to earth from her golden chariot, made so by erudite wit and money so that one could say she was, in a sense, under permanent hypnosis. She told Sylvia to open the package.

"I can't fault you, Sylvia." Mrs Belmont had her forearm upright, chin resting on the back of her hand, eyes on the box of cards. "I would have done the same thing." She turned to her daughter, "I'm glad we have them". Getting up from the bed, as light as her Halston dress, seeming to float, she said, "Find a safe place for them my darling. I don't need to tell you I don't want them leaving the house".

Sylvia knew she had practically gotten away with murder. If her father found out, there would be hell to pay.

The five met in the south-facing sitting room to view the cards. Sylvia carried the sacred object, wrapped in blue velvet, to a round table, where she unveiled it so they could all admire it. The clock on the mantle ticked. They remained silent, even Dinky, clutching onto the table edge, eyes on the treasure.

"I haven't touched them — the cards." Sylvia spoke in hushed tones. "Do you think *she* was the last one to touch them?"

From Dora, reverently, also whispering, "We'll never know."

And then Sylvia, "What should we do?"

Silence and the clock ticking.

"Maybe we could tip them out of the box and make a spread using a chopstick to touch them?" Harlow spoke, voice lowered.

"Why not just use gloves?" Dora proposed.

This seemed like the best solution. Sylvia left the room, with Dinky sailing through the air behind her, then returned from her mother's bedroom with red velvet elbow-length gloves. Dinky flew up and perched on a chandelier, chirping, dropping excrement onto a chintz sofa below.

"Maybe we should look at them face up, so we can see the last positions the cards were in?" Madison suggested.

"And take photographs." Sylvia put the gloves down, then exited again to get a camera and her Bolex. When she returned, she began filming at the doorway, moving closer to the four girls at the circular table in the shot, vaults of light acid washing the furniture, the air alive with dust motes, Dinky flying in and out of the frame, doing aerial acrobatics as though he knew he was being captured for posterity. Harlow was chosen to spill the cards out.

The Star — a card everyone knew was one of André Breton's obsessions[28] — flew out of the box, face up. Harlow gasped. Tears ran down Aurora's face. They hadn't come from any source of emotion. They came out of nowhere, like a ghost turning on a tap.

"Sylvia is here." Sylvia spoke from behind her camera. The frame focused on the card, then moved up and in an arc, capturing the faces of the girls. "We must kneel," Sylvia's husky voice commanded them. Everyone obeyed, the camera following their actions, its view lowering below the table, pointed down at the oriental carpet, evoking a posture of reverence and contemplation. After this and a moment of silence broken by Dinky's cry and the sound of his wings flying from the chandelier, each girl rose to her feet around the table.

---

28. It is the subject of Breton's prose poem *Arcane 17*, referring to tarot card 17, the Star, to which Breton's imagination brought new associations, linking the naked female figure on the card with the legendary figure of Mélusine, a mermaid who became a symbol of the difficulty to reconcile "reality" and "magic". Breton expresses the hope that the "inexhaustible" urns depicted on the cards can renew our disenchanted world. Indeed, even though the pond gives off the "pestilential odor" of social conventions, it still longs for "a new dream". The fragile butterfly in Breton's *Arcane 17* illustration on this card, designed by Roberto Matta, is another symbol of "consoling mystery".

Holding the Bolex, focused on the card, Sylvia narrated for the camera, "Historically a symbol of being open, a return to nature, purity, honesty, the Star card is an acceptance of one's body and desires. It is generosity, luck from heaven, intuition from a higher plane — a flow from a pure source. Reversed, it signifies naïve optimism and wishful thinking, exposing oneself to danger or abuse, difficulty in setting proper boundaries, squandering, wastefulness".

The girls waited for Sylvia to finish, then Harlow spoke. "You think she's here?"

"I think it's obvious."

"What do we do now?"

"Pour the rest out."

Harlow revealed the next cards with a gloved finger, The Moon, The King of Swords, VIII of Cups, VIIII of Cups, V of Clubs, Ace of Coins, VI of Coins, Temperance, III of Clubs, The Knave of Money, II of Clubs, The Chariot, and on through the remainder of the deck with Sylvia filming and stopping to take photographs.

"Alright. Now mix them up and we can each take one," Sylvia continued with her hold on the reins, directing their next play. Each girl had a turn with the gloves on, mixing the cards and choosing:

Dora: The Ace of Swords, virility, self-confidence
Aurora: V of Cups, separation and tears
Madison: Knave of Clubs, ambitious, hardworking person, always grateful
Sylvia: The Chariot, moral strength, intuition, lofty ideas, talent

Harlow: Knave of Cups, passionate and fickle young girl

Not sure what to make of this, whether it was coming from the cards, the unconscious, the stars, Sylvia Plath herself, or a combination, three of them were happy with the reveal; two were not.

"To be honest, I wouldn't really say I'm ambitious, hardworking, and always grateful."

"Am I a passionate and fickle young girl?" Harlow gritted her teeth, on the verge of tears.

"No, I wouldn't say those were your defining characteristics," Sylvia responded, her eyes tense, pupils retracting into hard pinpoints.

"At the end of the day, we're all passionate, fickle young girls." No one argued with Dora.

"Maybe we're supposed to look at them collectively. As though we're all part of a whole and they apply to all of us." This came from Aurora and was met with closed lips, contempt, contemplation.

"Let's put them away. I don't think we're ready for this yet," Harlow hammered the nail into the coffin with the ice in her voice. She took the gloves off and set them on the table.

"Agreed. I don't know what the fuck that was." Madison crossed her arms. "If you're listening Sylvia, you're one crazy bitch."

"Jesus Christ Madison, there's no need to be rude!" Sylvia put the gloves on, "I can't believe you just said that." She pushed the cards back into the box, wrapped it in the velvet and went to a wooden panel in the wall that hid a safe she had decided to appropriate. Her parents hadn't found a use for it yet and in fact, her father didn't even know the safe existed. It was here she kept her diaries.

"What now?" In Madison's voice was the steel and air of exasperated dejection.

"It's the full moon again. So we're going to do our invocation for a Master." Slightly peeved, Sylvia turned to walk out of the room. "C'mon, we've got to prepare."

"I thought we were going to do this by ourselves. No gurus, remember? I thought we decided that gurus were creepy."

"We're not asking for a guru. We're asking for a Master. A celestial being. Not of this earth. Hopefully, wherever she is, Sylvia can send one to us."

"Who said the Master was going to be a man?"

"We have Diana and Aion."

"Do we?" Sylvia narrowed her eyes, "We only saw them once. They haven't come back."

"That's true. And it's clear no one was protecting us when we took the mushrooms."

"Exactly."

"I think we've gone as far as we can or should alone, without a guide."

"I agree."

"Who doesn't agree?"

Silence.

"It's settled. We'll do an invocation for a Master."

They fasted for the rest of the day, drinking only Diet Coke and smoking the rest of Harlow's clove cigarettes. After much consideration, they decided to make bird masks and wear Sylvia's mother's silk chiffon Halston dresses so that they could fly with the fire, like the ancient druid Mogh Roith, into the firmament to find what they were looking for. Sylvia chose a spot she knew well in the forest and had the groundskeeper dig a fire pit, fill it with wood, kindling, and pine fronds for their night ritual. Sylvia found a heap of fire-gel fuel for fondue sets in the kitchen to get the fire started. In bed, sedated, with her silk eye mask on, Mrs Belmont did not notice the five entering her room and padding into her walk-in closet where they each chose a fur coat and Halston evening dress in floaty, gossamer fabrics.

Wrapped in furs, their moon boots on, pine fronds made into crowns, bird masks covering their faces, they walked over the frozen, blue-tinted ground, tree roots and dead leaves, their breath silvering in the beams of moonlight. One by one, following Sylvia with her lantern, the Milky Way overhead — a mass of glowing, blue-white-violet ectoplasm streaked across the dark star lit sky – they trudged through the snow until they came to the fire pit. Sylvia set the lantern down. She went to the firepit and threw the fondue fire starter gel in among the branches, then ignited the Zippo Typhoon matches one by one on a nearby rock, each hissing into flame, going up like mini flares, diving headfirst into the morass of flammable material, setting it alight. As the fire spread, they sang their hymn to turn into birds and find the Master, the stars glittering and flashing through the dark outlines of branches above. Shedding their furs they danced, circling round and round the bonfire, their bodies lighter and lighter[29] until they felt they might float above the treetops, to the stars.

29. The elementals still had not let go of Aurora and were in their element here in the forest, under the full moon and stars...

4.

In fact, the Master[30] was on his way. He had begun his journey before the five girls had ever met. He walked from the desert into the mountains and forest, across the plains, through prairies and farmland, surviving on mice and insects and whatever else was available; following his instincts in a north-easterly direction with the knowledge he was going to have to walk a very long time before he reached his final destination. Something was calling to him, an invisible force, tugging on the strings of his heart — a magnetic charge. This Master, if you've not already guessed, was Tu-tu. Or rather, Tu-tu became the Master after becoming something else.

As you may or may not know, almost every cat is psychic. The logical, or most practical path is not always the best, or the one that is most necessary. Cats in general are well aware of this fact. The moment Tu-tu knew Aurora would leave the trailer park, he set out immediately, certain that if

---

30. A Master can refer to a female, male, hermaphrodite, someone who is androgynous, or as is H. P. Lovecraft's Cthulhu, neither male nor female. I'm going to refer to this Master as a "him" because the body it inhabited was male. This particular Master had been almost everything in its existence and could identify with anything it put its mind to.

he did not respond to the calling there and then, he would never see Aurora again. In the desert, Tu-tu had found cool places to sleep during the heat of day and travelled mostly at night. He passed petroglyphs among the ochre rocks at dusk, padding beneath and beside them as he moved through the hills, between the scented scrub, up and down paths in the red, rocky dirt, through smooth-faced sandstone caverns, rivers that ran the colour of jade. His vision at night took on sharp lines, highly detailed in the platinum light.

As he climbed higher, the stars shone brighter and bore down harder, silvering everything, brimming from the depths where they appeared to be moving slowly, taking part in the construction of the universe. In these mountainous, rocky, forested parts were many dangers: coyotes, cougars, rattlesnakes, birds of prey. Tu-tu moved as quickly as he could, following a magnetic sense of direction, keeping to a north-east arc, watching the stars. Being black was an advantage, camouflaging him in the night. However, closer to towns and farms, wherever there were people, his colour was a problem. People, as a general rule, do not like black cats. In his encounters with other felines, females in heat were the friendliest, although they could be very cold, even vicious after the act, which was in the end an advantage because he did not plan on hanging around. Male cats despised him, all except for one: a farm cat who preferred the male sex and tried to entice him to remain with offerings of mice.

In the mountains of northern New Mexico, near the Rio Grande, Tu-tu was captured by a coven of witches. He was lured by mesmeric, flashing objects (a trail of crystals hanging from tree branches that led to the house), the scent of sardines, and music especially made for cats — slow, sombre, hypnotic, back and forth sawing melodies with electronic sounds that mimicked different timbres of purring. He entered their lodge lit with candles and came upon the women dressed in white — one playing a cello, another at an electric keyboard and the others dancing in a circle. They had flowers in their hair, and were humming and chanting, one with a drum across her shoulder, beating out a rhythm; another with a rattle shaking out a soft cadence. A terrible incense burned, the stench supremely offensive to a cat, but it did not deter him from entering and eating the sardines left on a plate by the witches who had put on this whole show in order to lure a vessel for their familiar.

The witches' activity fascinated the cat. In a goblet full of garnet liquid, an intense boiling created white rockets that fell back and broke into a violet mist that rose from the glass in the shape of Medusa's gorgon snakes, writhing around one another. The sphere of their ecstatic, ritual energy swathed Tu-tu in invisible caresses and made his hair stand on end so that he began to purr and jump from one piece of furniture to the next, wandering around the women, through the paces of their invocation, rubbing up against their ankles as they danced and played their instruments. He could not remember why he had set out, or where from, with no idea of where he was going, or where exactly he was, except that he knew he was precisely where he was meant to be.

During the course of the night, the witches were successful in opening a portal to the spirit realm through which an entity entered the lodge, enticed by Tu-tu's handsome form, longing to experience the sensations of a cat.

The entry of this entity into Tu-tu's body was brutal and excruciating. Fitting a spiritual mass of this magnitude, a mass which has been allowed to spread out larger than our solar system, into a human body is torture and hell. It was far worse for Tu-tu, whose small, feline body convulsed and froze in the throes of this agony, foaming at the mouth, tongue lolling.

Once the entity was trapped, the witches began the ritual to keep it there, binding it to the spirit of the cat. This went on for several days. Finally, the two spirits grabbed hold of one another. The witches were quick to notice the change in energy and found themselves speaking telepathically with the supernatural being who was also now the cat — one who held secrets to the universe, formulas, techniques it had acquired in its millennia of existence.

This was the second time they had facilitated the creation of a cat familiar. The previous attempt had ended badly, their spell to conjoin the entity in the feline body had not held and they had been attacked, battling with the creature from the Unseen realm for eight days. It had taken them eight months to recover.

This second entity, who was now inside of Tu-tu, had had its most recent incarnation in the future, spending the last millennium visiting here and there in the cosmos of the Unseen realm. It had been many things throughout its existence. On earth it had been insects and birds, molecules of water, predator and prey on land and aquatic. Hundreds of thousands of times, it had experienced the human form, been initiated into the arcane arts, slowly building its occult powers. As the witches trawled the psyche of their prisoner, they found they had enlisted a formidable ally in their search for knowledge and power. They rejoiced.

The lodge was sealed, the windows and doors shut; salt was poured in a circle around the house. Candles were kept lit at all hours. The women's hands were always busy, handling objects, rocks, feathers, making fire and smoke appear, settling in planes in the air, making everything foggy.

The sun and moon rose and set. Tu-tu was fed like a king, stroked, brushed, left alone to explore the lodge, walk among the herbs, candles and ceremonial statuettes. He sat for hours on end staring through the windows. Outside was the wild. The complex energies at work out there fascinated him. He followed movements on the ground and in the trees, lizards, birds, mice. He slept in sunbeams that poured through the glass, convalescing from the reverse exorcism. Aurora had not been entirely erased from his memory and floated as if adrift in his mind. The witches' charm was not potent enough to rub her out.

After a month of rest, sardines and cat milk, Tu-tu's body began to recover. The entity gained more and more control of the cat's mind to reveal a creature like none the witches had ever had the fortune to behold. Once the transformation had taken full effect, everything Tu-tu had experienced was accessible to the entity. Tu-tu was no longer in control, but a passenger, his spirit allowed the feeling of life, the sensations of living, but without free will. The spirit from the Beyond was now in authority.

The entity took up the life of the cat, walking among the idols, musical instruments, and furniture in the lodge; observing the witches' ceremonies, sleeping on pillows, eating sardines with relish, being brushed and stroked and massaged by his three female companions. He was pleased to find every whim and need was taken care of. For example, he defecated in a box filled with sand, and a moment later it disappeared. Choice cuts of poached fish were placed before him; fresh water flowed from several fountains around the house. The witches tended to his every need. Sometimes at night he would find himself staring at the witches' sleeping faces thinking of stealing their breath, sluicing their souls through their humid eyes.

When the telepathic channels between the cat and the witches were shaky and wouldn't open properly, the cat would communicate through a Ouija board. The cat was fond of reading and looking at art books. Life inside the lodge began to feel constricting, however. The wild called to him. He often stood on his hind legs at the window, imagining himself outside, his full attention on the forest bristling with wind and animals, dancing with light, the sparkles of dust, the sky changing colour — birds and bats in flight. In his mind's eye he saw flashes of a girl, or young woman, accompanied by a longing, a pressure overlapping with the need to hunt, to stalk, to hide, to take his prey with tooth and claw, alive to dead, warm and bloody.

Slowly, he began to register that the girl had something to do with the cat, with his previous life, before it had been possessed. The cat had been, in fact, in the process of walking across the country to be with this girl. He could see she went to a distinguished place of education in New Hampshire and was involved with four other novices in gaining occult knowledge. His curiosity was piqued. Between this and Tu-tu's soul, crying out to be reunited with Aurora, the entity in the body of a cat left the lodge under the cover of night. The witches thought that by keeping the doors and windows locked shut and encircling the house with salt they could keep him from escaping. They were mistaken.

To be in the wild — to have the earth and grass beneath his feet, drunk on the world of scent, the wind in his fur, the electric buzz of life all around — was ecstasy. After the mountains, the cat came to grasslands with magnificent buffalo, then moved onward to farmlands and towns. He hunted rodents, slept in crevices and holes in the ground or rock faces, anywhere that was hidden, generally avoiding the farms where other cats would be protective of their territories. He rode in a box car for a time, hopping off as the train slowed down. When his paws began to ache, he invoked air elementals to carry him, much to the surprise of birds he killed in mid-air, grabbing them by the wing, delighting in eating their ripe, succulent hearts, letting their bodies fall to the ground, leaving a trail of feathered carcasses in his wake. The air sprites took him on a scenic tour over Missouri, the Mark Twain national forest, along the borderlines of Illinois, Indiana, and Kentucky, then into West Virginia, above the Blue Ridge Mountains, over towns, power stations, until the capricious sprites had had enough and scattered, tossing Tu-tu into a grassy ditch, where he continued on foot.

Yes, he could have teleported himself onto the prep school grounds, but it was necessary to make the journey. What may appear quick and convenient doesn't always make it the best choice. Part of being a Master is knowing that doing the wrong thing at the wrong time can ruin everything. At this point, his mission was to walk across the country. And also, to try not to die, for even though he was powerful, he was not all powerful and could not avoid death. If he lost the cat's body, that would be the end. He could not simply possess another cat and continue the mission. The memory of the previous incarnation is always erased and not given back until many, many years have passed. By that time Aurora would have been long dead and buried, or cremated. This was a window, if he died, he would forfeit. So, mortality was a concern. He was always anticipating dangers: wild animals, humans, cars, inhospitable landscapes, rat poison, etc. As more of Tu-tu's spirit became glued to the spirit of its possessor, so reared the thorny heads of these longings for Aurora, the dominant spirit savoring the pure love the cat had for the human girl, in its pain and ecstasy.

Steadily and stealthily, Tu-tu made his way north-east, stopping here and there to kill shiny winged insects, making them into necklaces he wore to look more elegant, imagining the moment he would be in his mistress's arms, cover her in his scent, marking her as his. Walking down Main Street in one of the more affluent towns, he came upon a cigar end, a trace of smoke curling from it. He picked it up with his teeth, tongue prickling with the delightful tang, held it with both paws and sucked, bringing it back to life. The heat and bright red orange embers delivered an intoxicating, calming mouthful of smoke. He was hooked.

Aurora crunched through the snow, walking home in the frigid dusk with Dinky dipping up and down through the air behind her. Worried Dinky would freeze to death in mid-air, she held her mittened hand out and tucked the little bird into the neck of her down jacket. Aurora felt like a tiny boat, cutting through the wind, made of balsam on the high seas, no destination, not a chance in hell of staying in one piece. She had escaped in the crush at the end of the ballet — a performance of *The Firebird*. Word of the five girls' superhuman fluidity and grace had reached New York. Scouts were sent to hide in the audience and emerge backstage to woo them. Sylvia spoke for all of them, graciously declining. Ballet wasn't their main discipline. Ballet wasn't even the highest form of dance. Aurora was the only one to consider the offers, not having her parent's wealth and security to fall back on, but decided that in the end, ballet was too risky. If she worked hard, she could get into the Ivy League. From there, she could go anywhere. And yet, she had already come so far. She'd been to Paris, to Rome, to London, Bermuda,

Aspen, L.A., Malibu[31]. She had stayed in magnificent villas, ranches, compounds, townhouses, hotels; eaten in the finest restaurants, visited the French and Italian Rivieras on a yacht. Yet to think of it all, this glittering, awe-inspiring world of luxury hardened into sheer pain.

Not wanting to celebrate with the rest of them, Aurora had escaped out the back of the theatre with Dinky. There were two more performances before the run ended. Each time it had been packed to standing room only. Aurora sent her grandmother a video of one of the performances. Her grandmother was unable to attend. She couldn't afford the flight, having stopped sewing and stuffing envelopes because of her arthritis; living solely on her pension. Aurora was relieved. She felt indebted to her grandmother for all she had done, but she didn't want anyone to see her. With that hick accent and mannerisms, everyone would know. She was white trash.

The evening mist had begun to congeal into frozen fog, the last light catching the icy, airborne particles, tiny

---

31. In this, her third year, she had gone with Sylvia and the Californians on their winter and summer vacations. If life was glamorous, it was also humiliating. She toured the world first class in Sylvia's private jet, on and her friend's parents' dime. She saw herself as a parasite. The girls passionately insisted again and again that it was nothing to bring her along, to buy her clothes — that their parents wouldn't care or notice. Why had their parents given them unlimited credit cards if they didn't want them to use them? Each one did her best alone, and collectively, to convince Aurora it was not anything to worry about as they took her on shopping sprees in L.A., New York City, Paris, London, Rome — buying her trinkets, paying for restaurants — all the while harbouring contempt. Aurora couldn't dislodge herself from the vicious cycle, feeling they were holding every little thing they bought for her against her, despite everything they had been through together. They were fickle, as Sylvia Plath's tarot cards had revealed.

prisms flashing out of nowhere, here and there. It was at this moment that a black cat appeared on the snow-shovelled sidewalk, running between the snowbanks. Aurora watched to see if it would cross her path. This was, supposedly, bad luck. Every time she saw a black cat, she couldn't help but think of Tu-tu. The anguish of not knowing where he was, alive or dead, burst through her chest, shot up and coiled around her throat. Every night she missed him, missed holding him in her arms and falling asleep to his purring.

The black cat did not move from the path. It appeared to be galloping toward her, tail up, flying along the icy sidewalk. Without thinking, Aurora sunk to her knees to receive it. She met the animal's head with her mittened hands, stroking it until it pushed its way up to stand on its hind legs, put its paws around her neck and bunted her with the top of its head. The cat wore a necklace of iridescent green and violet beetles. Dinky flew out from Aurora's neck and flitted around them, landing on top of a rock wall nearby, looking on.

Tears rolled down Aurora's face. She looked into the cat's eyes — green-gold, glowing with markings like ridges of sand on the sea floor. They reminded her of Tu-tu's.

Out of nowhere, Aurora heard a voice in stereo all around her: "Yes, it's me. I've travelled across the country to find you". The cat's mouth did not move, yet the words seemed to be coming from the cat. It rubbed its cheek against hers.

Thinking the voice was the product of her imagination, Aurora saw the animal had no collar, aside from the strange beetle necklace. She picked the cat up, which it allowed, and walked back to the house. Maybe she was going mad, but maybe it was Tu-tu. Maybe he'd found her after all this time. She'd heard of cats who left their homes and returned several years later. Aurora unzipped her coat, slid the cat in, pulled the zipper back up, careful not to catch him in it, and held his warm body fast to her chest, her face wet with tears, freezing in streaks down her face. "Tu-tu, you have no idea how much I've missed you." She pressed her face into his fur, delirious. She wanted to believe he had found her.

Again, she heard the voice. "It is I, Tu-tu, your cat, in many ways, but along the journey to you, I found myself with a coven of witches who brought a spirit — my spirit, into the body of your cat — and our essential beings are now conjoined.

"I know many things you and your friends, the members of your fledgling coven, have been searching for. I have come to guide you, to initiate you and protect you in the realms Beyond the Veil, if you accept my tutelage."

Aurora could not decide whether she was in telepathic communication with the cat or going insane.

A blast of heat hit them in the face upon entering the house. Dinky alighted on a hall table, head moving this way and that. Aurora again heard the voice: "Tropical!" She set the cat on the tiled floor, where he did a jig on his hind legs — something she had never seen Tu-tu perform — as she pulled off her bag, jacket and boots. Aurora bent down to the cat's level, asking, "Are you hungry?"

"Indeed! Do you have any chopped liver?"

"No, but I think we have some tuna."

He flicked his tail back and forth, and his eyes took on a hard edge. "Too much tuna causes kidney disease in cats, but I'm hungry. I'll take it. Just a bit couldn't hurt. Perhaps you have some sardines?"

They went to the kitchen, the animal following behind her, Dinky flitting through the air, chirping, leading the way. "My grandmother used to give you tuna all the time. I hope your kidneys are okay."

"Hmmm. I was wondering about that — whether I need a transplant."

"Maybe we have some salmon."

"It would have to be poached. Cats can't tolerate salt, like smoked salmon, for example."

In the kitchen, Dinky took refuge on top of the refrigerator while Aurora poured the cat a glass of water and rummaged through the fridge for something it could eat. The cat hopped from the floor to the countertop as if by levitation and began to drink from the glass. "You're in luck. There's sushi with salmon." Aurora pulled strips of raw fish from the tops of the rice mounds and set them on a saucer. The cat ate the salmon delicately, with relish, making cooing sounds, then sat up and licked his paws when he had finished.

"You must be tired."

"Yes, I am. However, I have a rather pressing, embarrassing problem — fleas. And worms. You'll need to get rid of them if you don't want the house infested. You can't do anything about the worms right now, you'll have to get special medication.

"As for the fleas, even the gentlest formulations of dish soap diluted in water have proven to be very effective at exterminating them. You're going to have to give me a bath." The cat walked to the sink, hopped in and turned on the taps to the desired temperature with his paws.

Aurora let the sink fill and squirted washing liquid into it, swishing the water around until bubbles rose to the top, then attempted to follow the cat's instructions, but he wasn't satisfied. "No, no, no, step back — I can do it myself." The cat then sat up on its hind legs, massaging his soapy fur, rubbing himself under his armpits like she'd once seen a rat on YouTube do, appearing to wash himself like a human. When he was finished the cat turned the tap back on — not too hot, not too cold — and proceeded to rinse himself off.

Drying the cat off with a dish towel, Aurora heard the voice again: "When you take me to the vet to get the worming pills, you should have me neutered. The constant drive to mate is enough to drive one insane. I've got more important things to tend to. It's too distracting".

"Sure. Okay. If that's what you want."

"I think it's best." The cat took the towel from Aurora, then rubbed himself under his arms. "Why don't you make a fire?"

They sat before a blazing fire in the drawing room, the cat still wet, standing upright, his belly to the flames, Dinky resting on top of a lampshade. "This is wonderful, thank you."

Aurora took the cat in — his lines, his sleek, muscled form, his extraordinary resemblance to her beloved Tu-tu. She wondered whether she was going mad.

The cat turned to her, "You aren't insane. Don't worry," then closed its eyes and turned back to the fire.

Here, they continued their telepathic conversation, which, to Aurora, sounded as though it was happening in stereo around her, prompting her to speak out loud. "To recap. You say you're Tu-tu. You've been possessed by an entity. Some witches made you their familiar, then you escaped and walked across the country to find me?" Her face contorted in disbelief. "And you say you're the Master we've been calling for?"

"Yes. I suppose I am."

"I'm sorry, but it's all just so unbelievable."

"I'm sure it is. Now what you've got to do is to make sure I haven't come with dark motivations. That I'm not possessed with some malignant entity." The cat sprawled out in front of the fire, its head tilting up toward his mistress. "You and the others must decide, if you want to let them in on this, you must determine whether I am friend or foe."

Aurora sat and reflected: "I don't think I could keep this from them. If they can hear you too, I'll know I'm not insane."

"Good thinking."

"How should I introduce you?"

"Call a meeting, tonight if you like. We'll see how many of them can connect with me via their mind, otherwise, if you have a Ouija board, I can point to the letters and numbers, although that is arduous. I can also sign, if any of you know sign language but I can't articulate very well, having paws instead of hands."

That night, the five gathered in the downstairs library — the cat on a padded footstool facing them, Dinky flitting around the room as usual, perching here and there on the backs of chairs, on bookshelves, hanging from the chandelier. Aurora began. "This will sound completely insane, but I've been having telepathic communications with this cat, who is also supposedly my cat — the cat I left behind in Arizona.

"I mean, he looks like my cat. Exactly like my cat. He claims to be my cat and says he walked across the country to find me here, but along the way was captured by a coven of witches who trapped an entity inside him to make him their familiar. He says he's the Master we've been calling for."

The girls turned their heads toward one another, incredulous, then to Aurora and the cat before them on the stool.

Staring into the face of eternity, the intellectual force is exposed to predatory blasts which disorganize it. The trick is to hold fast to Ariadne's string of reason in this onslaught, to not let it snap, or you will fall into oblivion and madness. This is what the girls were dealing with. If one succeeds, one can gain access to knowledge which elevates the human experience. With the string held fast, you will find your way back. But the 'you' you were before will not be the 'you' you are now. You will have grown wings. And then you must decide whether you will fly with the angels or devils. Each girl realized this on a gut, subconscious level that cannot be put into words (in fact when one first encounters something of this nature, one generally becomes mute — the intellect frozen into submission).

Sitting on his hind legs, the cat spoke. "It's true. Something pulled me here. I was already with a coven of witches who treated me like a king, in a beautiful lodge in the Rocky Mountains. These witches caught on quickly, which is always a dream for a teacher. Repetition is so dull. They seemed very happy with my teachings and even kept the doors and windows locked, and a circle of salt around the house, thinking that would stop me from escaping.

"I am offering my knowledge and guidance in the world of the Unseen. As you already know, it's a dangerous path. Your eyes, and all your senses, will have to open to that which few people pay attention to, because to do so risks losing one's mind, and in some cases, one's life.

"Only a crackpot would undertake becoming a sorceress willingly. Normally, apprentices are practical. Rational people must generally be tricked into it. To be a good sorceress, one must be sober able to withstand the pressure. Reflect on this. Reflect hard before deciding whether you want to undertake such a task." The cat began licking its paw.

Aurora turned to the girls. "Did any of you hear any of that?" Hoping against hope she wasn't the only one.

"Yes, I heard a voice," said Harlow.

Madison's face went pale, smacked with the shock of dismay. "He called us crackpots."

Dora and Sylvia had not been able to receive the entirety of the message, but they had heard words and phrases in a voice that seemed to come out of thin air. Harlow and Madison filled them in on what they had missed.

Aurora felt less insane, but nonetheless, overwhelmed, as did all of them. The Master had finally arrived, in the form of a cat, no less — it was more than they could process.

"There will be times when you'll only get parts of my messages. It's always like this with telepathy," the cat continued. "So far, you've done almost everything wrong. That stunt in the forest with your silly brooms fabricated out of heather when you tried to call a storm by the river nearly cost you your lives.

"You were successful in calling something up, but not what you thought. You attracted the attention of something much more dangerous, even than elementals. You didn't see them, but they were there. So incredibly reckless." He then hopped down from the footstool, and disappeared out the door, into the shadows.

The five girls remained in silence. Aurora sat on the floor by the fire, deep in thought. Tu-tu had found her, but this was not the Tu-tu she knew. Was this a hoax? Her unwitting self, sending out telepathic messages, pretending to be the cat? It could not be ruled out. And then, if Tu-tu had been possessed, was this spirit there in good faith, or to cause menace? Aurora expressed her concerns to the four others.

As the days wore on, evidence mounted that the cat was not simply a cat. The things it was capable of were well beyond a cat's abilities. It spelled out sentences with the Ouija board, not to mention smoking cigarillos, playing the drums, watching television — mostly PBS, the news, and other educational programs he found by using the remote. He blocked Fox News with the parental controls. Sometimes he watched a film or two on HBO. In the music room, the cat took to the bongos, beating himself into a trance for hours a day while he communed with entities Beyond the Veil. At his request, Dora bought him an electro-acoustic Celtic harp. He played so well, he became the sixth member of their band. Harlow presented him with a diamanté collar, glittering with Swarovski crystals that shot out rainbow rays when hit with the light, making stars on the walls in the sunshine. The collar made Aurora think of the alien cat from the Disney movie, *The Cat from Outer Space.* As a child, she secretly wished Tu-tu was from another planet, fallen to earth, that he would talk to her like the cat in the movie. Now he was.

At the cat's insistence, he was taken to the vet to be neutered. Madison offered to put a pair of prosthetic testicles on her credit card, but the cat would hear nothing of it. They would only get in his way.

More and more, as the months went by, Aurora believed he was her beloved Tu-tu with an entity inside him. His aberrant behaviour and magical feats also convinced the others. Still, the question remained: was the spirit there to aid or destroy them? It was possible it would do both.

At night, Tu-tu sat on each girl's chest while she slept, tending to the aspects which existed beyond the bounds of reason — transmitting lessons through their subconscious and dreams. If, while awake, they did the arduous work the rational side of themselves required, these lessons would surface at just the right moment and activate the "will" or "will to power", which would turn them from ordinary women into sorceresses, capable of extraordinary feats. But of course, this was something that takes years and lifetimes, and does not happen overnight.

From the outset Tu-tu sniffed wafts of artifice, jealousy, and egotism in the air and was aware the girls were on a path of turning against Aurora and himself. Nevertheless, he was bound by one of the tenants of sorcery — impeccability — to fulfil his promise until they decided they no longer wanted his tutelage, or until they did something stupid and killed themselves.

Every Wednesday, the five gathered in the downstairs library with a fire going, installed themselves on sofas and chairs and listened to the cat's lectures. Tu-tu paced the fireplace mantle, his diamanté collar sparkling. "The key to sorcery is stopping the internal dialog! It is this dialog which holds up the 'normal', rational perception of the world, which is only half the picture. You might as well be walking around with one eye closed.

"When we are born, we are born with two rings of power. As we grow, the rational ring gets bigger and bigger, constructing our perception of reality, which is what we will call the 'ordinary world'.

"However, there is another world, the other ring — a way of perceiving that is chaotic and awesome and terrifying. It defies reason. And it holds great power. It is also a part of the human experience!

"This other world seeps into the 'ordinary world' when reason is overwhelmed. When reason cannot explain, the other world becomes apparent. Reason has its limits. And paradoxically, reason is also ultimately unknowable!" Tu-tu would pause for effect and then do something to jolt the girls, like flying through the air and catching the chandelier where he would continue his lesson, swinging from the crystal drops. "This 'other-worldly' perception surfaces again and again in moments of ecstasy and terror. It is the art of reason to suppress any manifestation of it, to obstruct and distract, to uphold rational reality, to maintain the internal dialog, the words which create this rational world!

"Mark me! A sorceress uses both rings of power to experience the totality of her being! She gains abilities which look extraordinary and impossible in 'everyday reality'. Ultimately, a sorceress achieves a better understanding of what the totality of reality actually is, even though it is inexplicable. Are you following me?" With this, he flung himself from the chandelier and dropped onto the armrest beside Madison. Tilting his head in a gesture of camaraderie, he put his paw on her shoulder. "Madison, I know you think I am 'batshit' and full of hot air. That I am over-explaining something that is really very simple, but I can assure you I'm choosing my words with care." The blood drained from Madison's face. She stood up and left the room. The others followed her exit with their eyes, then turned back to Tu-tu who jumped onto a side table, where he picked up a burning cigarillo from an ashtray and set it between his teeth, the end of which exploded into flame. "Mark me, young women! The difference between a warrior and a sorceress is one of temperament! I do not want you to simply become sorceresses — those morbid, indulgent, low-lifers, one step away from being trapped in any number of prisons. To be free, one must be a warrior!

"What is the difference you ask! A sorceress uses the information she gains to perform feats, which are seemingly impossible to our rational selves, and revels in this.

"Whereas a warrior learns everything a sorceress does, then takes another path. You must not, I repeat, must not, get drunk on the powers of the sorceress! A warrior is always sober." He jumped onto the sofa's armrest with the cigarillo still in his mouth and gave each girl a long, scrutinizing look, squinting his left eye, leaving them with the sensation of a shard of ice piercing just below the navel, which was not unpleasant.

"There are sorceresses who accomplish incredible feats, who turn themselves into animals — wolves, birds, mountain lions — whatever you like. They can be in many places at once. They can develop a double who can go anywhere they like in the world — in splits of seconds. They communicate telepathically — they can bend your will, make you do and feel things beyond your control. And much, much more.

"However! A true warrior doesn't get caught up in the fireworks. Instead, she uses what she's learned to free herself! To experience the totality of her being, the balance between the two rings of power — the rational and the inexplicable." The cat disappeared into thin air, then reappeared next to a small dinner gong on a sideboard, curled his tail around the mallet with the deftness of an octopus arm, and struck the instrument several times. When the vibrations dissipated, he ended the lecture. "We shall continue tomorrow on the same note. I bid you goodnight." Diamanté collar sparkling, he disappeared in a puff of cigarillo smoke.

As time went on and the evening lectures continued, Dora, Madison, Harlow and Sylvia harboured a loathing of the cat. He had rubbed them all up the wrong way. They found his act smug and outdated. He spoke of being sober when they wanted to be drunk – drunk on life, on wine, dancing in Bacchanalia. The prospect of listening to the stuck-up creature babble on for years before they were able to do anything of any significance, to endure its glittering eyes that reached into their guts and squeezed, was torture. They weren't masochists, after all. They didn't need a Master. Diana and Aion could guide and protect them better than any entity trapped inside a cat. If they wanted to unlock the Mysteries, all they had to do was to go back to worshipping the goddess and the god. If they had done it once, they could do it again.

Still, they feared the cat. They'd seen what he could do. Knowing he could read minds, they did their best to keep their heads as clear and reflective as possible to hide their true feelings. It was exhausting. They had become prisoners inside their own bodies. It was a violation, the cat always watching them from the inside. As for Aurora, the entity also creeped her out. What was fantastical was also terrifying and repulsive. Tu-tu was in there, but she only saw flashes of him. The entity had total control. She wanted Tu-tu back — set free, as he was.

More and more, Aurora felt the atmosphere in the house begin to close in around her.

In your affairs, create suspense. Admiration at their novelty means respect for your success. It's neither useful nor pleasurable to show all your cards. Not immediately revealing everything fuels anticipation, especially when a person's elevated position means expectations are greater. It bespeaks mystery in everything and, with this very secrecy, arouses awe.

Aurora ran lines from *The Art of Worldly Wisdom* through her mind again and again. She'd clung to the words in the book for a means to exist, to keep herself from drowning in a tar pit of uncertainty and self-loathing. To fit in. To gain respect. Clearly, it wasn't working. She still felt singled out — a target, a threat. A fraud[32]. They knew. They all knew the truth about her. That she would never be one of them. She was going off the rails. She was talking telepathically with a cat. There was no denying

---

32. In fact, it was not the case that the others saw her as a fraud. They saw her as an enigma — possibly in league with the entity inside the cat. Out of nowhere her cat had shown up, claiming to be the Master. It was suspicious. It made them afraid. It infuriated them. Yes, Aurora was an enigma that could sometimes be aggravating, and which instilled a sense of fear, wonder, rarity, and electricity they didn't know what to do with. She made their heads spin, their hearts race, their blood boil. On top of this, they were annoyed she'd brought the cat into the house and into their lives, as well as the bird, which was cute, but which shat all over the place.

it. The four had completely turned against her and were busy wrapping a crown of thorns around her head, around her naked body, preparing to roll her down a hill. What was once a fissure was widening into an abyss. Any last warmth and solidarity of sisterhood that had remained, was now a place where something putrid seethed. To Aurora, the words they used were loaded with the violence of what wasn't being said. Even things they didn't mean as violence enraged her. Their entitlement. The ignorance of their own ignorance. Rather than having it out and expelling her from the house and their lives, Sylvia and the Californians preferred to hold her captive, playing with her as a cat plays with insects. They maintained a line, so that things didn't escalate to the point of Aurora leaving. Aurora knew that if she decided to quit the house and the fledgling coven it would be received as an act of war, which would only sap her energy, when there were other — more important — matters that demanded her attention. She had to do well in school, in ballet; maintain her grade point average.

Aurora pretended to drink their poison. She knew she wasn't like them, and now she didn't want to be. She was trailer trash, but not trailer trash. It was perhaps time she owned it. She thought of telling them, watching them squirm and curse her with their eyes. It seemed so long ago, when she and Sylvia lived in the dorm together. When they went to Paris and Cannes. The sound of Sylvia breathing, the heat of Sylvia's body against her as they slept. They had showered together, used the same shampoo, conditioner, shower gel. Aurora wore Sylvia's clothes, used her lip gloss, borrowed her shoes. They brushed each other's hair with the same brush. They had fought off the entity in Sylvia's mirror together. Aurora confessed the horror of the exorcism she endured at the hands of the pastors — something she hadn't told anyone else. Not even the librarian. Now when she looked at Sylvia, her blood ran cold. It wasn't the same Sylvia. Her Sylvia was gone. Aurora, herself, was gone. She was not that girl anymore. The spell between them was broken forever.

In an effort to keep herself from being destroyed by bitterness, instead of allowing their infected arrows to rot her from the inside, Aurora tried to go back, to view the girls as they had first appeared to her, when she was enchanted by them and their world. Before she had gotten to know them, they were curiosities. Beautiful creatures from the upper echelons, shining, smelling of silk, crisp hundred-dollar bills, cashmere, soft as butter calf leather, expensive perfumes, looking like they had stepped out of the pages of *Town & Country* or *Vogue* magazines. She had wanted to emulate them, to slip into their skin, their luxury fabrics, their world. She did all she could to keep this view of them in every encounter. But she was sure now that she was not and would not be one of them — they were not of her. She would never fully inhabit their realm. She had knowledge of their world — she knew their customs, the code words, the movements — but her past would never allow her to live in the illusion — harder than glass, hard like diamonds, virtually unbreakable — that kept them from being able to touch the reality she had known in her blood, in her bones, the things she had seen, the impossibilities she faced without unlimited funds behind her, without the pedigree.

Despite all this, despite everything she'd seen and realized, she spent tortured, sleepless nights thinking of how she could win the girls back. Among her classmates she had been deified, along with the four others; cast into the cold outreaches of the stars. Anyone who tried to get close found themselves stranded in the optical illusion of space. They would never reach her co-ordinates. She was truly alone. She had only Tu-tu and Dinky.

To her benefit, Aurora kicked herself into survival mode. She realized she had to stop spending so much time brooding, contemplating all of this. She had to get out of the line of fire. Make herself flame retardant and bulletproof. She spent her time in the library, burying her head in her studies while Dinky flew through the stacks of the brutalist building, perching on Euclidean-shaped wooden, metal and concrete pieces in the architecture – twitching her head from side to side, looking down on the movement below, diving through the warm shafts of air, heavy with the scent of the slow death of books: cellulose, lignin, benzaldehyde, vanillin, ethyl hexanaol, toluene, ethyl benzene, releasing a smoky, woody, sweet aroma.

Top grades were Aurora's priority. She had to maintain her GPA and win another scholarship if she was going to get into the Ivy League. Whenever there was a remark at the house about Aurora being absent from their band rehearsals, shut away in her room or always in the library, she had to remind them she needed to concentrate, to work extra hard if she was going to get into the Ivy League. Like this, her star displaced itself from the constellation the others had formed, and everyone felt a chill.

One late afternoon, just before dusk, the five girls followed the cat to a cemetery on the banks of a river, not far from the Academy grounds, on the other side of a bridge. The road that looped through a cemetery had been ploughed with the snow banks piled up on either side and paths shovelled between some of the graves. There were a few trees here and there, their branches encased in ice. They trod along the frozen paths and tried not to slip, then veered off into the deep snow with Tu-tu jumping from tombstone to tombstone until he stopped and sat still on the left side of a cross. The moon was full, ringed with a rainbow stained a yellowy, tobacco hue. Clouds passed, obscuring it, breaking apart and floating away, leaving thin veils behind. Stars sparkled in the deep blue with bands of orange and yellow at the horizon line.

The cat asked the girls to form a crescent around him, knee deep in the snow. Perched on the cross, Tu-tu sat up like a meerkat and gesticulated with his paws as Dinky darted around him. "A warrior is keenly aware of her own death! This is what separates her from ordinary people going day to day about their ordinary tasks. If you choose to continue the path of sorcery, to become a warrior, you will be confronted with imminent annihilation every step of the way, as some of you have already experienced. (Here Dinky flew to the head of a nearby angel and rested.)

"Knowing that death is there, just over your right shoulder, stalking you, ready to sink its claws in — it is THIS that gives the warrior the necessary potency and concentration to transform her life from one which is commonplace to one that is imbued with magical power!

"At the same time, to be focused on death is morbid and debilitating! Instead of the idea of imminent death becoming an obsession, it must become an indifference. To do this, you must detach yourself from everything. I'm not telling you to become hermits. Being a hermit is self-important. What I want you to do is to get rid of self-importance!

"Stop throwing yourselves around with wild abandon! Make strategic decisions! Let Death advise you." Here the cat brought its paws together in what looked like a prayer. "When Death becomes your friend and you listen, not with your REASON, but with your BODY, you are on your way to power.

"When a warrior has entered into this friendship with Death, when she can sit with Death and be advised by it, she has acquired patience and is on her way to will. Will is responsible for the acts of power that defy rationality. When you have acquired will, you will be able to perform the extraordinary feats you have dreamed of. You will realize your full potential, your true form. Your true form is not solely informed by reason! It is also informed by that which is inexplicable and unknowable, beyond words, beyond the intellect!

"Tonight, I will give you an example of the fruits of power. Something straight from your *Magic and Mystery in Tibet*. What you are about to see feeds on self-importance. In order to come out of this encounter intact, you must banish your arrogance! I'll give you a few minutes to collect yourselves and concentrate. Cease your internal dialog."

The wind hissed across the frozen surface of the snow; icy branches clicked. The girls fell into a deep meditation, shutting off the interior dialog. A strange noise found its way into their ear canals and made their skulls vibrate — a sound like the sputtering of an outboard motor in the distance. As the noise approached, they noticed it changed scales, like a musical tone, making an eerie rhythm. Then it stopped.

"That was the moth," the cat's eyes shined in the darkness. "A warrior considers herself already dead, so there's nothing for her to lose."

The unnerving sputtering began again, coming closer, increasing in volume. The girls strained to determine what it was. It wasn't the cry of a bird or the call of a land animal. The tone of the reverberation varied from low and deep to high and piercing with a rhythm that also altered. At points, it sounded like a single unit of sound, then sprayed out into hard, dense machine gun-like machinations.

When it ceased, the cat spoke, gesturing with its front paw. "Out there, there is only knowledge. The moths are the heralds, or rather, the guardians, of eternity. On their wings is the gold dust...of knowledge and eternity." The cat smiled, his fangs shining in the moonlight.

The drone began again. The girls felt sick to their stomachs — a cold, metallic sickness like mercury being poured into their veins. Their tongues sparkled with electricity and the taste of ozone. Above the tree line, from out of the sky, came a figure like a Rorschach inkblot with two red pinpoints of light for eyes. Its wings beat slowly; it seemed to hover more than fly. The humming, buzzing, syncopated tones vibrated the air around them as the creature approached, the pressure palpable on the girls' skin. Then came a roar like a jet plane, increasing, with a sharp, metallic whizzing. The girls wanted to put their hands to their ears, but found they were captives, paralyzed by the noise. As the creature got closer, the din softened and transformed into a mesmerizing, melodious sound. The thing's hypnotic eyes pulled each girl in, distorting her thoughts, freezing her to the spot, filling her with the terror of lambs to the slaughter.

The creature was perhaps eight feet tall with a wingspan twice this size — the body shaped like a man's, covered in fur, its face the face of a gigantic emperor gum moth with large antennae shaped like leaves or feathers. After inspecting the terrified girls, the creature rose perhaps fifteen feet into the air, creating an influx of wind so powerful they were lifted out of the snow and violently scattered. Harlow slammed into the cross Tu-tu had been using for his sermon, got the wind knocked out of her and landed in the snow, struggling to breathe. Dora hit her head on a tombstone. Madison and Sylvia were sent flying across the surface of the snow where they narrowly missed a cement angel.

Aurora was thrown the furthest, then caught mid-air by the creature like an eagle catches a rabbit. The thing smelled of pollen and fur and held her close to it with the talons on its feet clutching her by the snowsuit as they sailed above the tree line, over the main road, over houses, eventually dropping her in the garden of the house where she landed in the snow on her back, her head sore from the shock. She felt something trickling down the nape of her neck. The sky was clear overhead, the masses of stars alive, glittering with every colour, appearing to move, in conversation, willing the construction of the universe. Aurora lay on the ground, arms out like a snow angel.

There were lights on in the house. Aurora entered through the back door to the atrium. She called out. No one answered. Dinky flew from the hallway and into the room, hovering around Aurora, little wings beating the air around her ears. She couldn't figure out how Dinky had gotten from the cemetery to the house. Aurora took off her boots, her mittens, her coat. She'd lost her hat. Her last memory was of standing in a semi-circle around Tu-tu knee deep in snow at the cemetery. Going from room to room, floor to floor, with Dinky fluttering around her, she called out. No response. Not even the cat. The house was still, no one was inside. Again, she struggled to recall what had happened before she had found herself in the snow in the backyard. All she could remember was the cemetery, Tu-tu standing on a cross, she and the others in a crescent before him.

Aurora decided to make a fire. She sat before the fireplace with the heat tightening the skin on her face and watched the fire spread through the logs. Tu-tu rounded a sofa, strutting toward her, tail quivering, eyes shining.

"Tu-tu! What happened? We were at the cemetery. I vaguely remember that. I'm here and can't remember how I got back. The house is empty. Everyone else is gone."

"The others have a problem with self-importance that may prove fatal. They're too sloppy and exuberant. Knowledge just taught them a lesson they hopefully won't forget. They'll be here soon." The cat sprawled out in front of the fire and began licking his paws.

"They all hate me now. How do I get things back to how they were before?"

"They don't hate you, they're jealous of you. They see you gaining power while they turn more and more bitter." The cat paused, then observed, "You were never happy, living beyond your means, in their debt. How things were before wasn't better."

"You're right, it wasn't."

The cat gave a look of consideration, "They want too much too soon. If they don't slow down and acquire some patience, they'll never achieve anything of importance. Plus, if they continue to chase after the secrets of sorcery with this mindset, I fear for what will happen to them. The world is dangerous enough without opening oneself up to the Unseen." Tu-tu gazed into the fire, then closed his eyes, relishing the heat on his face. He turned to Aurora. "Let's play Snakes and Ladders while we wait. It's under the bay window seat."

"Why not." Aurora got up and found where the board games were hidden. She went through them until she found the one she was looking for. Back in front of the fire, she set up the board. It was an old version, the kind the Victorians had used with squares of virtue: Faith (12), Reliability (51), Generosity (57), Knowledge (76), Asceticism (78); and squares of evil: Disobedience (41), Vanity (44), Vulgarity (49), Theft (52), Lying (58), Drunkenness (62), Debt (69), Rage (84), Greed (92), Pride (95), Murder (73) and Lust (99). The markers inside were Monopoly tokens. Aurora took the Scottie dog; the cat took the top hat. Aurora rolled the die. They began their game. Halfway in, the front door opened and closed to stomping feet and the noise of the girls returning. They kicked off their boots, got out of their snowsuits, threw their mittens and scarves to the side, some of these articles stained with blood from their injuries. Leaving everything strewn about the front hall, they stood in their silk thermal underwear, tired, dazed, then sauntered down the three steps into the sitting room off the entry hall, drawn by the fire Aurora had made.

"How long have you been back?" Sylvia stopped where she stood. Her tone was accusatory.

"I don't know, not long before you." Aurora gazed up at them, not really looking, then back down to the board, pretending to play the board game against herself. She shook the die in her hand and threw it. The cat had disappeared. Dinky flew from a side table to the moulding around the door and clutched onto it, eyeing the girls, then flew off among them, eventually landing on the back of a sofa.

"What are you playing?" The left side of Dora's head had swelled to the size of a grapefruit, distorting her face dramatically. She looked hideous. No one seemed concerned. Dora took her socks off and threw them in the direction of the hall they'd just come from.

"I'm not sure."

"Where is that fucking cat?" Madison narrowed her eyes, glancing around the room.

"I don't know," Aurora looked up at the four of them again, this time paying attention. "You're bleeding!"

"Yeah, we're all sore, bruised and bleeding because of that cat. I'm going to get some ice. Does anyone want hot chocolate?" Harlow gently touched the bruise on her forehead, waited for a response, then turned to go out.

"I'll go with you. My head feels like it's blowing up." Dora left the room with Harlow.

Madison sat on a club chair; her face slashed with an ice burn. Sylvia took a place on the sofa, and wrapped herself in a throw. Her face was also scorched. "We're finished with that cat," Madison stared ahead, something of a burnt-out fuse about her. "Did you see Dora? She looks like a monster. I didn't dare say anything to her. She's going to freak out when she looks in the mirror." They then heard a scream. All assumed it was Dora. "Harlow will take care of her."

"That thing. That thing in the cemetery. Your cat is a black magic cat. This is serious. How could we have let it in here? It's all your fault, Aurora." Sylvia was tired, her words slow and heavy. "That evil thing it made is going to come back."

"We've got to tell Harlow's mother about this, she'll know what to do," Madison pressed her fingers to her temple. "Unless you can get rid of it, Aurora. It might listen to you."

"I'll do anything, yes I'll speak to it. I'll get it to leave."

"Good. I'm going to bed." Madison got up and walked out of the room like she was drunk. Sylvia had fallen asleep on the sofa.

Aurora folded the gameboard, put the Monopoly pieces back into the box and stored it underneath the bay window seat. To look at Sylvia made her skin crawl. She climbed the stairs to the third floor, Dinky following, to her bedroom. In there, she was safe. Not entirely because it didn't belong to her, but then, after all, what belonged to her, really? The Virgin Mary statue? The clothing the librarian had bought her, which she stopped wearing because she knew Sylvia and the others didn't think it was good enough? She went to the desk and turned on the light. At the full-length mirror in the corner of the room she stood and practiced her poker face, careful not to stare too long. After what had happened at Sylvia's house, mirrors were no longer safe. She risked falling in.

Exhausted, Aurora sat on her bed and was able to recall the creature they had seen in the cemetery. It was covered with hair that was powdery, with the delicate scent of honey. This fur was also on its wings, like a moth. When it flew toward them, there had been the dark outline with huge antennae the shape of feathers. Out of the night, its eyes had shone — two pinpoints of piercing red light that felt like a searing blow to the head.

The cat had conjured the creature up[33]. He knew things, unimaginable things which could bestow great power upon the girls, but it was plain, they wanted nothing more to do with him. And who could blame them. Aurora wondered how she was going to get the cat to leave. She thought of leaving herself, going back to the dormitory.

She stared at the painting she'd submitted for her fine arts class inspired by James Dean's fatal car crash, propped against the wall. It was so big — she didn't know what she was going to do with it. The painting struck her as morose and indulgent now. But it had earned her an A. She thought of burning it in the backyard, making it into a vehicle and a weapon as she had intended, somehow drawing Little Bastard's evil spirit into the canvas like a genie to a lamp, then setting it on fire it to rid the world of the entity. This was of course idle fantasy — conceptual. There was no way in hell she was going to be actively calling evil spirits into her sphere ever again. She had learned her lesson. She was finished with sorcery.

---

33. Each time a physical or mental action takes place, currents or waves of force are produced. For the average person, this force is minimal. It doesn't do much. But for one trained in the art of concentration, such as the entity inhabiting the cat, these waves of energy can be put to use in astounding ways, for good or evil. "Guardian angels" are formed in this way. The life of such a creature is akin to a battery, its force slowly leaking out by means of radiation unless it is recharged, eventually weakening and dying out. However, this can take time and it can wreak havoc if left unchecked. The whole question of making, charging, recharging, or destruction of these artificial elementals is an important one in practical occultism.

"Some men put the wreckage behind a false wall in a building in Whatcom County, Washington State." Tu-tu sat sprawled at the end of the bed.

"James Dean's Porsche?"

"Yes." Tu-tu sat up and began licking his paws. "Also, Dinky is a male. It's difficult to tell the male from the female Eurasian blue tit."

"Oh." Aurora closed her eyes, breathed in and opened them again. "Do you know the girls want you to leave?"

"Yes. I came here for you, Aurora. Do you want to leave?" The cat's eyes gleamed.

Aurora looked sideways at the cat. "Where would I go?"

"You could go back to the dormitory."

"That would be acknowledging that there's a problem. I don't want to make waves. I get the feeling they'd make a big deal out of it if I did. Even though they don't like me anymore and find me annoying. I don't want to escalate the situation."

"Ultimately, they don't find you annoying. They're annoyed with themselves and their lack of discipline. They're too self-indulgent. They have no patience. As long as they keep the grip on their self-importance, they aren't going to be able to pay attention to the world around them." The cat rose, did a little sashay reminiscent of *Singing in the Rain*, then sat in front of Aurora like a Sphinx, whipping his tail back and forth. "You need to extricate yourself from them, go off on your own. You're doing so well already. I've been impressed by your stalking abilities." The cat admired how cunningly Aurora maneuvered through each day — at the house, in every encounter she had with others outside, in the classroom, in the cafeteria, with the girls in ballet, absorbing and repelling the subtle jibes and jabs that came from all corners. She had maintained her composure, playing her role with precision, unscathed.

"What do you mean?"

"A warrior must learn the art of stalking, 'Know how to be all things to all men. A discreet Proteus – a scholar among scholars, a saint among saints.' You have the right idea. One must be fluid in order to exist as a warrior-sorceress.

"Ordinary men and women's lives are formed of deeply engrained habits and behaviours. When one changes one's perspective, one changes one's world. A ballerina or a gymnast performs feats that appear impossible, defying gravity and reality. However, when one becomes a ballerina, or a gymnast, when one engages with the reality of what the art entails, one finds, through ruthless discipline and hard work, how such accomplishments are possible. It's the same with sorcery.

"When one diverges from, and challenges, these ordinary habits and behaviours, a new way of perceiving emerges, one which opens onto vistas and modes of power unavailable to ordinary people." The cat turned his head to the beam of light from the table lamp and winced. Immediately, the light went out. "When one becomes a stalker, one becomes a hunter of power, like death itself. The first principle of stalking is that a warrior stalks herself. She learns her disguise so well that no one knows she's in disguise. She must do this ruthlessly, cunningly, patiently, and sweetly.

"She must be ruthless, but charming. Cunning, but nice. Patient, but active and alert. Sweet, but lethal. Change your behaviour, and you change everything. Just as you wanted to reinvent yourself to fit in — but fitting in is not the point. Listen to me, follow my advice and you will not only fit in — you will captivate. You will accumulate power. Power, which you will be able to use for extraordinary achievements.

"To further specify, the ruthlessness mustn't be harshness. The cunning mustn't be cruelty. The patience cannot be negligent. The sweetness cannot be foolishness. A hunter must be humble and alert, invisible, until that last moment, when it's too late. Do you understand what I'm getting at?" The cat, still facing her like a Sphinx, swished its tail back and forth. Dinky dive-bombed the cat from his place on top of the door moulding, chirping and snickering all the way and was quickly smacked out of his trajectory by a paw, flung into the bathroom.

"So, you change your behaviour, and you change everything. And you must be ruthless, cunning, patient, and sweet, like you said, this is part of the technique. Isn't this like being an actor?"

"It's similar." Tu-tu sat up and began licking his paw. "But what I'm teaching you goes further than acting. This technique changes something fundamental in how you perceive the world, which is everything. It allows you to see more deeply, more completely into the reality, into the nature of things. It gives you freedom you wouldn't have had otherwise. It's a way to stalk power, to gain power, insight." He walked across the bed and jumped onto the windowsill, where he looked out into the night, "By practicing stalking, the effects are cumulative. Eventually, the apparatus with which we perceive reality shifts to another view, which is just as real. Through this view, one learns secrets about the nature of reality, which allows one to perform the feats of a sorceress.

"The mode of stalking, this system of behavior, protects against becoming petty and capricious. It reflects and sustains the morality and sense of beauty that differentiates sorceresses from plain witches. It forces one to be impeccable, to conserve one's energy.

"Without excess energy, sorcery isn't possible. The average person doesn't have enough power to be a sorceress, let alone a warrior. The warrior must be on permanent guard against the coarseness of human behaviour. She is magical and ruthless — a maverick with the most refined taste and manners. Her task is to sharpen yet disguise these cutting edges so that no one will ever suspect her ruthlessness." He jumped back onto the bed, holding Aurora with his gaze. "Stalking is an act of positive trickery. The point is to shatter the mirror of self-reflection. To go beyond the self — beyond reason, the tales we tell ourselves. Because there are other realities, as you know. Realities that have nothing to do with reason. You aren't going to understand this now. I'm planting a seed."

Aurora's eyes widened. "Christ said to his apostles, *Behold, I am sending you out like sheep among wolves. Be as cunning as serpents and as innocent as doves.*"

"Yes. Correct. Christ was a sorcerer." The cat looked at Aurora with a glimmer in his eye, then batted her on the forehead, sending her into a deep sleep.

Several weeks later Sylvia got wind of a party from a childhood friend who was now boarding at Choate Rosemary Hall. It was going to be an affair unlike Aurora or the nouveau riche Californians had ever attended. This was old money — American aristocracy. It was to be held on an estate owned by the family for generations. The Californians were beside themselves and went to work excavating their closets to find something suitable to wear. Aurora assumed she wasn't invited, that they didn't want her to come, but as it turned out, it was in the interests of sabotage to cajole her into doing things she couldn't afford, spending her precious study time on frivolities.

Sylvia was exasperating, making the point again and again that this kind of party didn't happen very often, that it would be a waste not to go — a great opportunity missed. The host was the most charming, well-connected person she knew. Sylvia wouldn't take no for an answer. It was important — a matter of urgency — that everyone attend. They would stay for the evening, not the weekend, and return to the Academy Sunday evening at the latest.

As the fever of excitement ran through the house, Aurora steeled herself, remembering the cat's lessons. Be ruthless, but charming. Cunning, but nice. Patient, active and alert. Sweet, but lethal. She chose a black Miu Miu pinafore dress and a sheer, white, ruffled, Victoriana blouse Madison had bought at a Chloé boutique in Paris, then decided she didn't like.

Tu-tu sat on top of Aurora's dresser, watching her prepare for the evening. "Be careful. Watch yourself. They're in the mood to tear your eyeballs out. You're lucky really. Petty tyrants plotting your downfall are the best way to test yourself and accumulate power." Since the night when the others had insisted Aurora get rid of him, the only place he had showed his face was in her bedroom otherwise, he was invisible. He was never spoken of again. Out of sight, out of mind. Of course, Aurora didn't want the cat to leave. In the end, he was her only true friend. She also had Dinky, whom she loved, but Dinky couldn't carry on complex conversations. The thought of Tu-tu gone, after three years of wondering whether he was alive or dead, was unbearable. Even if it wasn't really Tu-tu.

The cat had no intentions of leaving Aurora either. He envisioned the rest of his cat life in her company and saw his role as teaching her little by little, bit by bit, the great knowledge he had of sorcery, so that one day she might become a warrior, free of the confines that bind the average human to their limited perception of reality. After all, this is what she had wanted — to realize her full potential — and he would help her. With the cat's falsified departure, the illusion of peace gained some traction and made Aurora's life slightly easier in the house. But Aurora knew this was only temporary. The veiled insults and whispers would no doubt return.

Each night, lulled by that part of himself — the spirit of Aurora's childhood companion — longing for his mistress over years of separation, the cat found ecstasy in being next to her at long last, where he belonged, purring to his heart's content, both falling asleep under the green glow of the Virgin Mary looking down on them from the top of the chest of drawers.

5.

I look down at these bloodied pages, scattered throughout the room, and realize I have been staring into space and have no clue how long it's been since I wrote a word. I notice that, at times, everything in me tends to go on to become something else — the space between the words, the flame in the lamp, the call of the owl outside in the wood. I actually got stoned on the level of cannabis today from smoking a large joint of wild lettuce. L-Theanine is pathetic compared to it.

My soul has been reduced to a ball of thread. Aurora. Aurora, you have done this to me. There are dolls bursting from my chest. Despite my best efforts, I am struggling to continue the story.

What comes next is not pleasant. It's the beginning of the end, and in fact, it's potentially soul-destroying. But Aurora is, I believe, a fighter. I would bet money on her. Even if she goes numb, into the cocoon to protect herself, I have confidence she will re-emerge as a creature with wings and fly away from the horror.

I have conversations with her in my head. I wonder what she'd think of the threads of setting sun cutting through the trees, of the light that shimmers and changes form on the walls and floor throughout the day, the tea-set with symbols from the suits of playing cards, the fox face moulding on the fireplace, the ornate copper fire screen with a pear tree design hammered into it.

What would she think of James M. Cain's opinion of Hemingway, that he wrote of "God's eternal mayhem against Man, a theme he worked into great, classical cathedrals"? Cain said of himself that his focus was on "the wish that comes true, a terrifying concept...the wish must really have terror in it; just wanting a drink wouldn't quite be enough." In this same prologue, he went on, "... my stories have some quality of the opening of a forbidden box...Their appeal is first to the mind, and the reader is carried along as much by his own realisation that the characters cannot have this particular wish and survive, and his curiosity to see what happens to them, as by the effect on him of incident, dialogue, or character. Thus, if I do any glancing, it is toward Pandora, the first woman, a conceit that pleases me, somehow, and often helps my thinking." Yes, Cain is a man I feel a great affinity with. My Pandora's box is right in front of me, made of glass, in the shape of a bottle. And inside floats Pandora. Ultimately, it is she who has control...

Inside the limousine, the scent of perfume and leather, bubble-gum and antiperspirant vie for attention and mix. They are drinking champagne from the bottle, passing it around, fixing their hair, looking into compact mirrors, testing their smudge-proof lipsticks, running their fingers over their lips. Aurora has Madison's Christian Louboutin red lip stain on — a foolproof way to keep her lips looking like cherry skin for at least seventy-two hours. So strong is the staying power, application requires a certain level of skill and precision. Removal requires time or an oil-based cleanser.

Blacker than ink, the limousine slips along, shining with the reflectivity and depth of the void, carrying the five young women from their off-campus house in New Hampshire to the estate in Upstate New York for the party. They stop at a diner for lunch. As dusk settles, a band of hazy tangerine fades into a deepening blue, they turn off the main road, headlights illuminating a corridor of pine, birch, dogwood, fir, thick on either side. They eventually reach the main house and the circular gravel drive. Sylvia instructs the driver to pull over, parking out of the way of the general pile up of cars, where he will wait until the girls want to be driven back to the Academy.

There is a veranda on the ground floor, terraces and balconies on the levels above. Porch lanterns light up the facade. People with glasses and bottles in their hands congregate on the veranda, spill down the front steps. Their puffs of breath disappear in the air with clouds of cigarette smoke. Dimmed lighting glows from the windows.

As they approach, Aurora notices aureoles around the hanging lanterns that disappear after her eyes adjust to the light. Dinky follows. Inside, it is warm and inviting

— the murmur of the guests and music, crystal glasses adding little chimes to the background. Fires rage in every fireplace. Guests are sitting and standing, walking up and down the curving staircase. On the landing, two stuffed bears stand against the wall on either side with crystal lamps hanging from their paws. Hired help dressed in black and white weave among the people offering champagne and hors d'oeuvres. Moving from room to room, the scent of wood smoke, cigarettes, marijuana, and fresh flowers, mingles with perfumes and colognes, old carpets, cashmere, leather, silk drapery. Sylvia goes to look for the host. The Californians scatter and disappear through various doorways.

Aurora finds herself alone in the middle of strangers. She lifts the first glass of champagne from the next passing waiter she sees, looks into her eyes and thanks her, then moves across the room. She tells herself she won't drink any more after this and savours the champagne sip by sip. She wants to keep her wits about her. She can't afford to lose more than one day to debauchery. She has three essays to finish and an endless amount of reading. She doesn't intend to take part in the séance or trip on psychoactive mushroom honey. She also very much doubts they will be returning home the next afternoon. But this is a once-in-a-lifetime chance. These are the sort of people who would never be so tacky or gauche as to have their photo taken for *Town & Country* — they are above even that. This is the true elite, the ones who rule their own little worlds in secrecy —worlds which contract or expand according to their will.

The guests appear slightly older and more sophisticated than the students at Aurora's Academy. Maybe it's the lighting, setting, and champagne. One room on the ground floor is dedicated to a feast laid out on a fifteen-foot table: aged beefsteaks, the largest and freshest shrimp money can buy, imported French cheeses, exotic fruits and vegetables, seared tuna and olive skewers, cherry tomatoes filled with crab and lemon mayonnaise, etc. Platters and pyramids of delicate pastries, bottle upon bottles of champagne, buckets of ice, whisky, gin, vodka, every spirit imaginable. Aurora wanders, observing everything, drinking it all in. She goes from room to room on the ground floor, mostly unnoticed by the groups in conversation, smoking, laughing, drinking, teeth gleaming, jewellery sparkling.

She passes through the next open door and is met with a smoking room where framed and mounted rocks with prehistoric figures and paintings of monsters hang on the walls. This leads to a sitting room, then through a door off to the right — a library. No one appears to be there. The library is even larger and more magnificent than the one at Sylvia's house — four floors of stacks, two wooden spiral staircases, stained-glass windows high up on the eastern wall. Everything looks old. In the fireplace a fire consumes oak logs. Aurora puts her empty champagne flute on a side table and makes herself comfortable on the sofa. Dinky flits up through the stacks, exploring. Without realizing it, Aurora falls asleep.

When she wakes, a young man is staring at her. She can smell the alcohol on his breath, the scent of his cologne (woody, aromatic, aquatic) from where he sits in an armchair across from her. Aurora turns to look him squarely in the face, terrified of what he might do to her. His eyes narrow as he takes in the elegant line of her neck.

"Sorry, sleeping beauty. I didn't mean to wake you." He leans back in the chair, spreading his legs, holding a champagne glass in his hand that hovers above his groin. "Where're your friends? They abandon you?"

"No, they're here somewhere."

"You're stunning. You're going to eat me up, chew me up and spit me out, aren't you?" Sitting there across from the radiant young woman, he feels pulled by a force he knows only as attraction, but which is far more complex and occult than he could imagine. Sinking into her sphere, he remains fixed to the object of his conquest — his eyes seeing nothing but the enticing creature before him. Little does Aurora know, he is the handsome, charismatic and ruthless son of a Russian mafia underboss — a first-class seducer of women.

"How did you guess?" A well-studied aloofness and warmth in her voice marks her out as a member of the elite. Dinky flies down from the second floor and lands on the back of the sofa next to Aurora.

"What's a bird doing in here?"

"He's mine. I rescued him in Paris."

The son of the underboss smiles. "Cute." He stares at her. "So, you've decided not to take part in the orgy going on out there?" He empties the champagne glass, not taking his eyes off Aurora.

"No. What are you talking about?" She smiles playfully.

Spiritous fire hidden underneath a virginal sweetness. A hint of corruption wrapped up in a caress, childlike and devout. These are not his thoughts; he is not capable of this kind of depth but this is what he senses without being able to verbalize it. "Some girls gave everyone psychedelic mushroom tea and now there's an orgy going on."

"I guess I'll stay in here then."

"Yeah, I don't touch that kind of stuff. We can just hang in here. I'll go get more champagne. Wait here." He cannot believe the treasure he's found; one he couldn't have conceived of existing just ten minutes earlier.

A booming voice in Aurora's head tells her to run, but instead, she curls up on the sofa and watches the fire burn.

True to his word, he comes back with a bottle of champagne in an ice bucket. "You don't want to go out there, trust me, some crazy shit is going on." He pours them both a glass and sits back down in the armchair. "So, you go to Choate?"

"No, the other illustrious one in New Hampshire. You?"

"I'm at Columbia. Law student."

"Nice."

"Yeah."

Aurora isn't convinced at first. She can sense he's lying. But later, as he pursues her and the night wears on, she can see very well that he is attentive, well-mannered, cultured, world-weary — a true man, protective. She doesn't sense the apocalypse that is about to happen. There hasn't been many men in Aurora's life, only a few of her teachers, the prep school boys, men in passing, fathers of her friends, men at the trailer park, in the street, policemen. Men on television. A soldier she saw in the trailer park from inside her grandmother's car made a big impression on her. This man is nothing like them. Maybe a little bit like the soldier. She likes his build and his floppy, curly dark hair; his green eyes. He isn't manoeuvring himself to get his hands all over her. He is cool and collected.

With dawn, the stained-glass windows glow. Coloured rays run through the room, dance across their faces. The son of the mafia underboss is as attractive in the light as in the semidarkness. In the light, Aurora shines. The son of the underboss is in awe of her beauty. He isn't going to let this one go without a fight.

"Do you think it's safe to go outside now? Do you think the orgy's over?" Aurora smiles as she says this; it makes the son of the underboss want to kiss her.

"I'm not sure. I could go out and check." There is something about this girl that drives him wild. Wilder than he's ever felt about anything, even driving his Ferrari at high speeds.

With sorcery, as everybody knows, there is no stopping it.

When the son of the underboss comes back, he announces the coast is more or less clear, then asks her if she wants to go and have breakfast with him, after which he'll drive her back to the Academy. Aurora doesn't want to be left alone, waiting for Sylvia, Harlow, Madison and Dora to emerge so she can get a ride. Not to mention the hours and hours back to New Hampshire she would have to endure in the car with them. She agrees to his proposal.

Walking through the house, the guests are in states of undress, draped over furniture, entangled in one another — broken champagne flutes, articles of clothing, undergarments, scattered on the floor. Dinky follows, swooping through the air. Aurora passes Harlow, completely naked with symbols painted all over her body in black marker, asleep or passed out on a sofa, in the arms of the son of the Supreme Court judge.

Outside, in the blinding white of day, Aurora approaches Sylvia's driver, taps on the window to wake him and tells him to let Sylvia know she's getting a ride back and not to wait for her. The son of the underboss's car is a Mercedes, which he implies he took from his father's fleet without permission. On the way, his phone rings again and again. He ignores it.

They have breakfast at a diner. Aurora realizes she hasn't ever been on a date before in her life. This is the first time she's been alone with an attractive man. They drink coffee, smoke cigarettes. Dinky stays at their table and pecks at Aurora's waffles. The son of the underboss smokes Marlboro Reds.

Aurora is more electrifying than any woman the son of the underboss has ever encountered. Simply having his hand on the table two inches from hers is a conduit for shocks of adrenaline that course through his body and threaten delirium. He has no choice but to sit opposite the source of this mania and submit to it, engorged with a delicious sense of submission. And, at sixteen, she is not yet a woman. Although, to look at her, she appears older, certainly the age of consent. But young, yes — she has the soft skin and rounded cheeks babies and adolescents have. Aurora weaves her web, trying out the powers Tu-

tu has taught her, instinctively, impeccably, ruthlessly, patiently, with cunning that isn't cruel and a sweetness that isn't foolish.

Over eggs, bacon, and waffles the son of the underboss asks Aurora about her upbringing. She tells him she's from Arizona, that her parents are dead, that she was raised by her grandmother, the same story she tells everyone who asks.

After he drops her off and says goodbye, he can't stop thinking about her. Flowers arrive at the house, three or four times a day. The entry hall looks like a flower shop; everywhere there's a table, flowers sit. The five girls are lulled to sleep each night by the scent of an exotic, impossible meadow.

The son of the mafia underboss installs himself in a hotel in town and picks Aurora up in a metallic grey Maserati, taking her to restaurants and the cinema. He moves in slowly, taking time before he touches her, and then just briefly, her hand, to help her out of the car; the side of his shoe, gently resting against hers in the movie theatre; the silk of her arm in passing. His thrill is the chase, the sinking in, the slow burn he hopes will turn into a raging massacre.

No man has ever lavished this amount of attention on Aurora. He buys her clothes and jewellery. He waits until he knows she's ready, more than ready, to kiss him. When he first kisses her, they're staring into one another's eyes, the closest he's ever been to her, leaning on the armrest between them, his shoulder pressed to hers. Her skin smells sweet, like apples. *Raging Bull* plays out in black and white on the screen. Aurora's eyes burn in the flashes of light. He returns her gaze, serious and welcoming, leaning in deeper, and takes the back of her head gently into his palm and kisses the lips he has wanted to taste from the very beginning, when he first saw her sleeping and fought hard not to lose control of himself. The son of the underboss thinks this kiss is the most powerful drug he has ever taken and can't even consider what it might be like to take her virginity in that moment because he fears he would spontaneously combust.

The next three times they meet, they share several more kisses. Aurora tells him what he already knows — that she's a virgin. She says she isn't going to sleep with anyone until she turns eighteen.

Sylvia corners Aurora in the kitchen and tells her she has it on good authority that her boyfriend is the son of a Russian mafia underboss. Aurora tells her the idea is ridiculous, that he's studying law at Columbia. Madison chimes in: "Don't say we didn't warn you." Harlow raises an eyebrow. Dora pretends she isn't listening to any of it.

Tu-tu also knows the association will not come to a good end, declaring, "What you're embarking on is highly dangerous. You're playing with fire and you're going to get burned. I can't speak any plainer." But Aurora can't stop seeing him. She's having too much fun. She has been starved of this kind of attention. His man chemicals make her drunk.

The frolic ends when Aurora finds herself in a hotel room tied to the bed, drowsy from the amobarbital the underboss's son has shot into her arm. He tells her that he knows everything — that she is trailer trash, that her mother was a junkie who died in a fire of her own making, that Aurora herself was a crack baby, that her father was shot dead in a drug-related incident and was suspected of being a crystal meth manufacturer. But she's special, because no one would ever guess. She had succeeded in her masquerade. To all intents and purposes, she is prime — one hundred per cent Ivy League crème de la crème. He's secured a buyer for her virginity.

The underboss's son looks down at Aurora with sad, twitching eyes. After a year, she will be allowed to go. She will send postcards telling everyone she's taking a year out to broaden her horizons, an au pair for a wealthy European family. She will call her grandmother regularly. He assures her that her grandmother will understand, adding that her grandmother's life depends on it.

For Aurora, time slows down — she has the impression she's drowning. Dinky is flitting around the room, the shadow of his wings on the walls and ceiling. Aurora thinks of moths. The son of the underboss's voice speaks to her from far off, as though from on high, in a cloud. None of this is real. This isn't happening. Drugged, white silk ropes around her ankles and wrists, dressed in a lacey white baby doll slip and matching underwear, the son of the mafia underboss leaves her there. A man in a business suit enters. He does not say a word, undresses, and rapes her.

...I'm not a sociopath or a sadomasochist, I'm not about to give fodder for some sicko to get off on, so here, writing this horrible event, I have to stop. I can't go any further. The details of the assault aren't possible for me to give, to this page, or anywhere. I'm trying to forget them.

Suffice it to say the son of the underboss lured her onto a private jet with the promise of a romantic four-day weekend in Greece by way of London where they were going to meet his father. The son of the underboss had brokered a seven-figure amount for Aurora's virginity with photographs and proof of her prep school provenance. He knew she would be useless as an escort after a year — even a year was pushing it. If she was lucky, she would fall into the lap of a billionaire who would take care of her. It was a decent deal for trailer trash who had tried to become so much more.

I need to collect myself, go back to the cherry pop, smoke some hashish...

There is always a hired gun who stands outside Aurora's hotel suite. Sometimes, he takes her outside the city to country estates. On these occasions two men go with her and don't take their eyes off her unless she's in the bedroom. They stand outside the door and wait.

It's useless to scream, to physically fight. The underboss told her from the beginning that if she tried anything, she would be pumped full of drugs and put in a basement until she settled down. If she doesn't play her part, she will go back to the basement. After the first week, Aurora doesn't see the underboss again. There are pills to keep her sedated, her eyes wide and soft, pupils dilated. There is a birth control pill every day at the same time. They check her mouth to make sure she swallows them. Her thoughts scatter like marbles. All over, she feels scorched, dirty, exposed. Sometimes, everything is warped like she's looking through gasoline fumes.

Aurora is stuck in the purgatory of wanting to be sick but knowing nothing will come up. Days and nights blur. Dinky keeps her company. She feeds him the food they bring her. She has no idea what day of the week or month it is. Breakfast is brought every morning, then lunch and dinner. The television has been removed from the suite. Aurora wonders if there are other girls locked up in the hotel. The medication makes her feels stupid. Thoughts move in slow motion like tennis balls hit underwater.

Outside, six floors below, sprawls Regent's Park and the London Zoo. She leaves the windows open to let Dinky come and go. She hears the owls at night and imagines she's somewhere else — a cabin in the woods. Wolves sing and howl. With sunrise comes the looping, crazed duets of gibbons, the honking of flamingos, the far-off roar of lions. Throughout the day and night, peacocks scream blood-curdling calls. When she lays her head down to sleep, a vein in her right temple pulsates. She is afraid it will explode.

Aurora knows she must rely on herself and her wits. This is not a game — she must use everything in her possession to exit intact. She needs to remember what Tu-tu taught her. She has to steel her heart. Change herself into the stalker who stalks herself. The men she entertains and goes to bed with pollute her. She tells herself she will never fall into a trap like this again. The way they lean in, their alcoholic breath, the weight of them, their repulsive skin on her naked body. She wants to kill them. Kill them all. Aurora has the impression she's trapped in the reoccurring, infinite hell of funhouse mirrors. Often, she fantasizes about dying. Life has become exactly as Baudelaire described, "An oasis of boredom in a desert of horror". Every day is a variation of the same. She takes endless baths in an attempt to purify herself, rubbing bath salts over her arms, her chest, her legs, her stomach. She dreams of murder. Her nightmares are filled with the rodents in the tunnels, bloody incisors flashing, claws in her hair, the stench of incense and faeces.

The lessons Tu-tu taught Aurora in the art of stalking have now become a matter of life and death. Aurora is battling for her soul. She has to stay alert. She uses her charms ruthlessly, cunningly, patiently, and sweetly, convincing the man at the door to let her use his iPad for an hour a day with parental controls restricting sensitive information, and watches jiu jitsu videos on YouTube. With practice, on her unwitting clients, she perfects a sleeper chokehold. Like this she doesn't have to endure intercourse for more than five minutes. The men remember entering her, passing out and waking up, never the wiser. However, the move is dangerous. If pressure is applied to the artery for more than fifteen seconds, permanent brain damage and death can result. Aurora has three accidents, killing two and turning one into a vegetable. The same two men come each time and take the bodies out. She has become a murderer, like in her dreams. Murdering is more horrible than she had imagined. The bodies go limp. The killings are in self-defence but killing is killing. A corpse is left behind smelling of cologne, urine, faeces. The threat is neutralized, but there will be more.

She spends hours in the bathroom being sick. She can't remember any of the black magic spells in *The Kybalion*. Anyway, they are useless because they require the eyeballs of owls and other ingredients that are impossible to get, plus the supposedly ancient book was written in 1908, which points to it being a fraud. Aurora entertains the idea of conjuring up an artificial elemental like Dion Fortune did in *Psychic Self-Defense*, when she accidentally formulated what she referred to as a "werewolf". According to Fortune, she was lying resting on her bed one afternoon, brooding over her resentment of someone, drifting along the borders of sleep. The desire to cast off all restraints and go berserk consumed her. At the same time, images of Norse mythology swam in her head. Out of this visual kaleidoscope rose Fenrir, the wolf-horror, pure evil, destined to swallow the sun and the god Odin at the end of the world. Instantly, Fortune felt a pull and a drawing-out from her solar plexus, and there, on the bed next to her, materialized the giant wolf, made of ectoplasm, grey and colourless. She could feel its weight against her and smell its musky dog odour. It snarled at her. Instinctively, she jabbed it in its hairy ectoplasmic ribs, telling it to go to the floor, which it did, as obedient as a guide dog.

After this, Fortune described the perils of creating such a monster, how she lost control, and how she had to have help in absorbing it back into her solar plexus before it caused significant harm.

Aurora thinks she doesn't care if she gives birth to an artificial elemental she can't control. She wants to destroy her aggressors. She wants to annihilate herself. She wants oblivion. What she doesn't want is to harm innocents. She lies in bed one afternoon, exhausted from crying in the bathroom, and tries to recreate Fortune's experience. She feels the pull into sleep. She feels herself sinking. She lets herself fill with rage at it all, at the son of the Russian mafia underboss, at all the men who have violated her. The rage feels like it is running through her veins. It is consuming her entire body. She realizes she is also raging at herself. She doesn't care if the wolf devours her along with her enemies. She tries to visualize Fenrir. She sees the giant wolf-god in her mind. Blood drips from its muzzle. It snarls. Its eyes are translucent, amber, they glow with an otherworldly light. She feels a chill. The wolf growls, baring its teeth, and backs away. Nothing happens in her solar plexus. She tries this exercise many times with no results.

After rendering unconscious another man who violates her, Aurora tries to use the sleeper chokehold on the guards but they have black belts in jiu jitsu, know what she's doing, and overpower her. Luckily, they don't report this. They don't want anyone to know they've been emasculated by a woman, especially one of her size, but she's no longer allowed to use their iPads. Over the telephone, the son of the underboss threatens to have her killed, to also kill her grandmother, but business is good. An unprecedented frenzy of men is in constant bidding wars for her services.

It goes without saying that Aurora is no longer the same. She is unrecognizable even to herself. When she looks in the mirror, she sees thousands of women and knows she embodies them all, even though each one remains, ultimately, unknowable to her. She cannot look long in the glass because she is still afraid of falling in.

She sits in an armchair in her hotel suite and extends her arm toward Dinky, who is perched on a lampshade. The sound of his wings and chirps as he flies across the room, his little talons clutching her finger, the tilt of his blue and yellow masked head from side to side when he looks at her — he is the only source of joy in her life. But it's not the joyfulness she had before. It's packed in cotton wool and always flitting away from her.

Aurora wonders why Tu-tu hasn't come. Maybe it's a test. Maybe he didn't ever exist at all. With the drugs inside her, with the galloping light across the walls of her hotel suite, things disappear in a puff of smoke. (What Aurora doesn't know is that Tu-tu's time was up. The night she disappeared, running home to her, he was hit by a car, one of the most common fates of a cat. Presently, he was being filtered through the Bardo.) If life was surreal when she stepped from her existence as trailer trash into the rarefied air of the Academy, it is even more so now.

She breezes through door after door of perception, and another, and another, one by one. She has the sensation there won't ever be an end, it will go on like this forever, reality unmoored. She sees the infinity of the funhouse mirrors over and over again. At night she dreams of a giant spider who wraps her in its cocoon, speaking in reverse so that she can't understand what it's saying.

Aurora knows she must grab hold of herself. Sober up. She continues to focus on remembering as much of Tu-tu's teachings as she can. They are all she has left. They are the Ariadne's string through the labyrinth, leading back to sanity. She sees his feline face, speaking out of the darkness, *You must be impeccable. Impeccable not only in a moral sense, but in a sense of conserving and storing energy. Self-importance wastes an incredible amount of energy. We talk the world into being and maintain it by continuing to talk to ourselves. Inner silence breaks this mechanism. When enough energy is accumulated, the will activates. This will is not like "will" as people generally understand it. It happens mysteriously, after many years of tribulation and toil. No one can tell you how it works, except the results of using it are astounding. A warrior knows this and waits for the will to be revealed to her. A warrior, ultimately, has only her will and her patience.*

The only reading materials are trashy books and fashion magazines in the living room area of the suite. She looks out the window for clues in the activity below to determine what day of the week it is. She hears Tu-tu's voice: *Stalking is an act of positive trickery. The point is to shatter the mirror of self-reflection. To go beyond the self, beyond reason, the tales we tell ourselves. If this behaviour seems contemptible, to me it seems laudable. Because we are imitating nature, which is changeable. Whoever imitates nature cannot be censured.*

Aurora tells herself she's going to have to adapt, to continue adapting, as she did before, as she is doing now. She cannot fall into the void. No matter how hard it pulls her. She must reach the place of no pity — cold and calculating, indifferent to her personal safety. Again and again, she hears Tu-tu's voice. *The world hangs in a strange balance; there is nothing you can add to it and nothing you can subtract from it. You must be impeccable in order to survive.*

Rising in an elevator with her bodyguard, Dinky in her handbag, all Aurora knows is that the next client is a famous pianist. She gazes at her reflection in the bronze-hued cube of mirrors, turning her face from side to side. As they slide upward, she feels her heart levitate. The drugs they give her have all manner of side effects. She makes herself empty as the lift continues toward the penthouse. She will play the game. The game is the only way she can gain any control. Emptying herself out. This is the first step in becoming the fantasy that is expected of her. It begins with a void, ironically, like in the Bible. Darkness on the face of the deep. Her M.O. is to construct her personality in split seconds from cues she reads and interprets from the client. However, the base is always the femme fatale. From this position, she can go anywhere — to the girl next door, for instance. Every irresistible woman has a certain concentration of this 'lethal woman' inside her, however innocent she may be.

The elevator doors open. Aurora steps out into the marble entry hall. The lights are dim. Chandeliers sparkle. The bodyguard steps to the side. He stands in the corner, heavy lidded, hands crossed over his groin, next to the elevator.

The pianist cuts a handsome form. Aurora is surprised to find him very attractive. Blood rushes to her cheeks. She steps forward, closer, but not too close. The pianist displays just a hint of nervousness, a little twitch at the corner of the eye; otherwise he's outwardly calm, even though the blood is quickening through his veins, his heart beating faster like a hunted rabbit. From where she stands, Aurora feels his agitation. She has this effect on people.

Through a thin veil of cocaine and vodka, the pianist remains mute. The young woman before him radiates more than anyone he has ever seen radiate. It is an inhuman radiation. Ethereal sounds rise, clear as bells. He's convinced she is an angel. Her presence makes him drunk with sonatas. He cannot make his lips move, or his tongue, or open his mouth to speak, not even a *Hello* and an introduction. He wants to write the music down, but it comes at such a pace he can do nothing but listen and wonder as he gazes at the exquisite creature before him.

The pianist finds his voice. He speaks to the bodyguard in a gentle tone, full of the manners of English gentlemen. "You don't need to be here, wait in the lobby, I'll bring her back down personally." The pianist takes out his wallet and gives the bodyguard two hundred pounds. The guard has a hard look in his eyes that intimates a great reluctance — he would probably be killed if he lost the girl, but he also can't argue with a client so he stays silent, turns around and takes the elevator down.

Aurora and the pianist stand in the entry hall alone. Before asking her into the sitting room, he looks sideways at her. She opens her handbag. Dinky flies out.

The pianist doesn't know what to say. Aurora stands still in the hall, letting him take her in. Her eyes have a Slavic aspect. He can't make out their exact colour. That is neither here nor there. He feels his entire being drawn to her with an inconceivable force. "Would you like a drink? I've just opened a bottle of champagne."

She nods her head and follows him into a large room with parquet floors, a grand piano and French doors that open onto a terrace. Dinky flits across the room, out the doors and perches on the railing. "Sit anywhere you like." She sits down on the nearest sofa. He pulls the champagne from the ice bucket, pours her a flute and hands it to her, then picks up his glass and raises it: "A votre santé". He makes sure to look her in the eyes and she does the same. Her eyes are green. She takes a sip as he takes a sip. She finds she's unable to read him. This destabilizes her. He seems to see through her and exalt in her at the same time.

The pianist doesn't notice, preoccupied with his own unease. "Do you always carry a bird in your handbag?"

"Always."

He smiles a boyish smile. "I don't normally do this. I don't actually know why I did. I suppose I was curious. A friend gave me your number. I -" He goes silent; his heart stands still. He looks down at the table, the small, white pile of cocaine, the rolled up twenty-pound note. "Do you want any of this?"

Aurora shakes her head.

"I didn't mean to offend you. Forgive me, I didn't mean —" The pianist refers both to the cocaine and to the fact he's made light of something that was supposed to remain unspoken — the fact that he has bought her time, her flesh, that she is there to provide a service. He has ruined the illusion with his stupid blathering.

"No, you didn't ruin anything." Aurora cannot maintain her defences. She's attracted to him despite everything. Fighting against it, tears pour from her eyes. She does not bury her face in her hands. She turns her cheek, closes her eyes and feels her eyes burn, become wet, tears making tracks down her cheeks.

The pianist is struck by the fact that she has read his mind but he doesn't say anything, he simply puts his champagne flute down. He moves to Aurora, kneeling at her feet. He places his hand on her knee, and then inexplicably on her cheek, wet with tears, his lips on hers — he sinks into the ocean, into the air. He is consumed by that fathomless place (gained by occult means), rendering almost everyone who comes in contact with her electrified, overwhelmed, enchanted, terrified and soothed in equal measure. The elements will not let go of her. No one who ever desires her can get enough. The pianist is no different from the others.

As she transports him, so he transports her. This is not like the attraction she felt for the son of the underboss. This is a transverberation, like St Teresa of Avila — a seraph with a dart, pushing through her chest, into her heart, a red-hot poker, again and again, so deep it goes through her entrails, cauterizing instantly, the pain so great it makes her gasp, so sweet that with the worst of it she doesn't want it to stop. Her soul is on fire. They go to the bedroom. She makes love for the first time in her life.

Lying in bed after sex, the pianist is so moved he takes Aurora's face in his hands and tells her he doesn't want to be without her. He says this without knowing what he's saying, without thinking of what he's going to say, but they are the truest words he's ever heard come out of his mouth. His father is a count with coffers full of gold. He'll pay anything for her freedom. He wants to know, there and then, if she will run away with him. Immediately.

The question startles her. Her heart jumps. She wonders if he's playing a game. The pianist assures her he hasn't taken enough cocaine to alter his judgement. Again, he asks for her hand in marriage. Aurora points out that they haven't even had a meaningful conversation. He doesn't know her. She doesn't know him. Although, after saying this, in this short space of time, she feels he knows her better than anyone, he has seen who she really is. She feels it in everything she is. She is finally her true self. He has brought her to the centre, to the crux. She doesn't want this to end. She can't turn back. She believes him when he says he will protect her with his life...They talk about music. They tell each other things about their lives, thoughts they've had that they've never told anyone else. They laugh. They kiss. They make love again. The spell remains unbroken.

...A chill gnaws at my heart.

There is thunder so close it rocks the cabin. I can feel it through the floorboards. Lightning flashes illuminate everything. Droplets of rain glisten as they are hurled through the open window by the wind. I like my windows open, even in rainstorms. I smoke hashish, continue to write, get cotton mouth and drink more and more of the fizzy cherry pop. I might do some cocaine. Because Victory is with Truth and Truth is ours. No, I must put a line through that because the truth belongs to everyone, yet most will never know it. I find myself upon the sands of that which I can no longer say... I'm not going to stop to listen to the rain beating down harder and harder as if something were going to collapse in the blackness outside.

...The piano prodigy gets out of bed to look for the champagne. He finds the cocaine instead, in a little pile on the glossy pitch-black surface of the piano. He uses the credit card next to it to crush up the glittering granules, sweeps a portion into a line, then picks up the fifty-pound note already fashioned into a straw, rolls it tighter, sticks it in his nose and inhales. This makes him want Coca-Cola. But even more than Coca-Cola is the urge to touch the piano keys, to let everything out through his fingers in the form of vibrating sound. Thirsty, he sits down and begins to play.

The music draws Aurora out of bed. Wrapped in a sheet, she cuts a small figure in the enormous rooms, padding across the marble floor; in her slanting, Slavic eyes, terror, magic, intelligence, anxiety, wonder, menace, promise. Her eyes are solar systems. Dinky meets her in the hall and flies with her into the living room, where the pianist sits playing a pianoforte — exquisite, ruthless, carving out pieces of her heart. Aurora stands within his line of vision, draped in the white hotel sheet, watching him through those upturned eyes of hers —the eyes of a cat.

"You are going to be my wife. We're going to have beautiful children. This is the most wonderful day of my life." The pianist speaks loudly, above the sound of the music. "I can't wait to marry you."

Aurora is now a radiant, smiling schoolgirl, opening her arms, holding on to the sheet edges to reveal her naked body, the fabric billowing upward as she spins and dances with Dinky circling above, flitting around the room, diving from the chandelier, chasing Aurora's bedsheets as they whip through the air.

This goes on for a time, both absorbed in the world of the music, Aurora dancing naked on the parquet floor with Dinky. Aurora has never felt more like herself than in this moment. She is human and angel[34]. Stars sparkling and blinking out the windows are sending her messages. She is in communication with them.

---

34. Or, actually, human and elemental.

All of a sudden, disordered notes fall from the pianist's hands. He chokes and spits up blood. Splatters hit the piano, mottle the keys. Aurora and Dinky race to him as he falls off the piano bench to the floor. Aurora feels his head hit the marble as though it were her own, the crack echoing in her skull. The piano prodigy has been tapped by death, the Death that has been stalking him, as it stalks us all.

On the shiny parquet floor, she speaks to him, cradling his bloody head in her lap as he convulses, leech-like globs of haemoglobin sliding from his mouth. He falls limp and stops breathing. She does not know CPR. His head is bleeding through her fingers, the blood coagulating in his hair. She takes the sheet off herself and bunches it up to make a pillow, pressing it to the wound.

Sobbing, covered in his blood, she gets up, knowing she has to clean herself up, get dressed, go and tell the man downstairs in the lobby what has happened. In the bathroom, she splashes her face. The water flowing from the tap holds complex, ethereal music that floats around the room. Rubbing the blood off her cheeks, washing it off her hands and arms with soap, she moves as quickly as she can. She thinks she sees tiny lights — balls of energy — bobbing in the air haphazardly. A flying beetle, with green iridescent wings, lands on the sink with a click. This startles her. Nothing is as it seems or what it has been.

Down, down, down, the mirrors make copies of her, on and on for eternity. The elevator hits the ground floor and opens. She looks for the man in the lobby. He can see things are not right, takes her by the arm to the car with the driver waiting outside, tells him to take her home, then disappears into the hotel.

Three months pass. During this time, Aurora learns the pianist is dead when she sees the newspaper headlines in the hotel lobby as she is led back to her suite after a "party" at a country estate in Oxfordshire. The three months are more like three years.

Aurora finds herself on a yacht with Saudi Arabian royalty. She hears Tu-tu's voice in her head. *When one becomes a stalker, one becomes a hunter of power, like death itself. The first principle of stalking is that a warrior stalks herself. She learns her disguise so well that no one knows she's in disguise. She must do this ruthlessly, cunningly, patiently, and sweetly. She must be ruthless, but charming. Cunning, but nice. Patient, but active and alert. Sweet, but lethal.*
Even so, Aurora feels like killing the Prince and setting the boat on fire, then moving on to the son of the Russian mafia underboss. The rage has not subsided. Even though she has tried again, the wolf ectoplasm will not materialized. She examines everything about the Prince when in his company. She studies and checks herself. She remembers the films with the femmes fatales and inhabits them, adding aspects of her own to make everything more real and immediate, in order to appear spontaneous and fit the glove the Prince presents. She feels she isn't giving her best performance. It's difficult to care about anything, except Dinky. She is losing hope in her ability to continue.

Aurora must call her grandmother every week from the cell phone one of the guards brings her. She hasn't stopped lying to her. When she hears her voice, she holds her tears back. She can smell the trailer and her grandmother's lotion, her home-made doughnuts frying, the whiff of her hairspray.

The son of the underboss checks in every month to make sure the calls have gone well. He wants her to know he is still out there. When the telephone is passed to Aurora and his voice comes on the line, she wants to claw her face and scream. She imagines retribution in the form of something like the sacrifice in William Blake. She sees herself among the naked daughters of Albion hacking at the shrieking, whimpering son of the underboss tied to a rock as they castrate him, open his chest, thrust their fingers in and rip out his beating heart with their bare hands, leaving him there to be eaten by vultures. Instead, she steels herself. She remains cunning but nice, sweet but lethal.

"Did you call your grandmother?"

Aurora imagines his bloodied heart in her hands. His voice is poison and makes her sick. "Yes. Three days ago."

"What did she say?"

"That she loves me and can't wait to see me again."

"What did you say?"

"That everything is fine. That I'll come to visit her as soon as I can. That I'm on the French Rivera and the children I'm taking care of are adorable."

"Good."

"Anything else?"

"Don't even think of trying any of that sleeper chokehold shit on the Prince."

"Obviously."

"I know where your grandmother lives."

"Yes. I know."

"Be good and you'll be free before you know it."

"You think I'm just a doll. A doll that's pink and light. A doll you can arrange however you want. You're wrong. Very wrong. What you think of me is only a ghost of time." *I am dangerous. And I will show you just how dark I can be.*

"Don't forget what I can do to you. Be good." The son of the underboss hangs up. No other woman has been able to mess with his head like she has. Just hearing her voice drives him to pitches of exquisite madness. She is right. She is always there, like a ghost haunting his psyche. She is the forbidden fruit. The one he himself has spoiled.

On the yacht, Aurora is left to her own devices for the most part, confined to five rooms with a terrace. A security guard sits outside her door, replaced every six hours. Room service meets all her needs. Food, clean linen, clothing, fresh towels appear, although Aurora never sees nor hears anyone bring them. They even bring sunflower hearts for Dinky. Sometimes, she feels a presence and calls out, but no one ever answers. She wonders whether she's losing her mind, being in confinement for so long.

A green, iridescent beetle seems to be the only other inhabitant of the suite. Dinky chases after it but it disappears into thin air. The beetle reminds her of the night of the pianist's death. There had been a beetle then, just like this one. There had been a beetle when the pastors performed the exorcism on her. The beetle also reminds her of the necklace Tu-tu wore when she saw him again for the first time. The insect makes faint, humming, whirring sounds and is always surprising her. It falls into her lap, dropping down onto the table out of nowhere, crawling through the strands of her hair...

And here, I will admit something — if you know my kind, you know we are capable of shapeshifting. We're generally known to take the form of a black dog, but really, we can be anything — a tree, a cat, a bird. You may have guessed — I was the beetle. But I was not the cat, or the entity inside her former cat. I was only this insect. You see, I cannot stay away from her. I reduce myself to an insect to crawl through her hair.

How did I go back in time and revisit the events of her life, you ask? Because, in fact, I met her at the end of the story I'm telling you. Going back in time isn't something all jinn can do. It's like getting a degree in astrophysics. Suffice to say, the *will*, when mastered and understood, is capable of a great many things that ignorant people call supernatural or magic.

I probably shouldn't have revisited her past, but my inquiring mind left me no choice, and now I find myself here with my bandaged fingers, my head exploding from lack of sleep and an obsession with a girl I never should have gotten this close to. I could have gone further. I could have possessed her, a painful and difficult process (due to the astral body of a jinn being much larger than the body of a human being). But I did not possess her. I had no intention of violating her in that way. I only wanted to observe her. In short, I was the beetle.

On the Saudi prince's yacht, somewhere off the coast of Norway, Aurora looks out to the sea. She can see an island with trees. At night, it's cool and breezy under hordes of stars, the Milky Way something like the aftermath of a beautiful explosion.

The days are calm and soft. Aurora can smell the sun-warmed pine and sweet grasses drifting in the sea air. Too often, she replays the night with the pianist in her head, staring into a horrified space. She can't sleep for days on end. Nightmares of the rodents with bloody teeth, bloody claws, bloody fur, tear at her. The slimy creature with tentacles returns. She wakes in a cold sweat.

Aurora is sure she's going mad. She summons her will to remain on the straight and narrow. She follows the phases of the moon and wonders how long it will take, how many months or years before she stops going over that night in her head. She thinks of the pianist so often and sees him in so many of her dreams and daydreams that a facsimile takes on a life of its own inside her. She is trapped. And now the pianist is trapped inside her. Aurora tells herself it's time to grow up, to put an end to this grief. The pianist is gone.

The Saudi prince comes to visit her every third evening, sometimes staying until dawn. His cologne is sharp and overpowering. They drink champagne. Occasionally he inhales bumps of cocaine from a tiny golden spoon while they listen to disco, R&B, hip hop, or house, according to his mood. Aurora dances. She dances herself into ecstasies and calls to Diana and Aion, who do not come. The Prince likes nothing more than to watch her, drink champagne, take a line of cocaine, then sit back, relax into the void. He never makes a move to sleep with her. In fact, he never even touches her. He devours her with his eyes. She steels herself for the day he wants her flesh.

After four weeks, and not having left the suite, Aurora asks the Prince if she can go swimming. He forbids it. His first wife drowned, as well as one of his brothers. They weren't getting in a speedboat and visiting the island, and she wasn't going swimming. She brazenly tells him she's beginning to feel like a genie trapped inside a bottle. This is their first true moment of tension. The Prince is visibly annoyed by the remark, but says nothing, communicating his displeasure with a hard, wild look in his eyes. Still, Aurora presses on and asks if he wants her to leave. She has nothing to lose, she no longer cares what happens to her.

"I've been very pleased with your company. I don't want you to go just yet, but it seems you do." The Prince stares directly into her eyes, challenging her.

"I would like to see my grandmother." She doesn't want to see her grandmother but knows this sounds innocent and sweet.

After glaring out to sea for ten minutes or more, the Prince speaks. "It's funny you should mention the jinn. I'm sure you know of the *Thousand and One Nights*."

"Yes, who doesn't?"

"What if you were to tell me a story every night, for a thousand and one nights. We wouldn't always be here; we would travel the world. On the last night, I will transfer a large sum, eight figures, to your bank account, or an offshore account I can have set up for you."

It is an offer of a place in his retinue for three years with enormous compensation. Aurora is horror-stricken. Does this mean he is going to give her to other men? She wants to dig her nails into her palm but stops herself. She will no longer be the property of the son of the Russian mafia underboss. The Prince is powerful enough to protect her from him. But what will he do to her? Three years. This is an eternity. Aurora's head spins. She knows these princes have unimaginable sums stockpiled around the world — so much money that they do preposterous things with them. Without thinking, words come out of her mouth: "I can't guarantee I'm any good at telling stories."

"You could instead recite a short poem. And every night, dance of course."

Calculating the chance of the prince remaining true to his word, Aurora stops and realizes she has no choice. She is a prisoner on the boat. The Prince and the son of the underboss are more powerful than she is. The Prince is only giving her the illusion of choice. He already has her fate in his hands. Aurora looks the Prince softly in his eyes. "Yes, I accept."

The Prince smiles.

And like that, Aurora finds herself in the company of the Prince for an extended period of time. The Prince has the son of the underboss's men, who had come with Aurora, escorted off the yacht. He will pay the son of the Russian mafia underboss off.

In Oslo, it takes five private jets to move the Saudi prince's retinue to Zurich, where he has a home in the forested foothills. Through the tinted glass of the Bentley SUV, rolling hills are scattered with doe-coloured cows feeding on phosphorescent grass, enormous bells around their thick necks. Behind the cows, bald rock mountains erupt, fringed in forests. They wind through medieval villages, past stone and wood houses with criss-crossing beams and wooden shutters carved with hearts. Aurora thinks of the pianist. She cannot get him out of her mind.

After more forest, a Palladian rotonda villa comes into view through the trees. The structure is built on metal and rock with domes shaped like Huns' helmets, shining white under the packed blue of the sky. This is the house Aurora is to stay in. The others in the Prince's retinue continue on in the fleet of SUVs, up the slope to the main house which is made in the same style but rambling, and three times larger.

Inside the villa, everything appears to be a replica of times as old as fairy tales. Elaborately carved wooden arches, beams, staircases, balustrades, doors are everywhere one looks. On the walls hangs silk wallpaper with a shining gold Greco-Roman revival pattern. Other rooms are paneled with oak. The Prince brings Aurora from room to room, all thirty or so of them, spread out on four floors with ten bedrooms, fourteen bathrooms, four reception rooms, two working kitchens and a guest cottage at the back of the house with its own kitchen, living room, bedrooms and bathrooms. His cologne makes her sick. The ballroom, on the top floor, has ten-meter-high cathedral ceilings that extend into intricately carved wooden eaves.

A treasure trove of art and artefacts fit for a museum is housed within the labyrinthine structure. When they come to a painting by Rothko, Aurora weeps. This endears her even further to the Prince. He knows he's getting too close, that only something drastic will make him stop. He ruminates on the fact that after three years the attachment will no doubt be much worse. Aurora dares touch nothing and acts as though there is a forcefield around each precious object, except for a bearskin rug with its head still attached, teeth bared. She can't stop herself from bending down to touch an incisor. The Prince installs Aurora in a bedroom fit for a princess and tells her he hopes she and her bird will be very happy there.

An Indian summer takes hold. Balmy breezes rustle through the delicate branches with their gold, red, and orange leaves, their exquisite scent mixed with damp earth and moss, game, fur, wild berries, the stench of foxes and other wildlife. Aurora and the Prince ride their horses through the forest, stopping at a transparent green lake hidden in the trees, boulders jutting from its clear depths. Flecks of quartz sparkle in the sun. The air is sweet and fragrant with the crystal tang of the lake rising beneath it. Leaves flutter all around, the colors of a blazing fire. They dismount and leave the horses without tying them to a tree, which strikes Aurora as odd. The prince points to where a lavish picnic has been set in the dappled light underneath the trees, gauzy mosquito netting hanging from the branches to make a tent.

"Aren't you going to tie the horses up so they don't stray?"

"They'll be fine," he says, gesturing to the air with his right hand, waving her along down the incline.

"I never see who lays food out for us," Aurora remarks.

"It's the jinn."

"The jinn?"

"They don't care what we do, they don't gossip about us, they're very efficient. They save an incredible amount of money. Free labour."

"You're kidding."

"No, I'm not."

"Do you command them?"

"You needn't concern yourself with things like that."

"Do you use a ring or the seal of Solomon, like in the *Arabian Nights*?"

"Don't be ridiculous."

"Do they grant wishes?"

"Yes, but we've learned to alter fate like that is inadvisable. Nine times out of ten, tragedy ensues. It isn't worth it. They are best for manual labour."

It occurs to Aurora that if this is true, perhaps one of them could bring her pianist back to life. Throughout the picnic, the idea consumes her thoughts.

"You seem very far away, my dear," notes the Prince.

"I only wish I could go swimming."

"You know how I feel about that."

Aurora strips to her underwear and walks to the lake edge. Poised on top of one of the boulders, she dives in. The prince does nothing to stop her. He stays silent, secretly delighting in her swimming and the grace with which she dives from the rocks. She reminds him of nymphs from Greek mythology.

Autumn gives way to winter with the first snowfall accumulating, transforming the landscape into a white and sparkling world, quieter than the one before. The nights remain unchanged. Aurora dances with Dinky flitting around her while the Prince sits by the fire, drinking whisky. No matter how hard she struggles to abandon the idea, Aurora is constantly attuning herself to signs of jinn, hoping she will make contact. Half the time she's worried she's going mad. The Prince isn't fond of conversation. Aurora holds her tongue around him. She goes from room to room, looking at things, studying the paintings and *objets d'art*. She remembers Paris and the girl she used to be. In the basement, she finds Masonite panels. Remedios Varo painted on panels like these. Aurora walks through a labyrinth of piled furniture, wooden crates, and other bric-à-brac, finding cans of wall paint, brushes, primer, sandpaper and a tarpaulin. She takes all of this to the ballroom in the elevator. She remembers she'd seen an easel in one of the rooms and goes to look for it. This takes over an hour to find. On the easel is *The Fisherman and the Syren* by Frederic Leighton, which Aurora finds twee and repulsive but somehow alluring. She removes it and steadies it against the wall, then takes the easel to the ballroom. Aurora sets the tarpaulin on the floor, places the panel on top of it and begins priming the surface.

Waiting for the primer to dry, she goes downstairs to the first library she comes to. It isn't the one she had been using before. She has no idea where that one is now. She looks through the shelves for something to read. Ideally, she wants to find a book on the jinn. Eventually, she finds one, *The Multitudes of Djinn* by Yolanda Greer. In it, she finds a section on summoning different jinn based on their types. She learns that the jinn are weakened by iron. However, upon reading the text, there is nothing practical that will help her. All it says is that there are ancient Arabic rituals predating Islam that can be used in conjunction with the Qur'an to contact the jinn and bring them to our world, but doesn't give any actual instructions, as this would be too dangerous.

Aurora flips through the book and finds another section that deals with radio waves to make contact. There is mention of something called an EVP recorder but since Aurora doesn't have a computer or the Internet, she can't research this lead. The book is useless. She goes back to the ballroom, sands the primed surface of the Masonite panel, brushes it off and sets the panel on the easel.

From sequestration and boredom springs violence and/or creativity. As she works, Aurora is murderous and imaginative. She flings wall paint at the canvas and watches it streak and splatter as clumps slip downward, falling onto the floor. She wants to get the nail gun she saw in the basement and shoot it at the panel. Then maybe start shooting at everything. Aurora screams but no sound comes out. Dinky flies frantically around the ballroom until she comes to rest on one of the wooden eaves.

More days pass. Aurora stretches on the ballroom floor and works on the painting. She ends up going back to the *The Fisherman and the Syren* and looking at the mermaid tail to make tentacles in her painting. She asks the Prince for oil paint. The next day all colors of paint imaginable materialize next to the easel, along with brushes and charcoal pencils. As usual, splendid food appears out of nowhere, breakfast, lunch and dinner. In the evening Aurora tells the Prince a story — but sometimes not. If she isn't in the mood or is too tired, the Prince doesn't insist. However, one night he demands one. Aurora tells him she's sleepy and can't think of anything. They sit in silence with the crackle of the fire, Dinky chirping from a chandelier now and then.

The Prince turns to Aurora, locks eyes, then offers to transfer the eight-figure sum into an offshore account if she tells him a story, then and there. However, it must be complex — a proper story, a story as good as Scheherazade would tell to save her life.

Aurora has nothing to lose and agrees. She tells a bizarre, true tale, with embellishment to give it a *Thousand and One Nights* flair. She relays an account her English teacher at the Academy told the class one day when tired of lecturing them on F. Scott Fitzgerald:

Once, over sixty years ago, there was a little boy who lived in Denmark. He foretold things, like Mrs so-and-so breaking her leg, or an accident in the capital before it happened, deaths in the village — these kinds of things. It happened so often, his parents called the local priest to have him exorcised. Everyone thought he had the mark of the devil. He didn't want to see these things; they came to him uncontrollably without rhyme or reason. He was an intelligent child — he pretended to be cured. He did not speak of the visions again.

The boy could also tell a person's future when he touched them — images came to him in flashes. And what was more terrifying, he could read people's minds. More and more, he realized he was cursed. He could read the thoughts of his neighbours through the walls, and they in turn could read his, not knowing they were hearing his thoughts, saying things he planted in their minds without meaning to. The amount of information he received, and its content, was unbearable.

The Danish boy stayed away from people as much as possible. He went to the woods for hours on end, camping out there. He preferred the company of trees and animals.

At school, he studies hard. He is accepted into a top university and throws himself into his studies — into mathematics and chemistry — determined to shut the world out and one day make an important discovery. Invention and creation are all that matters to him — the world beyond his head being too much to bear.

Eventually, in graduate school, he has a breakthrough. It is so pioneering, he is offered a position in the chemistry departments of several prestigious American institutions on both the East and West Coasts of the

United States. He chooses New York University for a reason he can't explain rationally. There is a pull.

In New York City, he develops ways to deal with the hordes of people. One thing he finds helpful is jazz. When he concentrates on the music, the thoughts and conversation of the people around him melt away.

Even though he isn't very sociable, in these jazz clubs he falls in with the bohemian set and meets Aldous Huxley, who is much older and something of a father figure — one who understands; one who can also read people's minds. The two carry on telepathic conversations together, which, for the first time in the young Danish chemist's life, feels natural and not at all traumatic.

Huxley wants to change the world. He believes in a geopolitical utopia ruled by an elite of intelligent, creative, benevolent leaders who swear an oath to act for the common good, so that there will no longer be hungry, homeless, uneducated people in existence. He thinks that psychedelics, like mescaline and LSD, are potential tools that could be used in humanity's enlightenment to usher in this paradise.

The young Danish chemist finds many of Huxley's ideas compelling but isn't wholeheartedly committed to them. Still, he knows he has much to learn from the great man and keeps his mind open.

The chemist's psychic abilities fascinate Huxley. They are much stronger than his own. Huxley can't stop wondering what the effect of LSD would be on his friend; he truly believes in the enlightening nature of the drug and feels that, in the right conditions, it might very well positively alter the chemist's life — facilitate an understanding and impart knowledge that would end, or at least ease, his suffering.

At this time, Huxley is involved with the CIA and their investigations into psychedelics. He proposes that he and the young Danish chemist go to a small facility in the Maine woods to perform some LSD experiments with their operatives.

The chemist falls in love with a beautiful, petite, raven-haired poetess he meets in one of the jazz clubs he frequents. He hasn't ever had a girlfriend before but decides he wants to marry her. She says yes. The fact that he can read her thoughts and always knows what's going to happen is exciting at first. They enjoy an idyllic four months together with the poetess writing prolifically.

Slowly but surely, the chemist's abilities begin to unnerve his wife. She finds herself ruthlessly policing her thoughts until she barely knows who she is anymore. The chemist does his best to behave normally and let events unfold without interfering, unless the situation is grave and he feels he can do something. However, he is always aware there's the chance of beginning a chain reaction, which will set off something else just as horrible. It nearly drives him mad on a number of occasions. The chemist discusses Huxley's proposal with his wife. They agree he should go to the Maine woods, to the CIA lab, and try the LSD therapy.

So off they go, to the CIA MK-Ultra facility in the backwoods of Maine, which looks like an ordinary farmhouse but has secret rooms and a laboratory underground.

After much testing, they find, tragically, that LSD is not therapeutic. It augments some of the chemist's abilities and scrambles others. He is plagued by acute nightmares and flashbacks and begins to have violent psychotic episodes. His condition worsens until he is admitted to an insane asylum.

After four years, his wife divorces him. At the asylum he is able to bribe some of the guards into bringing him the materials he needs to continue his experiments. He makes a lab in the corner of the basement for which he pays an extortionate sum. The numerous patents he'd filed before he went insane have been sold for millions. He can easily afford whatever he desires, his freedom from the mental institution notwithstanding. The doctors and his wife believe he needs to remain at the hospital.

One night, while working late in his lab, the chemist senses he isn't alone. He gets up and scans the area, peering behind shelving and into each corner of the room. Perhaps it's a rat, he thinks.

The next thing he knows, something or someone is breathing down his neck. There is a tap on his shoulder. His heart freezes. He turns. No one is there. The chemist goes back to his work, rattled, his hands shaking as he arranges the solutions on his lab table.

And then it materializes, the form, perhaps seven feet tall, like a human but also like a goat, powerful and glowing. It tells the chemist it is a jinn — many centuries old, all powerful, yet powerless to return to the world of the jinn, in an alternate dimension.

The jinn is convinced the chemist has something to do with his abduction. An evil jinn, who had previously put him in a coma for a thousand years, is also involved. He is sure the chemist knows this jinn.

The chemist does not. The entity is furious. It threatens to torture the chemist if he can't find a way to send him back to where he came from. The chemist tries to convince the jinn he has never met any other jinn before. The jinn laughs outrageously, shaking the walls and everything in the laboratory, then says, "I know — I can read your mind".

"I can read human minds, but I can't read yours," the chemist offers, then realizes the jinn knows this as well.

The jinn explains that his kind are more evolved in certain areas and have access to more dimensional frequencies.

The chemist tries again and again to convince the jinn that his experiments have nothing to do with the jinn's displacement. He has been working on mind-altering compounds he hopes will restore him to sanity. He explains it's more likely the jinn is a hallucination and he's having a psychotic episode.

"I can assure you, I am real. And what I will do to you if you don't help me will feel very real. I will crack each bone in your body, one by one, then play your nerves like a harp until you scream bloody murder."

The chemist has an idea. He asks the jinn if it is true about the three wishes, like in the *Arabian Nights*. The jinn says yes, it's true. The chemist proposes the jinn give him three wishes, the last of which he would use to send the jinn back where to wherever it was he had come from.

The jinn agrees it's worth a try, spins like a whirling dervish and glows red like a hot coal, his voice commanding the chemist to make his first wish.

The chemist wishes he hadn't ever gone mad. The walls dissolve. He finds himself in bed with his poetess, his wedding ring back on his finger, the levitating jinn glowing beside him.

The chemist doesn't know what else to wish for; he has everything he wants, so he wishes for world peace.

Before making the third wish, the chemist sees the jinn's future flash before his eyes — the jinn's enemy will be waiting for him upon re-entry and has a posse who will beat him to death. The chemist relays what he's seen to the jinn but the jinn has seen it too, as he's read the chemist's mind. And so, the jinn stays on with the chemist and poetess and tells them stories of the world of the jinn each night, for a thousand and one nights, until the chemist has a vision the coast is clear, makes the wish, and sets the jinn free.

At the end of Aurora's story, they both sit in silence. The Prince looks at Aurora, waiting to see if it is in fact the end, because it doesn't seem like a proper ending. It's the oddest story he's ever heard. It's completely unsatisfying and leaves the Prince cold. But judging from the length of the silence, and Aurora's body language, it is indeed the end. The Prince speaks. "I don't know what it is you've just recounted." He sighs.

Aurora fixes her eyes on his. She doesn't care whether he thinks it's good enough to pay her and let her go. If she has to stay, at least that would give her more time to make contact with the jinn and perhaps bring back her pianist from the dead.

"I'll transfer everything I owe you into an account, then you are free to go when you wish. Just say the word. I'll have all the arrangements made." The Prince hesitates for a moment. "But you can stay on a bit longer, if you care to. I'm due to be in London in a week and a half and could take you with me. You could leave from there to go to your grandmother."

This option suits her. She still has hope of contacting the jinn. "Yes, perfect."

The Prince nods. He knows he should have dispatched her earlier, that he has become too attached already. The huge sum he is going to pay to her is worth every penny. She has touched his heart and his spirit in ways he never thought possible.[35]

That evening they eat and retire to their respective bedrooms. After falling asleep, Aurora finds herself sitting up in bed, on edge, wanting a cigarette. Nothing seems real. It doesn't seem possible she will soon be in possession of a great sum of money, a sum which she doesn't even know the exact amount of. It could be ten million or

---

35. If anyone is wondering why the Prince never made any sexual advances toward Aurora, it is because he is asexual. He is also a violently jealous person and would never have given her to any of his friends or colleagues or brothers to amuse themselves with. He wanted her to remain his secret treasure.

ninety-nine million. She reasons it will probably be more like ten million. She won't let herself get excited or believe it until it happens. Aurora wanders down the hallway with Dinky fluttering around her, taking the stairs to the floor below, where she remembers a room with wood-paneled walls and bookshelves built into them — a library of sorts where she thought she'd seen a pack of cigarettes sitting on top of a side table. The room evades her, but she comes to another which looks promising, plenty of furniture with drawers where a packet of cigarettes might be hiding. Dinky flits around the room, landing here and there, as though he is helping Aurora look. Aurora sees ashtrays and finds a silver lighter. On top of beautifully crafted furniture sits wondrous *objets d'art*.

Aurora speaks to the air, asking the jinn if they could please send her cigarettes, as she wanders around the room. On a table there are three similarly-shaped, different-sized blown glass decanters with orb-like stoppers of bubbled glass. Aurora continues to scan the area for cigarettes, holding a small, crystal ashtray in her hand.

The jinn don't appear to be listening or are ignoring her. She looks in drawers and cabinets. Eventually, she finds an open pack of Lucky Strikes in a place she thought she had already looked, out in plain sight. As she smokes, she is drawn to the decanters. She takes the smallest in her hand and pulls the stopper out.

The room becomes ice cold — she can see her breath. A handsome man appears out of thin air and introduces himself. He is a jinn. He thanks Aurora for releasing him from the bottle. They stand before one another. Aurora is speechless, the jinn bearing down on her with his bewitching gaze, searing as a cold fire, lapping up against her. "Do you want to know if you get three wishes?" he asks.

"Would that be possible?"

The jinn takes the burning cigarette from Aurora's hand and stubs it out in the ashtray. "Yes, of course."

"If I were to make a wish to bring back someone who's died, would they come back the same as when they'd left?"

"It isn't certain that they would, no."

"Do you know what happens when we die?"

"We know there are dimensions. But even in the land of the jinn, no one knows what the details are, exactly. Not for certain, anyway."

Aurora sits down in a chair and smokes her cigarette. The jinn studies a Rothko on the wall. After ten minutes, she has decided. "I wish for my pianist to come back to life as he was, as though nothing had happened."

...In case you haven't figured this out already, I am the jinn Aurora freed from the bottle. The bottle which sits before me now. I had vowed to send the person who broke the seal to hell, as that was the condition of my release by the jinn who trapped me. And now it is she who has me caught in a trap, and I her. Her image will be forever stained across my face. Like the shroud of Turin. *To see is to stain.* I admire her resolve and her willingness to be flung into the unknown for love, even a love misjudged or imagined...What I'm sure you are not aware of, because

I have been careful not to divulge this fact, is that since arriving at this cabin and beginning this account, I have taken the form of her lover, the pianist. Don't judge me for this. I couldn't help it, just like I couldn't help going back in time and like I cannot stop myself from drinking the artificial cherry pop...

After Aurora makes the wish, the next thing she knows, she's on a terrace with cliffs and the glowing azure sea below. There is music, Chopin, the clear, minimal notes heart-breaking, fortifying, drifting from the French doors behind her, open, fluttering at the edges with flimsy white, transparent curtains. Aurora steps through them, into the room. Dinky follows, flying past her, and alights on the back of a chair. The pianist is at the bar, pouring two gin and tonics with sliced cucumber. She stands before him, both engulfed in the beauty of the music, tears running down her flushed face, breathless. The pianist turns to her. She is next to him. She can feel him exhale on her face; he puts his hand to her cheek. "Chopin. *Nocturne in F minor, Op. 55, No 1* variation with the piano, violin, and cello. The first time you hear it, it rips you apart."

Something moves in the corner of the room. Aurora turns to see me, open-mouthed, eyes glowing red, rough, gorged with horror.

By the force of my will, I suck her soul from the marrow, pitching her into a pit of regret following nothingness, into the bottle which sits before me now, along with the bird. Inside is the void — neither heaven nor hell. It is the truth. One ceases to exist, there is no sense of time. Or so I imagine. It's different for everyone in there. I sit here and wonder whether I would in fact prefer to return — to exchange places.

Who knows if the same actions which set me free and entrapped Aurora into the bottle will repeat themselves? This is not like clockwork. If I unstop the bottle, there's no guarantee I'll be sucked back in, and Aurora expelled. Any number of scenarios could occur. There isn't a universal science to these spells, each practitioner has their own way, capabilities, imagination. There are multitudes of outcomes...

After much consideration, I've concluded there is nothing else to do but open it. I am a bucket. A cosmic bucket with a cosmic hole. I am preparing myself for my part, getting into character, twisting the top out from the neck of the bottle. It is open. There is the chill, soft and sweet... the bird has flown out...and now...Aurora

Acknowledgements

I would like to thank Dodo Ink for their tireless efforts, dedication, and vision, my agent Jessica Craig for everything that she does, copyeditor Andrew Gallix, publicist Nicci Praca, Dan Stiles for the magnificent cover artwork and design, my sister Ariel, Mary Quirolo, my parents, Ugnius Uzkuraitis, Nyx, James Miller, Sheri Fowler, Susanna Crossman, Venetia Welby, Houman Barekat, Antonet Verschuren, Daria, Teresa & Francesca, Stephen S Thompson, Masa Masuyama, and Michael Sayeau.

I'm indebted to the works of Carlos Castaneda for the ideas present in the character of the Master embodied in a cat and to *The Master and Margarita* by Mikhail Bulgakov. Below is a list of sources which have been important in the crafting of the novel:

Alexandre De Dánann (2009). *La magie de la rose-croix d'or: traduction de La croix d'or, ou, Bréviaire de la Confrérie de la rose-croix d'or dans le seul manuscrit connu du XVIIe siècle avec ses psaumes et caractères magiques une introduction sur l'origine de la confrérie et la traduction intégrale de ses statuts, 1678.* Milan: Archè.

Antonin Artaud (1965). *Antonin Artaud Anthology.* San Francisco: City Light Books.

Bauduin, T.M., Ferentinou, V. and Zamani, D. (2017). *Surrealism, Occultism and Politics: In Search of the Marvellous.* Routledge.

Breton, A., Seaver, R. and Lane, H.R. (2008). *Manifestoes of Surrealism.* Ann Arbor: University Of Michigan Press.

Chénieux-Gendron, J. (1990). *Surrealism.* Columbia University Press.

David-NéelA. (1931). *Magic and mystery in Tibet: Discovering the Spiritual Beliefs, Traditions and Customs of the Tibetan Buddhist Lamas, an Autobiography.* Pantianos Classics.

Debertolis, P., Gullà, D. and Savolainen, H. (2017). Archaeoacoustic Analysis in Enclosure D at Göbekli Tepe in South Anatolia, Turkey. *Human and Social Sciences at the Common Conference.* doi:10.18638/hassacc.2017.5.1.240.

Evans-Pritchard, E.E. and Gillies, E. (2014). *Witchcraft, Oracles, and Magic Among the Azande.* Oxford: Clarendon Press.

Faivre, A. (2000). *Theosophy, Imagination, Tradition: studies in Western Esotericism.* Albany, Ny: State University Of New York Press.

Ferentinou, V. (2011). *Ithell Colquhoun, Surrealism and the Occult.*

Hanegraaff, W.J. and Kripal, J.J. (2008). *Hidden Intercourse: Eros and Sexuality in the Hstory of Western Esotericism.* Leiden ; Boston: Brill.

Harris-Logan, S.A. (2006). *Singing with Blackbirds: the Survival of Primal Celtic Shamanism in Later Folk-Traditions.* Girvan: Grey House In The Woods.

Jung, C.G. (2015). *Psychology and the Occult.* London: Routledge, Taylor & Francis Group.

Leiris, M. (2013). *Aurora and Cardinal Point — Surrealist Novels by Michel Leiris.* Atlas Press.

Lepetit, P. and Graham, J.E. (2014). *The Esoteric Secrets of Surrealism: Origins, Magic, and Secret Societies.* Rochester, Vermont: Inner Traditions.

Mabille, P. (2018). *Mirror of the Marvelous: the Surrealist Reimagining of Myth.* S.L.: Inner Traditions.

Maria De Naglowska and Traxler, D. (2013). *Initiatic Eroticism and Other Occult Writings from La Flèche.* Rochester, Vermont: Inner Traditions.

Mckenna, T. (1999). *Food of the Gods: A Radical History of Plants, Drugs and Human Evolution.* London: Rider.

Narby, J. (2003). *The cosmic serpent: DNA and the Origins of Knowledge.* London: Phoenix Press.

Rakoczi, B.I. (1970). *Forseeing the Future.* Castle Books.

SERAPHINA MADSEN

DODGE AND BURN

DODGE AND BURN
By Seraphina Madsen

We were told that our mother's life was terminated by killer bees while vacationing in San Marcos, Mexico with Dr Vargas at his family home.

After her mother dies in bizarre circumstances, heiress Eugenie Lund is abducted by Dr Vargas, a charismatic Svengali-like figure who educates her according to his own philosophy, an esoteric blend of anthropology and psychiatry. Isolated from outside influences, Eugenie's life is spent on the run across North America and Europe, existing on the fringes of society, always trying to keep one step ahead of her past. Taking in Mexico, Las Vegas, and the underground rave scene, *Dodge and Burn* is a psychedelic road trip recounted in beautifully crafted prose that pulses with frenetic energy.

Inspired by the likes of Carlos Castaneda and Hunter S Thompson, this is an exciting, iconoclastic debut novel from a remarkable new voice.

'A graceful, droll and absorbing book, Madsen's nimble prose winds around your mind and heart, leaving you breathless.'   Emma Jane Unsworth, author of *Animals*

'Seraphina's writing is vital, exciting and above all, original. *Dodge and Burn* marks the arrival of an exciting new voice.'   Lee Rourke

'Madsen writes like a fallen angel from another world; intoxicating, strange, super-charged with occult knowledge and a mystical sensibility. *Dodge and Burn* is an unforgettable tour de force of avant-garde writing. You've never read anything quite like it.'

James Miller, author of *Lost Boys*

'Mesmerising, episodic, full of wonder and very cool dialogue ('Let's hit the road, Terror'), *Dodge and Burn* is deeply committed to exploring the possibilities of language and describing unconventional experiences.'

3:AM Magazine

About Dodo Ink

At Dodo Ink, we're book lovers first and foremost. From finding a great manuscript to the moment it hits the bookshop shelves, that's how we approach the publishing process at every stage: excited about giving you something we hope you'll love. Good books aren't extinct, and we want to seek out the best literary fiction to bring to you. A great story shouldn't be kept from readers because it's considered difficult to sell or can't be put in a category. When a reader falls in love with something, they tell another reader, and that reader tells another. We think that's the best way of selling a book there is.

Dodo Ink was founded by book lovers, because we believe that it's time for publishing to pull itself back from the brink of extinction and get back to basics: by finding the best literary fiction for people who love to read. Books shouldn't be thought of in terms of sales figures, and neither should you. We approach every step of the process thinking of how we would want a book to be, as a reader, and give it the attention it deserves. When you see our Dodo logo, we'd like you to think of our books as recommendations from one book lover to another. After all, aren't those the ones that we take the greatest pleasure in?

At Dodo Ink, we know that true book lovers are interested in stories regardless of genre or categorisation. That's how we think a publishing company should work, too: by giving the reader what they want to read, not what the industry thinks they should. We look for literary fiction that excites, challenges, and makes us want to share it with the world. From finding a manuscript to designing the cover, Dodo Ink books reflect our passion for reading. We hope that when you pick up one of our titles, you get the same thrill—that's the best thank you we can think of.

www.dodoink.com
Tw: @DodoInk